The Lure of the Falcon

The Lure of the Falcon

JULIETTE BENZONI

Translated by Anne Carter

G. P. Putnam's Sons
New York

FIRST AMERICAN EDITION 1978

First Published as *Le Gerfaut Des Brumes*
Copyright © 1976 by Opera Mundi, Paris

Translation © 1978 by William Heinemann Ltd. 1978

SBN: 399-12048-3

Library of Congress Cataloging in Publication Data

Benzoni, Juliette.
  The lure of the falcon.

  Translation of Le Gerfaut des brumes.
  I. Title.
PZ4.B483Lu   1978   [PQ2662.E5]   843'.9'14   78-13154

PRINTED IN THE UNITED STATES OF AMERICA

Contents

PART ONE

A Wind of Freedom

1779

'

There is something in us that can be without us, and
will be after us, though it is strange that it hath no
history what it was before us, nor cannot tell how it
entered in us.

Sir Thomas Browne

1

The Siren of the Estuary

The ebb had been running for some time already. The month was September and the spring tide, strong and full, was carrying the blue-grey waters of the Blavet out into the Atlantic along with the sea water which flooded busily into the two channels of the estuary twice a day, jostling the little river aside and mingling with it to thrust deep into the Breton landscape for three leagues and more, bearing the red-sailed fishing boats proudly all the way to Hennebont.

It was the time of day when a fat orange sun was just sinking below the dark line of the horizon, the time when waders were wheeling slowly above the river, waiting for the mud flats to emerge for them to land on. Now and then a gleaming splash marked where a gull had dived swiftly in search of supper. The sky deepened to mauve and the fat, broad-beamed boats moved sedately out towards the open sea for the night's fishing, like a stately procession crowned with a snatch of song borne on the freshening breeze.

Gilles bent and picked up the line that lay coiled at his feet. He checked that the ten-ounce lead weight was fast and fixed a lugworm to each of his two hooks. Then, grasping the line with both hands, he whirled the weighted end round his head and sent the lead whistling out as far into the water as he could, where it sank.

When he had cast the line and drawn it taut, holding it between two fingers so as to catch the faintest tremor of a bite, he sat down on the grass and took no further notice of it, waiting and trusting in the sensitivity of his fingers to strike when the moment came.

The fishing fleet had passed out of sight, hidden by a bend in the stream. Only the echo of the song still lingered and but for that Gilles could have thought himself sole master of earth and sea. He loved this melancholy hour when the sun departed from one world to seek another. The water in the river became smooth as glass and the sky put on fabulous colours, like an actor decking himself in his most magnificent costume for the last act of a pantomime. One by one the daytime noises died away, until there was only the distant tinkle of the Angelus . . . It was always a particularly sweet and precious time of day but tonight there was something magical about it, something out of the ordinary which the boy could not define. It might have been in the great arrow-headed clouds that came with the setting sun or in the scent of the grass and the faint smell of angelica that mingled with it . . .

A slight movement at his fingertips called the fisherman's thoughts back to his line. It had stirred almost imperceptibly, but not enough to matter and he was letting his mind wander again when he saw the boat.

It was drifting, all alone, down the centre of the stream, borne seawards on the tide, a small boat scarcely deeper than a raft and empty, quite empty.

Someone must have moored it badly, Gilles thought. He'll be upset when he finds it gone. The tide is running fast tonight . . .

The little boat was certainly moving very fast. Thinking of the trouble its loss would be to some poor man, Gilles rose from his nest of grass as it came level with him and tied his line to a bush.

He was beginning to pull off his shirt when he saw something a little way behind the boat which drew an exclamation from him. It was a head, the hair, too long for a man's, catching a ray of the dying sun and spreading like a coppery stain in the dark water.

The boy's quick wits deduced at once what must have happened. The boat had not simply worked itself loose. The woman must have taken it but, either through clumsiness or inexperience, had fallen into the water. She might well have hurt herself, for she seemed to be gliding along on the current

4

without the slightest movement, like one drowned. Perhaps she was already dead . . .

In another second, without pausing even to pull off his shirt, Gilles plunged into the water. So perfect was his dive that it did not even disturb a tall, grey heron absorbed in the search for worms. Swimming with all his might, he sped after the ruddy speck floating along with the tide and very soon caught up with it.

His fingers grasped the long, trailing hair, like fronds of seaweed. He tugged it towards him. There was a scream, quickly smothered as the head went under. He thrust out his arms and clutched blindly at a smooth, slippery body. He was aware of naked skin as it struggled frantically against him and the pair of them sank together below the surface.

Accustomed by long practice to swimming with his eyes open under water, Gilles saw a youthful face grimacing inches from his own and propelled it hastily towards the surface so that it might breathe. Since, however, as was frequently the way with drowning persons, the face's owner continued to struggle, it seemed to him that he must immobilize her before she took him with her. He therefore stunned her with a quick blow to the chin, so as to be able to tow her ashore safely. Then, swimming with one arm and supporting the head above water with the other, he made his way back to the bank, scrambled for a foothold on the muddy sand and dragging the rescued girl after him, laid her down on the grass.

He almost dropped her then, with the shock of his discovery that the girl – she could not have been much more than fifteen – was stark naked but for the long hair that fell about her, a fact of which her rescuer had been quite oblivious in the heat of the moment but which now brought an instant blush to his cheek and caused an alarming disturbance in the region of his heart. But he pulled himself together and laid the strange girl down on the grass as gently as he could, then dropped to his knees beside her, trying to see if she were still breathing, and uncertain whether he should go or stay. Suddenly he seemed to hear, thundering on the evening breeze, the stern voice of the Abbé Delourme, deputy head of St Yves College at Vannes, where he was a pupil. 'The beauty of Woman is a wicked snare

5

to entrap Men's souls and minds. Fly from women, all you who would serve God alone . . .'

He shut his eyes in terror and crossed himself several times, muttering the prayer against evil spirits. But he did not run away and after a moment or two reopened his eyes.

He knew then that if he lived to be a hundred he would never forget what he saw, for it was the first time it had been granted to him to behold a naked female form and as luck would have it the one before him now was exquisite. A far cry from the occasional glimpses he had caught down by the harbour in Vannes.

The girls who loitered outside the shuttered houses, hailing the sailors as they passed, had a trick of whipping their gowns open to show a thigh or breast. But from the moment he had first seen what they were about, Gilles had always turned away, sickened by the heavy, sagging and frequently none too clean flesh. The sight of them bore out the deputy head's dire warnings, excepting only that it was hard to envisage them as any kind of snare. But with the girl who lay there on the sun-browned summer grass it was a very different matter, for she seemed made of a wholly different substance . . .

She was all pink and gold with skin as soft as the petals of a flower. Her graceful body was as slim and fine-drawn as a thoroughbred's and her waist incredibly slender above the smooth swell of her hips and gold-shadowed abdomen. Her breasts, though small as yet, were exquisitely formed and tipped with delicate rose pink. The only faintly jarring note in the whole symphony of loveliness was where her arms and her long legs, to elbow and knee, were distinctly darker than the rest of her, as though from long exposure to the sun.

'Some fisherman's daughter, surely,' Gilles said to himself, but he could not really think it. For one thing, he knew all the fisherfolk and their families and this pretty sea nymph was a stranger to him. For another, her shapely hands and feet, long, slender neck and the dainty little nose joined by the slightest dimple to her upper lip, with the unconscious grace of her attitude, all contradicted any such hasty conclusion. This girl had never endured the hard life of a fisher lass. She was a creature of a quite different essence.

Quite suddenly she opened her eyes, huge, dark eyes flecked

with gold, though Gilles was given little opportunity to judge their colour, being almost immediately the recipient of a ringing box on both ears which rocked him back from his kneeling position to sprawl on the grass, while the girl, shrieking like a fury, hurled herself upon him with the evident intention of scratching out his eyes.

They struggled for a while, the youthful fury pressing home her attack and abusing him so roundly that Gilles was unable to get a word in. He succeeded in overpowering her at last, and pinned her to the ground with both hands clamped fast behind her back. Helpless but by no means resigned, she spat up into his face like an angry cat and her eyes blazed at him in a frenzied paroxysm of rage.

'You filthy clodhopper!' she screamed. 'Let go of me this instant or I'll have the skin of your back and throw it to the hounds!'

Her childish features were so screwed up with rage that they had ceased to look remotely threatening and were indeed simply funny. Still without releasing his grip, Gilles started to laugh.

'You have an odd way of thanking one who saved your life, Mademoiselle!'

His calm voice and gentlemanly speech had their effect on the youthful fury. She ceased spitting and frowned up at her rescuer through half-closed lashes.

'Why should you think my life in danger?' she retorted, with an unconscious alteration in her tone. 'Is it no longer possible to bathe but one must needs be pounced on by some bedlamite, knocked senseless and dragged ashore?'

'Bathe? In the estuary? On a falling tide, with the currents that there are? It was sheer madness. And you were not even swimming.'

'No. I was letting the tide carry me. It was so delightful!'

'Quite wonderful, to be sure. Unfortunately, that can carry you straight into the next world. Anyone else in my place would have done as I did. Where are your clothes?'

She laughed, on a shrill note that betrayed her anger.

'Where should they be but in the boat, of course? You have only to go after them—'

Gilles sat up and peered through the twilight. The boat was already a long way off. Caught in a swifter current, it was almost out of sight and in another moment would have reached the open sea.

'Not a chance,' he said absently, his gaze returning, as though drawn by a magnet, to rest on the girl's body, which she made no move to conceal. On the contrary, she stretched herself full length on the grass and yawned, revealing a pink mouth and small, white teeth.

'There it is, then,' she sighed, and there was so much malice in her smile that Gilles suspected her of secretly enjoying the situation. 'I shall have to go back to the château as I am! I wonder what they will say to that!'

'The château?'

She jerked her head in the direction of the tall grey rooftops looming beyond the trees.

'Over there! The Château de Locguenolé, of course! The Perriens are my cousins and I am on a visit, but since they are inclined to be a trifle stiff about such things there is nothing else for it. You must give me your clothes.'

Her words fell on deaf ears. His fascinated eyes were following every supple movement of her naked flesh. Something strange and terrible was awakening within him, sweeping away all his preconceived ideas. The blood was beating in his throat and temples, blurring his sight and obliterating will and reason. He felt that this body had belonged to him since time began, that he must be close to it and cling to it so that they might never more be parted . . . His need was something almost painful, like hunger or thirst. His whole being reached out to her, yearning to seize her, to hold her and possess her.

The sudden change in his face warned the girl. Her smile faded and she sprang lightly·to her feet in an instant and withdrew circumspectly behind a bush. All that remained visible to Gilles was a discontented young face crowned with a tangle of red-gold hair, eyeing him above the blazing gorse.

'Well?' she said sharply. 'Did you hear me? Give me your clothes, I said.'

Gilles came back to earth so suddenly that he grimaced with the shock, as if he had physically hurt himself.

'My clothes?·And how am I to get home?'

'I don't care. All that matters is that I shall not be obliged to return to the château stark naked. Quickly, now – and don't

8

tell me they are wet, because it is of no consequence. If you don't do as I say, I shall scream so loudly someone is bound to hear! Then I shall say that you assaulted me – and you will certainly be flogged for it, perhaps even hanged!'

Gilles shrugged, unimpressed by her threats, but he acted without hesitation. She was quite right when she said she could not go back to the château naked. The Comtesse de Perrien, Locguenolé's owner, was said to be a lady of such strict principles that she might well have a fit. For himself, he could wait until nightfall and then get back to Kervignac unnoticed and that would be that.

Swiftly, he ripped off his shirt and sopping canvas breeches and tossed them over the gorse bush, leaving himself with nothing but his close-fitting linen drawers. He turned his back to the girl, feeling much more self-conscious than she had been a little while before. Weren't they for ever telling him at school that nakedness of any kind was an intolerable shame? He longed to run away but something stronger than himself held him back. Then he heard a voice say quietly :

'You have no need, to be ashamed. You are very handsome. It is only when one is ugly that one needs to hide oneself.'

He turned round then and looked at her and laughed with a sense of profound relief. Dressed in his clothes, which were far too big for her, she was at once absurd and charming. But she was not laughing. She was considering him with some perplexity, as though she found him a knotty problem.

'I have not seen you before,' she said at last. 'What is your name?'

'Gilles. Gilles – Goëlo. I live at Kervignac.'

Lord, what it cost him to bring out that name! He would have given anything, in the presence of this girl whom he guessed, for all her strange manners, to be of noble birth, to be able to style himself Rohan or Penthièvre. Worse still, he could sense from the slight pursing of her lips, the faintest shrug of her shoulders, that she was disappointed.

'Oh,' was all she said. Then, without another word, she turned on her heel and began to run in the direction of the château grounds. At that, Gilles cupped his hands to his mouth and called after her :

'And you? What is your name?'

She stopped then and turned but in the gathering darkness he could no longer see the expression on her face. But he did sense a hesitation before her voice came to him, cold and distant.

'I had rather you forgot it,' she said, 'but I have no right to withhold my name from you. I am Judith de Saint-Mélaine!'

With that, she was gone, vanishing into the trees without another glance, while Gilles, feeling angry and humiliated, as well as freezing cold, turned his steps across the heath towards his own village of Kervignac, some three miles distant.

He was by no means clear whom he was most angry with. Which one did he blame the most? Himself, for being fool enough to stun a harmless bather who had not asked him to interfere (even though she was undoubtedly putting her life in danger). Or the little red-haired harpy with no more shame than a real siren, whose smile had such charm but who had shut up like an oyster, just when she seemed on the point of making friends, as soon as she discovered he did not belong to her hidebound, aristocratic world? Or the malign fate which had brought them together only to make him more conscious, when for the first time in his life he was attracted by a girl, of the unbridgeable gulf that would always lie between himself and that lovely creature? Judith de Saint-Mélaine had been disappointed by his plebeian name. How would she have reacted had she known that it came to him only through his mother, and that his birth was illegitimate? As he pictured her pursing up her soft lips and wrinkling up her little freckled nose with scorn, or even with disgust, the boy felt a murderous anger welling up inside him. Why had God done this to him?

Once, in a fit of rage, when he had put that question to the old servant, Rozenn, who had all but brought him up, she had only smiled fondly at him and patted his cheek.

'I dare say he wanted you for himself, my child, even before you were born,' she had said then. 'You know that you must dedicate your life to his service.'

For a long while, that explanation had satisfied him. But for the past two years, ever since he was fourteen, it had been no more than a theory, and one which he had been bending all the powers of his youthful logic to break down. God could not have decided, even before a person came into the world, that he was destined irrevocably for the Church. Or if he did do it, he would at least take care to inspire his chosen servant with a real vocation.

Yet this was far from so in Gilles' case. He was genuinely, even deeply religious, but no more nor less than any other young Breton of his age. God, to him, was a vast, mysterious being, frightening and rather cruel, the best of whose servants were bound to renounce absolutely everything that was most wonderful in that very God's own creation: the world and all its vast wealth and infinite delight. The older he grew, the more Gilles was repelled by the austerity of that difficult service. He could see himself far better in the braided cocked hat of one of the king's soldiers than in the narrow black habit, worn shiny with age, of a man of God! Unfortunately, his mother had decided once and for all that he was to be a priest.

His mother! Whenever he conjured up the image of Marie-Jeanne Goëlo, Gilles was filled with such a strange mixture of feelings that he could never decide which one predominated. There was a kind of devotion mingled with fear and, from the onset of adolescence, a kind of angry resentment also. In return for a little love, had she so wished it, the child would have given her all the affection and adoration that were in him. But that Marie-Jeanne had never wanted.

As far back as he could remember, Gilles had been held at arm's length by a mother who had never kissed him and the two of them, though bound by the closest of all blood relationships, would have lived together in almost total silence until the boy's departure for the college six years earlier, but for Rozenn's warm presence, so full of bustle and affection.

It was from Rozenn, also, that Gilles had learned something of the events leading up to his own birth which had shattered his mother's life and brought him into the world a bastard. It was a common enough story, the classic tale of a girl seduced and abandoned, except that Marie-Jeanne's own fanatical character had raised it to the level of Greek tragedy.

Marie-Jeanne Goëlo was the daughter of a retired ship's surgeon, invalided out in consequence of a naval engagement and settled in the small town of Pont-Scorff. She had never known her mother, who had died when she was born, but she had been the prettiest of the waiting women serving the Comtesse de Talhouët-Grationnaye, whose château of Leslé was not far from Pont-Scorff. It was the Countess who had made the match with Ronan Goëlo and she who had taken charge of the little girl after her mother's death.

She had seen to it that the child was given an excellent education at a good convent in Quimperlé, where the Talhouëts passed the winter months. Marie-Jeanne was a grave, reserved, yet attractive child, beautiful in an austere way, with her pure features, thick brown hair and very beautiful eyes of the same colour. Above all, she was extremely religious and it soon became an accepted thing in the Talhouët family that when Marie-Jeanne grew up she would quit her rather worldly convent only to enter another and much stricter one belonging to the Benedictines of Locmaria.

And then, at the end of one of those summers which took the Talhouët family and Marie-Jeanne with them back each year to Leslé, the thing happened. The nun-to-be was found to be pregnant. Dry-eyed but with a deathlike countenance, she herself broke the news of her condition to the Countess but it proved quite impossible to get a word from her about the circumstances of the disaster or the name of the man responsible. Immured in a ferocious silence, the sixteen-year-old had rejected both blame and pity. What she sought from her benefactress was rather a sentence than any form of assistance.

And the Talhouëts, who had four children of their own and entertained a great many young people, could only fall back on guesswork, for no one had ever observed any unusual intimacy between Marie-Jeanne and any of the guests at the château.

That winter, Marie-Jeanne did not go back to Quimperlé. She remained hidden away at Leslé in the care of the housekeeper, Rozenn Tanguy, and in May 1763 brought Gilles into the world. But Leslé, for all its lakes and woods, was not so far removed from the world that no rumour could leak out, and a fortnight after the clandestine birth the one-time naval surgeon Ronan Goëlo was found hanging from the kingbeam of his house, above a collection of empty rum bottles.

Realizing that there would be malicious gossip to contend with and that Marie-Jeanne and her baby might not be safe on her own estates for much longer, Madame de Talhouët set about finding them a refuge. Her younger son, the Abbé Vincent, who had insisted upon standing godfather to the child,

12

had been obliged to return home after the dissolution of the Jesuits and had just then been installed as rector of the nearby town of Hennebont. He it was who took charge of mother and baby. They removed to Hennebont and settled in a small house by the ramparts, taking with them Rozenn, who had become passionately fond of the little boy.

But Marie-Jeanne longed for still greater silence and solitude. Regret for the cloister bit deeper than ever in her shuttered heart. She loathed the noises of the harbour and the town. And so, with the small legacy left her by her father, she bought a house and garden hidden away behind thickets of gorse and blackthorn near the moorland village of Kervignac. There she shut herself away with Rozenn and the baby to live a life of self-denial centred chiefly on prayer.

Gilles grew up a solitary little boy with an uncaring mother whom he had never known to smile. He learned to play quietly so as not to disturb the meditations of this would-be nun. On the rare occasions when she talked to him at all it was all of God, the Virgin and the saints, to teach him his prayers and try to inspire him with a disgust for this world. And the better to convince him, she taught him very early that he was not like other children but a kind of outcast who could find peace and salvation only in the bosom of the Church.

'The world will reject you with loathing,' she would tell him. 'Only God will open his arms to you.'

In the teeth of the Abbé Talhouët's remonstrances and despite the tears of Rozenn, who could not bear to see her nursling made unhappy, Marie-Jeanne Goëlo strove, week after week and year by year, to instil into her son's head the belief that in this world he must be either a priest or an outcast. Unless he chose the devil's path which could lead him only to the scaffold.

She was only partly successful. The child had eyes to see with and although he was told that the world was wicked, corrupt and dangerous, he could not bring himself to see it so. There was all the beauty of the countryside in spring, there was the sea, the wind, the starry nights, the smell of sun-warmed earth, birdsong and trees and all the animals that filled the little world of any peasant child. There were horses, those great, splendid beasts he adored instinctively, like creatures out of legend. And then there were Rozenn's songs and the countless wonderful tales of old Brittany, of which she seemed to possess an inexhaustible fund.

He had been told so often that he was not like other children that he sought the reason for it, and learned that it was because he had no father. Then he wanted to know more and pestered Rozenn with questions the poor woman could not possibly answer.

'A gentleman, he was,' she admitted one day, 'but his name I don't know, for your mother would never tell it.'

Over the years, the image of that father about whom Rozenn would only speak so guardedly began to haunt Gilles' imagination, becoming ever more highly-coloured. Perhaps because his mother denied him the love which, like all children, he had a basic need for, he grew the more attached to his missing parent, rejecting the picture of an unscrupulous seducer and clothing him in the glory of a great adventurer and a man with a passion for freedom.

And so, as the figure of this faceless father grew within him, there grew up also a still unrecognized yearning to rejoin him somehow, beyond time and space, and become as though one with him. At this point he ceased questioning Rozenn, who in any case had no more to tell him, out of a vague fear of coming across something which might spoil his private hero for him. He was silent, too, whenever his mother happened to refer to the time when he would commence his theological studies.

Become a priest? He had never really wanted it. But tonight, as he ran across the moor where the great standing stones stood like the petrified sentinels of some mysterious kingdom, he set his face against the alien thought once and for all. How could he freely offer God a heart possessed by the shameless vision of a little siren with a head of flaming red hair?

When at last he reached his home, crouching like a big cat in a small hollow, surrounded by may trees, brambles and gorse bushes, he paused for a moment, alarmed at the thought of encountering his mother in his present scanty attire. When he pictured the icy way she would look at his nakedness, he felt a shiver run down his spine.

He crept cautiously to the little, low window winking out like a big eye into the night, hoping that Marie-Jeanne would have retired already to her chamber, to her prayers, by this late hour. In fact, she never took much notice of what he did with himself in his holidays and would sup when it suited her, without waiting for him, for Gilles would be out all night sometimes at sea, fishing with the sons of the pilot, Le Mang, who were the only friends he had ever made in the village.

Pressing his nose to the window, he saw that the room was indeed empty, except for Rozenn, seated on a settle by the hearth telling her beads and dozing intermittently, as her habit was, her head nodding forward from time to time upon her chest. The long, polished oak table was set for one.

Gilles smiled at the reassuring picture, opened the door quietly and slid inside as noiselessly as a cat. Three strides took him to the big chest which ran along the carved wall where the box beds were concealed. He opened one section of it, took out a coarse shirt, similar to the one he had lost, and a pair of trousers to go with it and put them on.

Then he crept back to the door, slipped out and came in again, more noisily.

'I'm late!' he called, 'but it was so lovely down by the river I forgot the time. I'm sorry!'

Rozenn started and blinked her blue eyes vaguely at the boy from under the pointed arch of muslin which she wore over her grey bun instead of a cap, in the fashion of the women of Auray.

'Eh! It's you!' she said, getting up with an effort. 'I think I must have dropped off for a moment.'

'Dropped off! I think you were fast asleep. Why didn't you go to bed? I'm old enough to get my own supper, you know.'

She shook her head, displeased at this revival of an old bone of contention between them.

' 'Twouldn't be right! How many times do I have to tell you, men of your breeding never have got their own food? Sit down and eat!'

'Where is my mother? Gone to bed already?'

'No. To church. There is continuous prayer. Your mother will be there all night.'

'All night? Surely that's rather a lot?'

The old servant shrugged, indicating her own opinion of Marie-Jeanne's excessive devotions.

'One of these days she'll be asking them to make her

15

sacristine, so that she can spend all day there, too. Blessed St Anne! There's no sense in the woman.'

Gilles nodded agreement and attacked his soup with the hearty appetite of his age. His rescue and his run across the heath had both made him ravenous. And he said no more because, although there were more questions he would have liked to ask, it was not done for a man to talk while he ate. So it was not until he had finished his meal that he glanced up at Rozenn, still standing by him, with eyes bright with curiosity.

'My mother never goes visiting and she sees no one,' he said, by way of an opening, 'but you know the whole country all the way to Hennebont and Port-Louis, don't you, Rozenn?'

'I've no call to be discourteous,' she snorted, rising on the defensive. 'If folks speak to me, I answer them! Why should you ask?'

'Nothing really. I was only wondering if you knew a family called Saint-Mélaine?'

The grizzled brows frowned under their little starched roof.

'Well – what of them?' she said suspiciously. 'Why should you want to talk about them?'

'Oh . . . no reason,' Gilles said, rising so as to forestall further questions. 'As I was coming by the park of Locguenolé, I met a girl who said that was her name and that she was visiting at the château. But it doesn't matter . . .'

And to cover his embarrassment he went out, saying he would make sure the hens were shut up because a fox had been seen hanging round. Curiosity was Rozenn's besetting sin and she would be sure to pursue her little inquisition to the bitter end. While he made his conscientious round of the small hen run, he was busy making up a tale about a fall into a ditch and a twisted ankle which should preserve both his own self respect and Judith's modesty.

His hope was not disappointed. Rozenn knew better than anyone how to put the most detailed questions without appearing to. She would have made an incomparable confessor because not only could none of the gossips for miles around resist her but she could even make the most taciturn old fisherman talk, the ones who only unclamped their toothless gum from their pipe stems enough to take in warming draughts of brandy or cider.

'She could wring a confession from the bishop himself – or even from my verger!' Gilles' godfather, the Abbé Vincent, would say, and he had known the old woman all his life. 'When I was a child, she could even make the poachers at Leslé talk and would take a share of their loot off them, then send them off with the remainder, plus a flask of brandy and a lecture.'

Consequently, Gilles very soon discovered all he wanted to know from her.

Judith de Saint-Mélaine had lost her mother some months previously and had been admitted as a boarder to the Convent of Our Lady of Joy at Hennebont, where the abbess, Madame Clothilde de la Bourdonnaye, and her Bernardine nuns undertook the education of young ladies of noble birth and little fortune and in general made nuns of them. Her father, an elderly gentleman and all but penniless, had been obliged to quit the small estate at Fresne, not far from Ploermel, which had been his wife's dowry and their sole property and move to an old, crumbling house in the walled town of Hennebont bequeathed to him by some forgotten cousin.

So the baron and his daughter had gone to live in the dead cousin's dark, cramped house and thanks to the good offices of the La Bourdonnayes, whose lands marched with those of Fresne, and also to her godmother, the Comtesse de Perrien, Judith had been admitted to Our Lady of Joy to embark on what, until then, had been a wholly neglected education. For with a mother who was a permanent invalid and two half-wild brothers she had grown up as naturally as a wild flower and with no more care.

'You see,' Rozenn concluded, taking up her knitting again, but giving the young man a meaning look which instantly set him blushing, 'this young lady of yours is scarcely luckier than you are. You have no father, she has lost her mother, she is nobly born but as poor as Job. You are to be a priest and she a nun. And so you may put her out of your mind.'

'What makes you think I had her in mind at all?' Gilles said sulkily.

Rozenn took off her spectacles and wiped them on a corner of her apron. Then she uttered a short, mirthless laugh.

'My poor boy! If you hadn't, you would have given me and my tales short shrift long before this, saying you'd lost interest.

But you heard me right out without a word, and your eyes like stars. Is she so very pretty?'

Gilles turned his back on her abruptly and began rumpling his thick, dark-gold hair as though seeking for some elusive idea.

'Yes . . . yes, I suppose she is! But after all, what difference does it make? You say she's no better endowed than I am, but you're wrong. Even if her future were not already decided, she could never be anything to me because she may be poor but she is still noble and if she has no mother, at least she bears her father's name. She was born in wedlock while I am nothing but a bastard. Which, in a world where birth is the only real passport to a proper life, is to say nothing. So we'll not talk about it again, ever . . .'

And rather than let Rozenn's distressed eyes see him give way to the flood of bitterness that was overwhelming him, he escaped from the house and roamed about the heath until late into the night.

During the days that remained of the holidays, before he was to return to college after All Souls, he did not mention Judith's name again, but he was rarely seen about the house.

Yet he no longer went to sea with the Le Mang brothers as he used to do, nor did he fish in the river any more. Even the ramparts of Port-Louis, the nearby naval fort, where he used to love to wander and the Eastern waterfront where he liked to go sometimes to breathe in the spicy odours of the great ships returning from the Indies, saw him no more. He would sit for hours by the banks of the Blavet, in the nest in the long grass to which, that evening, he had dragged an unconscious form, watching the moving waters flow past but with no thought of casting a line.

Two or three times, he went as far as Hennebont and wandered for a long time along the path between the river and the high walls of the convent, and then walked back to Kervignac without so much as calling on his godfather, although he loved him dearly, both for his inexhaustible goodness and for his ever-watchful care. Too watchful, perhaps, in the present case. Gilles was chiefly afraid that the priest's shrewd eyes would very quickly discover his secret.

He returned to the house only after dark, to swallow some

food and fall asleep without uttering more than a dozen words. He had become as taciturn as his mother, although she was not the one to notice it, plunged as she was in her own interminable prayers. But Rozenn worried for both and studied the young man's face for the progress of a disease which she divined all too well.

She caught Marie-Jeanne one evening as she was putting on her black cloak to go to evening service.

'Take your mind off heaven for a while and look at this world,' she told her roughly. 'Look at your son. He doesn't eat any more, he no longer laughs, he hardly even speaks . . . Can you not see he is unhappy?'

Gilles' mother was thirty-three and looked fifty, but her narrow face lightened in a smile and the dark eyes below the widow's cap which she had worn ever since the birth of her child shone with a fanatical flame.

'Unhappy? Because he has heard the Voice which turns him away from the world and its vanities? He no longer laughs or talks, you say? Rejoice, then, you stupid creature, instead of bemoaning it. If he is silent, it is the better to hear God calling him. Blessed be His Holy Name to all eternity! Now leave me. I am late.'

And away she went, almost at a run, before Rozenn, disheartened, could make a move to detain her. After all, it had been foolish to have tried to interest this broken-hearted woman in the child of whose existence she seemed for the most part scarcely aware. Now that he spent most of his time at school, she hardly spoke to him, except to bid him good morning and good night and to inquire if he had said his prayers. Apart from that, her glance rested on him no more than if he had been made of glass, like the window panes.

'She sees nothing and hears nothing!' the old woman fumed. 'God! Heaven! The Church! She can think of nothing else and at this very minute she will be telling her confessor, the Abbé Séveno, and the rector in the village that Gilles has been touched with grace! And what does it matter if the child is miserable! Grace? A likely tale! And a fine priest he'll be making if he's lovesick already!'

But Rozenn knew that there was nothing to be done and for the first time in her life she found the holidays too long for her

19

and felt that the time when Gilles must leave a place so full of peril and return to Vannes could not come soon enough.

She did not know it but in this she was at one with Gilles himself. The boy could not understand what was happening to him, the dull ache that had lodged itself like a tiny gnawing worm in his chest, the image that haunted him day and night, the burning desire to see again, even for a moment, the face which obsessed him. He had come a long way from the Abbé Delourme's stern warnings, inveighing against woman and her wiles. No echo of those reached him now, he only thought that God was both cruel and unfair to have let him see Judith when she could never be more than an impossible dream to him. And, in his innocence, he longed to go away for ever . . .

But his need to see the girl again was stronger than reason. On All Hallows Eve, the day before he was due to go back to college, he made up his mind to do his duty and attend the mass for the dead at Nôtre Dame du Paradis, the principal church of Hennebont. He knew that the whole town would be there.

And Judith, of course, was there, leaning on her father's arm. But at first he hardly recognized the little fury who had done her best to gouge his eyes out in the demure young lady, her curls tucked away inside a brown hooded cloak, who moved sedately and with downcast eyes up the nave towards the seats reserved for the nobility and gentry.

Hidden behind a pillar, he saw her smooth hair shining like copper in the candlelight and when she raised her eyes to the altar their brilliance, sparkling like black diamonds, pierced him to the heart.

All through the interminable service he remained rooted in the shadow of his pillar, without so much as a glance for the choir and the officiating clergy in their black and silver copes, with the agonizing feeling that his life would end the moment he took his eyes from Judith.

But when the final Requiem thundered out under the ancient arches, swelling from the strong throats of the good people of Hennebont, he did what any young man does who sees the girl he loves in church and literally hurled himself towards the holy water stoup to be ready to offer it to her as she passed.

He waited a long time, in the growing fear that she might have gone out by another door, for he had seen her father go by with old Madame de La Foret, who was as deaf as a post and crippled with rheumatism, on his arm.

He saw her finally, among the last of the congregation, walking with a girl of her own age who was as dark as she was auburn but with a pair of very bright green eyes. Gilles stepped forward quickly and, plunging his hand so eagerly into the granite basin that his sleeve was wet to the elbow, held it out to her all dripping.

A tremor ran through her and for an instant her dark eyes met the young man's blue ones, then came to rest austerely on his wet hand.

'Still as clumsy as ever, I see,' she said, making no move to lift her own to meet it.

'Eternal rest to all departed souls,' he murmured, aware to his horror that his voice was shaking.

Judith made no answer. She simply stood and stared at him insolently from a few feet away while her companion, clearly thrilled by the adventure, whispered something in her ear.

'Amen!' Judith said at last. 'But our prayers for the dead do not give you the right to offer me holy water! Oh Azénor,' she added forcibly to her friend, 'do stop pestering me to introduce this young man to you! One cannot present every Tom, Dick or Harry to a gentlewoman! As for you, Sir, I thought I asked you to forget you ever knew my name? Much less my face!'

'But who is he?' young Azénor persisted, evidently unable to contain her curiosity. 'I have never seen him before!'

'It doesn't matter. But if you must know, his name is Gilles Goëlo. He is going to be a village priest. Come on. We mustn't miss the procession.'

And she moved on, out into the grey daylight, borne on the last rolls of the organ.

Gilles never knew how long he stood there, by the holy water basin, his feet rooted to the cold flagstones where a few withered leaves swirled in the rain-laden wind, his hand still in the air, shattered by her contempt and with a weight like lead about his heart.

He might have stood there until Judgment Day if the pealing of the bells and the shrill voices of the choristers breaking into a psalm had not dragged him out of his trance. He saw the procession coming towards him from the far end of the church, the great silver cross swaying forward slowly against the blue of the banners, the solemn-faced priests with mourning vestments on their backs. An unfamiliar lump came into his throat, a lump which may have been to do with fear. It was as though the church were performing the obsequies of his own life and hopes, reminding him of his fate.

'Going to be a village priest! Going to be a village priest . . .'

The scornful voice filled his ears, rising above the tolling of the bells, the din of choir and organ. A kind of panic seized him and he fled then, pushing past the groups of people standing by the graveyard, awaiting the procession, and hurtling down the steep hill to the river until the foggy November air had swallowed him up.

Reaching home, he found Rozenn busy laying the table with a white cloth, ready to put out the cider, pancakes and curds for the dead who, that night, were permitted to revisit their old homes on earth. But Gilles paid no heed to her.

He went straight to the chest where his clothes were kept and dragged out all his possessions, stuffing them into an old seaman's duffle bag, working with such nervous haste that the old woman was alarmed.

'Blessed St Anne! What ever are you about, child? Are you going away?'

'Yes . . . I'm going . . . now, this minute! I must go . . . I must go back to school—'

'But there's no hurry! The coach for Vannes does not leave until tomorrow. And your mother—'

Gilles gripped Rozenn's arms and kissed her on both wrinkled cheeks, knocking her muslin coif askew.

'Say goodbye to her for me! Tell her – tell her I'll write to her. It will be all the same to her. I'm going down to the waterfront. In three hours the tide will be up and I'll find a boat to take me back to Vannes. God bless you, dear Rozenn!'

She was frightened suddenly by the catch in his voice and by the white, drawn face which at that moment had lost all its childish curves. She put her arms round him and hugged him, in an effort to make him stay.

'Gilles! My little one . . . Are you truly going to Vannes? You promise me?'

He gave a harsh little laugh, so sad that it made her want to weep.

'Oh yes, to Vannes! Where else should I go? I must go back to school and continue my studies. Am I not to be a village priest one day? Who wouldn't be impatient with such a brilliant future ahead of him?'

He wrenched himself out of the old woman's arms and the door slammed dully behind him. Rozenn sat down abruptly on a settle, listening to the fast-fading footsteps of the boy whom she loved like her own son, more perhaps, since her love was given of her own free choice.

'Dear god!' she murmured. 'It is worse than I thought.'

And all night long, while she tended the fire which had to be kept burning until daybreak so that the dead souls might warm themselves, Rozenn sat in the chimney corner and listened to the passing bell, for that, too, must keep tolling until dawn, and praying in her simple heart for God to be merciful to Gilles and not test him too cruelly.

'He is so young,' she muttered, over and over again. 'So young! He has not learned to suffer . . .'

2

The Man from Nantes

St Yves College, originally a Jesuit foundation, stood in the
faubourg of Auray, outside the walls of Vannes. It was not an
inviting place. It comprised a large, gravelled courtyard, overrun with weeds and some austere, somewhat dilapidated buildings which, situated as they were on the downhill side of the
courtyard, were prone to collect the water on rainy days, trans-
forming the classrooms into a succession of swamps. A square
tower, known as the 'Barbin', in one corner, served as a place
of punishment and occupied a sufficiently prominent position
to keep its function constantly before the inmates. The classrooms themselves were rudely flagged and furnished with high
chairs, which had at least the advantage of keeping the teachers
dry, and rows of wooden forms on which the pupils sat with
their books on their knees. There they froze in winter and sat
with their feet in the water whenever it rained and the concierge
forgot to put straw on the floor.

They were taught French, mathematics, physics, history and
geography in small doses and Latin in enormous ones. Discipline was strict and intellectual activity narrow and sternly
controlled. For picking up a fragment of a news sheet in the
street one day and slipping it into his books, Gilles had received twenty strokes of the cane and spent an hour in prayer
on his knees on the hard stones of the chapel.

To all this he returned without enthusiasm yet at the same
time with a curious sense of security. Within St Yves' leprous
walls, echoing with the rolling periods of Cicero and the say-
ings of Ecclesiastes, Judith's tantalizing image faded into the

mists of legend. She seemed to belong to the mysterious world of lakes and trees and to the people whose slender forms haunted the nearby woods of Paimpont, once the old forest of Broceliande. She was a fairy glimpsed in a dream, she was Morgan, she was Vivian . . . she was no longer altogether Judith and that in itself was some help to the boy's peace of mind.

As regards his studies, he could not have been called devoted to them. History, geography and the natural sciences he loved, but his reports were bad on account of his unshakeable aversion to the inevitable Latin, and also because his masters could not view the combination of daring and independence in his character with anything but alarm. That apart, he did not dislike the arts, while as for mathematics, he looked upon them like relations, useful if not visited too often. All in all, he was an average pupil but not one the good fathers of St Yves looked to to shed academic lustre on the college.

He returned to the same small room in the Rue St Gwenael that he had always lived in, in the house of a spinster who, in return for a modest rental, provided him with bed and a none too lavish board. The bed was in a cramped, ill-furnished room, devoid of curtains or carpet, although the tall window and dusty panelling smacked of better days. Morever Gilles could roast chestnuts in the hearth in winter to fill up the corners left unsatisfied by his hostess's meagre fare. In fact he felt much more at home there than in his mother's house because he could be alone here with his dreams and the modest treasures which constituted all his worldly goods, a few clothes, sadly plain, various toilet articles and some shells and curious stones picked up on his wanderings along the shore and about the countryside. These were books, too, mostly those he needed for his studies but including two works shockingly unsuitable for a future priest. There were *The Age of Louis XIV* by Monsieur de Voltaire and *Emile* by Jean-Jacques Rousseau and he revelled in both of them.

These things made up the little private world in which Gilles hoped to find himself again after his flight from Kervignac. But he soon realized that this was impossible, for Judith invaded even his reading. Alexander the Great's beautiful captives or Queen Cleopatra all took on a curious likeness to her, with flaming hair and smooth, luminous flesh. Then he would hurl the book furiously into a corner and all night long would toss and turn on his seaweed mattress, unable to go to sleep. Sometimes, towards morning, he did manage to doze off. But the dreams that came to him with this sudden awakening of his manhood carried him into unsuspected chasms from which he awoke panting and drenched with sweat, with his heart pounding in his breast.

These wretched dreams left him deeply worried and ashamed. So much so that when Christmas approached he dared not tell them to his father confessor and failed to put in an appearance at Confession as the college rules required. On the day when he should have presented himself, along with the rest of his class, for this ritual cleansing of the soul, he stayed at home, feigning illness. Nor was it entirely feigned, because the mere thought of evoking Judith's unconsciously voluptuous form in a dark and dusty confessional, reeking of damp and the stale breath of the unseen priest, made him feel sick. And he swore to himself that if, when he went back, he were obliged to go to chapel after all, then he would say nothing about the things that haunted his nights and filled his heart, even if it meant lying to God Himself.

He knew that this was dealing a severe blow to the contract his mother had made with Heaven in his name, but he found himself taking a kind of bitter delight in his new rebellion, like a taste of revenge. He felt as if he were confronting God face to face.

On the day after his pretended illness, he left the house in the Rue St Gwenael at his usual time and was walking past the cathedral in the cold greyness of the early morning on his way to St Yves when he met one of his schoolfellows, a boy named Jean-Pierre Quérelle, the son of the best shipwright in the harbour. Jean-Pierre had his books under his arm but he was running as fast as he could in quite the opposite direction to the college. Gilles, partly out of a natural waywardness and partly from pride, was not in the habit of making friends with those of his fellows who possessed proper fathers, but his curiosity got the better of him and he called out :

'Where are you off to so fast, Jean-Pierre Quérelle? You know you're going away from St Yves? Lost your compass?'

The other boy halted.

'Never mind college,' he said, with a shrug. 'Didn't you hear the guns at cockcrow? They say the *St Nicolas,* Monsieur de Sainte-Pasane's ship that has not been heard of for so long, has just entered harbour. I want to see it! Are you coming? She's from the East Indies—'

Gilles needed no second invitation. In the eighteen months since France had been at war with England and the two countries had been laying into one another with great quantities of chain shot and cutlasses all over the Atlantic, a ship returned from the Antilles had become a rare occurrence, especially in the port of Vannes. For the most part the great pyramids of sail that beat about the oceans of the world would put into the quays of L'Orient, home of the Great Indies Company, or of Nantes, capital of the French slave trade. But Sainte-Pasane, with the stubborn independence of a true descendant of the old Venetii, was a shipowner who had never seen the point of bringing home his vessels from whatever part of the world to any anchorage but that outside the tiny bottle-glass windows of his own counting house.

Despite the mist and the cold, which was unusual for this part of Brittany, for it was freezing hard, a crowd had gathered at the port. It was a joyful crowd, echoing with the click of sabots and crested with white caps like the sea in stormy weather.

The *St Nicolas* was there, huge and broad-bellied, settling into the misty river like a hen onto her nest. Only this hen had had a hard time of it. The colours of her hull were worn with salt. Her sails, now being furled by the skeletal seamen performing acrobatic miracles on her yards, were patched and dirty. As for the seamen themselves, with their prophetic beards and dirt-ingrained skins, they looked more like savages than honest Bretons. But not all the scars of their sufferings could extinguish the joy of this triumphant return, their holds full of indigo, sugar and precious woods to be exchanged for gold crowns chinking on mahogany counters, and silver coins gleaming in calloused palms, and made into fabulous tales to be told amid the smoke of the long clay pipes and the smell of rough cider in Mamm'Goz's tavern.

Perched on a bollard where they had clambered for a better

27

view over the crowd, the two boys craned their necks to watch it all with sparkling eyes. Jean-Pierre was the first to speak. Gritting his teeth, he declared abruptly :

'I want to go to sea! Next time the *St Nicolas* sails, I shall go with her.'

Gilles looked at him in surprise.

'I thought your father was sending you to school to become a lawyer? They say he has saved up for it all his life—'

'I know. Well – he can keep his money. I don't want it. All I want is to go to sea. All my life I've seen him building great, lovely ships and never knowing the places they would sail to. Well, I'm going to see them. To hell with being a lawyer!'

And Jean-Pierre spat like an angry cat to show his contempt for the whole profession. Gilles said nothing for a moment. He was studying his schoolfellow's freckled countenance, the washed-out blue eyes under jutting brows, the short but stocky figure, and he could not help smiling. Jean-Pierre was as much fitted by nature for sitting in a comfortable office drawing up legal documents as he himself was to say mass and hear old ladies' confessions. And he felt all at once very close to the lad with whom, until that moment, he had been on the most distant terms. The invisible link which had been forged so suddenly between them was made by the sea, that familiar yet unknown sea which had figured like a tumultuous paradise in his dreams from babyhood, the forbidden sea his mother would never permit him to embark upon. But looking at this ship which carried with her all the fierce aroma of distant horizons, he thrust the thought of Marie-Jeanne away from him, as if her mere image was an insult to the voyager from afar with her glorious scars.

'And I,' he said at last, as though the words were dragged from him by some unknown force. 'I, too, shall go to sea some day.'

Jean-Pierre gave him a crooked grin and jerked his shoulders with a hint of scorn.

'You? You're even worse off than I am. You're going to be a priest.'

His grin broadened but at the cold rage in Gilles' glance it faded and he turned dull red.

'A priest?' young Goëlo said, with dangerous softness. 'That,

28

let me tell you, I shall never be. And I won't have anyone say it to my face again. You understand?'

'All right,' the other conceded. 'Only – what are you going to do? They said your mother had decided—' .

'So she has, yes. But I don't want to – not any longer. And I'm going to write to her tonight.'

'But what if she refuses to listen to you? Suppose she insists on sending you to the seminary? She'd be within her rights, you know, to have the constable take you there by force.'

'Then I should run away.'

There was silence as the two boys scrambled down from their bollard. All the seamen had come ashore by now and the crowd had dispersed to seek the warmth of home or tavern. For a moment, Gilles and Jean-Pierre stood face to face, looking at one another as though meeting for the first time. They felt suddenly shy, as embarrassed as though the years of indifference stood in the way of their friendship.

They were rescued from speechlessness by the clock of a nearby church striking the half. Jean-Pierre smiled awkwardly.

'I suppose we ought to go,' he said. 'We're shockingly late already. I dare say we'll get a spell in the "Barbin",' he added, with a comical grin.

Gilles returned his smile readily. 'That's for sure! But don't you think it was worth it?'

The two of them began to run back up the steep street, more to warm themselves than out of any real fear of the beatings in store for them. Both were too familiar with those to attach overmuch importance to them.

But when they came in sight of the great, two hundred-year-old gateway of St Yves, Jean-Pierre, who had not spoken all the way, suddenly stopped.

'Tell me,' he said, 'did you mean it just now when you said you wanted to go to sea?'

'Of course I meant it. Why?'

'Listen, then. Meet me this evening after the cathedral bell strikes nine at the corner of the Rue des Halles, by Vannes and his wife. Ask no questions,' he added quickly, seeing Gilles start to speak. 'I'm going to take you somewhere that will interest you. Now, let's go and take our punishment. See you tonight!'

'Tonight! I'll be there.'

Gilles received a double punishment, for having missed confession on so febble an excuse as illness. He was also commanded to go straight to the chapel on being released from the 'Barbin' and present himself to the officiating priest, and to say two rosaries in addition to whatever penance was imposed on him. He bore it all without protest, sustained by the new vistas which Jean-Pierre's words had opened up to him. He made deliberate omissions in his confession and in so doing broke with the conscientious scruples he felt he had outgrown and which no longer applied to the man he was becoming. And on the last stroke of nine o'clock, with a back still smarting but a heart full of hope, he was pacing the greasy cobbles of the little square, dark and deserted at this late hour, brooded over by the two small tutelary figures of the city. For the first time since his plunge into the Blavet, the thought of Judith had loosened its vicelike grip on the young man's mind. It was of a future misty with the blue haze of adventure that Gilles was dreaming as he paced up and down in the cold, dark night.

Jean-Pierre popped up out of the darkness like a jack in the box, making no more noise than a cat.

'Come on,' he said simply.

As they had done in the morning, the two lads made their way towards the harbour, the only part of the town that still showed signs of life, for Vannes was a good and pious city where life was regulated by the bells of the cathedral and religious houses.

'Where are you taking me?' Gilles asked, as the two of them emerged from the Porte St Vincent.

Jean-Pierre's only answer was to indicate an ancient building by the quay, its upper storey jutting like heavy brows over the two small windows blinking redly into the darkness.

'There.'

Gilles made a face. He had never entered any of the harbour taverns but he knew enough to be aware that the *Hermine Rouge* was one of the most disreputable.

The landlord, Yann Maodan, was not particular in his choice of customers, the more so since he had himself spent three of the best years of his wild youth at the oar of a galley, the only effect of which had been to give an added hardness to his already cunning and slippery fingers. The smuggler seeking new recruits, the jealous husband in search of a spy, even the thieves' captain desirous of reforming a gang broken up by the law, could all be fairly sure of finding what they wanted in his house. But it was naturally not a haunt much frequented by the pupils of St Yves. So that when Gilles saw his companion descend the steps that led to the low doorway with the ease of long familiarity, he could not help clutching at his arm.

'You've been to this house before?' he said accusingly. Jean-Pierre shrugged and would not meet his eyes, but there was a note of defiance in his voice as he answered.

'Of course. If you want to get aboard a ship without anyone's knowing, you can't afford to be choosy. There's a man here who can help us—'

'You know the *Hermine Rouge* has an evil reputation! But have you even thought what would happen if your father, or the Head, learned you had been seen here?'

'Don't worry. I've thought. But you can't make an omelette without breaking eggs. Now, if you're afraid of what people might think, you are quite free to turn back. Only I'm beginning to wonder if you had not better stick to being a priest—'

'When I need your advice about my future, I'll ask for it!' Gilles retorted curtly. 'And now, lead on – since you seem to know what you are doing.'

He took a deep breath and entered the tavern on his friend's heels. He had expected to walk into a hell of noise and anger, full of quarrelling, shouting and drunken singing. But the noise was less than in many a classroom at St Yves.

From the threshold, he got a glimpse through a blue haze of pipe smoke of variously coloured backs and heads of varying degrees of hairiness, all bent over tables on which elbows and beakers of rum jostled for room. All these men were talking quietly among themselves, discussing in low voices business which, however shady, was none the less of paramount importance to them. And not even the presence of two serving wenches in bodices cut almost indecently low moving to and fro between the tables carrying heavy trays could give the place anything approaching a festive air.

Yann Maodan himself was leaning, both elbows on his grimy walnut wood counter and surveying the assembled company with an imperious eye that missed nothing. The eye took in the two boys, creased into an expression which might conceivably have passed for a smile and swivelled across the room, coming to rest at a table in the far corner where a man sat alone.

'Hey! Nantais!' he called. 'Someone for you!'

The man addressed pinned a smile to his face, which suited it like a rose in the teeth of a crocodile, and removing from his square-shaped head a splendid, gold-braided tricorne which had certainly never been made for it, waved it graciously in the direction of the two boys threading their way towards him among the tables.

'There you are then, lad!' he cried thickly, revealing three astonishingly white teeth in a mouth full of dark brown stumps. 'Come to tell me that you've thought it over?'

'Yes, sir. And I've made up my mind.'

An amicable flourish of the cocked hat.

'Good! And who's this?'

'A friend. We're in the same class. And he has made up his mind also—'

'Just a minute,' Gilles said. 'I'd still like to know what I'm suppose to have made up my mind about.'

He did not care for the Nantais. His steel-blue eyes narrowed swiftly and searched the man's face coldly, as though striving to fathom his secret thoughts. The face below the square skull was a fleshy face that smiled too broadly, a long nose with widely flaring nostrils and small black eyes as bright as beads of jet. The face was clean and well-shaven and would have been not unpleasant but for a certain elusive shiftiness about the eyes and the Nantais' disturbing habit of licking his lips with his tongue all the time, like a cat after meat.

A flash of anger gleamed in the shifty eyes, but only for an instant, then it was gone, like a candle snuffed out by the wind. The man shrugged and gave a shout of laughter.

'Made up your mind to go to sea, by heaven! Like this bold lad here who's burning to win fame and fortune on the high seas and feast his eyes on all the wonders of the world.'

'And you have it in your power to give us all that?' Gilles said coolly.

An expression of deep grief came over the Nantais' face and he turned to Jean-Pierre reproachfully.

'What's this, boy? Have you not told him?'

'No, sir! I thought it better you should! Besides, you urged me to be discreet.'

'True, son, very true! Discretion is a great thing. My poor mother always used to say that in great matters it was better to confide in God and His saints! Well, sit down, lads! And listen to me. Hey there! Manon! Two beakers for these young gentlemen!'

One of the serving girls came up. Lifting his eyes automatically, Gilles saw that she was blonde and pretty and surely not much older than himself, also she was looking at him. Silently, but without taking her eyes off him, she set two pewter tankards on the table and departed with a sigh, as though unwillingly, while the Nantais took up the big black bottle that stood in front of him. The aroma of old West Indian rum filled the boys' nostrils like a subtle reminder of those distant lands the Nantais had spoken of. At the same time the man embarked upon a kind of grandiloquent speech wholly designed to persuade his youthful listeners that he alone had power to offer them a brilliant future.

But his introduction was too long for Jean-Pierre, despite his evident respect for the man.

'We are both only too grateful to you, sir,' he broke in. 'But tell us, if you please, about America – and the Rebels!'

Gilles, who had been beginning to find the Nantais not merely antipathetic but tedious, felt his interest reawaken. News of the outside world was rarely discussed in the classrooms at St Yves, or in the main streets of Vannes, where people had small interest in the affairs of a parcel of savages on the other side of the Atlantic except, of course, when commercial interests were at stake. The war with England taking place in home waters was of much more pressing concern to a city which had not yet forgotten that it was once the seat of the Breton parliament. Even so, the younger dwellers in the Rue Latine and the Rue St Gwenael had not failed to glean some adventurous rumours percolating from the house of Monsieur de Limur, the Lieutenant-General of the Navy, or from the barracks of Walsh's regiment.

For some months past, and especially since the outbreak of the war with England, the talk had been full of sympathy for the revolt of the thirteen English colonies in America which, since 1776, had flared into open war. The unrest had been simmering for years, ever since England, exhausted by the Seven Years War and endeavouring to wipe out a national debt amounting to a hundred and forty million pounds, had attempted to shift the greater part of it on to her American colonies. The representatives of all the colonies, meeting in New York, had declared their rejection of a tax they had not voted for. English reaction had been prompt. And so the unrest, going from bad to worse, had turned into open rebellion and had driven the colonists to demand independence and declare war on the mother country.

These determined men led, it seemed, by a soldier of genius named General Washington, were known in Europe as the Rebels and they had long been petitioning the King of France for aid. Three years previously the people of Vannes had actually seen the Rebel ambassador put up one December night at the inn of the *Dauphin Couronné*. He was a stout, good-natured old gentleman, neat and bespectacled, with long white hair surrounding a bald crown on which he wore a curious kind of fur hat. He had his two young grandsons with him and announced himself as Benjamin Franklin on his way to Paris. He was said, moreover, to be a great scholar, known the world over and to have power over the lightning, so that the Bretons had decided he must be some kind of wizard. The ancient forest of Broceliande was close at hand and the memory of the enchanter Merlin ever-present to men's minds.

People said, with a kind of exasperated indulgence, that a young officer from the Auvergne in attendance at court, who was as hotheaded as he was highborn, had freighted a vessel in spite of the King, at that time by no means determined on a breach with England, and had gone to fight for freedom in America, and that he had returned, broken in health but with enough strength left to implore Louis XVI to send aid to the Rebels. And now of late the rumours running round the barracks whispered that the King might be going to reward the hopes of the American Congress by sending the men and money it so sorely needed.

All these rumours inflamed the young hotheads of St Yves. Especially such new and uplifting words as liberty and independence. To Gilles, in particular, coming back to Vannes with a heart full of bitterness, they were like a cool shower after a day of blistering heat. La Fayette's exploits haunted his dreams and, except for Judith, there was no one in the world he longed more eagerly to be with.

Therefore as soon as Jean-Pierre uttered the magic words America and the Rebels, he became passionately interested.

'Lord, what a hurry you young men are in!' the Nantais sighed, draining his tankard at a draught. 'I was coming to it. But first, you, the new lad, what do you call yourself?'

'Gilles Goëlo.'

'Well, my boy, I'm telling you that there are those in Nantes who believe America should be free and are willing to do all they can to help her. The biggest of them is a very wealthy gentleman, a great shipowner in Nantes, the owner of a royal château, a personal friend of Mr Franklin, who lives in his house when he is in Paris – and my master!' This last was uttered with such pride as to suggest that, among that list of impressive titles, it was by far the greatest. 'This gentleman, who has devoted much of his wealth to helping the Rebels, is at this moment fitting out his largest vessel in the port of Nantes, ready to sail to Boston. All those young men at court who wish to serve a noble cause and at the same time seek adventure and their fortunes may sail in her. And it is my especial task to select those in these parts who seem to me most worthy of so high a destiny – Will you be one?'

'I ask nothing better,' Gilles answered. 'But what are you doing here, in this tavern where, between ourselves, there can't be many such? One would say you were hiding from something! Why don't you go to the *Chapeau Rouge* or the *Dauphin Couronné* and have the town criers proclaim your master's offer? What is his name, by the by? I don't recall that you told it to us.'

'Precisely, because it is not to be spoken in such a place as this,' the Nantais answered sternly. 'As to your other questions, my young friend, they prove that you are both observant and quick-witted but unused to the ways of politics. Have you yet seen our worthy King sending troops to aid the Rebels? I do not mean Monsieur de La Fayette, who went of his own accord, but proper troops, with generals and guns?'

35

'No. But it may be—'

'That is where the shoe pinches. It may be – but it cannot be yet! And my master is risking the King's displeasure by determining to send his own aid to those good folk. He is risking his reputation and a host of other things which compel him to secrecy. Do you understand?'

Gilles nodded. 'I think so, yes. All the same, I should like to know what this wonderful man is called, even if it is sacrilege to utter his name here.'

The Nantais sighed like one resigned. Then, placing an arm round each of the boys' necks to draw them close, he cast a conspiratorial glance around him, as though expecting police spies to pop up everywhere, and finally whispered : 'His name is Monsieur Donatien Leray de Chaumont! Does that satisfy you? But forget it at once and so wipe out my shameful indiscretion. And now that we are agreed, let us come to the arrangements. You go aboard at high tide tomorrow night—'

Gilles started and drew back.

'Tomorrow? But that's impossible!'

'And why impossible?'

'Because – well, it's much too soon! Jean-Pierre, tell him! We don't mean to sneak away from Vannes like criminals. At least give us time to see whether our families won't change their minds and let us abandon our studies.'

'For my part, it's already done,' Jean-Pierre said grimly. 'If I refuse to be a lawyer, my father means to disinherit me. And if I don't take ship at once, he'll set the law on me. I'm off tomorrow!'

'Well, not so I! You didn't tell me we should have to burn our bridges quite so fast. Only this morning, remember, you were talking of going with the *St Nicolas* when she sailed!'

'I didn't know this morning that you had the same idea as I did. I was right to be cautious. Quite right, as it turns out – if you're scared!'

Gilles leapt to his feet, rocking the table. His eyes were flashing and his face was hard as stone.

'Never say a thing like that again!' he said. 'By my soul, I'll not stand that from anyone! I am not scared and well you know it. Only I don't want to break my mother's heart unless I'm sure she will leave me no choice. All I ask is a few days to

36

be sure. If you had told me you were thinking of leaving at once, I would have told you.'

Jean-Pierre, who had risen also, let the flush fade from his face. He even tried to smile.

'You are right! I'm sorry. The trouble is we don't know each other well enough yet. Very well. We'll wait for a few days.'

The Nantais, who had been following the exchange with more interest than he allowed himself to show, now clicked his tongue irritably.

'Wait! Wait! How you do go on! The ship puts to sea very soon. As for the next vessel, I don't know when that will be. I'm willing to give you a few days, boy, but it will be better, if your friend is ready, if he goes at once. After all, he can as well await you at Nantes and can even make sure that a berth is kept for you. Besides, I did not know there would be two of you.'

Gilles and Jean-Pierre looked at one another, obviously undecided. In the latter's eyes there was so much impatience, such evident haste, that Gilles guessed what a sacrifice waiting would mean. He smiled in his turn.

'He's right. You go first. I'll be joining you, in any case, and it's no good two of us wasting time.'

'Really? You don't mind?'

'Not at all. Things are not quite the same for both of us. Go and don't worry.'

'Thank you. In that case, sir, tell me what I have to do,' Jean-Pierre added, turning to the Nantais. But the man shook his head.

'I am going to tell you. Only, with things as they are, your friend must leave us, for you never know when one may say something indiscreet! There's no offence in this, my boy, only simple prudence. When you've made up your mind, then come back here and find me and I will tell you what you must do then. Agreed?'

'Agreed! I'm going. Good night, Jean-Pierre. I'll see you tomorrow. And God be with you.'

'God be with you, Gilles Goëlo. Until tomorrow.'

Leaving his companion still seated at the table with the Nantais, Gilles left the *Hermine Rouge* without a backward glance and with a curious sense of relief. After the heavy aroma of spirits, the cold outside seemed delightful. He took two or three almost voluptuous breaths of the sea air, with its lingering odours of seaweed and fish. But it was far from warm and he set off at a run along the harbour in the direction of the Rue St Gwenael.

He had almost reached the archway of the Porte St Vincent when he heard someone running after him. At the same time a girl's voice, gasping and breathless, called out:

'Stop! Please stop! You are running too fast for me!'

He stopped and, turning, saw a red skirt and the white head-dress of the women of Vannes caught in the yellow beam from a lighted window. To his surprise he recognized the young serving girl the Nantais had addressed as Manon. A black shawl was clutched round her shoulders and she was running lightly on the uneven cobblestones.

'Was it me you wanted?' he asked, as she came up to him.

'Yes! I must speak to you – only I have not much time. I said – that I was going down to the cellar – to get oil for the lamps! Hurry! Come in here.'

He felt a cold, firm little hand in his, drawing him with surprising strength into the darkness of the archway, while above them St Vincent Ferrier, in bishop's robes, endlessly blessed the harbour.

'What is it you must say to me so urgently?' Gilles asked, intrigued.

Manon breathed in two or three times to get her breath back. She was so close to him that Gilles could feel the hurried beating of her heart beneath her shawl, while even after running in the fresh air she still carried with her, lingering in her clothes, the smell of the tavern, a mixture of alcohol and tobacco. She had not released his hand. On the contrary, he could feel that her grip had tightened.

'Do not go with the Nantais!' she whispered hurriedly. 'I heard what he was saying to you. He is a bad man, a brigand – and he does not work for any great shipowner in Nantes.'

'For whom, then?'

'I am not quite sure. I think it is for a Spanish smuggler who, they say, sometimes drops anchor in the bay. We hear things at the *Hermine Rouge*. But they are always better forgotten.'

'But surely the Nantais—'

'Is a devil of a man! Listen! He came to this town once before, two years ago, and three young lads disappeared. They were said to have taken ship at L'Orient and sailed to the West Indies – but a seaman from Auray who had been captive in Algiers and ransomed by the Fathers of Mercy told me, in his cups, that he had seen one of them there – a slave to a rich blackamoor. Instead of sailing from L'Orient, he had been taken aboard the Spaniard's ship one night and the Spaniard had sold him to the Barbary pirates. The same fate awaits you, if you go! Don't go, I beg of you—'

The girl's words chimed too closely with his own instinctive distrust of the Nantais for Gilles to feel a moment's doubt. Besides which, there was an eagerness and sincerity in her voice which carried conviction. Yet there was something he did not understand and he could not help asking her : 'How long has the Nantais been here?'

'Two or three months – perhaps more. I don't know exactly.'

'Have other boys come to him in that time?'

'Yes – three or four, I think.'

'And – did you warn them?'

He heard her breath come a little faster and felt her hesitate. But not for long.

'No,' she said. 'It was too dangerous. If the Nantais knew – or even my master, Yann Maodan, I might disappear also.'

'Then why are you taking that risk now? Why for me?'

'Because—'

She left the phrase unfinished and pressed herself suddenly against Gilles. Her arms went round his neck and he felt her warm lips against his. It was done quickly and lightly, but with passion. For an instant, Manon's body lay close to Gilles' from knee to lips, then she jerked away as if he had burned her and her voice was murmuring breathlessly : 'Don't ask me why. I don't know myself, except that I like you as I have never liked a boy before. When I saw you with the Nantais just now, it was like seeing a seagull caught by birdlime. And I felt that if I let him make a slave of you I should never sleep again. Now, I have told you everything and I must go back. Take heed of my warning – but be sure and let no one ever know I gave it you, unless you want my death on your conscience.'

She turned to go but Gilles detained her, almost instinctively. It might have been because of the strange feelings aroused in him by that brief contact of their bodies, feelings that recalled what he had experienced the first time he saw Judith.

'You have saved more than my life. Tell me how I may thank you—'

He heard her laugh and saw her teeth gleam in the darkness.

'By cutting the rope the day they come to hang me.'

'Why should they want to hang you, Manon?'

'I belong to Yann Maodan and one of these days the law will take him. When that day comes, I shall have to follow him to the end.'

'Are you his mistress?'

'Yes. And he is fond of me. But it is to you that I would give what he takes every night. Listen – there is a single-storey cottage hard by the Porte du Boureau, on the right. My sister lives there. She is crippled and spins flax for a living. I often go to see her there on Sunday nights, after dark, to save her reputation. Come to me there one evening, if you want me. I think, after all, that might be the best way of thanking me! Just knock five times, that's all.'

She ran off, leaving Gilles feeling a little sorry, as well as deeply grateful. The thought of what had lain in store for Jean-Pierre and himself if the girl had not taken this sudden strange fancy to him, made his flesh creep. He thanked God and Manon that it was not too late to avert the danger, but he still had to warn Jean-Pierre and stop him going to his perilous meeting with the Nantais the next day.

He walked back towards the *Hermine Rouge* in the hope of meeting his friend, but stopped short of the tavern so as not to alarm Manon. He huddled in the angle of a doorway, both for warmth and to keep out of sight, and waited for Jean-Pierre to come out and pass by on his way home.

He waited like that for more than an hour and when, his patience wearing thin, he made up his mind to go and peer through the tavern's grimy window, he saw that the Nantais' table was empty. The man had gone and Jean-Pierre also . . . Perhaps, after all, he had gone home by another way, avoiding the Porte St Vincent, during the time that he had been talking to Manon.

It was getting late and thinking that his friend would be at school the next day and he would have plenty of time to warn him then, Gilles decided to go home. He flung himself on his bed without even troubling to undress and slept uneasily until cockcrow.

He was at St Yves among the earliest, but he looked in vain for Jean-Pierre. The boy did not put in an appearance and to Gilles, devoured with anxiety, no day had ever seemed so long. When evening came at last and the college released its pupils, he ran straight to Master Shipwright Quérelle's house in the Rue des Vierges.

Since he and Quérelle's son had not been friends, Gilles had never been there before but he was ready to dare anything to save the rash boy from the fate in store for him. Unfortunately, although he knocked again and again on the closed door, no one came to answer. Only a neighbour, drawn by the noise, came to her door and told him that Master Quérelle and his family had gone away to Loudéac the previous morning to attend a cousin's wedding.

'But Jean-Pierre has not gone!' Gilles protested. 'I saw him last night!'

The woman was evidently not the sort who liked to hear her word doubted. She stepped back inside and closed the door on him, crying: 'Go away, then! I've told you what I know!'

Gilles did not persist. In any case, he knew well enough. This explained Jean-Pierre's haste to be gone from Vannes. He was taking advantage of his parents' absence. It could not have been difficult for him to get permission to stay at home because, by what they said, Master Quérelle took his son's studies seriously and would probably not hear of his missing his lessons for so frivolous a cause as a cousin's wedding. But where could Jean-Pierre be now?

With a heavy heart and a dreadful sense of loneliness and impotence, Gilles allowed his legs to follow where his thoughts led until he came to the harbour. Jean-Pierre was to embark on the evening tide and the tide would be full at ten o'clock. And he would be sure to meet the Nantais at the *Hermine Rouge* as before.

By the time he reached the tavern, Gilles was ready for anything. He would snatch his friend away from this dreadful

41

place before he could go aboard, whatever might follow. Such was his fear for Jean-Pierre that he gave no thought to his own danger.

On the threshold he paused briefly to cross himself and then pushed open the door.

The scene was so exactly as it had been the night before that Gilles felt as if he had stepped back in time. There were the same backs, the same smoke, the same faces. Yann Maodan leaned on the counter in exactly the same attitude and the two serving girls were flitting among the tables precisely as before. Yes, everything was the same – except for one thing : the table where the Nantais had sat was empty.

Gilles' heart beat a little faster but he set his teeth, squared his shoulders and advanced with a firm step to the counter, Yann Maodan watching him with a frown.

'What do you want, boy?' he asked roughly. 'You're a mite young for rum or wenches.'

This was not encouraging. Yann Maodan had too good a memory to forget a customer from the night before, but Gilles did not give up.

'I want to see the Nantais,' he said coolly.

The landlord wiped his nose on an arm as hairy as a bear's, cleared his throat, spat and uttered a short laugh before he condescended to reply.

'That's a pity, because he ain't here.'

'But he told me yesterday I could find him here if I wanted him.'

'That's as maybe. All I know is he ain't here now, nor he won't be here tonight. What do you want of him?'

Gilles ignored the question. He clenched his fists and the eyes that met Yann's hardened a little.

'That is between him and me,' he said. 'Can you tell me where to find him?'

'No!'

The word was almost a roar and Gilles was suddenly aware that silence had fallen and everyone was looking at him. He was aware, too, of Manon, standing stiff with terror at the other end of the counter, her two hands gripping her tray. But his own gaze, icy cold now, never left Yann's which flickered suddenly, like an animal mesmerized. The ex-galley

42

slave had never seen such eyes, especially in one so young. They were like two steel blades driving into his head, stern and implacable, hawklike and unblinking. He wanted to be free of their power and his uneasiness expressed itself in anger.

'What are you waiting for? I tell you he ain't coming. As to where he is, I don't know. Gone to the devil, I shouldn't wonder! He's left the town, that I do know. Be off with you now, and don't let me see you in here again. I don't want no trouble with the law when someone starts tellin' 'em I'm serving babes of your age.'

'You are grown very scrupulous since yesterday,' Gilles observed.

But then his eye fell on Manon's horrified face. The girl was on the verge of fainting and he took pity on her, shrugged his shoulders and turned away.

'Very well. I'm going.'

He went out, full of bitterness, not even hearing Yann Maodan's harsh voice calling: 'What are you up to, Manon? What have you forgotten now? Get on and serve the customers.'

That night, Gilles did not go back to the Rue St Gwenael. Driven by helpless anger and fear, he roamed unceasingly from end to end of the harbour, from one end of the Rabine to the far side of Calmon-Bas, watching for the slightest movement in the boats and always hoping against hope to catch a glimpse of Jean-Pierre's stocky figure. He even went down river as far as the Pointe de Langle, studying the gleaming black waters for a sign of a ship about to sail. But with the high tide had come a sharp, cutting wind, laden with snow, that whined about the tossing heads of the pine trees and no one left the harbour of Vannes that night. Gilles felt neither cold nor wind, nor tiredness. He wanted to cry out, to call to the boy who had been an unregarded part of his life for years and who had suddenly become like a brother to him, a boy he would never see again and was powerless to save.

When the dawn broke, grey over a grey sea and the mud flats left by the receding tide and the trees on the small island of Conleau loomed vaguely through the mist, Gilles rose at last from the rock where he had come to rest at the end of his solitary vigil and, forcing his numbed legs to walk, turned his steps slowly back towards the town. His head was aching and his heart empty of hope.

The bell on the island ringing the Angelus brought him to himself. He remembered suddenly that it was Sunday and this was the day when Manon went to the little house by the Porte du Boureau to see her sister, the little house where she had asked him to meet her. With that, he began to run.

By the time he reached the Rue St Gwenael, it was the time for early mass, attended by servant girls and pious old maids who, indeed, would go on to hear high mass later. Black figures were hurrying cautiously over the thin covering of crisp snow that felted the cobbles and outlined gable ends. Gilles lurked in the shadows of the old hallway until he had seen his landlady and her maid pass by, so as not to be recognized.

Then, sure of meeting no one else, he went up to his icy room to rest and wait impatiently for evening.

Fortunately, night fell early in winter. In that overcast weather it was even earlier than usual and it was full dark by the time Gilles, wrapped in an old cloak of his godfather's, made his way to the flax spinner's house.

It was not far. He had only to go round the cathedral and take the narrow alley that went under the Porte du Boureau and came out on the far side of the ramparts. The street was empty and utterly silent and but for the snow he would have needed cat's eyes to see his way. However Gilles soon spotted the cottage, like a malignant abscess swelling from the great wall behind, with its front walls bulging and its roof all askew like a drunkard's hat. The yellow light filtering from its two closed shutters looked like peering eyes. But Gilles was determined to discover more about the inhabitants of the *Hermine Rouge* and so he stepped up to the narrow doorway with its judas window and knocked as Manon had taught him.

The window in the door opened almost at once. The light of a candle behind the bars fell on a pale face with anxious eyes which brightened instantly.

'Is it you?' Manon whispered. 'I did not hope for you so soon— Wait a moment and I'll open the door.'

There was the dull sound of a bar being withdrawn and then of a well-oiled bolt and the door swung open soundlessly.

44

Just as in the shadow of the Porte St Vincent, the girl's rough little hand seized his and drew him inside.

'Come in quickly and don't make a sound. My sister is asleep in there,' she said, jerking her head towards a closed door at the far end of the passage. The whitewashed walls were dazzlingly bright.

'Perhaps I'm too late and you were just going out?' Gilles stammered, seeing that Manon wore a big, brown, hooded cloak round her shoulders. But she shrugged carelessly and laughed.

'Too late, no! Only I had not expected you to come tonight and I was just going back to the *Hermine* because I was bored. But you are very welcome!'

She led him to where an open doorway threw a bright rectangle of light on the tiled floor. And suddenly Gilles found himself in a world far removed from what he had expected of a humble tavern wench. The room before him was small and low beneath its huge dark beams, but it was charming and almost elegant. A Persian rug covered the flagged floor. Long curtains of Indian muslin hung above the bed with its pink silk counterpane. The white walls were adorned with flower engravings and there were some pretty pieces of furniture, painted grey, while next to the hearth, where a good fire blazed, stood a work table with an unfinished piece of lace upon it.

Manon, delighted with the effect produced, was watching the expression of surprise upon her companion's face.

'You like it?'

'Indeed I do! Only I was not expecting—'

'To find a room like this in the humble home of a poor girl like me? I don't let Yann Maodan maul me with his fat hands for nothing! At the *Hermine Rouge* I am his servant, but here, I am the mistress. And I have some fine dresses, too, you know. Wait, and I'll make myself beautiful for you! Sit down and close your eyes.'

She flung off her cloak and, running to a painted coffer like a captain's sea chest in a corner of the room, she pulled out a cloud of rose-coloured material and began feverishly tugging off her embroidered fishu. Gilles stopped her.

'Listen! I haven't come for the reason you think.'

45

Manon's hands fell like stricken birds and she lifted great sad eyes to his.

'Oh? Why, then?'

'Because of my friend – the boy who was with me the other night. I searched for him all day and all night. I wanted to tell him not to go to meet the Nantais. And I couldn't find him.'

The disappointment in the girl's eyes was replaced by suspicion. She shook her head, as if to drive out some unwelcome thought.

'Then forget him! Immediately!' she cried. 'No one in the world can do anything for him now. And I shall not say another word on the subject.'

'But—'

She moved towards him so quickly that he recoiled instinctively. But she only clasped both hands on his raised arm.

'Hush! Not another word. I want to live, do you hear? Live! Yann Maodan is rich. He gives me gold and with gold one can get anywhere, even out of prison. I am putting money away against the day when, God willing, I shall be free and can forget the *Hermine Rouge*. I gave you some good advice because I liked you and because it hurt me to think of you beneath some blackamoor's lash, but don't ask any more of me. It's too late!'

'He is my friend,' Gilles protested hotly, yet with a kind of relish also. It was the first time that he, the bastard whom even the humblest looked down on, had felt able to use those words. And he could not resist the pleasure of saying it again, a second time, more quietly : 'He is my friend.'

'You will have others. You are the sort that easily wins men's friendship – and women's love. How many women have you had already?'

Gilles stared at her in amazement and a good deal of shock.

'Women? Why none! I am a pupil at St Yves,' he added austerely, as if that alone were sufficient reason. But if he had hoped to impress Manon, he was disappointed because the girl from the *Hermine Rouge* broke into a peal of laughter as natural and unforced as his own surprise had been. She laughed so much that she was forced to double up, her hands holding her middle, while the tears started from her eyes and

46

fell upon the chest. The boy reddened slowly as the joyous waves of mirth flowed over him.

'I don't see what's so funny about it,' he muttered angrily. 'The fathers at St Yves teach us that woman is the instrument of the devil, false, treacherous and dangerous, and that—'

'And that is why certain of those same worthy fathers sneak out into the alleys of the harbour and the arsenal at night, dressed like lawyers with their tonsures hidden under a wig, just to see how dangerous those girls are who traffic in their bodies. Really, though? You've not had a woman? Never?'

'Never! And as to what you just said, I don't believe it. Or, if it's true, the reason must be a holy one. The fathers are used to confront the devil and face up to perils. They must go where Satan lurks!'

'Well then, let's see if you can be as brave. You look to me as if you, too, were made to face up to perils?'

As she spoke, Manon took off her cap and began quickly pulling out the pins that held her hair. She unfastened the scarf at her neck and slipped out of her dress. In a twinkling she was dressed only in her pale blue stockings clasped about the knee by pink garters with lace rosettes.

Her body gleamed like pale silk in the warm glow of the candles and the firelight. Not so slender as Judith's, it was more rounded and disturbing in its femininity. The swell of her hips was soft above her rather strong legs, her full breasts just yielding enough to hint at a long familiarity with caresses. Manon took them in her hands and stroked them gently so that the nipples hardened, then she laughed.

'Well? What do you think of the serpent? It is all yours now—'

She stepped out of the circle of her dress and came towards him where he stood in silent fascination, watching her, and reached up on tiptoe to brush his lips with first one light kiss, then another and then a third, whispering against his mouth: 'I don't think much of your clothes. Let's see what you have underneath—'

With the ease of long practice, she slipped off the black coat and the long waistcoat, undid his shirt, which had more darns than embroidery, and slid her hands down the boy's body. They were warm and rough-skinned and their touch was like an electric shock to Gilles. At the same time Manon's belly, pressed against him, began undulating gently, awaking the boy's manhood with a suddenness that brought a smile to the girl's face.

'Well, well,' she said mockingly. 'It was high time I took you in hand—'

But he did not even hear her. The unknown devil within him which had been making such strange turmoil of his nights was suddenly unleashed. Grabbing the girl round the waist he threw her on to the bed and fell on top of her and began kissing her with clumsy eagerness, while his hands kneaded whatever flesh came their way.

Pinned down and half-smothered, Manon pushed him off vigorously and protested, laughing:

'Mercy! How you do go at it for a novice! Let me breathe, at least!'

He drew back, flushing.

'I'm sorry. I didn't mean to hurt you,' he said with contrition.

'You didn't hurt me. It's just that you're in such a hurry. You don't know anything about lovemaking – but the first thing is that if you are to do it properly you must take your time. Tell me, do you play any musical instrument?'

'No. But I'm fond of music,' Gilles said, not seeing the connection.

'Well, never forget that a human body is like an instrument. You have to learn how to play it – and I am going to teach you.'

Young as she was, the little serving girl from the *Hermine Rouge* was an excellent teacher. She was both active and sensitive and Gilles enjoyed his first lesson so much that he had no sooner roused himself from a moments blissful unconsciousness following on an altogether novel sensation than he was demanding a repetition, which was generously granted him, and then a third. Only this time the pupil took charge and justified himself so admirably that Manon, still gasping, whispered in his ear:

'You had better not come here too often, for I should not be safe if I were to fall in love with you.'

'But I want to come back. There are some lessons one can go on learning for ever,' he said happily.

'You've little enough left to learn already. What will you do when you have to go to confession? They say they're very strict about that at St Yves.'

With a careless gesture, Gilles swept away a whole vista of floggings and painful sessions on the stone flags of the chapel.

'I shan't say anything, that's all! Better to say nothing than to promise not to do it again – and then break my promise. But tell me, Manon? Did you learn all these pretty arts from Yann Maodan?'

Instantly, the look of happy relaxation faded from the girl's face.

'You ought not to have reminded me of that brute. Of course it wasn't him! My first lover was a cornet in Walsh's regiment. He was young – and handsome, like you. And he was kind, too. I was madly in love with him, and of course I thought nothing of Yann.'

'What happened?'

'The tide washed him up one morning. He had been stabbed— They never found out who did it.'

There were tears in her eyes and all at once she flung herself on Gilles and pressed her lips to his.

'I don't want to think about it any more. Love me again. And come back – whenever you want to, come back! I'll wait for you every night after work. I need only say that my sister is ill and I must nurse her.'

When, very late that night, Gilles left the flax spinner's house at last, his legs felt weak and his body very tired, but his mind was extraordinarily clear and liberated. He could not understand in the least why it was the fathers should make a crime of anything as simple, as natural and as delightful as love. And for the girl who had revealed this to him, he felt a gratitude not far from love.

It was very quiet and the cold bit more keenly than ever. Gilles began to run to keep warm. But just as he came to the Porte du Boureau, invisible hands seized him and flung him down on the hard snow, while others rained a hail of blows upon him while he strove vainly to defend himself. Blinded, his head ringing, he tried to kick out at his assailants, but to no avail. At last a heavy body reeking of dirt and rum, crashed down on him. Hands, rough as pumice stone, caught him round

49

the neck and began to squeeze slowly, a blast of evil-smelling breath took him in the face and a muffled voice hissed at him.

'We'll let you go this time, my young whelp,' said his attacker, 'but if you ever dare to visit this house again – or even to mention the name of a certain tavern, it'll be the end of you. And of that slut Manon also. One word from you, just one, or even so much as a look, and you'll both be in the river with a twenty-pound cannon ball tied to your feet! There are some things—'

'That will do,' broke in another man whom Gilles could not see at all except as a darker shadow on the snow. 'Not so much lip! Hurry! He knows now he'd better keep his mouth shut.'

The hands were loosed from about his throat but before Gilles had time to appreciate the change a violent blow to his chin plunged him into instant, if somewhat less than blissful unconsciousness. So that the two men carried an unresisting body to the edge of a ditch some small way off, and there abandoned it to the cold night.

3

The Open Door

That first night of love and its unfortunate ending left Gilles
with little worse than a protracted stiff jaw, a great many
bruises and a certain difficulty in swallowing, all minor dis-
comforts which he was able to ignore. But the effects on his
mind were deep and irremovable. In the short space of a few
hours he had discovered the most uplifting of human pleasures
and the most abject humiliation. He had learned what it was
to be a man with a woman – and a mere boy in the face of a
gang of ruffians. That, at least, was how it seemed to him,
although if he had had a little more experience, been a little
less innocent, he would have realized that Yann Maodan's
men had treated him as no negligible foe.

Barricaded into his room and only opening the door to let
the maidservant give him his bowl of broth and jug of water,
he brooded on his anger and mortification. The injunction laid
upon him never more to cross Manon's threshold weighed on
him like lead, and if no one but himself had been involved he
would have gone back to the house by the Porte du Boureau
that very night. But it did not seem to him that he had any
right to bring what he divined to be a terrible danger on the
girl. He could not repay the hours of pleasure she had given
him with such perilous coin. Besides, would Manon dare to
open her door to him again?

Hour after hour, he indulged in feverish dreams of leading
an attack on the *Hermine Rouge,* of descending on Yann
Maodan and the Nantais, sword in hand, and cleaning out that

rat's nest once and for all, although as to the flaming sword, he could barely handle an ordinary hanger competently.

There was, of course, the possibility of laying a complaint with the city provost, but the role of informer, even against a lawbreaker, was not one that appealed to him. No, what he needed to do now was to learn how to pay them back in kind, to fight and to become the kind of formidable man, like certain famous privateers, respected equally by the law and those outside it. And in order to achieve that he was going to need more help than a pail of holy water and a sprinkler.

Like a traveller examining the condition of his baggage and the state of his purse before taking to the road, Gilles sat down with his elbows on his knees in front of his meagre fire and reviewed his assets. His scholarship, though mostly derived from books, was sound, if not brilliant, except for an excellent grounding in English which he had from his godfather. On the practical side, though, the account was virtually a blank. He could certainly swim like a fish and could sail a boat as well as any fisherman's son, and his strength was well above the average. But he could not ride – he, who adored horses! He knew nothing of the art of war, could not even fight with his bare hands and had never touched a weapon in his life. His mother, continually obsessed with her own mystical ideas, had even forbidden him to take part in the age-old Breton sport of wrestling, which involved no weapons at all.

Concluding from all this that it was high time he changed his way of life, he then wrote two letters, one to his mother and the other to the Abbé de Talhouët, in which he begged to inform them both, very respectfully, that he desired to abandon the Church and prepare for the entrance examination to some military college, such as the artillery school at Metz, which would accept boys of no birth.

This was not a decision he had arrived at light-heartedly, for if he went to Metz he would undoubtedly be condemning himself to something not far removed from purgatory. He would certainly have to spend a long time kicking his heels in some lowly rank, even supposing he was far enough from home to conceal his shameful birth from his fellows. But what had happened to Jean-Pierre Quérelle had given him a sharp lesson regarding the perils of rash adventuring. Before he set out to conquer the world, he meant to acquire those skills which at present he so sorely lacked.

He hovered for a moment on the verge of writing a third letter, to Manon, to tell her how sorry he was he could not see her again, but then he thought that Yann Maodan had probably visited some of his anger on her already and that any such note might only add to her troubles. He therefore gave up the idea, while promising himself to return to Manon later, when things should have calmed down. In any case, it was odds on that Manon could not read.

With his decision taken and his bruises fading somewhat, Gilles went back to school with an easier mind. He suffered without flinching the chastisement earned by being absent without excuse and flung himself into his studies, especially mathematics and geography, with an unprecedented enthusiasm, in order to distract his mind from waiting feverishly for a letter from Hennebont. By dulling his senses with fatigue, he also hoped to try and forget Manon's arms.

When the winter drew towards its end and still he had received no answer to either of his letters, Gilles was in a fret of impatience. In an effort to overcome it, he spent more and more time hanging about the barracks of Walsh's regiment and picking up the news, which was growing daily more exciting. The American expedition was decided on, the King was sending money and a force which was to assemble at Brest under the command of General the Comte de Rochambeau, some regiments were already on their way to Brittany to embark. A fleet had put to sea on February 2nd under M. de Guichen, to replace Admiral d'Estaing's in the Caribbean. Finally, it was rumoured that the famous Marquis de la Fayette was also going, but from Rochefort, where he would take ship to rejoin Washington. There was an odour of gunpowder, spices and the sea in the air, in spite of the nasty drizzling rain which had enveloped Brittany ever since the new year.

The smell was so intoxicating that Gilles, all his warrior's instincts roused, found himself regretting his letters. What need had there been to talk about schools when the noblest adventure of all was unfolding her great wings right beside him?

His dreams had reached this point one tempestuous March

morning as he sat in his place in the icy classroom, letting his mind wander away from St Augustine's *City of God* and gallop after the two regiments which had passed through Vannes the previous evening, when an usher came into the class to tell him that the vice-principal, the Abbé Grinne, wished to see him in his study immediately.

Gilles got up in surprise and went out, amid the kind of expectant, inquisitive silence which falls on a room full of boys when one of them is singled out, whether for triumph or disaster. In Gilles' case, the general feeling was in favour of disaster, for he was not over-popular. Besides his illegitimacy, which they all knew about and which made him somewhat shocking, a child of sin, the other boys disliked his cold reserve, his secret pride in his irregular birth and even his slightly arrogant bearing.

Gilles, for his part, was wondering what the Abbé Grinne could want with him. For two months, he had worked as he had never done before and, as far as discipline was concerned, his conscience was clear. He had not, in fact, so much as seen the inside of the Barbin again.

The vice-principal was, in any event, a good deal less awe-inspiring than the Principal, and so it was with no particular apprehensions that Gilles tapped on his door.

The door, which was of oak blackened with age, creaked open. The Abbé François Grinne was seated at his desk, writing. At the boy's entrance he raised tired eyes behind big metal spectacles, smiled faintly and murmured, without interrupting his work: 'Sit down, my child. I will be with you in a moment.'

Somewhat disconcerted, both by the smile and the invitation, Gilles seated himself on the edge of a rush-bottomed chair which, with the black wooden desk, the bulging bookcase and a large Spanish crucifix on the wall, constituted the entire furnishing of the room. Thereafter he employed the respite granted him in studying the man opposite him whom he had, in fact, always rather liked. At thirty-nine, the Abbé Grinne presented the appearance of a serious but not a stern man, scholarly without pedantry and wise without ostentation.

After a few minutes, the vice-principal stopped writing, reread what he had written, uttered a little grunt of satisfaction and put down his pen. Then he took up a sheet of paper from the table and, holding it between his clasped hands, looked up and smiled at Gilles.

'I am sorry to have kept you waiting,' he said, as politely as though he were addressing an equal, 'but I had to finish this – it is a letter to the Head of the Great Seminary.'

When the young man said nothing, he went on, with a slight wave of the paper in his hand : 'We had a letter from your mother yesterday. I have it here.'

Gilles stiffened, surprised and a little startled.

'My mother? She has written – to you?'

'Why yes. You have always been aware that it is her greatest wish that you should enter the Church? Now, for reasons best known to herself, she is asking that you should be taken to the Seminary at once in order to begin your theological studies and prepare for your entry into the priesthood.'

Gilles was on his feet in a moment. He felt a choking sensation, as though chains were being suddenly drawn tight about his chest.

'At once? But this is only March, and the school year not yet over. Besides—'

'You may complete it at the Seminary more profitably than you could do here.'

'Possibly. But that is not really the point. My mother is exceeding her rights in requiring me to enter the Seminary straight away.'

Now it was the Abbé Grinne's turn to stiffen. He was not accustomed to hearing a pupil take this tone.

'What do you mean? Are you and she not in agreement as regards your future?'

'By no means! Of course she has never made any secret of her wish to see me wear the cloth, and when I was a child I saw little enough against it. At first because I scarcely knew what it meant and then because I liked the idea of copying my god-father – and my teachers. But as long as a year ago I made it clear to my mother that I was not sure of my vocation – and two months since I wrote to her, saying I wanted to do something else with my life. Admittedly, she has never answered my letter.'

'Had you talked to her about it before?'

55

Gilles smiled bitterly. 'There is no talking to my mother, sir. She seemed to listen to what I was saying to her but I wonder if she even heard! But all the same, the fact remains that I do not wish to be a priest and she has no right to force me.'

François Grinne did not answer at once. He studied the young man, while his thin fingers, stained yellow with the tobacco which was his only indulgence, rolled Marie-Jeanne Goëlo's letter thoughtfully between them. He was not particularly surprised by this violent reaction, for from the day when he first learned that the boy was destined for the priesthood he had watched him discreetly and had formed his own doubts as to his supposed vocation. Gilles' was a passionate, occasionally violent nature, but reserved also and oddly controlled in a way far beyond his age.

The Abbé studied his pupil in silence, with as much attention as if he were seeing him for the first time, yet with a curiosity altogether new. Gilles was very tall, both for his age and for a Breton. There was still something bony and unfinished about his long legs and broad shoulders, but the arrogant way he carried his blond head, with its unruly curls and the natural grace of movement which enabled him to carry off even his ugly black suit with elegance, all promised a man of great assurance and for the present marked him out from his companions.

When he reached the face, the Abbé had the curious impression that he was looking at it for the first time, perhaps because he had not really seen it for a long time. It was no longer the childish face it had been but a man's face already, despite the youthful softness of the thin, sardonic lips. The features were delicate but clean and proud, there was power in the jaw and arrogance in the slightly aquiline nose, while the eyes, so light a blue as to be almost grey under their straight, faintly upward-slanting brows, the eyes whose gaze Yann Maodan had found so disconcerting, contained a glint of ice. The hands, too, though ill-cared for, were excellently shaped . . . Everything, in short, about this careless-looking youth proclaimed the passionate vitality of a breed not easy to discipline – combined with an attraction perilous for a man of God.

If his mother hopes to make a country priest of him, then she can never have looked at him, the Abbé thought, amazed and somewhat alarmed by the result of his examination. The women will all run mad after him, and that will cause trouble in plenty. Of course, if he could hope for a bishopric or an abbey it would be all to the good. Unfortunately he will be prevented from rising by his birth. Looks like a lord but born the wrong side of the blanket. Not a good augury.

Uneasy at the long silence, Gilles plucked up courage to ask: 'You are very silent, sir. May I ask what you are thinking?'

The Abbé repressed a sigh. His duty to the mother did not permit of his taking sides. So he merely observed quietly: 'I was thinking that you are mistaken. In actual fact your mother has every right over you, even the right to have you taken to the Seminary by force — and brought back by the law should you take it into your head to run away! Which you are very well aware of! But tell me why you do not wish to serve God.'

Gilles levelled bright eyes at the young priest.

'Is there no other way to serve God than in a priest's robe?' he asked insolently. 'I had thought that every man who did the work he was born to and obeyed God's laws was a good servant of His!'

'I do not deny it. But your mother believes that you were born for just that life — and she loves you.'

'No!'

The word shot out, almost taking the Abbé in the face. He uttered a horrified protest.

'Say no more! How can you blaspheme so?'

'Why should the plain truth be a blasphemy? My mother loves only God. Not only did she not want me, my coming wrecked a life she had intended to be wholly divorced from this world. It hurts her even to look at me because for her I am sin incarnate, the image of the man who came between her and divine love, forcing her to remain a prisoner of a world she detests. That is why she insists on my becoming a priest, because that way she will be forgiven, sanctified. Sacrifice for sacrifice, Father! But she is not Abraham and I do not believe that God has ever asked my life of her.'

Once again there was silence. Disarmed, the priest felt suddenly heavy-hearted and there was a bitter load on his conscience as he looked at the young rebel, obstinately refusing to take on himself a sin that was not his. He felt that the mother's intransigence was doubling the weight of original sin on the child's soul and that for her the tonsure would be the only true baptism for her child. And he was aware of a great pity. But it was a pity he had no right to express.

Emerging from behind his desk, he went to Gilles and laid a hand on the boy's arm, feeling it tremble under his touch.

'Go back to your class and prepare yourself,' he murmured with a sigh. 'I will take you to the seminary myself in an hour's time. That will be better than sending you with the Father Censor. Afterwards – and this I promise you – I will come back here and write to your mother to tell her my private opinion. That is the best I can do for you.'

He did not say what that opinion was. Gilles bowed his head, overwhelmed by what he saw as his condemnation, and, too depressed even to give the vice-principal a proper bow, he turned and left the study.

Out in the courtyard he came up against the storm which had been sweeping the bay since early morning, a foretaste of the equinoctial gales. In that enclosed space, its violence seemed concentrated. The wind raced across the ground, flattening the winter's dead weeds and picking up the gravel. A window somewhere, left unfastened, banged with a tinkle of broken glass.

The future seminarist stood for a moment in the midst of that broad open space, letting the raging wind buffet his body and take hold of his hair, so that it streamed out like a pennant from a masthead. He wished he could remain there for ever and never have to move, a figure turned to stone. The storm did him good, he would not have liked to see what he considered as the wreck of his life taking place to soft sunshine and birdsong. This was a fine introduction to hell.

All at once he heard a dull crash behind him, a deep, echoing boom like a drumbeat. He turned and saw that one of the great double entrance doors to the college had yielded to the pressure of the wind and was banging against the wall. The porter whose job it was to watch it must have fastened it badly.

Through the gap, Gilles saw dead branches and other rubbish being swept along the street. Everything the gale picked up in its passing, seemed to be on the run, as though moved by a life of its own. It was then that Gilles first saw that miraculously open doorway as a sign, as a kind of invitation, because he knew now that nothing and no one could turn Marie-Jeanne Goëlo from her purpose and that if he once let himself be shut up in the seminary, no power on earth but open flight would ever get him out. So what was he waiting for?

The door banged again, as though impatiently. Without another moment's thought, Gilles darted towards it, suddenly afraid that the porter would emerge and heave it inexorably shut again. In one bound he was over the threshold and sprinting down the street towards the cornmarket.

Forgetting the resentment which had kept him away from it for two months, he made instinctively for the harbour, as representing sanctuary and also escape to far-off places. His first thought was to hide in some warehouse until nightfall and then slip aboard the first vessel he came across. There could be no question of returning to the Rue St Gwenael because that was the first place they would look for him. He had not much time, for within an hour he must be in a place of safety.

But as he was speeding as fast as his long legs would carry him through the Porte St Salomon, the smell of hot pancakes assailed him and made him pause and almost deflected him from his purpose by reminding him how hungry he was. The bowl of broth he had swallowed at dawn was a long way away, especially since his landlady's parsimony encouraged the maidservant to make it elegantly thin. Moreover he had left the thick hunks of lightly buttered brown bread which should have sustained him until evening in the classroom, along with his books. And when Gilles was hungry, his brain was less efficient.

He slowed down and felt mechanically in his pockets in the hope that the few farthings which constituted his whole wealth might miraculously have multiplied themselves. His mother, of course, had always regarded pocket money as a snare of the devil. Naturally, he found no such luck, but he did manage to scrape together enough to purchase two big maize cakes.

They were gobbled up in an instant, leaving a delicious fragrance of salt butter on the young man's lips and a great gaping void still in his stomach.

But the brief pause necessary to eat his slender meal had

given him time for thought and he realized the foolishness of his initial plan. What would he find at the harbour beyond fishing smacks or perhaps, with luck, the odd coaster which could put him off somewhere on the Breton coast, whereas he was dreaming of America? If he did not fall a prey to scoundrels like the Nantais who would ship him off in quite the wrong direction.

Besides, his combative nature and the need he had to look things in the face made him reluctant to run away until he had played his last card. And that last card was his godfather. The Abbé de Talhouët loved him enough to understand his lack of a vocation for the religious life and to help him at need. Several times already the abbé had tried to warn Marie-Jeanne tactfully against a too hasty decision. The rector of Hennebont was a friend and confidant to Gilles, a man whom he had now and then permitted to glimpse his deepest aspirations and the humiliation he felt at being unable to lay claim to a father. And although the abbé had twice prevented his godson from going to sea, once with M. d'Orvilliers' fleet at the start of the war with England and again the previous year when the Duc de Lauzun sailed from Quiberon for the reconquest of Senegambia, it had been more in the nature of a pious hope than a definite prohibition.

'Wait a while yet, child. You are not ready and life at sea is hard. You would not go very far, or rise very high; a lowly rank and menial tasks to perform. You would need some great occasion—'

And now that great occasion had arrived : a great country was fighting for its freedom, a lion was held captive by a mouse. Surely among such people even a bastard should be able to redeem himself! But if he was to seize the chance he must see the abbé again, and that meant going back to Hennebont, with the risk of coming up against Marie-Jeanne and getting the law set on his heels. It was a hard choice, and not one he had time to examine closely.

Nevertheless, Gilles retraced his steps, back from the fish market towards the upper part of the town, cursing himself for a fool as he went because in order to reach Hennebont he would have to pass by St Yves again and that was a grave disadvantage, to say nothing of the waste of time.

He was still hesitating when a shout went up suddenly from the other end of the street he was climbing.

'There he is! Catch him!'

An icy shiver ran down Gilles' spine. The ringing cry had come from a police sergeant who was now sprinting rapidly up the street with two men at his heels. In a flash, Gilles saw that he was lost, he would be recaptured, dragged to the seminary, locked in, perhaps flung into a lightless, airless cell until he consented to accept the tonsure. His flight had been discovered already and that unconscionable hypocrite the Abbé Grinne, for all his show of sympathy, had not hesitated to set the law after him. He was going to be taken up publicly in the street, like a common vagrant.

He swore through his teeth, crossing himself automatically as he did so, and cast a desperate glance around him. Then he saw the horse. It was the most beautiful one he had ever seen. In fact it was so beautiful it seemed like a miracle. It was as if it had sprung out of the ground for the sole purpose of coming to his rescue.

It was standing under the archway of the *Grand Monarque* inn, tied up there, no doubt, to wait until its master, some wealthy traveller, had dined. But to the young fugitive it was like a vision.

Gilles did not give himself time to think. He no sooner set eyes on the miraculous animal than he literally swooped upon it, quite forgetting that he had never ridden anything more challenging than a donkey or the abbé's mule. To unhitch the horse and leap on to its back, with more agility than skill, was the work of the moment and it all happened so quickly that an ostler who was ambling up with a nosebag on his arm stopped dead, too startled even to cry 'Stop thief'. Digging his heels hard into the animal's sides, Gilles was already bearing down on the approaching policemen, knocking over a harmless citizen who had been keeping his head down against the wind and had not seen him coming.

The sergeant's men stepped aside just in time to let him through.

'That's a damn fool way to go on!' grumbled the sergeant, who had been obliged to flatten himself uncomfortably against the wall to avoid being run down. 'What's more, he's made us lose sight of our quarry. If I wasn't in a hurry, I'd have a word or two to say to that young man!'

With that the three men, who had in fact no interest at all in Gilles, went on their way in pursuit of a chicken thief they had caught sight of in the market. Meanwhile the young man thundered past St Yves, convinced that every law officer in France was on his heels, and on into open country, already fighting what was to become an epic struggle with the elements and his unfamiliar mount.

Because things were not going by any means smoothly for him. The rider was worse than inexperienced, the horse mettle-some and furthermore wholly terrified by the gale. As luck would have it the animal had not been unsaddled and Gilles, clinging to the bridle, was occupied first in trying to stay in the saddle and secondly in doing what he could to steer his mount in its blind career. He found himself fighting the first real battle of his life for mastery of the beautiful creature which had laid its spell upon him. Three times his feet left the stirrups but he never lost his hold on the strip of leather gripped in his hands, not even when the horse was dragging him along the ground where the worn stones of the old Roman road still stuck up here and there. Three times he got somehow back into the saddle, bruised and shaken, his clothes torn and covered in mud, but filled with a fiercer determination, so that in the end he got the better of the animal. By the time the two of them reached St Anne d'Auray a kind of truce had been established, due perhaps in part to a certain exhaustion on the part of the horse, which had slowed to what, for an unaccustomed rider, was a more or less tolerable canter. As they passed the old church of St Anne's, its grey tower lost in the racing clouds of a sky scarcely lighter in colour, Gilles muttered a grateful prayer to heaven that he had been saved from breaking his neck, even though he had been indulging in nothing more nor less than highway robbery.

Somewhat disturbed by the unpleasant thought that after this he was little better than a gaol bird, he promised himself to make his peace with heaven as soon as might be. Then he put the matter right out of his mind and thought instead, with a kind of delicious guilt, that he was on the road to Hennebont and that in Hennebont was Judith!

It was the first time for a long while that he had allowed himself to think of her, and to think of her with a kind of tremulous hope. He discovered now that she had been at the bottom of almost everything he had done since going back to school and that the great longing for fame, fortune and independence which possessed him had no other aim than one day to compel her admiration and transform her scorn into marvellous love. Until then, he had banished her picture from his mind, especially at night when the memory of Manon set a fire in his loins. It was too easy to substitute her body for the servant girl's and that, to Gilles, seemed a kind of profanation.

After St Anne, it was necessary to slow to a walk, for the old Roman road degenerated to little more than a rutted track. The ruts were fresh, deep and slippery, indicating that heavy wagons had passed that way. Gilles thought of the troops that had passed through Vannes the previous night, the guns of Anhalt's regiment and the battalion of Turenne's whose fine uniforms and gleaming weapons he had envied. They could not be far ahead, for the marks were very recent, and would certainly be encamped at Hennebont that night.

The fugitive was glad of it. Amid all the excitement caused by the coming of the royal troops, the unaccustomed manner of his own arrival would pass almost unnoticed. The horde of religious ladies who flitted like bats about the rector's house would have other things on their minds.

All the same, he was glad to find that dusk was falling before his eyes lit on the familiar landscape, the hills that formed a natural amphitheatre round Hennebont, the calm waters of the Blavet with the boats coming in slowly from the sea, the harsh cries of the sea birds and the melancholy chime of evening bells. A sudden surge of happiness filled his heart, as it did every time he came home to the town of his childhood, only that night it was more intense than ever before, almost more than he could bear, because it was mingled with an intoxicating feeling of freedom, a freedom he did not intend to be robbed of ever again, and with the excitement of having burned his boats. For Gilles, that burning had been the theft of the horse. He could never go back to Vannes, where even at that very moment they might be searching for him to hang him. He could forget all about the seminary and think about life and the future – about Judith. And he discovered also that he loved every stone of Hennebont.

The ruddy stones of the curtain walls and ancient towers of the old castle where he had so often hunted the ghost of Jeanne La Flamme, the age-blackened stones of the ramparts where fine trees now made a pleasant promenade for peaceful citizens, the stones of the steep alleys of the Old Town making a blue network around the handsome church of Notre Dame du Paradis, and of the restored houses in the New Town, and finally the mansions of the Ville-Close beneath whose tall gables dwelt a proud nobility to which he himself belonged by blood but which, with few exceptions, turned from him with scorn, that evening all these worn stones took on the fragile, threatened aspect of things one is about to leave for a long time.

After traversing the old walled town, Gilles emerged suddenly into a scene like a Flemish fairground. The two regiments whose traces he had seen on the road were indeed in the town, filling it with the cheerful din of a campaigning army. A host of bright coloured uniforms, white with yellow facings for Turenne's regiment, blue and red for Anhalt's, made Hennebont like a spring meadow in the torchlight. The men were bivouacked around their fires, their muskets stacked within reach, dicing on drumheads after their supper. Groups of officers, their black cocked hats encrusted with gold lace and white cockades, were strolling idly in the direction of the dark mass of the Bro-Erech, the walled town, guarded by its great prison-gate, where their own supper would be awaiting them in the wealthy houses where they were billeted. The air smelled pleasantly of wood smoke, straw, draught cider and cabbage soup. The morning's high wind had given way to a cool, moist breeze that already carried with it a scent of spring.

There was no presbytery at Hennebont. The building known as The Priest's House stood in the Rue Neuve, which, despite its optimistic name, was a good two hundred years old. It was a grey house with tiny windows and an arched doorway, so low that one had to bend to enter it. But Gilles did not go in that way. As a familiar visitor, he made his way down a narrow passage alongside the house into a back yard, where he knew there was a stable. It was a small place, for hitherto its sole occupant had been the abbé's venerable mule, Eglantine, but there would be room for two.

He was about to lift the latch when the door was opened from within and a boy came out. He was surly and unkempt and dressed in a goatskin waistcoat and wide, gathered trousers, so stained that it was impossible to say what their original colour had been, and he was carrying a large lantern which he all but hurled in Gilles' face in panic when he caught sight of the fantastic double silhouette of boy and horse. He uttered a yelp of terror and crossed himself hurriedly before retiring with a moan into the safe darkness of the stable.

'*Spered-Glan! An Diaoul!* Holy Ghost! The Devil!'

Gilles shouted with laughter.

'No, you poor idiot! It's not the devil! It's I, Gilles Goëlo, the rector's godson. Come out of there and let me get in. There's no room for two.'

Still half-afraid, the other stammered something incomprehensible and trembled so that he almost dropped the lantern in the straw.

'Hold it steadier than that!' Gilles protested, grabbing his arm. 'You'll set fire to the stable and roast us all four, you, me, this horse I've brought you to look after, and poor Eglantine here as well.'

Gilles saw no need to enlarge on these orders. Indeed, he knew that he need not have said so much, for Mahé might be dirty, idle and surly, and constitute, in his role as the rector's body servant, an additional penance for that holy man, but however little he might relish brushing his master's wigs he was passionately fond of animals and horses, with him, were almost a religion. This he inherited from his father who had been groom to M. du Bois-Guehenneuc until his death. Mahé took the stolen horse's bridle with a kind of reverence and forgot Gilles altogether as he started crooning softly to soothe the noble animal.

Relieved of his anxieties on that score, Gilles crossed the yard and went through the back door into a flagged passage which divided the ground floor of the house. There was a staircase leading up from it and two doors, one on either side. The young man chose the one from beyond which came a rattle of saucepans. He entered and stopped dead in the doorway, startled by the sight that met his eyes.

An old woman in black petticoats and a white coif was striding up and down in front of the huge hearth where a small, black pot hung over a blazing fire, like a priestess of some obscure cult, addressing a flood of imprecation to an invisible adversary and now and then brandishing an angry fist. From time to time she would pause to aim a kick at the logs, and then resume her pacing with still greater fury. At last she stopped, snatched a whole string of onions from the chimney breast and stuffed them into the pot, without so much as peeling them. Then, as though relieved by the act, she sank down on the hearthstone with her knees drawn up to her chin, laid her arms upon them and her head on her arms and burst into resounding tears.

At this unexpected sign of grief, Gilles cast himself on his knees beside her.

'Katell! What is it? Why are you crying? – Has something dreadful happened?'

The old woman started and cast a streaming glance at him out of a pair of astonishingly bright blue eyes which still managed to convey a great deal of anger.

'Blessed St Anne!' she cried. 'That's all it needed! Where have you sprung from, you wicked rascal? And just look at the state you're in! You look like a tramp and as filthy as a pigsty! Well? Let's hear where you've come from?'

'Let's say I've dropped from heaven. And it's been raining all day. But I still don't know why you are crying?'

'You can blame heaven for that, too! And if you are its latest gift, then the good Lord must have a grudge against me. I'd best go to confession . . . Come along, up with you! Get those clothes off! Draw some water and wash yourself! You're making my kitchen filthy. And to think you're supposed to be studying to be a priest— A fine priest you'll make! You're as bad as Mahé—'

Forgetting her tears, Katell, who was Rozenn's sister, set about the cleansing of Gilles. She skinned him like a rabbit, tossed his clothes disgustedly into a corner and scrubbed him down before the fire. Then she went to a big chest and pulled out some garments, old but clean, which had belonged to the rector's brother-in-law, the Vicomte de Langle, whose wife had donated them to charity. In this way, Gilles found himself decked in an old bottle green hunting coat with brass buttons and deep cuffs on sleeves and pockets, a pair of maroon plush knee breeches and striped stockings which fitted him well enough. And while she refurbished him, Katell at last consented to explain the cause of her great rage : the rector had taken the supper she had just cooked and given it to a poor fisherman whose wife had just given birth to their eighth child.

'He'll give away even the shirt off his back,' the faithful servant complained wrathfully. 'If it wasn't for my lady his sister, he'd be going about naked, and he must be one of the poorest of all our rectors. And him with his health not good—'

With a pang of regret for the vanished supper, for he was hungry enough to have eaten the table it stood on, Gilles asked whimsically : 'And is it for the good of his health that you mean to make him eat his onions with the skin on?'

The effect of these words was astonishing. The hot-tempered Katell swooped upon the little black pot like a hawk and, snatching it from the fire, opened the window and hurled the boiling contents out into the street, without so much as a glance to assure herself that no one was passing. Then she cast the pot into the sink and wiped her hands on her apron, muttering : 'I'm ashamed of myself! But I was so angry.'

Gilles started to laugh wholeheartedly.

'I do understand a little,' he said. 'Only now there's no supper at all. And I'm so very hungry. I'm even sorry about the onions.'

'Don't be. I have a – a little put by for times like these. You shall have pancakes, and some oatmeal porridge and perhaps a—' She broke off at the sound of a door closing, pursed her lips as though she had been on the point of giving away a state secret and, seizing her largest pan, began hurling a good bushel of oatmeal into it. Footsteps were approaching, dragging heavily on the flagstones in the passage, as though someone were very tired.

Seeing him enter the kitchen, his big black cloak sodden with rain, Gilles thought that his godfather had changed since Hallowe'en. The Abbé Vincent-Marie de Talhouët-Grationnaye was only forty-three but he looked much older. He walked with a slight stoop and the clear-cut features between the white wig and the black soutane, so open and kindly always, bore the marks of constant toil and great weariness.

'The weather is changing again, my good Katell,' he said with a gentle sigh, shaking his wet shoulders. 'Now the wind is bringing us more rain.'

He broke off as he saw the figure waiting for him, outlined against the glow of the fire. His grey eyes widened for a moment with surprise and a trifle of worry.

'You here? What brings you? Have you had bad news? Your mother is not—?'

Gilles bowed as deeply as to the king himself.

'If I have had bad news, at least it concerns only myself, sir. I've no reason to think my mother is other than well. But forgive me for coming to you thus unannounced.'

'You know you need no announcement. This house is always open to you, especially when, as I think, you have something serious to tell me.'

'You are right, sir. Something very serious, although it will not, I think, come as a surprise to you.'

The abbé shook his head and looked still more worried.

'Well then, let us go into my study and leave Katell to her kitchen.'

They left the big warm room where Katell, still muttering, was beginning to set the table and made their way to the upper floor, where the rooms of the rector and of his three curates in residence opened on to an icy landing. The fourth curate, the Abbé Duparc, had particular charge of the hamlet of Sainte-Gilles and lived in the vicarage there.

M. de Talhouët's was a panelled room, very simply furnished, with neither carpets nor curtains. Its one luxury, in addition to the fire in the hearth, was a small bookcase containing a number of fine books, their bindings, polished with much use, gleaming softly through their tarnished gilding. Most were devotional works, or histories, but among them were several by Voltaire, a legacy from a humorous-minded parishioner out of which the abbé had kept only those least shocking to his devout soul.

He sat his godson down in the one armchair and settled himself on the bed instead of at his desk, so as to avoid any appearance of sitting in judgment.

'I am listening,' he said, 'but am I wrong in thinking that this visit has some connection with the letter you wrote me two months ago?'

'You are not wrong, sir. Will you permit me to ask why I had no answer to it?'

The abbé smiled. 'The young are so impatient! I could not send you any answer until I had reached some conclusion with your mother. And you know quite well that she is not an easy person to argue with where her beliefs are concerned. But I do not despair, in time, of bringing her—'

'No, sir,' Gilles interrupted him. 'She will never change and it is because I have had proof of that today that I have come to you.'

And he described what had passed in the Abbé Grinne's room. He did so with brevity, calmness and a firmness which impressed his companion. Like the vice-principal earlier, M. de Talhouët was suddenly aware that he was dealing with a different person, almost a stranger. He felt no great surprise but a kind of sadness mingled with the curious excitement felt by a spectator in a theatre before the rise of the curtain.

He heard Gilles out to the end without a word. And even when the young man ceased talking, he let the silence prolong itself between them while he rose and poked the fire and threw another log on it. Only he did not return to his place on the bed but remained standing by the hearth, holding his hands out to the warmth.

'I did not know that your mother had written,' he said at last, 'nor do I know all the reasons which prompted her letter. But are you yourself quite certain that you cannot comply with her wishes? Youth is eager and hasty. Even I myself once dreamed of serving the king in the cavalry.'

'I am quite sure of myself,' Gilles exclaimed hotly. 'And you know it, sir, for you have twice prevented me from taking ship. Have you forgotten how desperately I wanted to enlist aboard the *Surveillante,* under your friend of glorious memory, M. De Couédic? You told me I was too young, that I should finish my schooling—'

'And I was right. If you had gone with poor De Couédic you might be dead, or crippled by now!'

'Or covered with glory, like the helmsman Le Mang whom

69

we all admire at Kervignac. And even if I were dead, that would be better for me than to be rotting slowly in some cloister or sacristy.'

The Abbé de Talhouët frowned.

'Gilles!' he said sternly. 'You forget yourself.'

Crestfallen, the young man accepted the rebuke.

'I'm sorry. I'd rather die than offend you, because I love and respect you. But, as I said, you know my inmost heart and when I wrote to you—'

'Very well. Let us come to that letter. Frankly, it did not surprise me because, between you and me, I had given up expecting Divine Grace to visit you. And I went to see your mother to try and plead your cause—'

'Try?' Gilles broke in in amazement. 'Do you mean to say – she would not listen to you?'

'Shall we say – she listened to me, but she did not understand. She told me these were the passing ambitions of a boy in constant contact with other boys destined for worldly careers. And that living near a seaport was bound to affect a youthful imagination. It will pass, she told me, once Gilles is properly set on the way he must go. And what if it does not, I asked? She merely smiled at me, as though she knew some secret I could not perceive, and then said, with complete conviction: "It will pass. I am absolutely sure of that. Have you forgotten that God can work miracles? It is a simple matter for Him to draw to Himself the stubborn soul of a child who knows Him not as yet." After that, there was nothing to say. I did not persist, thinking that it was not yet time for you to leave St Yves and I could return to the subject later on. But I was mistaken. And I even wonder if it was not my doing that she determined to hurry matters on. Now it appears,' he added with a faint smile, 'that you have been even more precipitate. But what are you going to do now? In your letter, you spoke of a military academy—'

Gilles' eyes blazed.

'Listen to the noises in the town tonight, sir! The king is sending troops to help the rebels! I want to go to America and fight with them! The opportunity is here in front of me. First thing tomorrow, if you give me leave, I shall present myself to the recruiting sergeant of Turenne's regiment and enlist. Or else I might go to Brest and take ship. It would be very nearly as easy.'

The abbé did not doubt it. The recruiting officers of both army and navy would be only too happy to get their hands on a sturdy youth who asked nothing better than to shed his blood. And after a few years – or a few months – he, the abbé, would see him come home again, old before his time, crippled per-haps— The light would be gone from the eyes now regarding him so straightly and nothing left in that heart but disillusion. Moreover, he had little faith in this American campaign which was being so much talked of. He changed the subject to give himself time to think.

'How did you manage to get here so quickly? Did you run the whole way?'

Gilles flushed brick red in an instant but he answered bravely enough.

'No, sir. I stole a horse.'

The abbé, who had been gazing pensively at the ceiling, started and choked.

'You – it's not true? I cannot have heard you right?'

'You heard me perfectly. I stole a horse. He is downstairs in your stable, with Eglantine. I know I ought not to have done so,' he added coolly, meeting the rector's eye, 'but there was some urgency. They were after me and I had to do something quickly. The horse was tied up outside the *Grand Monarque*. I jumped on to it and off we went. I hope you won't blame me,' he added, uncomfortable, in spite of everything, at the sight of his godfather's appalled expression.

For a moment the abbé sat speechless and unmoving, hardly able to draw breath. Then a sudden idea struck him and he demanded abruptly : 'Tell me, how much have you had to do with women?'

Gilles stiffened, taken by surprise.

'What do you mean?'

'Just what I say. How much have women to do with your refusal to be a priest? No, don't look so offended. You are quite old enough to discuss the subject. So, let me put my question another way. What do they mean to you?'

Silence. The abbé had the feeling that his godson was closing up like an oyster. And indeed, after a moment's

71

thought, Gilles put up his chin and, looking him straight in the eyes, said with unexpected coolness : 'By your leave, I will not answer that. In fact it is a subject I prefer not to discuss.'

The abbé realized, from the slight huskiness in his voice, that he had touched a sensitive chord and that behind this great longing for freedom and a normal life there lay some tale of love. A tale which Gilles was not ready to confide to him.

'As you like,' he said with a sigh. 'Very well, then. Let us go down to the stable. I want to see this stolen horse of yours.'

4

A Mother's Heart

Armed with a lantern, Gilles followed the rector without comment and even with a kind of relief. He was glad his godfather had not pursued his inquiry into the subject of women because, under the influence of strong emotion, he had been on the verge of betraying his secret. The violence of his own inward reactions had surprised him. His heart had sounded the alarm in very much the manner of a watchful sentry keeping guard over some great treasure or well-defended fortress. And this little excursion to the stable was welcome in so far as it gave him a chance to recover his self-control.

With an effort, he drove out the image of Judith which had been going to his head like a fever and also the infinitely more disturbing vision of Manon, and pushed open the wooden door. He breathed in the good stable smell of fresh straw and held up his arm to light the interior. The horse's gleaming hindquarters, beautifully groomed by Mahé, shone like silk in the glowing light. The abbé stepped forward, a sudden brightness in his eyes.

He examined the animal in silence, like a man who knew what he was about, for M. de Talhouët had been an enthusiastic horseman before taking orders. Indeed, his love for horses had at one time troubled his father, who doubted if it were compatible with a genuine vocation. Then young Vincent had offered that love to God, as he had offered every other sacrifice, with a smile. And quiet Eglantine, docilely munching her heap of gorse alongside the handsome newcomer, was in her way the image of that sacrifice, for ever since he had put on a priest's habit the youthful centaur of Leslé had contented himself with a mule. But he could still take the same pleasure in the sight of a fine horse.

At last the abbé straightened up, forcing his glowing face into an expression of sternness.

'You have good taste, my boy. When you steal you don't do the thing by halves. This is a magnificent animal, a mount fit for a lord.'

Gilles dropped his eyes, feeling uncomfortable none the less.

'I know, sir. All the same, I swear to you I did not choose him. I should have jumped on the first slug I saw just the same.'

'Come, come! There must have been other horses in the vicinity, but you saw only this one. Perhaps because you sensed that he would be fast and you were in a hurry?'

Gilles' honesty rejected this proffered excuse.

'I don't think so. I should have preferred a quieter mount because it took us some time to reach an understanding, he and I. To begin with, he was trying to throw me off.' He sighed. 'You know,' he said, 'that I am a wretched horseman, since my mother would never let me learn to ride. She used to tell me I should never have to ride on anything but mules and donkeys. I think that was when I first began to jib at the future she had arranged for me. I love horses so much—'

He stopped, flushing, but the abbé did not notice, being lost in his own thoughts which were far from charitable towards Marie-Jeanne. With the best will in the world, the poor woman had certainly been doing her best to give her son a dislike of the religious life. But then, had she ever tried to discover what was going on inside the child's head?

Seeing him lost in thought, Gilles plucked up courage to add very softly : 'I know I have no right – that it would be a bad beginning to the new life I want to make – but I should so like to keep this horse. I love him already—'

The abbé glared at him.

'And what gave you the idea that such wickedness deserves reward? Do you realize that you could be sent to the galley for this? There are lads of your age in convict gangs in Brest for doing far less.'

74

'I know. Do you want me to give myself up to the law, then?'

'I don't want anything at all – except my supper and bed. And time to think. We'll go in now. I'll tell you tomorrow what I have decided.'

But neither Gilles nor the abbé were fated to sit down to supper at a reasonable hour that night, for when they entered the passage they found Katell there, obviously upset. With her was an elderly peasant woman, weeping like a fountain, open-eyed and with the tears pouring unchecked down her grey face and on to her black cloak.

As soon as Katell perceived her master, she literally flew to him.

'Oh, rector, sir, it's Marjann! She says that my lord baron de Saint-Mélaine is much worse and in need of the last rites.'

Gilles started at the name as though he had been struck but the abbé exclaimed incredulously.

'Much worse! Why, I did not even know that he was ill. Has a doctor been sent for?'

It was the elderly Marjann who answered him, still weeping: 'He would not have it, rector! He would not have it. He always said that when an animal was worn out there was nothing to be done. But as to being ill, oh, that he was. And for a long time past. But, by our blessed lady, he would not say so! Not even to you or the young lady. He made me promise not to say a word to anyone. And now he's dying. You must come, rector. You must come quickly—'

And she began to cry more than ever, while Katell muttered under her breath about the folly of trying to hide one's poverty to that extent.

'I'm coming,' the rector said.

'And I,' Gilles cried, without thinking. Then, at his god-father's questioning look, he added in an undertone: 'You'll need a choirboy to go with you, at least. It's late and the weather is dreadful. It's no night to take a child out, and since I'm here—'

'Hmm,' was all the abbé said, but the glance he gave him brought the colour to Gilles' cheeks, for it said clearly enough that in his view a boy in a state of sin was scarcely the most

75

desirable escort for the holy sacrament. However, since he was unaware of his godson's real motive, M. de Talhouët merely ascribed his offer to an earnest wish to redeem himself. He nodded.

'I am going to church to make ready,' he said. 'Come to me there in ten minutes. But first go and ask Dr Guillevic to call on M. de Saint-Mélaine immediately.'

The boy was off almost before he had finished speaking.

Ten minutes later, the abbé in surplice and stole but with sabots over his shoes and clutching the viaticum to his chest, was almost running in the direction of the Ville-Close, followed closely by Gilles wielding a large umbrella and a bell which he swung regularly. The rain was still falling. It pattered on to the stretched silk. But despite the lateness of the hour the town was still awake. In fact it presented a spectacle of unaccustomed gaiety, thanks to the lines of army tents along the Blavet. The lights within them give them the air of a Venetian festival, while the camp fires struggled bravely against the rain. There came the sound of the sentries' regular footsteps and their voices calling to one another from time to time.

God, Gilles and the abbé passed beneath the great gateway, walked on a little way and stopped before a tall, narrow house with only three windows in the front but adorned with an elegant balcony wrought in the previous century. The rust which had eaten it away and the cracks in the façade were partly concealed by the darkness, but Gilles' sharp eyes noted them as he passed.

Two steps led up to the door, which was standing open. Old Marjann was on her knees in the doorway, waiting for them, candle in hand. As soon as they were inside she rose, more nimbly than might have been expected from her decrepit bones, and led them quickly down the passage and up a dim staircase, holding the candle high so that its light fell mercilessly on the damp-stained walls and cobwebby ceiling.

The house was icy cold. It reeked of poverty and Gilles' heart was wrung as he thought that this was the palace of his proud Judith. Even the classrooms at St Yves were more comfortable. At least they put down straw there in winter.

The room that opened to them was minimally brighter, thanks to the fire of broom twigs burning in the hearth, but the peeling paper made strange acanthus leaf shapes on the walls and the huge, old-fashioned bed, like a temple with its four solid oak columns, enclosed a desert of torn sheets and patched coverlets in which the frail figure of the dying man was all but lost.

Gilles scarcely recognized the man he had last seen in church at Hallowe'en. Without the white wig, which now stood on a wig stand on the mantelpiece, he was seen to be nearly bald with a long, red nose which stressed the tragic pallor of his face. The purple-veined lids were stretched over his sunken eyeballs and a continuous rattle came from the open mouth with its one tooth. A man in a brown suit was at the bedside, short-sighted eyes peering behind steel spectacles, bending down to examine the thin chest with a frown.

Seeing the abbé in his vestments, he straightened with a sigh, then got to his knees.

'You come in good time, Abbé,' he said testily. 'It is too late for me.'

The priest's eyes went from the doctor to the dying man and then back to the doctor.

'How is it that he never sent for you, my friend?'

Dr Guillevic shrugged his shoulders.

'The answer is all around us. He was poor but he was proud. I would have treated him for nothing, of course, and he knew it. All the more reason, in his eyes, why he should not ask it of me. He is all yours now.'

'Not for long, I fear. We must make haste.'

While old Marjann set out the small items needed for the rite of Extreme Unction and the abbé began the prayers for the dying, Gilles, mechanically uttering the responses, gazed at the dying man before him.

He was no more than a shadow, the mere suggestion of a man, a fragment of stretched skin and bone that no longer seemed to contain any human organs. Yet from that shrunken body had once come that other he could not wipe from his memory, that glowing young girl's body, demoniacal in its vitality and yet instinct with gentleness. Judith was flesh of this wretched flesh. Such a thing seemed inconceivable.

He was picturing the girl in his mind so intensely that he was scarcely surprised to see her appear suddenly in the dark

77

doorway, like a portrait come to life by magic. The figure of a nun loomed behind her but remained outside.

Judith uttered a cry of grief. She flung herself so impetuously at the bed that she bumped into the priest who had not seen her come in. Nor did she seem aware of him. She dropped like a wounded animal, her knees thudding on the wooden floor, and grasped the hand lying motionless on the sheet. They heard her moaning softly: 'Father! Father! What is it? Father, speak to me. Please, speak to me. You won't go away – you won't leave me – for pity's sake, say something. Speak to me!'

'He cannot speak to you, my child,' the abbé said, bending over her. 'You must be brave.'

'But he is not dead. I can see he is not. He is breathing!'

'Yes, but he can no longer hear you. Let us pray together. That is all that we can do for him—'

But Judith had no wish to pray. She jerked herself upright and in the light of the candles Marjann was lighting, Gilles saw her dark eyes glittering angrily.

'Why was I not told? Why did I know nothing?' she cried, without troubling to lower her voice. 'I thought he was quite well, only a little tired because he was old. And now, this evening, they come to tell me he is dying and that I must make haste. Was there no one to look after him?'

Her tone and her eyes were accusing. Then Dr Guillevic spoke up sharply.

'No one told you, young lady, because nobody knew. Not even ourselves. Your father insisted on keeping his condition a secret. You must know how reserved, how withdrawn he was—'

'And you must know how poor we are. My father was not withdrawn, as you say, he was proud. He would rather die than ask for help. But because he could not go out or entertain, no one bothered to find out how he was. If he had been rich, then the whole town would have flocked to his doors if he only sneezed!'

'You are letting your grief run away with you. Your father would not see anyone and we could scarcely force his door if he refused to open it. He could always find an excuse to avoid being visited, even by the rector. And you will hardly accuse

78

him, who spends his life among the wretchedest hovels, of scorning your father because he was poor.'

The girl's mouth turned down as though she had just swallowed something bitter. She shrugged.

'Visits of charity! Don't you understand how he must have hated that? He, a Saint-Mélaine, the honour of Brittany, to be treated like a crippled sailor or a worn-out labourer. To have to be humbly grateful for a good word, as they say, and accept a few provisions left, as though by accident, on one corner of the table, or one of those grey woollen mufflers people knit of a winter's evening as they sit by the fire eating pancakes and mulling over the latest gossip – or – or perhaps even a few silver coins – for Christmas! That's not what I meant. But a friendly visit, such as one makes to one's equals, the true, warm, noticing kind of friendship that can recognize death lurking at the back of tired eyes. He would not have refused that. But you left him in his dreadful loneliness with only that crazy old woman who believes in fairies and in goblins and sees the devil everywhere! Oh, I hate you! How I hate you! All of you!'

Her angry cry ended in a sob and the tears welled up and poured down her strained face. She was shaking like a leaf, on the verge of hysteria, and her shrill voice rang through the almost empty room. Then the doctor stepped forward and slapped her twice, quite calmly, then took hold of her bodily and forced her to sit down in the one armchair, where she collapsed in a heap, shaking with convulsive sobs.

'Someone get me some water,' the doctor growled. 'And you, abbé, finish your business. This is a shameful scene.'

The abbé nodded and smiled sadly.

'Oh, grief knows no shame. The poor child is beside herself. She does not know what she is saying, you know. And there may be something in it after all. We ought to have tried to force our way in. I fear that we have been gravely wanting in charity.'

'Don't try and blame yourself for a fault you've not committed, Abbé. You knew the Baron as well as I did. If we had forced our way in, he would have hurled the first thing that came to hand straight at our heads. He never went to church except at Christmas and Easter and he did not go out. But for

79

the devotion of poor Marjann here, whom his daughter so unkindly calls a crazy old woman, he could have died alone and no one even noticed, and it might have been weeks before anyone found the body. But let no one come and tell us anyone knew what was going on – even his daughter who seems to have been sitting in her convent thinking that all was for the best in the best of all possible worlds.'

Contrary to what might have been expected, Judith showed no signs of resenting this indictment. She might not even have heard. She was huddled in her chair, her head in her hands, weeping softly.

With a sigh, the abbé moved back to the bed and resumed the interrupted sacrament, but he had to shake Gilles to get him back on his knees. Overwhelmed by the violence of the scene and by the girl's grief, he was staring at her with a dreadful sense of helplessness.

What she inspired him with, in addition to a recurring, painful hunger, was an odd mixture of affection and anger. He hated her for the unmitigated contempt which she so unjustly heaped on him, but he could not resist her charm and the tenderness which enveloped him whenever he thought of her smile and of the shadow of her lashes on her cheek when she lowered her eyes. That night, seeing her suffering, watching her sitting in the chair as though in the pillory, it was tenderness that won. He would joyfully have banished all his resentment to have the right to protect her, even against herself, and to dry the tears that flowed so endlessly.

When the last prayer was at an end, he emerged from the dark corner where he had been ever since her entry and moved towards her, as though drawn by a magnet. A board creaked under his foot and Judith looked up.

For a moment their eyes met and locked and for a few brief seconds the wondering Gilles found himself believing that they could never part again. In hers there was neither anger nor contempt, but only the misery of a little girl lost, only a pathetic appeal for help. It was like a miracle. Everything else had vanished, the handsome, poverty-stricken room, the dying man, the priest and the doctor. They were alone in a world which belonged to them alone.

A tear rolled slowly down Judith's cheek. Her lips parted,

trembling, as if she were about to speak. But then a rattle from the bed broke the wonderful silence, and the doctor's voice said : 'It is the end. Come, mademoiselle.'

She was on her feet in an instant. The moment of grace had passed. Judith's head went up, her lips tightened and her face set hard again.

'You have no business here,' she said frostily. 'Be gone!'

Gilles shuddered, dragged from the gentleness of a moment before by the cutting contempt in the girl's voice. Moving so close that he could look down on her, he rasped out : 'No! The rector brought me here and it is for him to tell me when to go. And if you mean to have your servants throw me out, Mademoiselle de Saint-Mélaine,' he added cruelly, 'I do not think their numbers need concern me.'

He thought for a moment that she would have hurled herself at him but already M. de Talhouët had intervened, looking from one to the other of the young people in surprise.

'Go and wait for me downstairs,' he told his godson. 'I will make arrangements for the laying out and for someone to watch the body before we go.'

An hour later, when the mortal remains had been entrusted to the Brotherhood of the Dead, godfather and godson faced one another across the table in Katell's kitchen, while she dished up great bowls of porridge, mulled cider and even an omelette, whipped up by some miracle out of her mysterious store, before retiring to the chimney corner with her knitting.

They ate for a while in silence. Gilles, his nose in his bowl, shovelled food into his mouth and struggled against sleep. His long ride, the bruises of which were beginning to make themselves felt, the excitements of the day and the late hour were all weighing him down. All he wanted now, once he had satisfied his protesting stomach, was to sleep, to sink deeply into that blessed oblivion which is the sleep of youth.

The abbé waited until he had swallowed his last mouthful of cider and then asked quietly, as though continuing a conversation already begun: 'How long have you known her?'

Gilles did not look up.

'If it is Mademoiselle de Saint-Mélaine you mean, sir,' he said bitterly, 'I don't know her. You are forgetting what I am A bastard cannot claim acquaintance with a noble young lady.

81

I have – met her, let us say, twice. And those two occasions were enough to show me where she puts a boy like me : beyond the pale! Outside with the servants! And in her eyes they at least have the good fortune to be born in wedlock. I have not.'

The abbé made an impatient movement.

'Don't exaggerate. Your mother and grandfather have not deserved such scorn. Before his misfortune, he was a man of property, even a worthy man. As for her, she can be stern, even ruthless, perhaps, but at heart she is nobler than many.'

'And my father? Why do you say nothing of my father? Why do you never speak of him?'

'My poor child! For the very simple reason that I have never known his name. But when I hear you talk so bitterly, reducing yourself to the level of a servant, although they, too, are also God's creatures like other men, I think that you are abusing yourself and your family. Illegitimate birth is a misfortune but it is not a crime.'

'Go and tell that to the people who live in the Ville-Close, to the parents of the boys at school – and to Mademoiselle de Saint-Mélaine! They'll tell you what they think of bastards. We are nothing and we have no rights – except to accept humbly whatever fate may allow us. The good old days in the middle ages when a bastard could live the same life as his half-brothers are long gone.'

'God's ways are inscrutable. As for Judith, well-born she may be, but she has no more power to choose her own future than you have. Less, perhaps, for she is poor. She is no more cut out for the religious life than you are, yet a nun she will be, for I can see no other course open to her now that her father is dead.'

'A convent? But why? They say she has brothers—'

The abbé got up and, fetching a long pipe and a tobacco jar from the chimney breast, brought them back to the table.

'That is true. She has brothers – unfortunately. You have never seen Tudal and Morvan de Saint-Mélaine, or you would know what I mean. They are coarse creatures with dark, unfathomable minds. As to their hearts, I do not think they have any. The way they turned their father and sister out of doors after their mother's death was truly scandalous. And the way they live now – well, no one knows for sure. But strange tales are circulating about their estate at Fresne. The people of La Bourdonnaye, whose lands march with theirs, say that none of the local peasants will go near Fresne after dark for love nor money.'

'What do they do, then?'

'I don't know. And none of it is anything but rumour. But the story is that no man's purse nor woman's honour is safe with them. But, as I said, it is all rumour, of course, and there may be nothing in it. Yet Judith begged Guillevic and myself this evening not to let her brothers know of their father's death.'

'But – how can you?'

'We can't. They must be told. Unhappily, they are all the family their sister has now. Tudal, the elder, will automatically become her guardian and no one can do anything about it, for it is the law. Only Judith is afraid of them. That is why I said that the convent is the only way out for her.'

'Afraid of them—'

Remembering the almost terrified anguish in the girl's eyes earlier that evening, Gilles knew now what it had meant. Men capable of turning their own father out into the street, could make their sister's life a veritable hell.

'But we – you? Can't you do anything?'

The abbé took a brand from the fire, lit his pipe and puffed at it.

'No. No one can do anything – except herself. If Judith wishes to take the veil, I do not think they will dare to oppose her. Especially as they wanted nothing better to begin with, so as to prevent the poor child from claiming her share of their inheritance. There is no reason why they should have changed their minds. As for Madame de La Bourdonnaye, she is determined to keep her as long as she cares to stay.'

'And – she?'

The abbé's eyes, through the pipe smoke, gazed into his godson's with a curious persistence. Then, idly, as though it were a matter of no great importance, he said : 'I left her resigned. She knows that there is no alternative for a girl with no dowry. After the funeral, she will return to Notre Dame de Joie – quite certainly for ever.' He rose with a sigh. 'Now go and sleep,' he said. 'You need it. And so do I. And tomorrow we shall both see more clearly. But I think you will have to go to Kervignac.'

Gilles started and felt his face grow pale.

'Please, don't ask me to do that! My mother will never give way. And who can tell what she might do if I defy her openly.'

'What are you afraid of? That she will give you up to the law?'

Gilles was silent for a moment. Then : 'N-no,' he said. 'Not really. I think, sir, that what I am afraid of is myself. I am afraid of what might be said, and that I may not be able to control myself. Most of all, I – I am afraid of proving that she has never loved me. Oh, it's not that I still have many illusions about that, only she has never said it and I am afraid that, if she is angry, she will give free rein to her real feelings. I would rather be wrong all along the line and still able to keep some tender feelings for her.'

There were tears in his eyes, but the abbé would not see them, even though it was the first time he had ever known this reserved boy to cry.

'Still you must go. You will not be able to respect yourself if you do not. You have no right to sneak away like a thief. Go and see her and, since you are determined to be a man, behave like one. Dare to face her, whatever the consequences. Who knows, in her anger she may tell you the one thing you are burning to know – your father's name.'

The Abbé Vincent knew his godson well and indeed the boy's eyes were sparkling now, although the tears had gone. He looked up and his light blue eyes met the old priest's.

'You insist?'

'Yes. That is the price of my help. Go and sleep now. You must leave tomorrow at dawn.'

When the door had closed behind the boy, he made the sign of the cross and then went to shake Katell who was fast asleep in the chimney corner, her knitting in her lap.

Gilles slept like a log but he was used to rising at cockcrow and dawn found him running across the heath towards Kervignac. His long legs made nothing of the level ground and he was scarcely out of breath by the time the grey granite finger of the village spire rose above the horizon. Veering to the right,

84

he plunged down a sunken lane hedged in with giant gorse bushes, at the end of which lay his mother's house.

He leaped the fence, raced through the paddock without loss of speed and came to the low door, which opened under his impatient thrust. A tall black figure turned towards him. He was looking at his mother, but the startled cry that went up from the far end of the room had not come from her.

They stared at one another for a moment without speaking, he surprised to find her so much paler and smaller than in his memory of the previous autumn, she with a kind of stunned concentration, as though she could banish the unwelcome vision by a simple act of will. At last she spoke, in a dull, cold voice that was infinitely more striking than a cry of anger.

'What are you doing here?'

'I've come to speak to you, Mother.'

'I have nothing to say to you, and no time to listen. Go back to the seminary. They ought never to have let you out.'

'They didn't let me. I ran away before they could take me there. And I ask you to listen to me, even if what I have to say seems to you a waste of time.'

The words were polite enough but the tone was so uncompromising that Marie-Jeanne frowned.

'You ran away, do you say? How dare you! Well, you can just run back again and take the punishment you deserve, that's all. Now, let me pass. I must go to the church and say farewell to Rector Seveno before I leave.'

But instead of making way for her, Gilles put out both arms to bar her passage. At the same time, his eyes travelled round the big, familiar room, where everything surely looked unusually tidy, took in Rozenn, in her outdoor clothes, backed up against one of the cupboard beds, and then returned to his mother's narrow face, framed in her dark hooded cloak, as if it was carved from ivory. The face was so ageless that it cost him an effort to remember that it belonged to a woman not thirty-four years old. Only the beautiful dark eyes with their thick lashes still had a look of youth. Everything else had the dead tinge of things kept too long shut up.

'So, you are going away?' he said at last. 'May I ask where – and for how long?'

'For ever. I am going to Locmaria, to the Benedictine convent.

They are expecting me. I wish to have nothing more to do with this world or with men. Now that you know, are you going?'

He shook his head and then, before she could resist, he took her by the arm and led her to the table, where he made her sit down. She obeyed him mechanically, subdued in spite of herself by this new authority in her son. Gilles, however, did not sit. Conscious of the advantage given him by his height at least, he folded his arms across his chest and considered his mother.

'So,' he said quietly, yet with a sadness he could not control, 'you were going to part from me, your son, for ever, without a word of farewell, with no regrets, without even seeing me? What kind of a mother are you, after all?'

'I did not ask to be a mother. It was forced on me. No prisoner loves his ball and chain!' she retorted harshly.

The brutality of the words struck the young man like a blow. A ball and chain! So that was all he meant to this woman whom he himself could not help loving in spite of everything. Never before had he felt so much alone, so wretchedly forsaken. A lump formed in his throat and he fought against it, knowing that it could break in tears, and he did not mean to cry.

Marie-Jeanne, meanwhile, had lowered her eyes and was studying the tips of her fingers as they emerged from her black crocheted mittens. Her foot, protruding from the hem of her gown, was tapping impatiently. Gilles sighed, trying to loosen the vice that had tightened about his chest.

'Well – thank you for telling me. That being so – since you seem to be telling me that you have never regarded me as your child, then I have no further need to abide by your decisions concerning my future.'

The dark eyes lifted suddenly, with a flash of anger.

'What do you mean by that?'

'That you have made things easier for me, Mother. You sent me to the seminary as a way of getting rid of an unwanted object. Only I do not wish to go to the seminary. That is what I came to tell you. I shall never be a priest!'

'What? How dare you—'

'Let me speak, Mother, while I can still call you so. You have never forgiven me for being born, as though it were my fault, and you made up your mind to punish me, unjustly, by burying me for life in a priest's habit. Well, I am not going to do what you want.'

Marie-Jeanne sprang up with the speed of a striking snake. Two ugly red patches burned on her cheeks. Her mouth twisted as though it hurt her to speak.

'Sacrilege! You miserable boy! What are you saying! Punish you! You dare to call it punishment, the noblest and happiest state a man could ever aspire to—'

'For you, perhaps. Not for me.'

'Then I am right and you are no son of mine, nor ever have been. And I knew it. Are you going to have the courage to tell me how you do wish to live, what you mean to do with yourself? Speak, then! Speak, if you dare to avow your shame.'

'There is no need for you to insist, Mother. I am not ashamed to admit it. I want to serve the king. I want to be a soldier.'

'A soldier!'

Marie-Jeanne literally spat the word out, like poison. It was a cry of rage. Then, abruptly, the violence left her. There was a moment's silence before she went on in a low toneless voice: 'A soldier – like the other! A creature of destruction and misery. A destroyer. A limb of Satan – like him.'

Gilles held his breath. His mother seemed to have forgotten altogether where she was. She was gazing at something very far away, far beyond the enclosing walls of the house. Perhaps she was going to divulge the secret he so longed to know.

'Like him?' he echoed softly. 'The man who fathered me was a soldier?'

'They are all soldiers. In that accursed family they always have been. All through the centuries they have never known how to do anything but kill. And plunder and ravish and rob and burn— Accursed, damned, they have defied God for too long. They are all alike – all the same, ever since their famous Gyrfalcon! All of them! And you, the last, the bastard – you are like them too, you want to follow their bloody road—'

She was on the edge of hysteria. With her white face and the great dark rings under her eyes, the hint of froth at the corner of her mouth, she looked like some antique sybil at the moment of revelation, as though she were suddenly reliving the tragedy which had destroyed her. Gilles, frightened, tried to put his arms round her but she pushed him away with unexpected strength, so violently that he almost fell and had to clutch at the table to save himself. As he did so, he noticed Rozenn. She was kneeling by the hearth, her beads in her hand, her head was bowed and she was praying with all her heart.

'Please—' he gasped, 'before we part for ever – at least tell me his name—'

'Never! Do you hear? I shall never speak that name again. I swore it by Jesus Christ. You can go to the devil, if that is what you want – what is it to me, after all? But you shall not know whence comes your damnation.'

'Do you hate him so much, that man— Did he maltreat you, force you—?'

'Hate him? Oh, yes, I hate him – I hate him all right—' Suddenly she rounded on her son, clutching at his coat and breathing a scorching breath into his face.

'Do you want to know why I hate him, why I curse his name, why I can never forgive him? It is because he stole my heart, my mind, my life away from me. Forced me, do you say? Yes, he forced me, but not in the way you think. He forced me to love him, he made me dote on him. He did not ravish me, you see. He only took my hand – and I gave myself to him, like the wretched bewitched creature I was. He was the Devil, I was his handmaid and I renounced everything for him. That is why I cannot forgive him, or myself, or you – you least of all because you are like him. Now, *my son*, do you understand why I never want to set eyes on you again?'

'And I—' Gilles cried. 'I loved you! I love you still! I so longed to give you the happiness that you have never had—'

She released him then and turned away. She walked a few steps and then turned again and looked at him. In a voice grown suddenly very tired, she murmured: 'Then do as I say. Go back to the seminary and take orders. There is no other way you can make me happy.'

He met her look for a moment and then looked away.

'Forgive me. I cannot.'

'Then go! I curse you – as I cursed him! You are no longer my son. You can go to the devil if you like. I do not care, for I shall never see you again in this life.'

She ran to the door and opened it and fled away to where

the church bell was striking mournfully in the distance. Unable to make a move to stop her or to go after her, Gilles watched the black cloak billowing in the wind until she was out of sight. His heart was so heavy, so poisoned with bitterness and grief that he no longer knew even what he really wanted.

A warm, dry hand was laid on his.

'Come away, child,' Rozenn's voice said brokenly. 'We no longer exist for her.'

'I, yes – but you, who have cared for her for so long?'

The old woman shrugged her shoulders resignedly.

'I am like you. I belong to a time which she would rather forget. Young Glénic's gig is to come for her in a little while to take her to the coach. It was to have set me down at the rector's in Hennebont, so that he could tell me what I ought to do. I would rather not wait for it now, but go with you.'

Rozenn was wearing her best Sunday gown and her most decorative cap but she looked all at once so old and so wretched that the young man's heart went out to her, for she had been a true mother to him. For all those years of devoted care, she was being repaid with indifference, the cruellest of all ingratitude. It seemed that there was no room in Marie-Jeanne's heart for anything but her own, very private God.

Overflowing with pity, he put his arms round his old nurse's shoulders and kissed her cheek. Still holding her, he said: 'You are right. There is nothing left for us here. Let us go where we are loved—'

Possibly because he had discovered someone to protect, someone worse off than himself, Gilles suddenly felt less wretched. More than that, as he walked beside Rozenn, her bundle on his shoulder, through the misty morning, he felt a strange sense of freedom welling up inside him, as if he were emerging from a thick, dark forest, full of wicked thorns and brambles. He was bleeding, but his wounds would heal quickly with the balm of a new life. And the mist-shrouded heath seemed all at once aglow with light. The sun was breaking through.

5

Blood of the Gyrfalcon

'She said she would never see me again as long as she lived – and then she cursed me.'

Gilles launched into his woes on the doorstep, without so much as troubling to lower his voice. The vestry smelled of beeswax, burnt-out candles, incense and starch. It was so dark, on this grey, lowering day, that the Abbé Vincent looked like a ghost in his white vestments.

As though his godson's tragic utterance were a matter of no great importance, he went on peacefully setting out the ornaments that he would need when they brought in the body of the dead Baron de Saint-Mélaine, merely remarking: 'I imagine you can scarcely be surprised? It was the only thing she could do. Here, get this incense burner ready for me. The verger has the influenza and the choirboys are all thumbs. And while you are doing that, you may tell me all about it, since we are alone.'

As he set out the little scented sticks, Gilles tried to remember as faithfully as possible all that his mother had said. Her words were too fresh in his mind for him to forget a single one. He was repeating her violent outburst against his father's family when the abbé interrupted suddenly, with great excitement.

'You are quite sure of that? She did say "ever since their famous Gyrfalcon"?'

'Yes, I'm quite sure. It was such an unusual word. But I didn't understand—'

'But I do. Quite simply, in her anger, your mother let fall the key to the riddle. I had hoped for something like this. I know now who your father is – or rather who he was, for I have no idea whether he is still alive.'

Gilles nearly dropped the incense burner in his astonishment.

'You know?'

'Yes. And I am going to tell you. We have a little time to spare. Come and sit by me on this bench. It won't take long, because I'm not going to tell you the whole history of your father's family here and now. It's a thrilling and terrible saga but tiresomely long drawn out. In any case, I've a family tree in my study which I'll show you.'

'I want to know everything,' Gilles cried, devoured with impatience. 'But first of all, what was this Gyrfalcon?'

'That is just what I am about to tell you. In the year 1214 – you see, all this did not begin yesterday – when he married the beautiful Edie de Penthièvre, Olivier de Tournemine—'

'Tournemine? Is that – is that my name?'

'The name you ought to bear? Yes – but if you keep on interrupting me, we shall never get to the point. Well, at the time of his marriage, Olivier de Tournemine was given as a wedding present by the Duke of Brittany a great white falcon sent from the far north. It was a magnificent bird and a great hunter. It became Olivier's almost inseparable companion and even his surest weapon. Taran, that was the falcon's name, was used to going for large prey and would attack man and beast alike, and when his master loosed him no one could hope to escape him, so swiftly did he fly. His talons drew the first blood and after that the baron's battleaxe had only to finish what the bird had begun. In time, Taran became a kind of extension of Olivier himself, so that the frightened peasants of Trégor came in the end to confuse the man with the bird. Both were called the Gyrfalcon, and each was as cruel and relentless as the other. Through them, the noble, simple coat of arms which the first Tournemine had brought from England, quartered or and azure, were all too often stained with blood – and, unhappily, Olivier's descendants followed his lead.'

'What happened to the lord and the bird?'

'They lived together for many years, growing each day a little more alike, a little more locked in their strange friendship. Taran wore hoods and jesses of pure gold. His ascendancy over his master was complete. But naturally he was not immortal and one fine day, he died. Olivier's grief was terrible. For days and nights, and weeks on end, he shut himself up within the turrets of the brand new castle he had built himself at La Hunaudaye, refusing to go out. He no longer cared for the chase, for war, for rapine and plunder. Even the women he had once pursued had lost their attraction for him. And it may have been in memory of the terrible bird that he took as his motto the three enigmatic words *Aultre n'auray*, I shall have no other, which has been the Tournemines' device ever since.'

'But surely he must have come out of his fastness one day?'

'Yes. To follow Duke Pierre and the sainted King Louis to the crusades. He was killed at the battle of Masurah. But his story became a legend in time and he has never been forgotten in Pleven, or in a great part of Brittany.'

'How is it that Rozenn has never told me of him? She knows so many tales.'

'I don't know. Perhaps she simply does not know of it. Or perhaps she had some suspicions which she kept to herself.'

'But – my father? Tell me about my father now.'

'Your father? He was the last of that fearful line of Tournemines who, for centuries, had swooped like birds of prey on whatever came within their grasp. An extraordinary collection of robber-barons, knowing and loving only violence. And even he did not belong to the elder branch, which died out two centuries ago. There was nothing left to him of the power or the immense riches which at one time made the lords of La Hunaudaye spoken of as little lower than the King in France. His name was Pierre and he served in the same regiment as my brother, the King's Infantry. I never met him personally, but I know that he was staying in our house at Leslé, with some fellow officers, in the summer in which you were conceived.'

Gilles' eyes were sparkling and his cheeks on fire as he drank in the abbé's words like a draught of fresh air. It seemed to him that a great window had opened suddenly before him, revealing a distant horizon where, before, there had been nothing but a high black wall. At last he could give a name to the unknown father he had sought for so long – and it was a fine name indeed.

Softly, almost timidly, as if he feared to break a spell, he murmured : 'Is it so very difficult to find out what has happened to him? If he was in the same regiment as Monsieur de Talhouët—'

'He would have to have stayed in it. But his visit to us was in the nature of a farewell. He was tired of poverty and had dreams of restoring his family fortunes and buying back La Hunaudaye, which is now in the possession of a Talhouët cousin of ours who presides over the Parliament at Rennes. With this object, he had decided to go to sea, to sail to the West Indies by way of Africa and engage in the slave trade. If I remember rightly, when he left Leslé, he went directly to Nantes to embark on a vessel belonging to the shipowner Libault de Beaulieu, bound for the Gulf of Guinea . . . Come, don't tremble so. One would think you had the fever.'

'I think I have. I should so like to find him.'

'You might as well look for a needle in a haystack. He never came back and he may even be dead. But if it will give you any pleasure, I will make inquiries. I will ask my family and I'll write to M. Libault de Beaulieu and see if I can discover anything. Now, we must go and welcome the dead. There is the passing bell beginning to toll. Help me to finish robing . . . I will tell you tonight what decisions I have come to concerning yourself.'

Realizing that it was no use to persist, Gilles did as he was asked, then left the church, taking with him the first fine youthful dreams he had ever had. But he did not go far. Coming towards him was the cortège bringing the body of the late Baron de Saint-Mélaine to lie in the church until the funeral service on the morrow. Concealed behind the clump of holly and box which marked the entrance to the churchyard, Gilles watched the little procession with a strange and quite novel feeling of pride. He might be still a bastard, but at least he now had a father. He knew whence he came, even if he did not yet know where he was going, and the blood in his veins, the blood of the Gyrfalcon, was older and nobler than that of most of the people coming towards him. His destiny, too, must be greater than theirs.

He looked for Judith among the bobbing heads but it was a man who first drew his eye. He was walking just ahead of the senior curate of the parish, the Abbé Gauthier who, mounted on the docile Eglantine, was preceding the coffin. He was built like a bull, his thick red hair was unpowdered and tied with a black ribbon on the nape of his neck, and he was carrying a small horn lantern containing a short, lighted candle. Custom decreed that the person who carried the candle should be the closest relative of the deceased and Gilles never doubted for an instant that the man with the lantern was Tudal, the elder of the Saint-Mélaine brothers.

This discovery gave him little satisfaction. The new baron seemed to be about twenty-five years old and his looks matched his reputation exactly: a hard-faced brute with a pair of eyes the colour of granite and about as soft, set beneath brows too low for any great intelligence. His figure was encased in an old-fashioned suit of puce which must have belonged to his father.

Knowing that the man had a brother, Gilles looked to the other side of the simple hearse, draped in white like the horse that drew it, on which lay the open coffin. He had no trouble in picking out an almost identical copy of Tudal, the only difference being that Morvan, the younger, was smaller in build and his dark eyes held a look of cunning. The only resemblance either bore to their sister was that of the unhewn block of stone to the finished statue of a medieval angel: the colour was the same, but the divinity was absent.

The girl was walking in the front rank of women, in between old Marjann and a neighbour. She was wrapped in her great black cloak and bowed as though under the weight of a burden too heavy for her, and Gilles would hardly have known her, so unfamiliar was her attitude, if it had not been for a wilful red-gold curl escaping from the edge of her hood and dancing in the wind.

But just as she came abreast of Gilles' bush, Judith lifted her head, as though prompted by some inner voice, and looked, as she had done the night before, straight into his eyes. There was the same look of anguish in her reddened, grief-drenched eyes as there had been then, only multiplied tenfold. This time it was fear, a fear not far removed from terror, which Judith let him glimpse.

A rush of pity drove out the last vestiges of resentment.

Behind that white-draped hearse, with the billowing wave of long cloaks trailing grimly after her, Judith looked so like one of those youthful captives drawn after the chariots of victorious generals in days gone by that Gilles had to exert considerable self-control not to leap into the middle of the cortège and snatch her away. But already the coffin was entering the deep porch where the priests in black and silver waited to receive it. Judith vanished with it and Gilles went on his way. He did not want his brand new happiness marred by funeral prayers. Moreover Judith would be engaged for a long time to come in the lengthy rites that would precede the funeral itself. He had no business in the church.

Just as in those days the autumn before, when he had ranged the country like a frightened animal seeking to rid itself of the arrow that had wounded it, he made for the banks of the Blavet, only now he turned his back on the sea and lost himself in the hills where the chestnut buds were beginning to burst. He had to share the great promise of joy that was in him with the earth, the hope which was as strong and vital as the rising spring. He stayed there for hours, sitting on a tree stump at the edge of a wood, his eyes following the swift flight of a small coal tit, his ears tuned to the curlew's cry, inhaling with delight the mingled scents of earth and sea. He felt as if the world belonged to him, the whole world, with one possible exception which was enough to mar his perfect happiness. For that exception was Judith. It would be a long time before he saw her again, if ever, if the rector were to be believed and she was obliged to take the veil as the only means of escape from her brothers.

Gilles had no very clear idea, in his rather wild dreams of the future, what place the girl was to hold. But he had the utter certainty of the very young and also the foreknowledge of those in love. He knew that a place was there and, for good or ill, Judith would one day come to fill it. And because she was the one link which still bound him to this land of Brittany which he knew that he was soon to leave, for it was highly probable that his godfather would send him somewhere a long way off, he swore to himself that he would not go without making one more effort to speak to her. As for what he would say, that, too, was something he was not very clear about.

Perhaps he would simply tell her that he loved her, even if she did laugh in his face.

He thought about her so hard all day long that, seeing her appear beside the river when he was going home as dusk was falling, he thought he was seeing things. Yet it was indeed she! And in such a state!

Both hands holding up her black skirt and the red-gold mass of her hair unfastened and tumbling down her back, she was running as hard as she could towards the main gate of Notre Dame de la Joie which Gilles had passed a few moments previously. She was not screaming or crying, but her whole bearing proclaimed her terror and Gilles did not need to look twice to find its cause. A man was chasing her, and the man was Morvan, the younger of the Sainte-Mélaine brothers.

Catching sight of a figure on the path, he called out: 'Stop her, damn you! Hi! You there! Stop her, do you hear—'

Gilles, naturally, did nothing of the kind. Instead he stepped aside as she came panting up to him to let her pass.

'For pity's sake,' he heard her gasp. 'Help me!'

But Judith's appeal ended in a cry of pain. Already tiring, the girl had stumbled in a rut, twisted her ankle and coming down heavily on the ground. Her pursuer, bearing down on her, greeted her fall with a yell of triumph.

'Ha! Got you!'

'Not so fast!'

Gilles stepped into the middle of the path and barred his way. Morvan was on him in an instant.

'Out of my way, bumpkin!' he roared, enveloping the younger man in a breathy blast oddly compounded of onions and cider. 'Stand aside!'

'Stand aside yourself,' Gilles retorted boldly. 'You must get by me first. Run, mademoiselle,' he added to Judith. 'I'll hold him off.'

'We'll see about that,' Morvan said, charging his unexpected adversary head down.

They met with a violent shock. Morvan de Saint-Mélaine might be smaller than his brother but he was still a powerfully-built man. As for Gilles, this was the first time he had ever used his own strength against another man, except for the inevitable fights at school from which he had always emerged with honour. Taller and leaner than his adversary, he had the advantage of agility and, above all, he was carried beyond himself by that most powerful of tonics, the exhilarating joy of fighting for Judith, with Judith looking on! And so he laid about him mightily.

The fight was over surprisingly quickly. It was all amazingly simple. Gilles, as happy as a king, scarcely felt the other's blows and used his fists as though he had done nothing else all his life. The two of them pummelled and grappled with one another, rolling on the ground and doing their level best to throttle each other, without success, then getting up and laying into one another again, until at length Judith's knight, taking advantage of his opponent's loss of balance on the slippery bank, delivered the final blow by striking him full in the face with such force that he toppled straight over into the Blavet.

Wasting no time on looking to see how he fared, Gilles turned back to Judith who was still lying on the ground, rooted there by surprise as much as pain.

'Let me help you up, mademoiselle,' he said, holding out his hand. 'Have you hurt yourself?'

All trace of fear had gone from the pretty face now lifted to his and it was almost eagerly that Judith's little hand reached out to rest in his. She even smiled at him.

'You again!' she said, with a little touch of mockery. 'You do seem very set on rescuing me.' Her face clouded again. 'Only this time,' she went on, 'I did truly need it. In another minute I must be safe behind the convent walls. It is only there that I can escape them.'

'Escape whom? Your brothers?'

'Oh! You know, then, that they are my brothers? Yes, from them. They want to take me with them tomorrow, after my father is buried.'

Gilles felt the hand that still lay in his tremble slightly. Her fear had returned.

'Take you with them? But I thought they wanted to make a nun of you?'

'They have changed their minds. They want to take me home with them and marry me to a neighbour of theirs, a horrible old man, but very rich, who, it seems, is in love with me. So

97

help me now. My foot is hurting dreadfully and, as I said, I must get to the convent quickly. Morvan won't stay in the river for ever.'

This was true. The cold water had revived Saint-Mélaine and he was beginning to swim towards the bank. Gilles shrugged contemptuously.

'He won't be able to get out before the bridge. It's full of mud here and terribly slippery. I've tried it and I know.'

'You don't know what they can do when they are angry. Oh, how it does hurt! You will have to help me to walk. Luckily, it's not more than a few steps.'

Gilles' only answer was to bend and catch Judith round the waist and under the knees, lifting her off the ground with no apparent effort at all.

'There!' he said gaily. 'The best thing is for you not to walk at all. If you'll just put your arm round my neck—'

She had already done so. With a thrill of happiness, he felt the softness of her cheek against his and her silken hair against his neck. At that, he dared to hold her a little closer and she did not protest.

Gilles' heart began to hammer wildly in his chest. Never had he pictured anything so sweet, so wonderful. This was not the arrogant, scornful Judith that he held in his arms but a new Judith, tender and yielding, neither rebellious nor proud, a Judith who might even love him in return. He could have wished the convent far away on the other side of the woods so as to prolong the delicious journey indefinitely, if it cost him his last breath.

All at once, he heard her sigh.

'You are strong and you fight well. What a pity they want to make a priest of you.'

He laughed. 'Ah, but that's just it. I am not going to be a priest. My godfather, the Abbé de Talhouët, will tell me this evening what he intends for me.'

He was tempted momentarily to tell her what he had just learned, to tell her what blood ran in his veins, if only to see her eyes widen in surprise. But he thought that it might also remind her of his bastardy and decided it was wiser not to. So he merely added: 'He may send me to fight in America. There is nothing in the world I want more—'

He felt the arms round his neck tighten very slightly and, bending his head, saw the dark eyes sparkling.

'America!' she breathed. 'Oh, how lucky you are! It is only men who are so lucky. All there is for me is a convent. And I do so want to live – a convent is like the grave—'

Judith's rebellious cry found its echo in Gilles' own heart. It was too like his own refusal to enter the seminary. The girl was rejecting the veil just as fiercely as he had rejected the soutane. The Abbé de Talhouët had been wrong in thinking her resigned, when she was simply submitting.

Gilles found himself wanting suddenly to tell her all about those last months in Vannes, about his fears, his refusal, his flight and even the theft of the horse, but there was no time for already they had reached the ancient, medieval-looking doorway in the wall that surrounded the convent grounds. Panic seized him. In another moment Judith would be on the far side of that door. He would no longer be able to see her, hear her, touch her.

Holding her tight in his arms, he murmured into her hair : 'Are you sure you will be quite safe in the convent, that your brothers will not be able to tear you away? They are your whole family now. They have absolute authority over you.'

'I know, but Madame de La Bourdonnaye will be able to keep me safe. She has my father's express wish, before he died, to see me take the veil at Notre Dame de la Joie. Poor Father, he thought he was making sure that I should be at least peaceful, if not happy.'

'But you are not bound to take the veil straight away?'

'Of course not. I have to finish my year's schooling and then there will be my noviciate, which may take two or three years. But why are you asking me all this?'

'Because I want to do for you what has been done for me, to give you your freedom. I swear, if God gives me life, that I will come and take you away from this convent when I come back from America. I don't know yet how I shall do it but if you will trust me, even a little, I am ready to give my life for you.'

Judith did not answer immediately. She unwound her arms gently and made him set her down and for a moment he was afraid that he had angered her. She was going to lose her temper again and pour scorn on him, throw his bastardy in his face. But she did not. She simply put both hands on his shoulders and stood on tiptoe the better to look right into his eyes.

'Why would you do that?' she asked, almost timidly. 'You have had nothing from me until now but scorn and unkindness—'

'You being who you are and I who I am, that was almost to be expected,' he said gently. 'On the other hand, I think I owe you a lot, for but for you I might have let them shut me up in a seminary. But you gave me an immense longing to be near you, to try and make myself worthy of you. I think – yes, I think I love you.'

The word uttered itself, as simply, as naturally as a bird singing and Gilles was amazed that the admission could have been so easy. He felt Judith's hands quiver on his shoulders. They moved suddenly and twined about his neck and then the girl's body was pressed close to his and their mouths had joined, though no one could have said who had begun it.

For an instant, the universe turned upside down. Judith's lips were fresh as a rose and tasted of her tears but her trembling body burned like a flame in Gilles' arms. Even so, it was she who recovered herself first. Almost tearing herself from their embrace, she darted to the gate, lightly enough to cast some doubt on the severity of the twisted ankle, and rang the bell. Then she turned back to him, tossing back the hair that had fallen into her eyes, and those eyes were sparkling like black diamonds. They were bright with triumph. In a breathless, hurried voice she whispered :

'I will wait for you, Gilles Goëlo. I will wait – for three years, and not one day more. If you keep your promise, I shall be yours and you can do what you will with me. If not—'

'If not?'

She laughed, a laugh at once hard and shaky.

'If not, I shall see what I can do to help myself. Only, let me tell you, I am not going to waste my life in perpetual renunciation. I am not going to wither away into a hopeless virgin behind these walls. If you do not come, I shall give myself to anyone who helps me escape, be he only the convent gardener. Go now, someone is coming.'

100

In fact the ring at the bell had set up quite a bustle within. The light of a lantern shone over the wall, and with it came the sound of footsteps. An aged voice quavered: 'Who is there? Who rang?'

'Sister Félicité! It's Judith de Saint-Mélaine!' To Gilles, she added in an undertone: 'Don't forget. You have only three years in which to deserve me.'

The door opened a little way and shut again with a dull thud. The footsteps receded up the garden path and the light which had shone on the treetops disappeared. Gilles wandered on, with no very clear idea where he was going. There was a ringing in his ears and he was half drunk with joy and amazement as he walked slowly back beside the convent walls to reach the town the other way and so avoid meeting Morvan as he clambered out of the river. There was nothing to be gained by creating a fresh scandal which might delay his departure. For now he was in a hundred times more haste to be gone than he had been before. Three years! He had three years to win his life and make a success of it! There was not a moment to be lost.

An hour later, the look of the whole world had altered for Gilles so that he could scarcely remember a time when he had wept for grief and loneliness. The great black wall which for months had hidden the sun from him had fallen once and for all, not to the sound of trumpets, like the red walls of Jericho, but at the quiet, gentle words of a man with a sympathetic heart. A vast landscape now stretched before his eyes, bounded only by the wide earth and infinite ocean. What did it matter that the bitter wind was still tearing down the steep streets, slapping the puddles and banging the shutters? What did it matter that the soldiers had left the town as dirty and glum as a harlot after a night's orgy? What did it matter that dark clouds, heavy rain, were scurrying across the night sky? In Gilles' heart, all was clear and bright.

In order to achieve this minor miracle, M. de Talhouët had not needed any long words or florid speeches.

'Tomorrow,' he said, 'you will leave for Brest where you will go to the house of my old friend Madame de Couédic with a letter which I shall give you. Madame de Couédic is in deep

101

mourning, for it is barely two months since we laid her illustrious husband to rest, but her kindness takes no account of grief or joy. Furthermore, at this time there is not a seafaring man alive, however lofty his rank, who would not count it an honour to pay his respects to the hero's widow. The Chevalier de Ternay d'Arsac, in command of the fleet assigned by the King to the duty of carrying the Comte de Rochambeau's army across the Atlantic, will be no exception. Madame du Couédic will commend you to him and ask him to use his good offices to present you to the General – possibly as a potential secretary, since you happen, fortunately, to speak English well.'

Gilles' heart was beginning to thump under the old hunting coat. America! There it was indeed! He was to be sent to America. In a little while he would be aboard one of the King's great ships on his way to the new world, borne simultaneously on the green ocean waves and on gilded clouds of dreams of glory. And there, in that fabulous country where men were fighting for a word that was, as yet, barely known in France – for Liberty! Once there, he would very likely meet the amazing Marquis de La Fayette and might even fight at his side. But most of all, before anything else, he would be able to force fate to give him his chance at last.

'What are you thinking of?' the Abbé Vincent asked, watching the reflection of his godson's thoughts on his face.

Brought back to earth, Gilles gazed at him for a moment with eyes shining with gratitude. Then he smiled.

'I was thinking, sir, that tomorrow you are going to fly me and that Olivier de Tournemine used to launch the white falcon, Taran, from his fist. I, too, am going to fight—'

The abbé frowned. 'Just a moment. I am sending you to fight, yes, but for the King, and in the King's name. I am not sending you out to commit murder or rapine. If you want to imitate your ancestor, let it be only in what was great in him – and especially in the last part of his life, for he was fighting for God when he died.

'To become a true gentleman will mean a longer and harder road for you than for others, but you must never forget honour, courtesy – generosity – and pity, none of which were known to the Gyrfalcon. Do not take him too readily for your model.'

'I shall not forget, sir, because that would be to forget what

I owe to you. It would be to disappoint you – and I would rather die than displease you.'

The abbé smiled at the seriousness in his voice. He slapped him on the back.

'Try and stay alive,' he said. 'You can't think how I dislike conducting funerals.'

6

A Swede Named Fersen

Gilles left Hennebont on March the tenth but it was not until the fifth of April that he sighted the bastions, ravelines, fosses, redoubts, ramps and star forts which made Brest M. de Vauban's masterpiece and an all but impregnable fortress.

If this seems a long time for a journey of some thirty leagues, especially on horseback, it should be said that the youthful traveller spent no more than three days on the actual journey. The rest of the time he spent in becoming someone else. Or, at least, in trying to.

The fact was that after a sleepless night divided between thoughts of Judith and apprehensions concerning the next encounter between his bruised posterior and the back of a blood horse, he went downstairs to say goodbye to his godfather and was surprised to find Mahé out in the street, looking dirtier and hairier than ever, and standing stolidly in between the fine horse and Eglantine. The thoroughbred had been groomed in masterly fashion but bore no saddle, only a bridle which Mahé had firmly in hand. The rector's mule, on the other hand, was saddled up as usual, and carried a small baggage pack as well.

At the sight of his godson's discomfited expression, the abbé burst out laughing.

'You did not really think, my son, that I was going to send you off into the blue without the smallest preparation? For today, you are going no farther than Pont-Scorff and our estate at Leslé, where my father's old groom, Guillaume Briant, is expecting you. You will stay at the farm with him for three weeks. That should be enough to teach you the rudiments of how to handle weapons, as well as to sit this handsome fellow well enough not to put him to the blush. Only then will you go on to Brest. Mahé will go with you and can bring back my mule, which I'll lend you for the journey so that you need not go on foot like a peasant, for I want you to know how seriously I regard the responsibilities I am assuming against your mother's wishes. From now on, I mean you to be a credit to the humble name that she has given you – in the absence of a better.'

Simultaneously disappointed, delighted, mortified and swelling with pride, Gilles ended up blushing scarlet with happiness. It had occurred to him that Pont-Scorff was no great distance from Hennebont and that he might be able to return secretly and see Judith. But, as though the abbé had read his thoughts, he moved a step nearer and his fingers closed with unexpected strength on the boy's arm, while he looked him very straightly in the eye.

'You will not return until you have become a proper man,' he said, 'and I want your word on that here and now!' Lowering his voice, he went on : 'The whole town knows already that Mademoiselle de Saint-Mélaine fled from her father's house yesterday and took refuge in the convent, and that she was escorted there by a young man, after he had fought the younger of her brothers. It is known, too, that the Saint-Mélaines have sworn to punish him for his rashness. They would have no trouble finding you—'

'How do you know?'

'You came home in a terrible mess last night, but your face was radiant. That is why I am asking you to give me your word. Are you coming back?'

Gilles lowered his head, defeated.

'You have done too much for me to disobey you. I will not come back until I have done what you expect of me. Only – take care of her, I beg of you!'

'That is for God to do. She is in His hand. For your part, you had better forget what you cannot mend. Farewell, my son, and God keep you.'

Gilles knelt to receive his last blessing and then heaved himself on to Eglantine's back with a sigh, while Mahé, proud as a king, led the new horse which the boy had not been deemed worthy to ride.

Three weeks later, matters had altered dramatically. But at what a cost! On the Leslé estate, where his mother had known first love and then dishonour and where he himself had uttered his first cry, Gilles underwent a fair foretaste of purgatory under the pitiless rule of the ex-dragoon, Guillaume Briant. Leathery-skinned and bristly, Briant, though well past sixty, was still capable of schooling a tricky horse and teaching many an experienced master-at-arms a thing or two about sword management. And for those three weeks, under his chilly eye, Gilles ran and jumped and fought and rode from dawn to dusk, learning to use a pistol, a musket, a sword and a sabre, all out in the open air in the fine drizzle which fell almost continuously and, for the most part, with no more encouragement than a volley of abuse. But after a week his tormentor permitted him to mount the beautiful stolen chestnut, which he had christened Merlin in memory of their first magical encounter, and finally, just as he was about to leave him, Guillaume Briant actually brought himself to utter a few grudging words of praise.

'I'd have been glad to have had you longer,' he told him, 'for you have some rare qualities. You've the makings of a fine horseman and one of the best blades in the kingdom if we only had the time. Try not to forget anything I've taught you. You know enough to put on a good show . . . especially as I've had orders to fit you out.'

And indeed, no one would have recognized the unkempt fugitive from St Yves in the youthful rider who, on that April day, was riding at an easy pace towards the Porte de Landerneau, the only one of Brest's gates open to wagons and pack animals. Dressed in cloth of iron grey with a ruffled shirt of fine white linen with a flowing black cloak over all, with black leather boots and hair drawn back neatly into a soft leather bag and tied with a ribbon and a plain cocked hat worn at a careless angle, Gilles sat very straight, guiding Merlin firmly through the press of cattle, vehicles and donkeys with women or monks on their backs which filled the roadway.

He went on quietly, without hurrying, enjoying the moment, simply happy in the new strength he felt in himself and, even more, in the sword of blue steel that Guillaume Briant had buckled at his side before slapping Merlin's rump a vigorous gesture of farewell. It seemed to him that his eyes could never open wide enough to take in all the spectacle before them.

Enclosed within its fortifications and guarded by its castle, green with time and weather, Brest itself was simply a small, grey town with narrow, picturesque streets. It was like a nut in the centre of some formidable shell.

Its granite houses were almost as grim as its walls but it was filled with soldiers whose gay uniforms rubbed shoulders with the white coifs and embroidered petticoats of peasant women and the gathered breeches and round hats of their menfolk, while sailors in striped jerseys and red-coated marines jostled the shabby overalled convicts in red or green bonnets, who worked as refuse collectors in Brest as well as in the various departments of the arsenal.

Accustomed to the quiet elegance of Vannes, Gilles did not consider Brest a beautiful city, but at the far end of the long Rue de Siam which cut through its centre lay the grey waters of the Penfeld bearing a forest of tall masts with multi-coloured pennons at their heads.

When Guillaume Briant had given him his weapons and a little money from the de Talhouëts, he had recommended the *Pilier Rouge* as a modest establishment kept by a cousin of his own and not far from the posting house of the Seven Saints, but Gilles put off the search for a lodging, being unable to resist the urge to take a closer look at the King's great ships at last. He went on to the harbour and stood gazing in wonderment at the splendid spectacle.

High wooden sides, painted red, blue or buff, stern castles with gleaming windows, carved like altars and gilded like missals, and wrought bronze lanterns, with their lofty, painted figureheads and embroidered silken banners, the vessels of his majesty King Louis XVI, the royal geographer with a passion for the sea, were like dream palaces moored for an instant on the dull shores of reality.

Gilles could gladly have stood for hours amid the seething throng that filled the waterfront if an angry voice close by had not dragged him from his thoughts.

'Why that's my horse! Hey, you, sir, will you tell me what you're doing on his back?'

Two young gentlemen were standing at the horse's head, regarding Gilles with a highly unfriendly interest. The one who had spoken even had his hand on the bridle and there was an ominous light in his bright blue eyes. Gilles felt himself turn pale and cursed the ill luck which had led him to fall in with the horse's owner, but he did his best to brazen it out.

'Are you quite sure, sir,' he asked quietly, 'that this is your horse?'

'What's that, am I certain? I paid enough for him to know him every inch, from nose to tail. He was stolen from me by some scoundrel in Vannes, when I left him outside the inn where I was dining on my journey.'

The matter was thus beyond a doubt, as also were the intentions of the young officer, who seemed to be aged about twenty-four or -five and spoke with a fairly strong foreign accent. Gilles took in at a glance the elegant blue and yellow uniform of the Royal Deux-Ponts regiment, the colonel's epaulettes, the powdered wig and gold-laced hat and realized that his dreams of glory were all too likely to come to an abrupt end. This man was going to send him straight to prison.

Nevertheless, he decided to play the game to its end. Coolly dismounting, he swept off his hat and bowed gravely.

'I am that scoundrel, sir. I did indeed er – borrow your horse on an occasion of dire need when I was obliged to flee in haste. Believe me when I ask your pardon.'

'And you think that is enough? Thanks to you I was obliged to finish my journey on a horrible slug. I all but died of mortification! And may I ask why you were under the necessity of this hasty flight? From the law, perhaps?'

'No, sir, from the seminary where I was to have been incarcerated against my will. Which said, I have the honour to beg your pardon for a reprehensible piece of behaviour which I am not at all in the habit of. If, however, you still do not consider yourself satisfied by this – and by the immediate restitution of your property—' Gilles laid his hand significantly on his sword hilt. It was the purest folly, for he was quite certainly no match for a practised swordsman such as the colonel, but he would a hundred times rather die than suffer the ultimate humiliation of an arrest. At least he would die as he would have wished to live, like a gentleman.

The stranger raised his eyebrows disdainfully and tittered.

'Why, how fierce you are, young sir! First you rob a man, next you would murder him?'

'Who spoke of murder? You have a sword, sir, and so have I. Use it—'

The other officer, who had so far said nothing but had merely watched the scene with evident amusement, now intervened. He was smaller than his companion, who was tall and slim and elegant in a way that could not help but appear slightly affected, with quick black eyes and a bronzed complexion which he must have acquired under some distant sun.

'Suppose you were to tell us first who you are?' he suggested. 'One cannot fight just anyone, especially here, where his lordship the Comte de Rochambeau is so strict in the matter of duelling. You have the look of a gentleman but that is not enough. Your name, if you please.'

The light, insolent tone caught Gilles on the raw. He looked down his nose at the speaker, who was a good head shorter than himself, and answered curtly: 'My name is Gilles Goëlo, sir. Is that enough for you?'

It was the turn of the dark young man to lift his eyebrows.

'By no means! What kind of a name is that? Are you even a gentleman?'

'No, sir!' Gilles exclaimed in exasperation. 'I am not, or not in the sense that you mean, for the name I bear is my mother's. My father, who was a gentleman, not having found the time to acknowledge me. If you prefer it, I am a bastard! Bastard of Tournemine, as they would have said in the middle ages. And now I have said enough. Kill me, sir. It is preferable to insulting me.'

The dark young man was about to answer but his companion intervened.

'Let be, my dear Noailles,' he said with a shrug and a light laugh. 'Since he insists, let us give him the pleasure! In any case, a little exercise in this chill wind will warm us up. Follow us, sir. You may leave er – our horse with my servant there.' He nodded in the direction of a man standing a short way behind. 'He will restore your baggage to you – if you should return alive. If not, it will be my unhappy task to restore it to your worthy mother. Have you any seconds, by the way?'

'I have but this moment arrived, sir, and I have an introduction to Madame de Couédic, but I know no one here. I have already told you that I ran away from Vannes.'

The stranger considered Gilles with some perplexity.

'You are a curious character, my escaped seminarist! May I inquire how old you are?'

'Seventeen.'

'No more? Almighty God, I had hoped for more. But then, if I kill you, surely I am going to appear an infanticide?'

His aggrieved tone drew a smile from Gilles and a quick bow.

'Fear not, sir. I am very much older than my years. And I think your friend is one who might fill the place of all the seconds in the world.'

The subject of this laughed and returned the bow.

'Upon my soul! That was bravely said and I'm much obliged to you, young man. I shall do my best. Come – only I warn you, it's some distance. Here, one can't fight just anywhere. It must be done in secret if you want to avoid being called to account for it.'

He took his friend's arm and they walked on to the ferry below the castle. Gilles followed, trying not to think and gazing wide-eyed on the martial and naval scene which, he felt sure, was soon to be extinguished for him for ever. Above all, he tried not to think of Judith, since he would not even have the consolation of a glorious death about which she would know nothing.

The three young men crossed the Penfeld whose shores, hemmed in by the fortifications and the magazines, were like one vast workshop, and came to the Quai de Recouvrance. From there, they made their way along the walls skirting the village. It was behind these walls that affairs of honour were regularly settled, being well out of the way of the prying eyes of authority.

They stopped at the foot of a bastion. The place was deserted, the ground level and the grass short. From it, one could see the magnificent panorama of the Channel and the roadstead with the dancing red sails of the fishing smacks. A big frigate out of Bertheaume was tacking as gracefully as a seagull. The sky was a soft grey and the sea a beautiful dark green and Gilles thought that he could not have chosen a nobler view to close his eyes on.

Calmly, he slipped off his cloak, tossed his hat away and took off his coat. Then he drew his sword and saluted.

'I am at your service, sir,' he declared firmly. 'Will you do me the honour of telling me who I am to fight?'

The young colonel's almost too perfect features were disturbed by a slight smile. The wind had put some colour into a face as pale and delicate as any woman's and his eyes had a brighter shine in them. He, too, had removed his coat and the wind was swelling his shirt of fine lawn trimmed with costly lace.

'That is fair. I am Count Axel de Fersen, a Swedish officer in French service, acting colonel in the Royal Deux-Ponts regiment and at present aide de camp to General de Rochambeau, as also is the Vicomte de Noailles here. Does that satisfy you?'

'Entirely, and honoured to cross swords with a gentleman of your quality. Believe me, I appreciate it. May I ask one last favour, however?'

The other's eyebrows rose again in slight disdain.

'A – favour?'

Gilles laughed. 'Oh, nothing for myself, never fear! It is simply that, since I know no one here, I should like news of my fate to be conveyed to the one person who cares about me, my godfather, the Abbé Vincent-Marie de Talhouët-Grationnaye, rector of Hennebont.'

'I will see to it, sir,' Noailles broke in. 'If your godfather is a Talhouët, then you are practically one of us. You may die in peace!'

Gilles thanked him with a smile and, murmuring a brief prayer inwardly, took up his position without more delay. The Swede engaged as coolly as if he were in the fencing school. The same faint smile lingered on his lips and he gave every appearance of one prepared to despatch the thief of his horse with all speed. But Gilles, who had few illusions about himself, was surprised to find that he could parry the first passes fairly easily. Some faint hope stirred in him and he did his best to remember all that Guillaume Briant had taught him and, above all, to curb his impatience. This was not easy, for the long, pale

111

figure opposite seemed activated by a kind of indestructible mechanical force and fought so neatly as to leave no opening.

All at once, he heard Fersen laugh and flushed angrily.

'Will you tell me what you find so funny?' he cried.

'Funny is hardly the word. It is merely that I should like to know how many duels you have fought before this, young sir.'

'You mean, I take it, that I am clumsy? Well, let me tell you, this is the first.'

'I thought so. And you are not in the least clumsy. But a novice, yes – that much is evident.'

'It need not induce you to spare me—'

Holding his point high, he was about to rush in wildly to the attack when Noailles threw himself in between the combatants, at grave risk of injury to himself.

'Sheath your swords, gentlemen, I implore you!' he cried. 'Look who is here!'

Two men had just come round the corner of the bastion and were advancing on the scene of the duel. The sight of them drew something like a groan from the Swede.

'That's just our luck! When I do break the law for once, it has to be the General himself who catches me at it! I'm for a court martial at the least—'

'And the Admiral with him into the bargain,' the Vicomte muttered. 'We are done for!'

'I beg your pardon, sirs,' Gilles broke in, uneasily, 'but do you mean that these two gentlemen—'

'Are our commander-in-chief, the Comte de Rochambeau, and the Chevalier de Ternay, Admiral of the fleet which is to carry us across the Atlantic. We have been caught red-handed and our jobs as ADC's are not worth a brass farthing. You, sir, are saved.'

Gilles was about to retort that his salvation was rather less assured than the Vicomte seemed to think, but those walking towards them were already within earshot. One, a very tall man of about fifty with a full face and regular features somewhat marred by a deep scar on the temple, showed a glimpse of the order of St Louis under his cloak. This was the General. The other, a wizened, sad-faced little man of uncertain age, wore the red waistcoat and dark blue coat and breeches of a naval officer. He was the Admiral. He walked with a stick on account of a limp caused by an old wound.

'My compliments, gentlemen,' Rochambeau said curtly. 'You arrived yesterday, you have been members of my staff since this morning and already you are contravening my orders? Duelling is forbidden. You know that and yet—'

Here Gilles, moved by a faint hope, was prompted to intervene.

'If you please, General,' he said hesitantly, bowing as respectfully as he knew how, 'but it was not a duel.'

Rochambeau turned and stared at him.

'Do you take me for a blind man or a fool? What, then, was it, may I ask?'

'A well-deserved lesson.'

'Indeed? And who may you be?'

'A presumptuous young Breton. Only yesterday, I was still a pupil at St Yves college in Vannes and I am but newly arrived in Brest. I have an introduction to Madame du Couédic—'

He recounted, with a fine assumption of innocence, how he had gone to have a look at the harbour and, meeting the two officers there, had asked his way of them and fallen into conversation.

'I told them it was my most earnest wish to sail with the army under you, General. At that, they fell to mocking me, saying that to fight a war you needed people who could wield something other than a pen, and I offered to show them what else I could do. I must admit,' he added with a smile, 'that these gentlemen were right. I am not very proficient with a sword—'

'Not at all, not at all!' the Vicomte interrupted, entering into Gilles' plan with enthusiasm. 'You acquitted yourself very well, young sir.'

The General's eyes rested coldly on all three young men in turn, but lingered on the Swede.

'And do you confirm this, Count Fersen?'

'Most definitely, General. The young man is extremely – er – promising, in every way. He could make an excellent recruit.'

'Very well. In that case, I will leave you to your amusements, gentlemen, and Monsieur de Ternay and I will resume our inspection of the defences. Ah, but I was forgetting you, young man,' he added, turning back to Gilles. 'You did say you had an introduction to Madame du Couédic?'

'Yes, sir.'

'Then you are out of luck. Madame du Couédic has left for her house at Kerguelénen. Brest was too painful for her after her husband's death. If you wish to see her you will have to go back to Douarnenez. Good day to you, sir.'

'But, General—'

Gilles' protest died on the wind. Rochambeau was already turning away to rejoin his companion who had strolled a little way off and was staring out to sea, leaving the commander-in-chief to deal with his subordinates as he thought fit. The two men strode off rapidly, their great, black cloaks billowing in the wind and Gilles watched them in near despair. His luck was going with them, for with Madame du Couédic away from Brest he had no other way of approaching either of the two commanders on whom his hopes rested. By the time he had been to Douarnenez, especially on foot, since he no longer possessed a horse, and returned again, the fleet would certainly have sailed.

A gentle cough reminded him of the existence of his chance companions, whom he had temporarily forgotten.

'Well, sir,' Noailles said. 'Are you coming, or do you mean to spend the night here?'

He turned and saw that the Swede had resumed his coat and was already fastening his cloak.

'Forgive me,' he said. 'I had forgotten you. Are we not to resume our fight?'

Fersen shrugged. 'Do you not feel we have done enough? It has been a close shave but I acknowledge that your presence of mind got us out of a tight corner. I thank you, and deem myself the more satisfied since you have restored the horse you – er – borrowed from me. Let us leave it at that and return to Brest.'

Without waiting for an answer, he began to stroll slowly down to the ferry. Gilles was left to finish dressing in his turn, feeling almost sorry in his disappointment that he had been deprived of a death which would have solved all his problems. He was watched interestedly by the Vicomte de Noailles who had remained with him.

114

'What will you do?' the Vicomte asked at last, when they were on the path. 'And what was it you expected Madame du Couédic, whom I know only by name, to do for you?'

Responding to his new acquaintance's sympathetic tone, Gilles explained, concluding, with no more than a sigh : 'Now, it is all done with. By the time I have been to Douarnenez and back, you will all be gone. I failed to speak to the General just now, and in any case he has no reason to take an interest in me. I shall never be his secretary and I shall never go to join Monsieur de La Fayette who, they say, is a hero worthy of antiquity. Unless I can enlist in one of the regiments that are going.'

'Don't pin your hopes on that. They are turning men away.'

'How can that be? It would surely be the first time a recruiting sergeant ever turned down a recruit. I've seen them at work often enough. They'll do anything to get more men.'

'Oh, yes. They'll take you with open arms if you choose a regiment like Karrer's or some other that is garrisoned here. But for America, they are turning people away. You see, there are too many troops already for the transport available. The Chevalier de Ternay, whom you saw just now, is always looking on the black side and he absolutely refuses to take more than five thousand men on board. There are nearly ten thousand here. As for the volunteer officers, I know of more than one who will have to stay behind in the faint hope of securing a passage at a later date. They'll not take you.'

Not wishing to repay the young nobleman's interest with a display of self-pity, Gilles struggled to put a brave face on and smiled courageously, even though there was death in his heart.

'Well,' he said, 'then that is the end of my dreams. But I thank you, sir, for your interest.' He made the other a bow.

They returned, as they had come, by the ferryboat. Fersen found his valet still waiting stolidly beneath the tower of La Motte-Tanguy, walking Merlin up and down. He restored Gilles' baggage to him.

The three men bowed and parted. But Gilles felt a pang as he watched the horse he had come to love being led away by the manservant. Now he would be truly alone.

115

At that moment, Noailles, his interest thoroughly aroused, turned back.

'Where are you staying, young man?' he asked. 'Lodgings here are as hard to come by as berths on the king's ships.'

'It hardly matters now. My best course might be to leave at once.'

He did not say where he meant to go, for the truth was that he did not really know. He had promised his godfather not to return to Hennebont until he had become a man. Perhaps, after all, Douarnenez would still be the best place to make for. Madame du Couédic might find a way.

'I should not advise it,' the Vicomte said seriously. 'Night is falling, and rain too. God forgive me! This is no weather to be travelling the roads – especially on foot, now that you are without a horse. At least spend the night here.'

'In that case, I was recommended to the inn of the *Pilier Rouge*, by the posting house of the Seven Saints. The landlord is a countryman of mine.'

'Go there, then, and don't stir before tomorrow. They say the night brings counsel. That is not always true but it does bring rest, at least, and you could do with that.'

'Noailles, what are you doing?' the Swede called irritably, retracing his steps. 'The weather's turning nasty and we shall be soaked. Let the boy go hang himself where he will. The matter is at an end.'

Gilles started forward impetuously, ready to hurl himself angrily at the insolent Swede, whom he was beginning to dislike exceedingly, but he was brought up short by young Noailles' hand on his arm.

'I'm coming,' Noailles said calmly and, in an undertone, he added: 'Promise me you will not leave Brest before noon tomorrow.'

'But I—'

'Don't go imagining things, but only promise me. If you have had no sign from me by noon, then you are free to go.'

'It will be a waste of time – but I promise, sir, and either way I thank you.'

Left alone on the quay, Gilles firmly refused to speculate further on the unknown Vicomte's oracular words and set out

116

to look for the *Pilier Rouge* without more delay. He had had enough disappointments for one day and preferred not to let his imagination run too freely.

However, another disappointment awaited him at the inn. When he made himself known to the landlord, that worthy raised his arms to heaven in a tragic gesture.

'A room? What does cousin Guillaume think I am? Does he think my house is as big as the king's palace? Not only have I no rooms left at all, not even for myself, but I have not even the smallest closet! In the ordinary way I take in country folk, small tradesmen and packmen, but with the city so crowded as it is now I am lodging officers. I even have a colonel – a Monsieur de something-or-other, all over gold lace. At home—'

Clearly, while he could not get over the honour of it, the colonel was also something of a mixed blessing. His demands were no doubt inconvenient.

'Listen,' Gilles pleaded, 'can't you find me just a tiny corner anywhere, not even in the loft? I simply have to stay here until noon tomorrow. I – I am expecting to hear from a friend. And I am very tired and hungry. Guillaume Briant told me you would look after me. I can pay, you know.'

Mine host Corentin Briant pulled off his cap, the better to scratch his head.

'It's easy enough to feed you. It's lodging that's the problem. Do you know there are people sleeping on the beach at this moment? On the other hand, if I let you sleep out, cousin Guillaume is not the man to forgive it . . . Very well, listen. If you can be content with a bale of straw and a corner of the coach house, maybe we can do it. There's not much room, because the coach house is full. The colonel's carriage is a great thing with fine cushions in it, and it fills the place completely.'

'That's all I need,' Gilles cried joyfully. 'Give me something to eat, quickly, and then show me my bale of straw.'

An hour later, his stomach the better for a rich and fragrant *cotriade* stuffed with every kind of fish in the Iroise, and a huge bowl of mulled cider, Gilles, much cheered, was crossing the *Pilier*'s small stable yard in the wake of the innkeeper who carried a lantern in one hand and a bale of straw in the other.

The coach-house door opened to reveal an immense apple-green chariot with its shafts in the air occupying almost all the available space. Gilles' jaw dropped.

'I'm not fat,' he said, 'but do you really think I can fit in there?'

'Why, to be sure,' the landlord answered calmly, scattering hay in a random way between the two huge wheels. 'It doesn't look like it but from this side, you see, you can even get the door open. Oh yes, it's a fine vehicle as fine vehicles go! And then the inside of it! I'd stake my hat on it, one could sleep in there as well as in a bed.'

This was said in such a way that Gilles stared fixedly at the man for a second, and then broke into laughter.

'I'm sure you are right, Master Briant! This straw will enable me to sleep soundly until dawn. I was always an early riser.'

'Then shut the door well and don't make a noise. The coachman sleeps above but he is drunk most nights and never awake before mid-morning. A fine sort of coachman, he is! If I were the colonel—'

Not many minutes later Gilles, comfortably settled on the cushions of the green berlin, had forgotten all his cares and was fast asleep. He dreamed that he, too, was a colonel and charging the convent gates at Hennebont at the head of his men, to snatch Judith away and bear her off on Merlin's crupper deep into a forest full of vast trees peopled with men of every colour.

The crowing of the cock roused him from this felicity to the uncertain present which, however, he was able to face with more confidence than the night before. And the first rheumy light of dawn found him stripped to the waist, washing himself at the pump in the stable yard.

He dressed and combed his hair with particular care and then, having breakfasted on a bowl of thick ham soup, settled himself in the common room of the inn to await developments – which might not even occur. However, noon had been set as the limit to his waiting. After that, he would see about taking the coach to Landerneau, whence it should be possible to reach Châteaulin and from there, Douarnenez and the château of Kerguelénen in Pouldergat, the home of his last hope. If he ran much of the way, he might still be back in time to catch the fleet before it sailed, and surely Madame du

Couédic would find some captain of a frigate or other vessel to send him to.

Gilles waited for a long time, keeping one eye on the long-case clock of chestnut wood whose loud ticking punctuated the whole life of the inn. Nine o'clock struck, then ten and then eleven, nibbling away at the hopes that rested in the young Vicomte's, admittedly vague, words.

All hope was quite gone and the hands of the clock moving towards twelve when the broad blue and white figure of a marine appeared in the inn doorway.

'Is there a gentleman named Gilles Goëlo here?' he bawled from the threshold, without deigning to enter.

He did not have to ask twice. Already Gilles was on his feet.

'I am he.'

'Will you come with me.'

'Where to, if you please?'

'To the Quartermaster General's office, where you are awaited most urgently. You must make haste.'

'Then I am with you.'

Entrusting his slender baggage to Corentin Briant, Gilles followed the soldier, aware that his heart was beating a good deal faster than usual. Not a word was spoken as they made their way in single file across almost the entire width of the city as far as the Arsenal and the imposing mansion with a military guard outside which served both as lodging and head-quarters for the man known as the White Admiral, the Deputy Quartermaster General, all-powerful representative of the Navy Office and absolute master of the docks and depots of the Grand Arsenal. The present incumbent of this office was the Comte d'Hector, a chronically nervous man who endeavoured to combat his frequent attacks of giddiness by long days hunting.

The whole house was in an uproar. Gold-laced officers and busy clerks with pens behind their ears moved here and there, running up and downstairs carrying papers and fat ledgers. The entrance hall and staircase echoed to the drumming of feet and a buzz of conversation.

Still following his guide, Gilles reached the first floor, where he was handed over to an orderly. He was led, by way of a short gallery and a long corridor, to a door which was opened to the announcement : 'Here is the gentleman you were expecting, sir.'

Somewhat dazed, Gilles found himself in a room whose lofty, uncurtained windows let in as much light as was possible on such a dreary day. The walls were covered with naval charts, diagrams and a rather fine painting of a naval engagement under a smoke-filled sky. Besides a large cupboard, the chief furnishings were two tables, a large one piled with papers and ledgers and a small one equipped only with writing materials. The man seated at the larger table looked up as Gilles entered. He was a thin, pale, lugubrious person with a pair of spectacles perched on his long nose, but his wig was powdered and he wore a suit of fine, chestnut-coloured weave with a plain stock at his neck.

He sat for a moment, silently nibbling the end of his pen and contemplating the new arrival who saluted him courteously, although in some bewilderment. At length he cleared his throat and, stroking his clean-shaven cheek with the quill in a thoughtful way, he spoke, somewhat patronizingly.

'It has come to our ears that you are soliciting an appointment as secretary to his excellency, the Comte de Rochambeau, young man. Is that correct?'

Gilles flushed. 'Quite correct, sir.'

'Hmm . . . Very well. You will appreciate, however, that to solicit such an appointment is not invariably to obtain it. You must first demonstrate your capacity. Good secretaries,' he added, stressing the words in such a way as to leave Gilles in no doubt of how he personally estimated the importance of such persons, 'are few and far between.'

The younger man repressed a smile.

'Believe me, sir, I am very sure of that. But may I derive some encouragement from your words?'

'Not so fast. It is true that fate seems to be on your side, for that position was occupied until yesterday by a most capable young man from Angers with a fine head for figures, but he has received news of an alarming nature from home which has obliged him to quit his post for what will undoubtedly be many weeks. The count was in some perplexity when one of his ADC's, the Vicomte de Noailles, most warmly recommended you. He seems to have a high opinion of you. We have decided, therefore, to give you a trial. Sit at that little table. Take pen and paper and be ready to write at my dictation. We have to see, first, how well you can write.'

Gilles obeyed mechanically arranging his papers, taking up a pen and assuring himself that it was well cut, and then waited. He was feeling somewhat uncomfortable, for he guessed that this pompous individual was about to put him through some kind of examination, and would not spare him, so that his palms were moist and there was a tiresome lump that kept coming and going in his throat. But when the secretary began to dictate, that small discomfort vanished. After all, it was a battle like any other and, while the pen might not be as noble as the sword, it could prove an effective enough passport to America.

The letter, addressed to the Minister for the Navy, M. de Sartines, began with a long string of formal courtesies enunciated with droning pomposity, and then launched into a lenghty requisition of supplies for the Chevalier de Ternay, concluding with an unequivocal call for money. But by then Gilles' pen was scratching away merrily, carried along by the new hope uplifting him.

When it was finished, the secretary peered down his long nose at it and read it through carefully before laying it down on his desk and subjecting Gilles to a fresh test. This time it was a long column of figures to be added up and otherwise dealt with in a variety of ways that made the young man screw up his face in anguish, for he was not overfond of mathematics. Even so, he acquitted himself creditably enough, or so he hoped.

After that, his tormentor went on without a pause to a further trial, consisting this time of a stream of point-blank questions on the subject of oceanography, posed with an alarming casualness and, what was worse, in English.

But if the secretary had thought to disconcert the candidate, he soon found his mistake. Thanks to his godfather, Gilles possessed a more than adequate knowledge of the language of Shakespeare and, if his accent left something to be desired, at least it was not too obviously provincial.

It was at this point that the door opened again and Gilles had barely time to jump to his feet, for the newcomer was none other than Rochambeau himself.

His cool gaze swept over Gilles and came to rest on his examiner who had stopped dead with his mouth open.

'Well, Monsieur Jego?' he inquired.

The secretary's thin back bowed obsequiously.

'We have almost finished, my lord. Indeed, I do believe that the young Victomte de Noailles' recommendation of this young man was fully justified. He expresses himself well, seems well educated, writes a fair hand and his English appears to me quite satisfactory.'

'We'll have Monsieur de Fersen's judgment on that. He speaks the language perfectly. Very well, sir. I'm much obliged to you. Will you leave me now to speak to the young man alone?'

The secretary effaced himself and the commander-in-chief was left alone with his would-be follower.

Rochambeau seated himself in the chair Jego had vacated and studied the young man attentively.

'It would appear, sir, that you are most fit for the post for which Monsieur de Noailles has recommended you. But you will understand that I should like to know a little more of you before making you a definite offer. Who are you, exactly?'

Instantly, Gilles took from his pocket his godfather's letter and the other papers he had with him, such as his certificates of birth and baptism, and held them out.

'Here are all my papers, General. And, with your permission, I should like to add this letter, which will certainly not reach its destination now. It is from my godfather, the Abbé de Talhouët-Grationnaye, and it is addressed to Madame du Couédic de Kerguelénen, however, since I am not acquainted with the lady I feel sure that it contains a full introduction. If that is not enough, I will engage to answer any questions you may care to ask me as fully as I can.'

The General took the letter in silence and read it carefully, which, since it was fairly lengthy, took some time. He then returned it to its owner, but for the first time Gilles saw the shadow of a smile cross his face.

'Ran away from the college at Vannes, eh? Good blood but no name – or as good as? I see. Tell me, though, what makes you so eager to come and fight with me overseas? Because, make no mistake about that – all my men are going to have to fight, even my secretary!'

The young man's eyes flashed.

'I hoped you might have said: "Especially my secretary",' he said with a youthful enthusiasm which produced an instant softening of Rochambeau's frosty eyes. 'As for America – I have a feeling that there is something waiting for me there. I don't know what, precisely, I only know that I must go there, at all costs!'

'Well, well. We shall see. Where are you lodged?'

'A – at the inn called the *Pilier Rouge*, in a way.'

'Why, in a way?'

'I mean I spent the night there, but the fact is that I slept in a carriage belonging to a colonel whose name I do not even know.'

This time Rochambeau laughed aloud.

'Most ingenious. However, I cannot feel that any colonel's carriage is a proper shelter for my secretary. Take your baggage over to my quarters in the Cours Dajot, in the admiral's house. They'll find you a bed. Settle in and come to me at two this afternoon on board the *Duc de Bourgogne*. We shall have work to do. Off with you, sir!'

A moment later, Gilles found himself, still dazed with his good fortune, in the passage leading to the main staircase. He was so happy that he seemed to be on wings.

In his elation, he almost precipitated himself straight into the arms of young Noailles who was pacing up and down the same corridor, evidently waiting for something.

'Hey there!' he called out, laughing. 'Steady on! Anyone would think you were in a hurry!'

Flushed equally with happiness and embarrassment as he realized that he had all but knocked down his guardian angel, Gilles endeavoured to regain his balance sufficiently to make his bow.

'Indeed, my lord, my humble apologies,' he exclaimed. 'I did not see you there.'

'So I see! You were not looking at anything at all! You were charging like one of Marshall de Saxe's Tartars at Fontenoy! It seems that all is well with you?'

'Wonderful! Thanks to you! Oh, sir, I am so grateful to

you! You see, I am appointed secretary to the Comte de Rochambeau – and given a lodging into the bargain!'

'I am delighted to hear it. But don't thank me too much. I merely put your name forward, that was all. You owe your appointment to your own ability and capacity to please. It makes me very happy. So now we are going to fight the English together! I think you will find some rare opportunities to better yourself there.'

'I hope so with all my heart. But – will you set the seal on your kindness by answering me one question?'

Noailles laughed. 'Oho! My kindness, is it? You do me too much honour. I am not kind, young man. Indeed, I can be quite nasty when I put my mind to it. But ask away—'

Gilles looked the Vicomte very directly in the eyes.

'Why did you help me?' he asked bluntly. 'The manner of our first meeting was scarcely in my favour. I stole your friend's horse. Moreover, I am neither of your rank nor of your world. I have no quality—'

'Rank can be acquired,' Noailles interrupted him seriously. 'Worlds are there to be entered. As to quality, I flatter myself that I have some skill in reading faces and I think you have more than you know, and that you will do credit to my judgment. And then—'

'Yes?'

'Well, you displayed such a touching reverence for our good La Fayette that I felt I must bring so stout an ally to him instantly. He has none too many, and you are quite the most enthusiastic I have met. Damnation! A lad who runs away from school and steals a horse to join him! Gilbert will be overjoyed.'

In his innocence, Gilles was on the point of stopping him and pointing out that joining La Fayette had not been his only motive in the business, but he checked himself. Especially as it had just dawned on him that the Vicomte had called his hero by his christian name.

'You call him Gilbert?' he said with new respect, for the name Noailles had meant little to him. 'Are you so well acquainted with him?'

This made the Vicomte laugh outright.

'Anyone can see that you are country bred! My dear fellow, he's my brother-in-law. We each of us married one of my

124

uncle Ayen's two daughters. But, alas,' he made a comical face as he spoke, 'I can see that my humble efforts have not made quite the same impression on the youth of Brittany as his! You dream about him and I dare say you haven't the faintest idea that, while he's been making love to the Rebels, I've been getting sunburnt with M. d'Estaing in Grenada? Oh, fame is a capricious mistress. It's true, of course, that I wasn't quite alone.'

It seemed to Gilles as if the heavens had opened. His saviour was a hero.

'You were? Oh, sir, you will never be rid of me now. I shall dog your footsteps until you tell me all about it. I am going to—'

'You are going to do precisely whatever you have been ordered, and quick about it!' Noailles broke in, clapping his young admirer on the shoulder. 'The General is a stickler for accuracy and he dislikes vagueness and unpunctuality above all things. As for my adventures, there will be plenty of time for those during the long days at sea! Run away, now. You won't have much free time between now and when we set sail. The General wants to be off in two days, but we can think ourselves lucky if we are away inside twelve.'

Gilles very soon found out that Noailles had not exaggerated. A gruelling work-load lay ahead of him that went far beyond merely dealing with the commander-in-chief's correspondence. He was up at dawn and dividing his time between Rochambeau, who shuttled back and forth continually between the ships and the cramped barracks where his troops were quartered, and the Quartermaster, M. de Tarlé, to whom the General obligingly lent him because of his quick understanding. M. de Tarlé was everywhere at once, since it was his task to collect the necessary supplies for an army of embarkation and assemble them in the port of Brest.

Gilles, in his innocence, had imagined that despatching an army to war was a simple and beautiful affair : troops in brand new uniforms with gleaming weapons being marched on board great ships, lovely as castles in a dream, then up with the sails and away they sailed to glory, with the sun shining and the bells pealing. He soon found out that before that sublime moment arrived, a good many people had to work like slaves in a thoroughly inglorious atmosphere of flour bags and ill-ventilated stores where every barrel of salt pork and even every piece of cloth had to be disputed with the rats. He discovered that a fleet was a many-headed monster with a belly that must be stuffed endlessly with food and ammunition, to say nothing of a host of other assorted supplies, ranging from cows and crates of chickens to communion wine. He was not the plumed servant of a noble knight quite divorced from sordid earthly cares, he was quite simply Gargantua's scullion.

Then, with a ledge or a roll of documents under his arm, he galloped away from the Quartermaster's office to the warehouses where blankets, shirts and shoes by the thousand were stored, along with tools of every kind, cooking pots, flour, fat, rice, oil, wine, salt meat, cabbages, dried peas and turnips, and from there to the quays along the Penfeld, where they were still working frenziedly on the unfinished vessels which were to carry all this gear.

The Arsenal, the rope walk, the smithies reddening the night with their great fires, the sailmakers' and all the other workshops involved in preparing the ships, some of which were still in dry dock, were scenes of frantic activity. Extra gangs of workmen and convicts worked day and night: in the rain which fell incessantly by day and at night by the light of guttering candles. Tired out and fractionally disappointed though he was, Gilles still had the feeling of being present at the birth of a giant. Brest was in labour with a fleet and an adventure.

From time to time, as he sat at his small table in the great after cabin of the *Duc de Bourgogne*, writing to the General's dictation one of the countless letters with which he bombarded the War Minister, the Prince de Montbarrey, Gilles would catch a glimpse of the brilliant little group of the six aides de camp, Damas, Dillon, young Rochambeau and Lameth, with Noailles and Fersen among them. But although the young Vicomte always had a smile and a kind word for him, the handsome Swede scarcely deigned to acknowledge him. Possibly he was still brooding over the theft of his horse.

He would respond to Gilles, greeting with an abstracted nod and then pay no further heed to him. But he had the reputation of being a cold and somewhat reserved person, always a trifle remote, as though wrapped up in some private thoughts of his own. He took little part in the lighthearted banter his companions indulged in freely as soon as their chiefs' backs were turned. At such times a hint of the frivolous atmosphere of Versailles invaded the austere world of the navy.

Now and then the cheerful group would be joined by the Duc de Lauzun, who commanded a legion of foreign mounted volunteers, and the Comte de Ségur, colonel of the Soissonais regiment to which young Noailles belonged. At such times Gilles would listen avidly, feeling himself transported by some magic into the King's very antechamber. Naturally, too, the talk turned much on women, for Lauzun was a great flirt.

But, except at these headquarters' conferences, it was rare for all the aides de camp to be together, for there was no lack of work and Rochambeau, who knew them well, always had some task for them, at least by day. At night, they were all of them determined not to be bored. Thanks to them, Brest, echoing to the lilt of violins from ballrooms, with the clink of glasses and the sound of drinking songs joined to the racket from the Arsenal, became easily the noisiest city in the kingdom. For a few days, at least, for the Chevalier de Ternay and the Comte de Rochambeau soon put a stop to all that by having each ship loaded as soon as it was ready. They were already quite sufficiently behindhand, as Gilles discovered for himself as soon as he took up his post.

The troops had, in fact, begun their embarkation according to plan on the evening prior to Gilles' arrival.

Hoping to set sail on the eighth of April, the Chevalier de Ternay had originally intended to embark the Royal Deux-Ponts on the fourth, Lauzun's legion on the fifth, and Soissonais regiment on the sixth, the Bourbonnais on the seventh and the three artillery companies of Auxonne, belonging to the Toul regiment, along with the Saintonge regiment, from Crozon and Camaret, on the eighth. They were to have assembled at Roscanvel and taken straight on board the *Ardent* and the transports amongst which they were to be divided from there. However, since nothing was ready by that date, this was altogether impossible, especially since the weather had turned very bad.

The winds were so bad, indeed, that on the tenth of April a

ship of the line, the *St Joseph*, and a Spanish fore-ship, the *Santa Rosa*, which had attempted to leave harbour both ran aground. The two commanders' faces grew longer and longer as they stared into a continuous barrage of rainy squalls.

But Gilles soon discovered that this delay could be very informative. As he watched the fleet and the cumbersome convoy it was to escort gradually taking shape in the offices of the Arsenal and in the harbour itself, and while he learned to recognize the seven ships of the line of the first two divisions, the supply ships of the third, the frigates and the twenty-eight transports, with the flags of their commanders and how the troops were distributed about this floating city, at the same time, in the after-cabin of the *Duc de Bourgogne*, he was sitting, stiff as a board and making scarcely more noise, sharing in all the hopes and fears of the two commanders and their reactions to the orders, frequently absurd, of their respective ministries, as well as the total lack of news from the rebellion to which they were committed to carry so many brave men. According to their latest information, which was already six months old, General Washington's position was by no means hopeful and the English under General Clinton still held New York. The Chevalier de Ternay's orders, nevertheless, were to sail to Rhode Island and Versailles seemed to be making no attempt to discover whether or not it was still in rebel hands.

Gilles gradually grew accustomed to the sight of the little admiral storming into the room after the arrival of practically every letter from the ministry.

'M. de Sartines is making a fool of me,' he exclaimed one evening, while the floorboards echoed to his uneven pacing. 'First he takes it on himself to order me on no account to leave Brest if the English fleet is lying off Ushant. Now he writes that the intentions of the English Admirals, Graves and Walsingham, are unknown to us and must therefore give cause for grave alarm. Since when, I ask you, have the English taken to informing us of their intentions? He might as well forbid .me to put to sea at all. Who does he think we're going to fight?'

Another evening, it was worse still.

'Do you know what I have here?' he cried, his voice shaking

with anger, thrusting a letter with a flaunting red seal under Rochambeau's nose.

'No, by heaven! Another order to postpone sailing?'

'Not this time, but it's very nearly as stupid. The minister, sitting in his office in Versailles, has despatched instructions as to the course I am to set : the Pointe du Raz, Cape Ortegal and Finisterre! As though I needed his advice! And he goes on to say that the English coast must at all costs be given the widest possible berth! It's too much! Who does he think he is writing to? Who has spent all his life at sea – M. de Sartines or I?'

And the one-time Knight of Malta crumpled the minister's letter into a ball and tossed it at Gilles' feet.

'Leave it!' he commanded as the young man bent to pick it up. 'You are too young to bother your head with ministerial idiocies!'

Rochambeau had begun to laugh but now he got up from his chair and, going across to where the little admiral stood quivering with rage, he laid a friendly, soothing hand on his shoulder.

'Calm down, my friend. It's an impertinence, I grant you, and not easy to bear. But don't forget we ought to be well at sea by this time, and the minister can't tell, after all, that the winds haven't changed and that you ever received his letter. Suppose we had already sailed and there's an end of it. You are much more your own master than I am, are you not? You are the leader of the expedition, whereas I am simply sent to General Washington to fight, I'll not say under his command, but according as he shall direct.'

Ternay shrugged his shoulders with a little smile.

'You're a tactful fellow, my dear Count. As if you didn't know that I've my orders to stay close to you. It comes to the same thing – All the same, your minister is easier to bear with than mine.'

The General said nothing but his expression was eloquent. He, too, had his problems. Only that morning he had received a distinctly curt letter from the Minister for War, the Prince de Montbarrey, in which that eminent person expressed his astonishment that so little effort seemed to have been made to accommodate the young Duc de Lauzun, who was complaining bitterly to his friends among the Queen's circle at court against a refusal to embark his horses.

'My men are cavalry,' he was protesting angrily. 'Hussars! What good are hussars without horses?'

'On paper, he's right, of course,' Rochambeau concluded, taking up his own ministerial epistle, 'but with the best will in the world it's quite impossible to give him his way and no amount of minister's orders can change that! What's more, I thought he had understood when I explained it.'

The General had indeed spent some time explaining matters to the fuming cavalry officer. To carry horses across the Atlantic special horse-transports were required. But there was only one of these, the *Hermione*, and she could carry no more than twenty horses, when what was needed was at least two hundred. Even then, the animals would not arrive in good condition, but on an ordinary vessel they would be unlikely to arrive at all. But it had been no use. Lauzun was obstinate and he had complained.

'So here I am,' Rochambeau concluded, 'forced to disobey my minister—'

'Let me sort that out,' Ternay interrupted. 'I don't mind making an enemy.'

That same evening, the young duke was told very forcefully by the Commodore to stop complaining and accept the situation.

'Horses, sir, you can find on the spot. You'll have no trouble remounting your men. Any we did take with us would not survive. Though we could always eat them, of course . . .'

Lauzun paled.

'You seem to forget, Admiral, that you, too, are responsible to a minister and that Her Majesty the Queen—'

'Her Majesty is not in command of this fleet that I ever heard,' the sailor interrupted him rudely. 'As for you, sir, you will do well to remember that aboard my ships I am sole master after God. However, if the discipline at sea is too harsh for you, you may prefer to return to the gentler pleasures of the Trianon—' Turning to Gilles, he went on without a pause: 'Have word of my decision conveyed to the Arsenal. We are taking no horses. The *Hermione* will carry such medical supplies as cannot be accommodated on board the hospital ship.'

Lauzun, white with anger, stared first at the young man and then venomously back at the Admiral.

'You will not always be able to order all things as you wish, Admiral! We shall not be at sea for ever.'

The Chevalier de Ternay looked at Gilles for the first time since he had been working aboard his ship. The shadow of a smile passed over his tired face.

'Monsieur de Lauzun disliked me before, now he will loathe me. But I fear, my boy, that I have involved you also in his loathing. He is not going to forgive you for having witnessed his discomfiture.'

The young man's blue eyes met the sailor's unflinchingly and he too smiled.

'While you are in command, sir, I have nothing to fear. Are you not sole master after God? And Monsieur de Lauzun is but a man – and not perhaps as strong as I am . . .'

Rochambeau laughed.

'Oho! If he could hear you! It's as well for you the Bastille is some way off! Can it be that you are a follower of Jean-Jacques Rousseau?'

Gilles blushed to the roots of his hair but he kept his head high.

'I have read his books, General, and admired them. But I'm not really a follower of his because what I have seen of men has given me little cause to look on them as brothers.'

'You know that, even at your age?' the Chevalier sighed. 'It has taken me a great deal longer to reach the same conclusion. Leave us now and take your message to the Comte d'Hector. And have a care to yourself, none the less.'

Gilles went ashore feeling happier than at any time since he had begun his employment. He might have made a powerful enemy in Lauzun but, on the other hand, he sensed that he had won the approval of his two commanding officers, whom he was coming to admire very much, and that weighed infinitely heavier in the balance.

The first person he saw when he set foot on dry land was Lauzun himself. The duke was evidently giving full vent to his anger and his impassive listener was none other than Fersen. Gilles moved into their field of vision and Lauzun no sooner caught sight of him than he cried: 'See, my dear Count, here comes the general's penpusher who is to turn our horse-transport into a lazar-house! If you were hoping to find a berth for that splendid animal I saw you with the other day and offered to buy from you, you may abandon the idea. Like the rest of us, you will have to make do with some American nag – supposing there are any to be had!'

The Swede looked calmly down from his blond Scandinavian height upon the Frenchman whom anger had made redder than his fine gold-laced coat.

'But there are,' he said gravely, with a lift of his eyebrows. 'I know you have been in Senegambia, my dear Duke, but I had thought you better acquainted with the uses and customs of America. What do you imagine our friends the English ride on? Donkeys? For my own part, I have heard that this General Washington, who is a gentleman of Virginia, is one of the world's finest horsemen. We shall at least have fresh horses.'

'You may be sure of that!' Lauzun cried furiously. He clapped his cocked hat with its white plumes back on to his head and, turning on his red heels, stalked off in the direction of the Rue de Siam.

The handsome officer of the Royal Deux-Ponts laughed softly and then turned suddenly to Gilles, who had halted, frowning, at the sound of his name, wondering whether or not it behoved him to challenge the Duc de Lauzun to a duel.

'Is this true?' he asked.

'Quite true, sir. Here is the order.'

'It is very tiresome. I had been hoping to take Magnus with me to the Rebels.'

'Magnus?'

'My – er – our horse,' the Swede said blandly. 'But I dare say you found another name for him?'

'Yes,' Gilles answered, with a touch of wistfulness he was unable to repress. 'I called him Merlin.'

'Oh, after the wizard?'

'Of course. He is a countryman of mine.'

'A pretty name for him. But none of this tells me what we are to do with him. After all, you are nearly as much concerned in his fate as I am and I confess I am loth to sell him. Since you belong here, perhaps you can think of someone who would agree to keep him and look after him as he deserves while we are at the wars?'

Gilles' eyes shone like stars.

'You would trust me?'

'Good God, yes,' Fersen said without hesitation. 'You did not steal him for profit but because you had need of him. Besides – you love him, I saw that at once. Those are things one horseman knows instinctively about another. So, what do you say? But let us walk on, for I believe you are forgetting your errand.'

So, while they walked towards the Arsenal, Gilles spoke of Guillaume Briant, of his passionate love of arms and horsemanship and of his low house and the meadows of Leslé. He spoke with such conviction that even before they came to the White Admiral's house, the Swede had made his mind up. One of his servants was to set out that very evening, taking with him some money, a letter from Gilles and another from Fersen himself, for the Talhouët estate.

'This evening?' Gilles said, amazed at such despatch. 'Are you afraid that Monsieur de Lauzun will try to buy him all the same and smuggle him aboard?'

For the first time, Gilles saw Fersen's rare laugh.

'He wouldn't dare. But I want to have the matter settled as soon as possible for a reason which, as the General's secretary, you must be aware of. My regiment, the Royal Deux-Ponts, is due to embark tomorrow morning, some on the transport ship, the *Comtesse de Noailles,* and some on the *Jason,* a ship of the line, which is where I shall be with other officers. General's orders,' he added with a sigh which betrayed how little he relished the prospect. 'I only hope we shall not have to wait too long before we set sail, and that we won't be lying at anchor indefinitely . . .'

Much to the Swede's chagrin, he was to be obliged to wait for some while yet. Rochambeau might write to the minister by his secretary on the seventeenth of April that 'if the weather clears, I shall take up my quarters aboard the *Duc de Bourgogne* tomorrow at the latest, so that, subject to the Chevalier de Ternay, we may take advantage of the first north wind . . .' But the north wind did not blow either on the eighteenth or on the days that followed, even though the General had in fact transferred his baggage to the flagship on the date announced. The ship's complement was now complete and included, in addition to part of the Saintonge regiment, with its colonel M. de la Valette, and his second-in-command M. de Charlus, two mysterious Americans who intrigued Gilles immensely but whom he was unable to get near.

One by one, the ships left the harbour to ride at anchor in the roadstead, waiting under strict discipline (no shore leave was granted at all) and in a state of total boredom for the order to set sail to be given at last.

Gilles was as impatient as any but for him there was at least some relief. From the moment of taking up his post, he had worked like a slave but once the *Duc de Bourgogne* was out in the roads, he found himself in a privileged position for, alone amongst those on board, he went ashore every day to carry out his chiefs' orders and, among other things, to fetch the official letters from the Comte d'Hector's office and any private ones from the Admiral's lodging. For himself, of course, there were never any letters at all.

Once only, in response to the enthusiastic letter he had written on the day of his appointment, he had received a long, friendly epistle from his godfather, full of encouragement and good advice, and this he guarded jealously as his one link with home. But he no longer suffered from the loneliness he had endured during the first few days. The two commanders who, when not attending conferences, whiled away the time playing chess, were very kind to him and, ever since the business of the horse, a kind of understanding had developed between him and Axel de Fersen which expressed itself on Gilles' side by the performance of a number of commissions on shore for the count who, immured aboard the *Jason* except for excursions to the flagship for meetings of the staff, was becoming very thoroughly bored. At last the belligerent Duc de Lauzun embarked also and occupied a berth in the *Provence* which was moored a few cables' lengths away. Not much was heard of him thereafter, except by way of the concerts which he made the band of his legion put on for him every evening as a distraction from boredom.

'He'd give a ball if he dared,' growled the Chevalier de

134

Ternay, irritated by the waves of music which filled the roadstead every evening after sunset.

'He'd dare fast enough if he could get permission to bring women aboard,' Rochambeau replied.

Sighing, the two men called for the windows to be closed and returned to their game.

Time dragged and boredom lay heavy on the fleet and on the motionless convoy, to which fresh units were added every day. On board the *Neptune*, young Noailles, with the second battalion of the Soissonnais regiment, killed time by quarrelling interminably with the equally young Arthur de Dillon whose Irish blood was fretted alike by inaction and by the Vicomte's occasionally biting witticisms.

Came at last the first of May which passed over Gilles like a meteor, leaving a fiery trail behind it.

To begin with, it was in the late afternoon that the long-awaited news swept through the roadstead like a power train : the wind was changing, at last it was beginning to blow from the north. A great cheer went up, starting on the ships and moving to the harbour and thence to the whole town. The whole fleet instantly became a scene of frantic activity. The Chevalier de Ternay let it be known that if the wind held they would sail at dawn and at once despatched a frigate, the *Bellone*, to reconnoitre the waters off Ushant to make sure that no English fleet had suddenly popped up in the vicinity.

Gilles had orders to go ashore for the last time and make sure that no further letters had arrived and came for the last time to the house in the Cours Dajot where the Admiral's and the General's personal correspondence was kept for them.

He was crossing the courtyard to call on the offices when he heard the porter calling him.

'Hey, you over there! Young man! Hey, Monsieur Secretary, if you please! There is a letter for you—'

Gilles stopped dead as though he had been shot.

'A letter? For me? What are you doing with it? It should have been with the rest of the post.'

The man's smile was at once sly and knowing.

'Come, come! One doesn't put a nice little letter like that in with an admiral's or a general's post. Such a pretty blue seal must be from a lady.'

135

The dainty missive which the porter was holding in his thick fingers was indeed artistically folded and sealed with a small seal on which Gilles, with a beating heart, made out the martlets that were the arms of Saint-Mélaine.

He was so shaken that he stood for a moment turning the letter over and over in his hands, unwilling to open it before the leering porter who was visibly consumed with curiosity.

'Well, to be sure,' that worthy said, unable to contain himself, 'you don't seem in all that much of a hurry to read it! Should be interesting, though.'

Gilles shrugged. Casting an angry glance at his tormentor, he turned back towards the main building and ran up the stairs two at a time to the refuge of the attic where he had lodged before going aboard. It was bare and unlived-in once more but it was still familiar and no one was there to watch him. Not until then could he bring himself to break the seal and unfold the letter. It was all he could do not to grin for pure joy.

The writing was clumsy and unformed, while for signature there was only a large, flamboyant J. The letter was not long but it seemed to him worthy of the greatest poets.

'I am told that you have begun well and that great things are to be hoped for you if you prove worthy of the trust reposed in you. Do not fail, for if you should you would grieve more persons than you think. And lose no time, for three years are soon gone.

Nevertheless, I pray you will take care of yourself, for it may be that the greatest danger in this war you go to will not come from the enemy. There is another, more treacherous, who is on the watch for you. Keep your eyes well open, for there are those, I know, who would grieve much should you fail to return . . .'

The mysterious tone of this letter was, naturally, alarming. But for the present Gilles paid no heed to that. He was overflowing with happiness. He kissed the big, sprawling J a dozen times over and read and reread the letter, seeing nothing in it beyond Judith's anxiety for him. She was warning him against some vague danger, something she dared not tell him openly, but it probably meant no more than that she was afraid for him

136

and longed to see him return alive. From there it was only a step to the thought that she must love him a little, and that step Gilles was very ready to take.

Stowing the precious letter safely in his bosom, between his shirt and his skin, he sped down to the offices, swept up the General's letters and rushed back to the Penfeld to rejoin his ship as quickly as he had come.

He was making for the boat belonging to the flagship which was now standing out into the roadstead with her copper-lined hull bristling with eighty-six guns and her soaring masts, when he saw a number of men coming towards him and recognized by their heavily frogged hussar jackets that they belonged to Lauzun's regiment. They were heading for a transport vessel, the *Françoise*, which had just that moment finished taking on water. In view of the large numbers to be transported, the Admiral had demanded three extra ships at the last minute. They were the *Françoise*, the *Turgot* and the *Rower*. The contrary winds had at least made it possible to effect this addition to their supplies.

The little group of men had to cross Gilles' path and, just as they were doing so, Gilles realized suddenly the exact nature of the threat Judith meant to warn him of. One of the men was looking at him, even turning his head to keep him in view, and he saw that the man was Judith's brother Morvan, whom he had so expeditiously tipped into the Blavet.

It was no more than a moment. Already, the men were crossing the gangway of the transport vessel and vanishing on board, leaving Gilles to make his way thoughtfully to his own boat. Here was a mystery. What was a gentleman from Brittany doing in a regiment from Saintonge? And what was Morvan, who had been described to him as something like a wild animal, quite incapable of enduring the slightest discipline and passing his days in a lair in the woods along with his elder brother, doing in the army? Was it the lure of the American adventure which had drawn him or the lust for vengeance – or something of both? Unless there were some other reason which was still hidden from him.

Judging from the red-headed man's ferocious expression, it seemed likely that Gilles himself had a good deal to do with his unexpected embarkation. Judith's letter only confirmed it.

137

But the presence of the younger Saint-Mélaine, far from alarming Gilles, actually delighted him. It was a good thing for Judith that her dangerous brothers should be separated, and it also meant that they considered him sufficiently formidable to pursue him half across the globe. He had become, in fact, someone to be reckoned with! As a result of which conclusion, Gilles stepped aboard the *Duc de Bourgogne* again with something of a swagger. His self-confidence was increasing hourly.

At five o'clock the following morning, the inhabitants of Brest jumped out of their beds in a body at the sound of the parting gun. Everywhere, people ran to the best vantage points to see the Chevalier de Ternay's fleet and its lumbering convoy put to sea. But while the clerks at the Arsenal and the officers of the garrison hurried to climb the castle's medieval towers, the streets were full of people running to the hills overlooking the Channel. At the same time, the red and blue sails blossomed from the masts of the fishing boats until the harbour looked like one gigantic flower bed.

The fresh wind swept the lightening sky in great, life-giving gusts, carrying the measured chanting of the men at the capstans far over the sea. Voices boomed through loud-hailers as they hauled on the anchor chains.

On the bridge of the *Duc de Bourgogne*, the little admiral stood stiff as a ramrod in his handsome dark blue coat with the gilded epaulettes, watching with a flash of pride in his deepset eyes, as mainsails, topsails and foretopsails were slowly unfurled, as his flag captain, the Comte de Médine, made the vessel ready to put to sea.

By half past five, the *Duc de Bourgogne* was under way and heading down Channel. Then, one by one, the forty-two ships of the fleet and the convoy which Louis XVI, by the Grace of God, King of France and Navarre, was sending to the aid of the Rebels slid after her towards the open sea and one of the noblest adventures ever undertaken by men.

To the frantic cheers of those who had worked so hard for them, M. Destouches' *Neptune*, M. de Lombard's *Provence*, M. de la Grandière's *Conquérant*, M. du Couédic's heroic vessel, the *Surveillante*, now by much labour refitted and placed under the command of M. de Gillard, and M. de la Pérouse's swift frigate *Amazone*, sea-birds all of them, now turned into watchdogs for the twenty-eight slower and heavier ships of the convoy, passed slowly out of sight.

Gradually the cheers and the drums died away and the guns of the forts of Bertheaume roared a last salute. Then there was only the sweet breath of the wind and the wide sea opening before the freshly painted and gilded figureheads that dipped as regularly as a troop of ballet dancers into the long swell of the Iroise towards the perilous waters of the Sein race.

Standing by the rail a little way apart from the gilded group of officers, Gilles watched Brittany and his childhood fade away.

PART TWO

The Guns of Yorktown

7

Scalp Hunter

As they drew near to the coast of America, Gilles spent long hours at the rail of the *Duc de Bourgogne*, tiring his eyes with peering into the distance for a first glimpse of a country which in his dreams had appeared to him as nothing short of fabulous. Helped by his Breton imagination, he was prepared for untold wonders, for vast forests, strange colours and peculiar people, like the Indians of whom he had heard tales almost every evening on that interminable seventy-day voyage. As far as landscape went, he was well satisfied, for it was spectacular and the forests more than majestic but the few townships they caught a glimpse of were scarcely encouraging: a cluster of white houses around a church spire, not much different from those at home, the people dressed in ordinary clothes and not a single canoe paddled by men in colourful feathered head-dresses. The uniforms of the French were infinitely gayer and more picturesque than the garb of the native Americans.

Their arrival at Rhode Island had done little to redress this feeling of disappointment. The French camp was situated on a headland overlooking the little town of Newport, between the harbour, from which it was divided by an area of marshland, and the narrow.

It was a very beautiful spot, with a view over the row of green islands between which the fleet had put chains, hermetically sealing off the approaches to Newport. Beyond lay the long, low island of Conanicut on which could be seen the remains of a fort, destroyed by the retreating British a year before, and the big, isolated house which served as a hospital for the army's four-hundred-and-twenty sick, who had been taken off the ships. There were also the shimmering blue waters of the huge bay of Narragansett, looking strangely peaceful since the war had interrupted Rhode Island's busy trade with Africa and the West Indies.

Not long since, vessels built by the people of Newport with their own hands would cross the seas to the Guinea Coast to pick up profitable cargoes of slaves, then back to the Caribbean, where the 'black ivory' could be exchanged for sugar and molasses to be brought home to Newport for the manufacture of rum – which would then be taken back to Africa for sale to the numerous petty black kings who provided the slave ships with their cargoes. Even though the greater part of Newport belonged to the strict Anabaptist sect, this trade proved so profitable that the governor levied a tax of three dollars a head on the slaves and was able to pave the whole town on the proceeds. But the war had put an end to all that. Newport had been captured and recaptured and was once again in the hands of the Rebels who had offered it to their French allies as a base.

It was not, perhaps, the safest of bases, for its inhabitants were still split into two camps: the rich tory merchants remaining blindly loyal to the mother country and the whig rebels, farmers and intellectuals, who dreamed of being simply Americans, each cherishing their careful copy of Thomas Jefferson's striking Declaration of Independence which the first Congress had voted and signed in 1776. And since no one yet knew quite how the wind would blow, both sides were doing their best to avoid proclaiming their beliefs too loudly. It was better to wait and see.

Rochambeau and his secretary were made aware of this when, accompanied only by the headquarters staff, they went ashore on the tenth of July. Gilles did not soon forget the strangeness he felt when M. de la Pérouse's frigate *Amazone*, which was to take them into the harbour, crept up to the long pier, shining with seaweed. It was nine o'clock in the evening. The sky was purple and only the white houses of the town seemed to hold some vestiges of daylight. A bell was tolling mournfully from the spire of Trinity Church but that was the only sound they heard, for no one came down to the harbour or out into the few streets to witness the arrival of the French.

Not only did the governor, or any other official, fail to put in an appearance, but every door remained obstinately shut as though in the face of an invader. The most they saw was the blur of an anxious face, the glint of a suspicious eye behind the small panes of sash windows. They could almost hear the whispering. The atmosphere around the little group of officers standing alone on the empty quay was so oppressive that Fersen could bear it no longer.

'Here's a friendly welcome! What do these people think they're about?' he exclaimed, glancing at his chief's grim face. 'Do they think we've been at sea for seventy days simply to look at closed doors? I vote we go back on board and make our landing in some more hospitable spot.'

'It is for me to decide, sir, what we shall do,' Rochambeau interposed calmly. 'My orders are to establish myself here and I shall do so. In any case, you should not complain. The people here sent pilots, after all, to guide us into the bay. Give them time to get used to us.'

'You are too good,' M. de Charlus said. 'But all the same, you will have to go back on board. The commander of the French expeditionary force can scarcely camp out in the town square.'

'With your permission, sir,' put in Gilles, for whom the idea of returning to the ship was like deserting, 'I think I can see an inn sign over there.'

A chorus of horrified exclamation greeted his words, but he went on undeterred : 'When you want to make contact with the people of a village, you always start by going to the inn.'

'Quite right, too!' Rochambeau agreed with a smile. 'To the inn, then! Lead the way, my friend.'

And thus it came about that the French headquarters staff spent its first night on American soil democratically at Flint's Hotel in Point Street.

For the worthy citizens of Newport it was a night of sleepless deliberation but it brought results. The whigs decided that it might be politic to show some consideration for men of such aristocratic appearance who had travelled so far. As for the tories, for all their strong attachment to King George III, they

145

could not but feel that prudence counselled at least the appearance of complaisance.

Consequently, it was quite a delegation which, the next morning, was led by Governor Wanton to pay its somewhat embarrassed respects to Rochambeau at the inn. Once past the barriers of suspicious guards and an unfriendly secretary who looked very much askance at them, they were met with a graciousness that surprised them. There were introductions and expressions of mutual goodwill, all the more heartfelt when the Frenchman indicated that his expeditionary force was soon to be followed by another, even then in preparation at Brest. There was more talk and when, at last, the ships' captains, with the Admiral at their head, came in to see how matters were progressing, everyone was in high good humour. The town's best rum was distributed on a lavish scale. Lanterns were hung everywhere, even on the church spire, there was a firework display and the junketings were kept up half the night with both parties very much pleased with one another.

By July 25th, fifteen days had passed since that memorable night and everyone had settled down to a rigid discipline, imposed by the General with an iron hand. The camp had been laid out, the four regiments on the left, the artillery on the right and Lauzun's cavalry in front. Headquarters were in the town itself, the thousand or so sick with scurvy or other ailments caused by the excessive length of the voyage, had been landed from the ships and put, some in the hospital at Newport, some in the big house on Conanicut Island, and a start had been made on the rebuilding of the fortifications destroyed by the English; all with a degree of discipline that was all the more admirable for being quite unusual. But the severest penalties were laid down for anyone caught looting, stealing or committing the smallest offence against the island's inhabitants.

There was, moreover, nothing else to do, for no news had yet arrived from the Rebel leaders and if Rochambeau had thought he would be able to go into action immediately, he was much mistaken. All that was known for sure was that La Fayette had arrived a few weeks previously.

There was, however, news of the English. Admiral Graves' strong fleet had appeared four days earlier and taken up a position outside the entrance to Narragansett. Rochambeau had

his work cut out to prevent the infuriated Ternay, with barely
a third the strength, from hurling his own force at it to hack a
way through.

'Through to where?' he asked. 'We don't even know yet
what they want of us. Besides, don't forget that Sartines requires
you to stick by me at all costs.'

The champing little admiral was brought to reason and,
since the English seemed in no way inclined to attack a position
so well defended, the two fleets might have remained staring at
one another like a pair of china dogs for a long time, rousing
the younger officers and the men who did not understand the
situation to a fury. To have the enemy in sight and not be able
to get at him was enough to make a man weep!

Gilles' thoughts were exactly like those of Noailles, Fersen,
young Rochambeau, Dillon, Damas and every other young
officer and he found himself wondering at last what they had
come there for. Ever since they sailed out of Brest, he had be-
guiled the tedium of the voyage improving his technique with
sword and sabre with the master at arms of the Saintonge
regiment and he had achieved a very pretty skill which he was
burning to put to use. Since coming ashore he had kept in
practice by daily bouts with no less a person than Axel de
Fersen himself.

In his silent way, the Swede had now admitted him to a kind
of fellowship. Seeing that the young man was embarrassed to
find himself almost the only civilian among a host of military
men, he had obtained Rochambeau's permission to enter him
in the Royal Deux-Ponts, so that he could at least wear a
uniform. Gilles nearly wept for joy the first time he put on
the blue and yellow uniform, even though it did belong to a
foreign regiment, because it meant that he was no longer
merely a dusty scribe but part of that enormous family, an army
in the field, far from its home base. What was more, this
promotion earned him a new respect from his friend, Tim
Thocker.

Tim was one of the two mysterious Americans who had
come aboard the *Duc de Bourgogne* at Brest. The whole of
their mystery lay, in fact, in their being the bearers of private
letters from Benjamin Franklin and Silas Deane to their
respective families. Young Thocker, son of the minister of

Stillborough, on the Pawtucket River, was particularly charged with those of the United States Agent who, being a native of Connecticut, was in some sort a neighbour but there was nothing of the secret agent about him. He was a simple, only moderately God-fearing young fellow with the curiosity of a cat and very nearly the same degree of stealth, for no one ever heard him coming and his ordinary rate of speech was no more than ten words an hour. Mention hunting or fishing, however, and Tim would chatter like a drunken parrot.

It was the urge to find out what the hunting was like on the other side of the Atlantic that had taken him to Silas Deane, ostensibly to bring him urgent news concerning his business interests. But he had quickly regretted his curiosity because there was a whole world of difference between the methods he employed to hunt deer, moose, bear and golden eagle in the vast forests of the New World and the refinements of the chase as practised in France and England.

'All that galloping about, thirty or forty horsemen on the tail of one wretched animal,' he told Gilles scornfully, 'it's well enough for ladies but not for grown men. With us, you'll see what it means to sweat blood for days on end over a trail faint enough to flummox an Iroquois medicine man and end up coming to grips with a beast three times as big as yourself.'

Simple as earth, tall as a tree and built on the same lines, Tim Thocker had the reactions of his kind. Hating the confined life on board, he looked for amusement and all but caused a mutiny by handing out an unofficial rum ration of his own, notched up one success by helping to retrieve a gun which had broken loose and was in danger of ramming the forward bulkhead and another by his handling of one of the three cows which the Chevalier de Ternay had taken on board. He had also developed a strong liking for the young secretary who could speak his language and, more importantly, showed a marvellous willingness to listen to highly-coloured descriptions of America.

With him, the taciturn Tim talked with a will and by the end of the voyage the young Breton could have believed that he had lived all his life among the cod fishermen of Nantucket, the Quakers of Providence or within one of the tribes of Indians that peopled the interior. He learned too that rum was a man's best friend when it came to crossing frozen rivers and that it was a matter of pride to be able to swallow a respectable quantity without loss of dignity. Consequently, it was with a good deal of regret that Gilles parted from his companion, who was obliged to go on and deliver his letters, on their arrival in Newport. But Tim reassured him.

'Just time enough to say hallo to my father, hand over Mr Deane's letters and take a look at what the red coats are up to round New York, and I'll be back. I'd like us to fight side by side.'

With that, Tim settled himself in the canoe he had borrowed from a cousin and set out to propel himself across Narragansett Bay by the power of his own arms, as energetically as if he had not just endured seventy days' privation at sea, and Gilles went to move into his new quarters.

Next morning, he began his day as he had got into the habit of doing. At sunrise, he left the tent which he shared with a Sergeant Weinberg, a native of Heidelberg with whom he was on the simplest of terms, since neither understood a word of the other's language. Having assured himself that the weather was perfect and the slight mist hovering over the sea promised a hot day, he made his way quickly down to Atton Bay to bathe.

In this land where everything was new to him, the sea was the one element that he really knew and he always felt as he plunged in as if he were coming home. Because of this, he swam for a good hour every morning, then walked up to a small spring to wash the salt off and allowed himself a few minutes lying in the sun before he got dressed. With this exercise, his body had not only recovered from the ravages of the crossing but had acquired a vigour and a fine biscuit colour which gave him something of the look of the woodsman, Tim. What was more, the swimming helped him to forget about a certain snowy night beneath the walls of Vannes and the delightful proximity of a feminine form. During his stay in Brest he had had no leisure to pursue his studies in those agreeable arts but once on board ship the subject had become one of consuming interest for women were the staple topic of all the men, soldiers and seamen alike, who were setting out on an adventure which none of them expected to include a life of celibacy. Throughout the seventy days at sea, Gilles had listened to nothing but talk of

149

love and his companions' eagerness to make the acquaintance of American women.

In the event, not only were the General's orders extremely strict, there was to be no trouble with the local inhabitants (hence no question of seducing their women folk), but furthermore, the pretty anabaptists of Newport seemed to regard the French as so many limbs of Satan whom it behoved them to keep at a distance. As for the whores who usually accompanied any campaigning army, there were none and there had, of course, been no room for camp followers on board. The French camp was therefore condemned to a most unwonted chastity, with the men's discontent held in check by the fear of corporal punishment. Gilles, for his part, sought relief in dreams and in intensive physical activity.

Leaving his uniform by the spring, he ran to the overhanging rock which served him as a diving platform and his head clove the smooth waters of the bay without so much as a splash. He swam on for a few minutes towards a bushy islet and then, turning on his back, let the current carry him, trying to make his mind a blank. He did not feel like breaking records this morning. The water was wonderfully cool and limpid. There was not a sound beyond the crying of the gulls and the gentle swish of the waves on the shore, and Gilles had a great sense of wellbeing. He was the first man in the world and this magical country was the realm which should make him strong enough to rival its greatness.

He was just thinking that it could be good to carve himself a place in the sun here and bring Judith back to live and love here, when something caught his eye and instinct told him that all was not well. Rolling over swiftly, he was just in time to see the stern of a canoe unlike any he had seen by the Newport landing stages disappearing into the long grass by the spring. It was small and painted bright red, with a big black and white eye just below the curved prow.

Tim's tales came quickly to his mind. The hunter had given him long descriptions of the Indians' light boats, made of birch bark and often painted in bright colours. But, according to Tim, the nearest tribes of Indians to Rhode Island lived in the Hudson Valley and northern Connecticut. They were mostly Iroquois in the pay of the English and deeply hostile to the Rebels.

Gilles' blood froze. The canoe he had seen disappearing must belong to a spy, come to nose out the strength of the French camp or even to a scout paving the way for an attack. It was being said that the great Mohawk chief Thayendanega, wholly won over to the English since his sister married Sir William Johnson the virtual ruler of the Six Nations of the Iroquois from his splendid residence at Mount Johnson, had unearthed the hatchet and gone on the warpath again, far from his camping grounds at Canojoharie in the Hudson Valley. It was said too that Sir Henry Clinton, defending New York against Washington, was concentrating his forces on Long Island, the big, low-lying isle that sheltered the besieged city, preparing for an attack on Rhode Island.

By connecting all these rumours, Gilles was able to form a very good idea of the possible nature of the suspicious canoe and, swimming partly under water, he reached the place where he had seen it disappear and wormed his way noiselessly through the long grass until he could see the spring.

What he found there disconcerted him a little. The canoe's owner was, as he had expected, an Indian, but he was only a boy, about twelve years old.

His copper-coloured body was naked except for a strip of deerskin sewn with coloured beads which went between his legs and was held by a leather thong round his waist, the ends falling like a narrow apron front and back. But his face and chest were painted with strange black and white patterns, making him look very fierce. His hair, which was jet black, was shaved on either side and the remainder hung in a long plait from the top of· his head and was fastened with a red band with a white feather stuck in it.

But Gilles wasted little time admiring his visitor's picturesque appearance for the boy was at that moment occupied in transferring his own uniform and weapons to the canoe.

The young man's muscles tensed and he sprang forward, snatching his shirt from the small thief's hands. Taken by surprise, the boy let go. But he was a lad of swift reactions because a second later he had snatched a feathered tomahawk from his belt and was brandishing it in his clenched fist, his face so contorted with rage under its paint that there was no

151

longer anything childish about it. All the same, Gilles started to laugh.

'You are too young to handle weapons, my lad! Put down that hatchet. You don't know how to use it.'

This was instantly and spectacularly contradicted. The young Indian gave a shrill cry and hurled the tomahawk. It hissed like a snake and only the instinct which made Gilles dodge just fractionally enough saved him. A split second later and the weapon would have caught him full in the chest.

He had scarcely time to be aware of it. Already the Indian boy had followed his tomahawk and flung himself upon him, waving a knife which he must have been carrying hidden under his rudimentary garment.

This time, Gilles lost his temper. This colourful child was beginning to annoy him and he had no intention of fighting him. To his mind, the only fit treatment for a boy of that age with such instincts was a sound beating but he soon realized that this was not going to be easy to administer, especially in view of the fact that he himself was stark naked and quite unarmed. The Indian boy was clinging to him like a leech.

Gilles could feel the other's skin against his, smooth and slippery and smelling unpleasantly of fish oil, and a body at once muscular and elusive. It was like fighting with an eel. But agile as the boy was and in spite of his fury and his knife, the contest was an unequal one. Once disarmed, the young savage was soon made helpless, much to his rage. He squirmed and spat ferociously as Gilles' hands pinned him to the ground, like a vanquished snake, and bellowed aloud.

To quiet him, Gilles had to resort to the same method which had succeeded so well in reducing Judith to silence after her mistaken rescue from the Blavet. One quick blow to the jaw and the Indian boy went limp. His eyes closed and he departed peacefully to dreamland.

Gilles' first move was to get dressed, keeping one eye on the lad as he did so. Then he explored the canoe. It yielded little enough: a blanket skilfully woven in garish colours, a bag containing some coarse, strong-smelling dark brown meal which he guessed to be the famous pemmican that Tim had told him of, and which the hunter seemed to set great store by, a child's bow, some unused arrows and finally a rope of plaited

152

fibre which Gilles used to truss his prisoner before he could come round and start to struggle again.

This done, he fastened the little boat securely, taking good care to conceal it among the rocks. Then he threw the boy over his shoulder and made his way up again towards the camp. But, instead of going all the way, he turned off along a path leading into Newport.

Child or not, his prisoner was an Indian and his very presence there could only mean that there was a tribe or encampment at no great distance. The General must be informed at once, for the news could be important. Headquarters had been established in one of the principal houses in the town and, in spite of the child's weight, Gilles broke into a run as soon as the spire of Trinity Church came in sight, such was his haste to reach his chief.

The house, which belonged to the Governor's son, John Wanton, stood in Point Street, the broadest of Newport's few thoroughfares. Like most of its neighbours, it was built of white clapboard with a pitched roof and small paned sash windows. It was set against the green of a large orchard full of knotty apple trees and graceful cherries which gave it a countrified air, even though it was the residence of one of the town's chief magistrates.

This house, just as it was, had been placed at the Chevalier de Ternay's disposal for use as naval headquarters and to house the expedition's exchequer. It also contained the military head-quarters, being situated approximately midway between the army camp and the fleet's anchorage.

By the time that Gilles arrived there with his burden, which had regained consciousness some time previously and was doing its best to wriggle free, he had acquired an escort of half a dozen urchins who trailed after him in mingled awe and admiration, making him a present of their comments. Then, just as he was pushing open the gate, he was joined by two horsemen, covered in dust, who came down the road from the north and reined in beside him. One addressed him sharply.

'Hey! You there! Are you mad, capturing an Indian child? Don't you know you're likely to bring the whole tribe down on the town? Let him go at once! Who are you, anyway?'

Gilles made no movement to obey but stood frowning at

153

him. The man had spoken French, and without the trace of an accent, but his uniform was strange to him. He had on a plain black coat relieved with white facings, white waistcoat and white breeches. The cockade adorning the tricorn, grey with dust, which sat on his curled white wig was black likewise.

'I might ask the same of you,' he retorted taking an instant dislike to the high-pitched voice. It belonged to a tall, loose-limbed young man with delicate features and a white skin adorned with a good many freckles. A high, receding forehead and extravagantly arched brows gave to his face an expression of perpetual astonishment and faint disgust. 'You speak French but you do not belong to M. de Rochambeau's army, for I do not know you.'

'True. I belong to the army of the United States. I am—'

Before he could reveal his identity, another person had arrived on the scene and was hurrying to embrace him.

'Gilbert, old fellow! Here you are at last!' the Vicomte de Noailles exclaimed joyously. 'We were beginning to wonder if you had forgotten us, by God! Where are you from?'

'From General Washington's camp, of course. And it's I who should rather be asking you that question. Do you know that you are a month behind your time? What have you been doing at sea all this time?'

'What you'd have been doing if you had to move a convoy of sea slugs loaded up to the gunwales! It's well for you to accuse us of dawdling, with your little corvette with hardly anyone but yourself aboard. But you are here, and that's the main thing. But now tell me why you are giving this young man the rough edge of your tongue, and without even troubling to dismount?'

'Why?' the other cried angrily. 'Can you not see that he has dared to lay hands on a young Indian, for a slave, presumably – or a souvenir. The poor child must belong to these Narragansett Indians who are so peaceful and so—'

He was beside himself with rage and Gilles gazed at him in horror. Gilbert! Noailles had called him Gilbert! Could this ill-tempered young man possibly be—

The Vicomte, who had been following the progress of his thoughts as reflected in his face with unholy amusement, now burst out laughing.

'Oh yes, my poor friend! This is your great hero, your precious La Fayette, who is honouring you with his displeasure. It can't be helped! As for you, Marquis, you ought to show a little more kindness to your loyal admirer. Here's a lad who has run away from college and crossed the ocean to be near you and you are almost insulting to him. Permit me to present to you our General's secretary, Gilles Goëlo, a Breton and a man of letters, wit and the sword.'

La Fayette smiled slightly but his eyes lost none of their coldness.

'I thank you for your good wishes, sir, but what the devil possessed you to steal this child away from those good Narragansetts—'

'Pardon me, my lord Marquis,' a drawling voice broke in, 'but this kid was never a Narragansett. He's a Seneca, of the Wolf clan, and I guess I'm not far wrong in thinking he's a young brother to Chief Sagoyewatha, a good friend to the English and the same they've been calling Red Jacket, ever since they gave him one of their red coats.'

Tim Thocker, an impressive figure in his grey deerskin garments and with his raccoon cap on his head, emerged like some sylvan deity in a melodrama from behind the horses, his long carbine over his shoulder and a brace of wild geese in one hand. As usual, no one had seen or heard him coming.

He beamed benevolently on La Fayette and then, handing his geese unconcernedly to Noailles, who took them automatically, took the Indian boy from Gilles and set him on his feet, directing a second, and much warmer smile, upon his friend as he did so.

'A fine capture, my boy,' was his comment. 'It would be interesting to know where you found him, and what he was doing on Rhode Island. It's a long way from his big brother's cooking fires.'

'I found him down at Atton Bay,' Gilles answered, 'and I was just taking him to the General so that he could see what he could get out of him.'

'Seeing that the General doesn't speak Iroquois or any other of these damned Redskins' confounded lingos, I'd be very much surprised.'

'Well, what about you?'

155

'Oh, I can speak them all.'

'Very well, then,' said La Fayette, his temper still more strained by the set-down he had received. 'Suppose you see what you can do. In any case,' he turned back to Gilles, 'this business of Indians can wait, for I must speak urgently to the Comte de Rochambeau and to the Chevalier de Ternay. The army has wasted too much time here already. It must go forward, damme, forward! The King did not send troops to have them sit down on the seashore and do nothing.'

Once again, Noailles broke into laughter.

'We all of us agree with you there! Only tell us where you mean to take us in such a hurry?'

La Fayette regarded his brother-in-law sternly and with a slightly pitying expression.

'Why, to New York, of course! Have you not heard that Clinton is holding the city? I can't understand why you have not gone there already. Take me to the General immediately.'

Followed by his aide-de-camp, the Marquis de La Fayette, major-general in the United States Army, swept into the Wanton house, giving the seamen on guard duty barely time to present arms.

Gilles and Tim were left looking at one another. The Indian boy stood between them, still in his bonds.

'Well!' the young Breton sighed. 'If that is all he has to say to my capture! When I think that he wanted to make me let the little beast go!'

'Oh, it's quite natural. All Indians are alike to him. He's one of those who think they know what they're doing and then ask an Algonquin and an Iroquois to dine together. And then they're surprised when, after they've finished up the maple syrup cookies for dessert, one of his guests goes off coolly with the other's scalp! But you're right. There's something mighty interesting about this little fellow.'

And with hardly any transition, Tim passed into swift speech, with broad accompanying gestures, directed at the young Indian, who seemed at first to pay not the smallest heed to him.

The boy's lips were tight shut to begin with and his face held nothing but unconcealed contempt. But as Tim spoke, he relaxed a little and finally uttered a number of sounds which, since they were not inarticulate cries, must logically have been words.

'What is he saying?' Gilles asked.

'Well, he's not really saying anything much, except that he is a warrior and we can put him to the torture but it will do us no good, because he'll only smile to show his contempt for us, even if we cut him in little pieces.'

'Put him to the torture? This lad? What does he take us for?'

Tim shrugged and nodded gravely.

'For worthy enemies. And don't go thinking that all this talk of torture is so much moonshine. If I know the Senecas, this lad, as you call him, has reached the age of puberty and is undergoing the ritual ordeals which will make a warrior of him. This visit to our camp is probably one of his tests.'

'And what does that mean?'

'That his brother may not have quit his camping grounds necessarily, but that he has journeyed a long way to find some adventure great enough to earn him the rank of chief in later life. An adventure which, in the meanwhile, can be told around the camp fires.'

'But what did he hope to gain by coming here? Was he going to make war on us singlehanded?'

Tim seemed to find nothing particularly startling in the idea.

'He belongs to a tribe of the Iroquois and the Iroquois are capable of anything. But it's simpler than that. The boy has merely come to collect a batch of scalps for himself. The more he takes home, the more highly he'll be thought of.'

'We might have something to say about that,' Gilles muttered, finding the thought singularly unattractive. 'In the meanwhile, none of this tells us what we are to do with him – or rather, what you are to do with him, because I am wanted elsewhere.'

This was true, for one of the men on guard at the door was calling his name. The General evidently required his secretary. Tim laughed.

'I'll do with him what he would do with us in our place,' he said cheerfully. 'Hand him over to the squaws! I'd like to see how this warrior stands up to Martha's doughnuts and jam.'

Martha Carpenter was the woodsman's sweetheart and indeed

157

the two seemed made for one another. She was a strapping, fresh-faced girl with a creampot fairness who ran the substantial chandler's shop bequeathed to her by her father, with energy and competence.

With a wink at his friend, Tim hoisted the Indian boy, still parcelled up for ease of transport, on to his broad shoulder, scooped up the geese which Noailles had abandoned and headed for the corner of Long Wharf Street where his beloved reigned over a world of ropes, anchors, fishing nets, navigational instruments and implements of every kind, to say nothing of pipes, barrels of tobacco, rum, gunpowder and everything else that could be required to fit out a vessel and make life tolerable for the crew that sailed her.

Gilles let him go with a sigh and turned to enter the Wanton house. He felt suddenly that he would much rather be listening to Martha Carpenter's deep laugh than to the high-pitched voice of the Marquis de La Fayette who was so little like the man of his dreams. Gilles had painted him like all his favourite heroes, and now he was discovering that La Fayette was really only one officer among many, not so handsome as Lauzun or so agreeable as Noailles, and a good deal less interesting than Rochambeau. But still the thing he disliked most about him was his voice.

This was in fact the only thing to be heard as Gilles entered the house, for it seemed to fill the whole building, reaching an almost unbearable degree of shrillness. It conveyed an impression of impatience barely tempered by respect and, with the best will in the world, it was impossible not to hear what it was saying.

'The position of the American forces is this : they are divided into three main corps. One, under General Gates, is operating in South Carolina and is suffering severely. The second is under the command of General Benedict Arnold, the victor of Saratoga, who holds the fortress of West Point and so guards the approach to the Hudson Valley. The third and largest, for it numbers some six thousand men and an equal number of passable militia, is the one commanded by General Washington. He is holding the Jerseys and considering attempting to take New York. I think, sirs, that your duty is obvious. You must make for that city without delay and—'

The grave voice of the commander-in-chief managed to make itself heard.

'My whole duty, my dear Marquis, is to obey such orders as I receive from General Washington. Do you bring me such orders?'

'Of course not. I have no direct orders. General Washington has desired me to make contact with you, to discover the precise strength you bring us and to assure myself—'

'Well, one thing I imagine you have been able to assure yourself of is that the English fleet has us bottled up inside the bay. To attack it would be madness, for our fire power is greatly inferior. What is more, our protracted voyage has left us with a great many sick whom we cannot abandon before they are recovered. Consequently, I think the first thing to be done is to repair the defences of Rhode Island for, if not, the English will take it again as soon as our backs are turned and it will be all to do again.'

'Yes, but—'

Thinking that he had heard enough and that it would not do to be caught virtually listening at keyholes, Gilles knocked gently and walked into the room. Inside, a limited council of war was going on. He saw La Fayette confronting the cool, stolid Rochambeau like a fighting cockerel, the Chevalier de Ternay seated in an armchair, tapping the toe of his shoe with his cane, La Fayette's aide-de-camp, Major de Gimat, effacing himself over by a window and finally Lauzun, arms folded and eyes bright as buttons, moving eagerly back and forth between the two opponents, obviously dying to bring matters to a head.

At the young man's entrance, he frowned and when Gilles bowed politely and made his way to his usual table he protested impatiently :

'Gentleman, we are discussing matters of the highest importance, and no business of junior officers. Surely we can dispense with this young man's presence? Our plans are not for the ears of all and sundry.'

Gilles flushed angrily and his hand went instinctively to his sword. The young duke's animosity had not abated during the long sea voyage and, since their arrival, Lauzun had lost no opportunity of making the young secretary aware of his open contempt and hostility. Nor had Fersen's friendship for him helped matters. The two men had brought an unspoken rivalry with them from Versailles, a rivalry whose mainspring was none other than the Queen of France.

But Lauzun's intervention cut no ice with Rochambeau. He glared at the young duke frostily.

'What is biting you, sir, may I ask? Do you presume to teach me when I may or may not make use of my secretary? I wish to dictate a letter to General Washington and, unless you would condescend to take up a pen yourself—?'

The Chevalier de Ternay uttered a short bark of laughter, expressive of his annoyance.

'Monsieur de Lauzun's understanding of military matters is admirable, of the written word, less so. Moreover, he is a little too inclined to take it upon himself to order things as he wishes. Come here, my boy, and be ready to write. We need you.'

The young duke was far from pleased at this sharp rebuke from the Admiral. His lips tightened and he asked, in an icy voice, for permission to withdraw. Then, with a stiff bow, he left the room. Rochambeau looked after him.

'He's a soldier through and through,' he remarked. 'It's a pity he has no idea of discipline, can't keep his mouth shut and thinks that he is still living in the middle ages.'

'He is Biron and Lauzun at once, and that explains it,' the Admiral retorted with a shrug. 'Men like him have rebellion in their blood. Rebellion – and tactlessness. Because, you must admit, he did you a service by providing you with an opportunity to bite his head off. You were none too pleased at having him present at this first, vitally important meeting?'

Rochambeau laughed.

'Nor you, my friend, to judge by the way you kindly came to my assistance? Confess it, you don't like him?'

'Monsieur de Lauzun holds me in dislike and contempt, and he takes me for a coward, without understanding in the least the reasons for my actions. I have no cause to love him. But to return to you, Monsieur de La Fayette. You must be finding our family squabbles very tedious.'

Washington's envoy, who had been observing this scene with some surprise and also a certain enjoyment, for he was no fonder of Lauzun than the two other men, smiled for the first time.

'I learned a great deal on those few occasions when I had the honour of being admitted to Her Majesty's circle of court,' he said, failing to keep a hint of wistfulness from his voice. 'Notably that Monsieur de Lauzun is over fond of giving orders, regardless of the place or of the persons present. Now, gentlemen, will you tell me what it is you wish me to report to General Washington? Are you ready to march on New York?'

'No, a thousand times no! Not now, and not until I have the General's explicit order to do so. By God, sir, I'll not conceal from you I'm disappointed. I expected Washington himself and he sends you, without a word in writing and without even an escort.'

'He is with his army, outside New York. He is in no case to be paying social calls.'

Rochambeau's temper seemed to hang by a thread. His fist crashed down on the table at which Gilles sat, assiduously cutting himself a pen while not losing a single word of what was going on.

'One would say, Marquis, that we do not speak the same language. You have certainly become much more an American than a Frenchman. I came here with everything your General needs, and I mean everything! My instructions were to position myself on this island. I had a right to think that someone would be here to meet me. But not only was I met with blank faces on all sides, I have waited a whole fortnight before anyone has come to me. Now you come, but you come alone and, if I may say so, you seem to me to represent no one but yourself. Have you brought me any orders, yes or no?'

'I am a Major-General in the United States Army,' La Fayette squeaked, his voice rising two octaves. 'General Washington has complete confidence in me and I speak for him—'

'Then show me some properly written orders! Have you any?'

'N-no, but—'

'There are no buts in war, sir. Not only will I not budge from this spot without written orders, for I regard this territory as entrusted to my care, but furthermore I require Washington

161

to send me, at his earliest convenience, a sufficient and wholly trustworthy force!'

At this, La Fayette nearly choked.

'Men? Are you then so fearful of your ability to hold Newport? Have you indeed come to aid the Rebels, General, or is it the other way about?'

Rochambeau's fist came down for the second time.

'Monsieur de La Fayette, I repeat that I need a force of armed men, American and reliable. And your general must know why. If he has not told you, then that is one more reason why I should consider you as acting now upon your own initiative – and not as his representative. Now, let us make an end. I think that after all this you must be dying of hunger, and Monsieur de Gimat also,' he added with a sudden smile, turning to the aide-de-camp who, ever since Lauzun's departure, had been rigidly propping up the doorpost, apparently deaf to what was going on. 'Here is the Chevalier de Ternay only waiting to take you on board his flagship, where a luncheon is waiting for you. As for myself, you will excuse me, I know, but I have a number of important letters to dictate—'

The Admiral rose to his feet at last and limped across to where La Fayette stood obviously on the verge of an explosion. With an aplomb no one would have believed the old sea dog capable of, he slipped an arm through his and led him out. But Gilles caught the knowing look which he exchanged with Rochambeau behind the back of Washington's emissary. Was it, after all, some kind of comedy that was being played out before his eyes? Gilles had the sudden feeling that someone here was being made a fool of, and that it might well be the Major-General of the United States Army.

Alone with his secretary, Rochambeau crossed over to a small table on which stood a carafe and some glasses and poured himself a long drink of water which he swallowed with evident satisfaction. Then, with what sounded like a sigh of relief, he came back and sat down in the chair the Chevalier de Ternay had just vacated.

'Go and tell the sentry that I am on no account to be disturbed by anyone. Then, when you come back, lock the door, Gilles. I want to talk to you.'

The young man flushed with pride. It was the first time the

General had called him by his christian name and there was an unaccustomed intimacy in his tone. It made Gilles all the more prompt in carrying out the order.

'Good. Now close the shutters. It gets hotter and hotter.'

The bright sunshine flooding the room gave way to twilight and Gilles returned to his seat at the writing table and took up a pen, ready to dip it in the ink as soon as the General began, as he expected, to dictate. But Rochambeau shook his head.

'Put that down. I said I wanted to speak to you. Tell me, my boy, have you heard any news of your friend Tim Thocker recently? Is he planning to return to Newport?'

'He has returned, General. He is probably waiting for me at Miss Carpenter's at this very moment, with a young Indian boy I captured.'

'An Indian? What is this?'

'I wanted to mention it to you, General, only Monsieur de La Fayette gave me to understand that you had more important matters to deal with than an Indian boy.'

'Monsieur de La Fayette will soon be thinking himself the President of Congress, it appears! Tell me about it.'

Gilles gave a swift account of his morning's adventure, his meeting with La Fayette, Tim's arrival and all that had followed. While he talked, the furrows in Rochambeau's brow seemed to relax.

'Excellent!' he exclaimed when Gilles had finished. 'This is just the excuse I was looking for. All I have to know now is whether I can count on you, on your loyalty.'

The flush faded from Gilles' face, leaving it very white.

'You insult me that you need to ask it, General. My life is yours. I give it to you gladly,' he said simply.

'I have never doubted it and I am going to give you proof of that. In a little while, you shall go and bring your friend Tim and this Indian boy to me. But first, listen carefully because I have an important mission for you.'

'For me?'

'Yes, and one that could be the foundation of your career. You will be better able to judge that when I tell you that it concerns a state secret, one vitally important to the conduct of this war. A secret which, until now, I have shared only with the Admiral . . . Listen, now. For almost a year now, Washington's greatest need has been for money. If you had been at Versailles and in Paris last winter, you would have learned, like everyone else with a concern for the Rebels, of the disastrous condition in which their army passed that winter. Their troops ill-clad, without shoes, without food and almost without weapons! This Congress of theirs signed an admirable Declaration of Independence but its members, some of whom actually support the English because they don't wish to give up any of their creature comforts, its members screech like stuck pigs if anyone asks them for money. They want to be free, but they don't want it to cost them a penny piece, and I cannot say how much I admire this Washington and his wretched army for holding out in such conditions.'

'Yet,' Gilles objected, 'the country seems rich.'

'So it is, and will be richer yet but, as I said, its merchants care more for their moneybags than their freedom. In their eyes the paper dollar is worth nothing beside English gold. They won't take it. So it's solid coin that Washington needs above all. And in the *Duc de Bourgogne*'s holds are three million pounds in gold. That is the secret I am entrusting you with. No one else but Monsieur de Ternay knows of it.'

'Except the King, I suppose, and his ministers—'

'The King knows nothing – officially. Monsieur de Vergennes, the minister for foreign affairs, knows but he would rather cut his tongue out than admit it. This gold has been amassed by a shipowner and financier, Leray de Chaumont, a fabulously wealthy man in whose house Benjamin Franklin has been staying since he came to France.'

Gilles shivered. He had heard that name before in circumstances too unpleasant for him to forget them. He had a lightning vision of Yann Maodan's tavern and the Nantais' pointed head, his little gleaming eyes and flaring nostrils. He heard his husky voice murmuring about a great gentleman who was fitting out a fabulous fleet to sail to America, the mirage that had caught Jean-Pierre Quérelle : 'His name is Monsieur Donatien Leray de Chaumont . . .' He had found out later on, of course, that the financier had nothing to do with the evil traffic to which his friend had fallen a victim, yet even to hear the name again evoked unpleasant memories.

Meanwhile, Rochambeau was continuing: 'Before we sailed, a messenger was sent to Washington by a swift cutter, but I fear that he can never have arrived, or we should certainly have found a proper reception committee, or at the least Monsieur de La Fayette would have brought a suitable escort for so large a sum of money.'

'But – how could so much gold be brought aboard without anyone suspecting?'

'It was loaded at night, while the ship was lying alongside the Penfeld. It was brought by trusty men of Monsieur de Chaumont's, concealed in bales of fodder for the horses.'

'The bales of fodder which were afterwards unloaded because we were not taking any horses?'

'Precisely. They had to be put ashore but the bags were already hidden behind a false bulwark at the back of the powder reserve. Now Washington must take delivery of the gold and the secret must be kept until then, because one never knows what treachery a rumour may set in motion – and our friends the English would attack us on the spot if they knew of the presence of this gold. It is too important to the Rebels.

'Now, this is what you have to do. On pretence of returning your young Indian to his tribe, so as not to set the natives against us and to try and win us a few friends among them, you are going to leave Newport, with your friend Tim Thocker as guide, since you do not know the country. You will go to Washington's headquarters and tell him what I have just told you. No more and no less. In the meanwhile, Monsieur de La Fayette will no doubt continue to quarrel with me over the men I am asking for ˙– and now you know why! Go and fetch Thocker and the Indian to me. La Fayette is on board ship and will not even see them.'

But Gilles did not make for the door at once. Instead, he stayed where he was. He was immensely proud of the secret with which he had been honoured but at the same time a deep sense of his own unworthiness made him slightly uncomfortable. Being incapable of guile, he confessed it openly.

'General, why do you honour me with this? Monsieur de La Fayette is a general and a great lord and one of your own kind. Surely he is more fit for this than I? Tell him all about it! He will go back at once and return with the escort you want.'

Rochambeau shot him a shrewd glance from under lowered lids.

'You think I do not trust him? Far from it, but it is not so with the man to whom this fortune belongs. Leray de Chaumont has no love for La Fayette and if he wanted to entrust the gold to him he would have had it put aboard the *Hermione* at Rochefort, rather than the *Duc de Bourgogne* at Brest.

'Monsieur de Vergennes, too, without whose authority I would never have agreed to carry the gold, wishes Monsieur de La Fayette to be kept out of the business as far as possible, since he regards him as a young hothead with dangerous ideas. I cannot say they are altogether wrong. The Marquis is young and hotheaded, and he does not always think as much as he should. Given his gilded plumes and his vanity, he would be perfectly capable of spilling the whole lot in front of Congress, just to show them how much aid he can bring to their cause. And then God knows how much Washington would ever see of it! Does my explanation satisfy you?' he added, with a touch of irony which at once re-established the distance between them.

'Perfectly, my lord. But one word more, with your permission?'

'Yes?'

'This Monsieur Leray de Chaumont – why is he so eager to assist the Rebels? It is a huge sum of money.'

'But he is hugely rich! One of the richest men in Europe, I think. One of the most vindictive also and he has nursed a grudge against the English for many years for the way they all but wiped out his slaving fleet. Finally, he is both a financier and a gamester. If the new United States are victorious and can win their independence and throw the English into the sea, then the potential of this vast, self-governed country will be equally vast. Leray knows that if that happens he will reap at least ten times what he has laid out. The game, as they say, is worth the candle. Now go, lad, for time presses.'

'At once, General.'

Almost before the words reached Rochambeau, Gilles was in the passage. The heat outside was staggering. Coming from the comparative coolness of the Wanton house, Gilles felt as if he were stepping into an oven. He wished he could have unbuttoned his thick waistcoat, but this was not the moment to be called to order for dereliction of dress. All the same, as he began to run towards Long Wharf Street, he had the feeling that the sky had opened and was pouring molten lead down on his head. The sea, drained of all colour, was a dazzling sheet of white.

It was with a real sense of relief that he plunged into the cool shade of Martha's shop, with its pleasant smell of new rope and tobacco. It was unusually quiet, even for this peaceful hour of day when three-quarters of the town was taking a nap, for Martha considered sleeping in the afternoon a deplorable and degrading habit.

She herself was accustomed to pass the time in a variety of feminine tasks about the house. With Rosa, her fat black maid who never slept, for company, she would sew gowns, make jam or concoct one of the enormous peach pies which were her speciality, with which she would regale her neighbours and the ladies of her sewing circle when they came to spend an evening. But the kitchen, adjoining the shop, was equally silent and when Gilles knocked gently no one answered.

He went in, nevertheless, and swore roundly as he saw Martha, a small mound of blue and white checked gingham, lying unconscious before her stove, on which a pan of gooseberries was simmering gently. On either side of her were the sugar-covered ladle which must have fallen from her hand and the heavy frying pan which had evidently struck her down.

In addition, an overturned chair, a cup of tea spilled on the table and the marks where a hand had scooped something up from the white sugar all combined to show that something had happened. But of Tim and the Indian boy there was not a sign. Rosa, too, was conspicuous by her absence.

Gilles began by lifting up the girl and setting her in the big rocking chair by the window, and after making sure that she was not hurt, he set about reviving her with the help of a drying-up cloth dipped in a bucket of water and manipulated none too gently.

His energetic ministrations very soon produced results. Martha opened her china-blue eyes wide, sighed once or twice and put a hand up to the bruise that was already colouring on

167

her temple. Her bewildered gaze went to Gilles who was busy chafing her hands.

'What happened?' she asked in the faint voice usual on such occasions.

'That's just what I'd like to know. Where is Rosa? Where are Tim and the Indian?'

The last word seemed to shed some light for Martha Carpenter. Recovering miraculously, she flushed brick red and leaped to her feet and began striding up and down her wrecked kitchen giving vent to such a spate of indignation that it was all Gilles could do to make sense of what had happened.

In the end he made out that when Tim had arrived with the young Indian, the boy was so quiet that he had untied him, after first relieving him of the weapons he used so readily. Then he had asked Martha to give him something to eat.

'I was not best pleased,' she said emphatically. 'I did not like the boy's looks, or his eyes. But Tim insisted and he was hungry too. I dished them up some pickled beef, doughnuts and a maple syllabub. God forgive me, but you should have seen that young savage eat! And now and then he said something in his own barbarous language—'

'Did he answer Tim's questions?'

'Yes, and without missing a mouthful. Upon my word, I ought to have given him ratsbane! When he had done stuffing himself, he began to look sleepy so Tim asked if he could put him in the outhouse with a blanket over him while he went to fetch the canoe from the place where you had hidden it. I said of course he could. Tim carried him out and locked the door on him and I went on making my gooseberry jam. Rosa is in the orchard picking peaches. I was just skimming the jam when something hit me on the head – and that's all I know. But it must have been that little wretch who did it. My head is ringing like a bell. Can you give me—'

'I'm sorry, Miss Martha, but now that you are awake again you'll have to look to yourself! Where is the outhouse?'

'Back of the house, on the right—'

Gilles was already outside. One glance was enough to tell him that although the door which Tim had locked was still as he had left it, the narrow window in the wall at head height

168

was gaping open, its wooden lattice torn out. The boy could not have been as sleepy as Tim and Martha had thought and must have found some tool inside the little shed to use on the window. Just to make sure, Gilles hoisted himself up and looked inside. The shed was empty. The Indian had made off.

'Yet the gap is far from wide,' Gilles muttered to himself. 'The boy is like a snake.'

But what mattered now was to find the snake as quickly as possible, and Tim as well, since Rochambeau was waiting for them both. Gilles hesitated for a moment, wondering what to do. The best thing might be to go to meet his friend. He knew the ways of Indians so well that he was bound to pick up the trail at once. But then it occurred to him that the boy, knowing that Tim had gone for his canoe, might have stayed in the town and be hiding there until nightfall when he might steal some fisherman's boat and get away from the island without having to pass the camp.

Pausing briefly at the house to tell Martha that he was going to search the harbour and to ask her to send Tim there when he came, Gilles started to patrol the length of the wooden quay, inspecting the line of boats moored to the piles below.

Except for three or four longshoremen snoozing in the sun against a stack of timbers, the place was deserted. Only a boat from one of the French ships blocking the harbour mouth was sculling ashore across the smooth waters. Fearing that it might be La Fayette, Gilles paused, shading his eyes with one hand against the glare, and studied the figures standing in the stern. But when he had recognized the stocky figure and cocked hat of Monsieur de la Pérouse and, beside him, the taller shape of Monsieur Destouches, the *Neptune*'s captain, he resumed his search with an easy mind.

He had just come to Flint's Inn, where Rochambeau had spent his first night ashore, when a tremendous uproar broke out within. It was the unmistakable clamour of soldiers off duty and getting out of hand. Knowing how strictly Rochambeau and Ternay were watching their men's behaviour, Gilles thought that he had better go inside and take a look, and try to calm things down before Pérouse and Destouches came ashore and heard it.

He pushed open the door and saw that it was high time someone intervened, and also that he had found what he was seeking. The Indian boy was there, lashed to one of the wooden
pillars supporting the inn's roof. His face was as impassive as
ever but as Gilles came in the boy turned to look at him and
the terror in his eyes betrayed his youth. The child was afraid,
as any child in the world would be at the mercy of a pack of
ruffians.

Seated at a table a few feet away were some thirty men of
Lauzun's legion, jostling one another to put down their money
in a game of faro.

'Come now, gentlemen,' shrilled a voice that Gilles recognized with a thrill of anger. 'Who'll have him? You'll have to
bet higher than that! This young, strong savage I have had
the good luck to capture will certainly fetch a higher price at
the next slave sale in Boston or Providence than any negro
child.'

'If he's worth so much,' someone growled, 'why don't you
keep him for yourself? Sell him yourself!'

'Because when you've been where I have, you need money
more than a slave,' snarled Morvan de Saint-Mélaine. 'And
you'd not be asking such stupid questions if you'd any left to
put down! Now, gentlemen, where's your nerve? You won't
get such a chance again.'

Gilles, standing in the tavern doorway, allowed himself a
moment to observe his enemy. He had not set eyes on Judith's
brother since their encounter in the port of Brest, the evening
before they sailed. But an examination of the army's muster
rolls which, as the general's secretary he had access to, had
assured him that no Saint-Mélaine was included in them and he
had concluded that Morvan had enlisted under an assumed
name.

This was unexpectedly confirmed during the course of the
interminable voyage. On May 26th, a signal had been received
from Monsieur de Lombard, the captain of the *Provence*, which
was carrying Lauzun's men, that one of them had been found
guilty of stealing rum and attempting, while under the influence
of drink, to set fire to the ship, and was sentenced to be keel-
hauled. The man's name was Samson.

Seized by a premonition he could not explain, Gilles watched the punishment through a telescope and saw that he was not mistaken : the man being plunged into the sea from the yard-arm was indeed Morvan.

Once ashore, he had made inquiries as to what had become of him and so discovered that the man had not died of his punishment but had finished the voyage in irons, as a result of which he had been taken to the hospital on Conanicut Island on arrival, along with the rest of the sick. He could not long have rejoined his regiment.

Absorbed in the game and in the growing pile of coins in front of him, Morvan had not seen Gilles come in. Gilles walked straight up to the wooden post to which the boy was tied, scooping a knife from a table as he went and slipping it into his pocket. His first impulse had been simply to release the lad without more ado but he remembered just in time that he could not afford the luxury of letting him run away.

Instead, he smiled encouragingly as he passed, making the child crimson to the roots of his hair, then pushed his way through the players until he stood facing the temporary banker.

'You are playing for something that does not belong to you, gentlemen,' he said coolly. 'This young Indian is a prisoner of war. He belongs to the Comte de Rochambeau who has sent me to fetch him. Pick up your money and get out!'

There was an instant silence, broken only by the clatter of Morvan's chair as he thrust it backwards in rising. The face under his red hair was white, with a curious greenish tinge about the pinched nostrils. But a flame of savage joy sprang suddenly into his dark eyes.

He let his breath out in a sigh of pure pleasure.

'The bastard! At last! The devil has saved me the trouble of looking for him and handed him to me on a plate! And, on my oath, giving orders, too! Cocksure young puppy! Hold him, lads! Don't let him get away before I've got even with him! We can finish the game later.'

'Just a minute,' one of the men broke in. 'He says the savage belongs to the General and, if he's the General's secretary, he ought to know what he's saying. I've no wish to be flogged for theft—'

'You poor fool!' Morvan roared. 'He's a bastard, I tell you. Lies are second nature to him and I tell you—'

'And I tell you,' Gilles took him up, as cool as ever, 'that you have no right in a tavern at this hour of day. Don't trust to the fact that everyone's asleep. They aren't. I can assure you, for instance, that Monsieur de la Pérouse and Monsieur Destouches are landing at the jetty at this moment. I saw their boat.'

He had no need to say it twice. Lauzan's hussars fell on the heap of money on the table and, each grabbing roughly what was his, escaped with it, at the cost of a few buffets, by way of the discreet rear door of the inn. From there, they fled between the houses like a flock of scarlet crows.

Three men, however, had remained with Morvan. All were clearly drunk. Their looks were so threatening that the land-lord, Flint, guessing that evil things were about to be done in his house, plucked up courage to emerge from the kitchen, whither he had fled with his serving maid for safety, and ask in quavering accents in his bad French :

'Soldiers go now?'

'We're not finished yet,' Morvan snapped, his narrowed gaze still fixed on Gilles' face. 'Shut the doors! And lock them! Then get back to your kitchen and stay there, if you don't want to end on your own spit.'

But fear for his property stirred one final spark of courage in the wretched Flint.

'If there's anything broken – who's to pay?'

'It's you'll be broken if you're not gone in one second!' roared a great black-avized lout who looked like the devil himself in his red uniform coat. The words were accompanied by a gesture expressive enough to elicit a moan of terror from Flint and send him scuttling to obey. He shut his doors and vanished like a rat into its hole.

Convinced now that he was going to have to fight for his life against the four of them, Gilles quietly drew his sword. Morvan gave a jeering laugh.

'What? Do you think I'm going to fight you? A trooper of the king's horse fight a bastard penpusher? Such as you are only to be touched with a cane or a riding crop! Come on, you men! Get him. We'll give him his deserts. Careful, now. Don't damage him too soon!'

Gilles' jaw set under the taunts and the surge of anger that

172

flared up in him drove caution to the winds. Regardless of his unprotected back, he lunged at Morvan with his sword.

'I'll show you who's the bastard, you damned craven scoundrel! Fight, damn you—'

A howl of fury drowned his words. Morvan clapped his hand to the long scratch that marked his cheek. His fingers reddened and he sprang back with a yell:

'Take him, in God's name! What are you waiting for?'

As one, the three men fell on Gilles and, taken in the rear, he was unable to defend himself. In another moment he had been overpowered, stripped of shirt and waistcoat at a sign from Morvan and lashed by the wrists to a rope flung over one of the ceiling beams. In this position he was hoisted up a few inches from the ground.

'What do you think you're doing?' His voice was as calm as ever. 'Must I remind you I was sent by General Rochambeau to fetch the Indian boy, and that he is still waiting?'

One of the men, impressed perhaps, muttered something about 'maybe better not make trouble' but Morvan only sneered.

'Trouble! What can the General want with a scrubby lad like you? And even if it's true? We don't have to know anything about it – especially since he won't be seeing either of you! Because get this into your head. There's not going to be much skin, or much flesh left on your bones when we've done with you! Scum! I'll show you what you get for throwing a gentleman in the mud.'

'You don't need me for that,' Gilles scoffed. 'As to being a gentleman – I'd no idea you boasted anything so exalted – Samson!'

All this time, the devilish-looking man had been unfastening his belt and wrapping the pierced end round his hand, leaving the buckle free. Evidently he was to be executioner. 'Samson' obviously had a knack of making the right friends, or accomplices.

Gilles' wrists were already painful from the whole weight of his body hanging on them. He tried vainly to grasp the rope with his fingers to ease them, shut his eyes and braced his muscles instinctively against the coming agony, praying with all his might that it should not drag a single cry from him. He would not give his enemy the fearful satisfaction of hearing him scream. The time had come for him to commend his soul to God.

A stinging pain seared across his back and his body swung a little from the force of the blow. Tears welled up under his closed eyelids but no sound passed the twofold barrier of his clenched teeth and lips. The belt hissed again and the pain was worse because the steel tang of the buckle tore his flesh, while the swinging increased the agony in his wrists. As he waited for the third blow, Gilles was feeling slightly sick. But the blow did not fall. Instead, Morvan came and stood before him.

'Now that you know what is in store for you, suppose we talk,' he said, in such silken tones that Gilles opened his eyes.

'Talk – I have nothing to say to you, you villain!'

'Oh yes, you have! A great deal . . . things that could mean you'll still have a shred or two of skin on your back when I kill you. And I'll make it quick, I promise you. You see, you did us a good turn by coming here. We were just going to look for you, my friends and I.'

'What for? Because you don't like Blavet water?'

'I don't, but that's another story. What interests me is the General's little secrets. You are his secretary, and must be somewhat in his confidence. So be a good boy and tell us about the gold—'

'Gold?'

'Come on, don't play the innocent. There was a seaman from the *Duc de Bourgogne* in the hospital on Conanicut muttering in his delirium about a huge sum in gold that had been brought aboard the vessel.'

In spite of his agony, Gilles laughed. But at the same time his throat tightened in terror. The secret! Rochambeau's great secret was known to Morvan. For all the secrecy with which it had been carried aboard, someone had witnessed it.

'Your seaman must have been raving, then. Every captain has a chest to defray the expenses of the vessel, but that is common knowledge.'

'I am not talking of that money. I am talking of a cargo taken aboard very mysteriously at dead of night in Brest, bales of hay that seemed peculiarly heavy and gave off a strange sound. I should say that the seaman's tale only confirmed a certain rumour I myself had heard at L'Orient. It was said that the Chevalier de Ternay's fleet would be carrying much gold. That was why I embarked, to look into it. As far as I'm concerned the Rebels, as they call them—'

The gesture which accompanied the words indicated very clearly what Morvan thought of the Rebels. He moved closer to his victim.

'So, you'll talk?'

'I don't know anything about it. You'd better ask this seaman of yours, since he knows so much.'

'We began with him. But he knew nothing more. He searched for it, naturally, on the voyage, but he found nothing.'

'Because there was nothing to find.'

'Or because it was too well hidden. But if there's one person who can tell us anything, it'll be you.'

'Supposing there were any gold aboard, how do you know it is still there?'

'The *Duc de Bourgogne* has never been alongside the quay, and you can't unload a weight like that from her anchorage. But it may not be there for much longer now. Young La Fayette will have come to collect it on behalf of his pals. So you'd better tell us where it's hidden, and mighty quickly too, if you want to make a pretty corpse. Why, I might even do you the honour of crossing swords with you. A fine, noble death for a bastard. But I'm a generous man . . .'

'You are a maniac! I know nothing of this phantom hoard.'

'You know nothing, eh? Grégoire!'

The torment recommenced. Two, three, five times the impromptu lash fell, leaving beads of blood. His back on fire, his stomach heaving, Gilles set his jaw and managed to bite back the shrieks of anguish for which his whole tortured body cried. Not a sound passed his lips. Now and then, Morvan would put a question to him, always the same. And then, suddenly, there was something like an explosion, followed immediately by two shots. The tavern door fell inwards, torn from its hinges by an irresistible force and on the threshold, growling ferociously, like a mastiff about to charge, Tim Thocker stood upon the ruined panels, a pistol in either hand. Grégoire, the man with the lash, and one of the other two lay dead, the first with a ball in his neck, the second shot through the heart. But Tim had already dropped his now useless pistols and drawing from its sheath the long knife that hung from his belt, he flung himself on Morvan while the fourth scoundrel, abruptly sobered and terrified by the appearance of so formidable a fire power, seized his chance to vanish through the gaping doorway without further ado.

Gilles, reviving miraculously, wriggled on the end of his rope, savaging his wrists still more, and panted: 'Don't kill him! He's mine!'

The knife had pierced Morvan's shoulder and Tim was already drawing it out, stained with blood.

'Sorry,' he said coolly. 'But don't fret. I've only damaged him a trifle. He'll be there when you want him.'

With that he picked up 'Samson', who was clutching his wounded shoulder with an agonized expression, by the scruff of his neck and carried him, one-handed, to the doorway. A resounding kick directed to the seat of his breeches sent him sprawling on the quay.

'And now for you,' Tim said, hooking a stool to stand on.

With unexpected gentleness, he supported his friend against him with one arm while he cut the rope and then lowered the bleeding body to the ground.

'Hey, Flint! Where are you? You can come out now. We need you.'

The innkeeper emerged at once, as white as his apron, but his maid was with him and she, at least, seemed to have kept her head for she was carrying water, lint and bandages. Gilles, mercifully unconscious at last, was laid face downwards on a table.

'They've certainly made a mess of him!' Tim growled. 'It's a good thing I happened to glance through the window when I saw the door was shut. Those damned curs! And they are Frenchmen! Cornplanter, chief of the Iroquois, couldn't have done better!'

Flint had been feeling the need for several glasses of rum as a restorative while his maidservant gently bathed the lacerated back with a mixture of oil and wine, but at this he started.

'My God!' he said. 'The Indian! Where is he?'

'The Indian? What Indian?'

'The kid the big red-headed one brought in under his arm. He tied him to that post, and now he's gone!'

176

Tim, busy trying to force Gilles' head up and make him swallow a few drops of rum, merely shrugged. He jerked his head at the little heap of rope lying at the foot of the post.

'That just shows that he untied himself. The day has not yet dawned when a trooper from Europe can tie up an Indian securely. No doubt he took his chance while they were looking the other way and is well away by now. Much good may it do him.'

'Idiot!' Gilles gasped, spluttering through a mouthful of rum but himself again. 'Go after him! We need him— The General says— God almighty! What are you doing to me? Are you trying to take off what's left of my skin?' he added, writhing under Molly's strong fingers.

'Yell all you like, sir,' the girl retorted, spreading on a thick layer of nauseating greenish-coloured ointment. 'You'll thank me tomorrow when your wounds begin to heal.'

'What a stink!'

'You can't expect it to smell like roses. There's spermaceti in it, and bear's grease, St John's wort – and a host of other things. This ointment is a secret I had off an old Narragansett medicine man, but it will heal you better than a needle and thread can cobble up your stocking. Now stop wriggling, do. Or you'll get it up your nose.'

Gilles did as he was told and while Molly made a sort of bandage round his body, he explained to Tim as best he could without mentioning the gold, why it was that he regretted the Indian's disappearance.

'What are we going to tell the General?' he finished gloomily. But it needed more than that to upset Tim Thocker's calm.

'The best way to find out is to go and see. If you can get up, let's go at once.'

In another minute Gilles, dressed and fortified with another drink, was leaving the inn, leaving Flint to deal as best he might with the bodies of the two dead hussars. It was a little cooler than it had been and the sea was slowly reverting to its normal blue. The harbour and the streets were coming to life again. Women in straw bonnets were entering the shops, holding by the hand small girls identically dressed. Martha, with a wide goffered cap on her piled-up hair, was standing in her

177

shop engaged in energetic argument with fishermen, an assortment of tobacco jars spread out before them. But none of this could take Gilles' mind from his obsession.

'Where can the boy have got to?' he muttered, gazing about him. 'He can't go unnoticed, at any rate.'

'Oh yes, he can! Indians are a common enough sight. But wait, there he is!'

They were just passing a pile of casks with a tall negro seated on top of them staring vacantly at the wheeling gulls, when the Indian boy suddenly rose up in front of them. He made no attempt to hide again, but came straight up to Gilles and stood before him. Then, raising his right hand to shoulder level, he held it palm outwards and performed a circular motion which brought it to a level with his black eyes which all the time stared fixedly at Gilles. Tim whistled softly.

'What have you been doing?' he murmured. 'He is giving you a greeting.'

But the boy had already begun to speak in short, clipped sentences which Tim made haste to translate, not troubling to hide his excitement.

'He says he wishes to be your friend because you are a true warrior! He says that he saw you laugh under torture as only his brother Indians know how to do, that he is your prisoner and proud of it. His name is Igrak, which means "the bird which never sleeps" and, as I thought, he is indeed brother to Sagoyewatha, whose name means "he who speaks to keep others awake". You've made us an ally there, my boy. If your General is not pleased with this, then he's a hard man to satisfy.'

Oblivious of his friend's condition, he was on the point of dealing him a hearty slap on the back. Gilles dodged in time but such was his delight that already the pain seemed less. He was, in fact, feeling much better. The giddiness which had affected him on leaving the inn had worn off. But he was still so pale that Tim insisted on stopping at Martha's for long enough for him to eat something and drink a cup of coffee.

'Otherwise you'll never get as far as the Wanton house.'

Rosa, Martha's fat black maid, was back and standing in the kitchen peeling peaches for a pie but she abandoned her task at once to produce an impromptu meal for the two men and Igrak, although not without much rolling of her eyes in disapproval at the latter. Martha was busy in the shop and did not appear.

'Tell her we'll be back in a while,' Tim said, swallowing the last of his coffee. 'And now for the General.'

They went on towards the Wanton house but were just crossing the road to enter Point Street when Axel Fersen stepped out suddenly from behind a tree and blocked their way.

'I was waiting for you,' he said. 'Don't go on. General's orders.'

'The General? But he's expecting us,' Gilles protested. 'We are late already.'

'I know. All the same, you must not be seen at the Wanton house. If you are, the General will have no alternative but to order your arrest.'

'Our arrest?' the two young men exclaimed indignantly with one voice. 'What for?'

'We can't stay here,' Fersen said quickly, drawing them into a narrow gap between the wooden wall of a big red-painted barn and a thick hedge of nut trees. 'We've not much time and you must be gone as soon as possible. You are accused of murdering two men of Lauzun's legion in Flint's tavern.'

'Mur—'

'Hear me out! Lauzun has been badgering headquarters for the past half-hour. He has with him two of his men, one wounded in the shoulder, and the three of them are kicking up the devil of a row! They say you attacked them in order to get hold of a young Indian, presumably the one with you now.'

Tim, who during this brief explanation had been turning all colours of the rainbow, now burst out: 'I swear on my father's bible, I never heard a more shameless tissue of lies! Murdered, eh? Let me tell you I killed those two scoundrels with my own hand and for my friend here I'd have killed the red-headed one too, and with great pleasure—'

'He saved my life, that is all!' Gilles put in indignantly. 'Look here!'

Eagerly, he pulled off shirt and waistcoat, grimacing with pain as he did so, to show the bandages, already stained with blood, which covered his back. Then, in a few swift words, he told what had passed.

179

'But for Tim Thocker they'd have beaten me to death,' he said grimly. 'And are we to be arrested for that? They might as well hang us!'

'Which is precisely what Lauzun is demanding,' Fersen retorted coolly. 'He is even threatening to embark his men again if he does not obtain satisfaction. I may add that the General does not believe a word of his tale and, as I said, it was he who sent me, in order to avoid having to put you under arrest.'

'Surely he and the Chevalier de Ternay are still in command? What can Lauzun do against his decision?'

'As I said, re-embark! And we cannot risk being deprived of his legion. Rochambeau would rather temporize, gain time. He has told me he was sending you on a mission which would keep you away from Rhode Island for some time. That will enable him to get at the truth and calm down Lauzun. I am to tell you to wait for him in one of the forts of the old English defences at the back of the town, the one directly in line with the church tower. He will join you there after curfew to give you your instructions.'

'That won't do,' Tim complained. 'A mission means a journey and a journey means the necessary equipment. My weapons are still at Miss Martha Carpenter's house. And my friend Gilles here has literally nothing fit for travelling in the forest. That red and blue uniform will make him as conspicuous in the woods as a parrot on its perch. Besides that, we'll need food for ourselves and our young friend, hunting gear – and some other, more suitable for Englishmen than hares—'

'All right, all right!' Fersen interrupted. 'You shall have what you want, only for the love of God make haste and get to a place of safety! And should you, by ill luck, run across any men of the legion, I beg you will curb your fighting instincts and take cover. They are quite capable of killing you on sight and a dead body never made a good messenger.'

Tim muttered something to the effect that it would give him great pleasure to wring the neck of a certain French duke but nevertheless he did as he was told and, followed by the other two, slipped along in the shadow of the hedge while Fersen, hands clasped behind his back, sauntered idly in the direction of the home of the Hunter family, prominent in the town, where he was a frequent visitor and passed his time paying casual court to the daughter.

Thanks to Tim's expert knowledge of quiet byways, untrodden paths, deep hedges and unfrequented orchards, the three fugitives arrived without incident at the old defence works which Rochambeau had not yet found time to put in order. Pushing their way through the thick vegetation with which it was overgrown, they found themselves inside a half-ruined enclosure with timbers roughly hewn from tree trunks emerging from piles of broken stones. There they selected an old casemate which was more or less habitable and settled down to wait for nightfall.

None of them had spoken since they parted from Fersen. Tim sat hunched up, elbows on knees, sucking at the pipe which he had pulled from his pocket without thinking and stuck in one corner of his mouth. He gazed absently in front of him, as though all that had happened were no concern of his. But Gilles was shaking with helpless anger and indignation, so that he even forgot the sting of his lacerated back. Only Rochambeau's direct order prevented him from hurling himself into Lauzun's camp, sword in hand, to rout out Morvan and purge the unworthy accusation levelled at his friend Tim, who had done no more than plunge into the hornet's nest in defence of his friend's life, in that wretch's blood. But he knew that he must obey his orders without question or be lost for ever. As for Igrak, he sat on a stone by the doorway, so still that he was almost indistinguishable from his surroundings.

Night was a long time coming. At last the sounds of the small town ceased one by one. When nothing broke the stillness but the call of the nightjar and the distant barking of a dog, cautious footsteps were heard in the undergrowth. Then the yellow beam of a darkened lantern flicked over the ruins, gleaming on the silver buckles and red heels of a pair of well-made shoes, above which loomed the tall figure of the General. Behind him came Fersen, loaded like a porter.

Rochambeau stood for a moment, studying the two men who had risen at his entry. His eyes rested gravely on Gilles' face which already showed the signs of pain and fever.

'Take off that coat,' he said. 'I want to see.'

181

But when Tim would have undone the bandages round the young man's body, he prevented him.

'No need. A man isn't bandaged like that for nothing and besides, it does no good to disturb it when it's been well done.'

'General,' Gilles cried, 'I swear as I hope to be saved that we are no murderers!'

'If I believed you were, my boy, I should not be here. But just at present it suits me to pretend I do believe it. However, carry out your mission to my satisfaction and you shall have justice. We'll see that Monsieur de Lauzun is made to see things as they are—'

'I do not ask so much, sir.'

'What do you ask then?'

'Your permission to meet the man who had me beaten like a cur and settle my account with my sword.'

'Do you need my permission for that? A duel between soldiers—'

'No. A duel with a gentleman who refuses to cross swords with a bastard. Samson is not what he pretends to be. He bears a great name.'

'And does no credit to it, then. You shall have your duel, Gilles, and I know who will be your seconds. Now, take this letter. You will give it to General Washington and then remain with him for long enough for me to sort out this business—'

'One more word, General. The man in question was trying to make me divulge a secret which was not mine to disclose. It seems that the nights in Brest are not so dark as it was thought. A sick seaman from the *Duc de Bourgogne* let fall some incautious words in his delirium in the hospital on Conanicut. The men we are talking of from the legion were showing a good deal of interest—'

'Can you name the men?'

'Their leader calls himself Samson. I don't know the others.'

There was a brief silence, then Rochambeau sighed.

'I see. In that case, my friend, you must travel all the faster. I will see that these men are kept under observation, and thank you.'

Then, he turned to the Swede who stood waiting calmly, apparently in no way discommoded by the weight of two muskets, powder flasks, pistols and a large, bulging sack.

'You may put that lot down, my dear Count,' he said with a chuckle. 'I dare swear no one has ever demanded such a service of you before.'

'But then there is no one quite like you, General. It is a pleasure to be a conspirator in your company. I wish you luck, gentlemen,' he added, turning to the two others. 'May I also say that I envy you? By going to headquarters, you will be gettting nearer the enemy. While we must go on playing whist with the good citizens of Rhode Island.'

'Your turn will come. Come along now. Our absence may be remarked on, and we promised to finish the evening at the Jeffries'.'

Fersen made a face and sighed deeply enough to bring down the remains of the casemate.

'Where Monsieur de Lauzun has promised to put in an appearance in order to describe to the ladies which novels are the Queen's favourites. I really would much rather go to bed, sir—'

'So would I, my friend. But you are not here to be entertained. We are at war. Good luck, the rest of you.'

Fifteen minutes later, looking like Tim's twin brother in his deerskin garb, Gilles followed his friend out of the old fortifications. Outside, the night was clear, warm and light, with the breath of sea air which can make even the worst of the dog days tolerable. Tim plunged into the long grass of a meadow that stretched northward along the island, ending in a small coppice. But when Gilles tried to urge Igrak after him, the Indian boy refused and Gilles had to call Tim back.

'I can't understand what he is saying,' he whispered. 'I think he said something about scalps!'

The hunter and the young Indian crouched in the grass and muttered rapidly. Tim laughed.

'He doesn't want to go home,' he explained. 'He says if he has no scalps to bring back he can never be a warrior, they will make him stay with the squaws and the papooses!'

'And you can laugh? Yet we can't leave him here, any more than we can let him go and get the scalps he wants.'

'Oh, if it were up to me, I shouldn't care if he were to go and scalp your friend Lauzun and some of his fellows. But I think I've a better idea. Go and hide in the spinney and wait for me.'

'Where are you going?'

'Don't worry. I shan't be long.'

Tim vanished, as noiselessly as a cat. The grass closed behind him as sea water closes on a fish. After half an hour which seemed like a whole week to Gilles, he reappeared, one hand carelessly gripping a whitish bundle with sinister dark stains. Gilles watched him hand it over solemnly to the boy and shuddered.

'What is it?' he whispered. 'You surely can't have—'

With no change of expression, Tim bowed deeply to Igrak whose eyes had begun to sparkle in the gloom, at the same time murmuring through his teeth : 'The hussars drink deep and sleep the better for it. I had no trouble relieving them of their wigs, and they'll be punished for their loss in the morning which brings joy to my vindictive spirit.'

'But – the blood? There's blood on them.'

'A belated chicken. I cut its throat over them. Looks pretty good, doesn't it? And just look at the kid. He's as happy as a king, and he believes in it. Of course, it will be harder to get his brother to swallow it, but I'll have a word with him. If you ask me, the boy has amply proved his courage. And then – well, we must be off and sufficient unto the day is the evil thereof! Come on! There is a fishing village opposite Prudence Island where we can get a boat to cross to the mainland.'

Gilles' laughter was echoed by the cry of an owl, disturbed in its hunting, but in another moment the spinney was quiet again.

8

The Captive Girl

'Three million! No more than three million!'

Startled, Gilles stared for a moment at the Rebel leader, wondering how to take this and whether it were some kind of private jest on the part of a gentleman who, at first sight, had made such a deep impression on him. But General Washington was rereading Rochambeau's letter with a care that ruled out any possibility of jesting, so that the younger man could not help echoing his last words.

'No more?' he said hesitantly. 'May I point out, sir, that that is an immense sum of money?'

The Virginian's stern, handsome face was illumined by a brief smile. Just for a moment, it held the charm of a wintry sea lit by a ray of sunshine. Washington liked the spontaneity of youth and he was amused by the faintly shocked tone of the young Frenchman in the deerskin jacket with his ready command of English.

'For a regiment, or even for a town under siege, yes, I agree with you. But not for an army which has been short of everything for far too long. We could do with thirty million— Not,' he added quickly, 'that this is not very welcome. It will enable us to deal with our most pressing needs. I'll give orders at once for a party to be sent to collect it, as discreetly as possible.'

Discretion again! The history of this cargo of gold was beginning to look like a comic opera. Rochambeau and Ternay bringing it in great secrecy and now Washington collecting it just as secretly, as if he were not master in his own house! The look on Gilles' expressive face did not escape the General's grey eyes.

'Is there something troubling you?'

Gilles flushed brick red.

'Forgive me, General. I am only surprised at so much discretion. Here you are in your own camp, amongst your own men. What have you to fear?'

'Nothing, to be sure, except for tradesmen, the suppliers of this very army. If it were known that I possessed so large a sum they would make me pay two or three times as much for what it has already cost me much trouble to extort from them at prohibitive prices. What is more, my men have had no pay for five months. They might imagine that the days of the fat kine have returned. Which is far from being the case! So I would ask you, too, to be very discreet. Leave me now, gentlemen. You have travelled a long way and must be in need of rest. I will see you again tomorrow. Until then, Colonel Hamilton will look after you.' He indicated his aide-de-camp who was standing blocking the doorway.

Gilles and Tim bowed and turned to leave the modest house which had served General Washington as headquarters since he and his army had arrived in the village of Peekskill on the left bank of the Hudson River. But the General called them back.

'Just a moment! General Rochambeau tells me he would like me to keep you with me for a little while. He says also that you have an interesting prisoner, the brother of an Indian chief?'

This time it was Tim who answered.

'Own brother to Sagoyewatha, chief of the Wolf clan of the Senecas who is—'

'I know who Red Jacket is,' Washington interrupted. 'That is what interests me. But I have to think. I will see you tomorrow.'

The two friends found themselves outside and, after collecting Igrak from the guard room, they followed Colonel Hamilton, whose age must have been twenty at the most, through the canvas city which the war had caused to spring up below the mountains, on the hill of Peekskill. Gilles looked about him with interest. The American camp was about the

186

same size as the French one at Newport but it looked very much poorer. The tents, their entrances concealed by odd-looking stoves, very necessary in winter, were sooty, patched and dirty. The soldiers were dressed all anyhow, many of them in rags and those that had them in grey uniforms and strange moulded leather hats with draggled plumes, like tufts of grass, at the back. As to their weapons, they were so obviously antique that they must have witnessed not merely the loss of Canada by the French seventeen years earlier but even the actual conquest of some of the thirteen states whose stars were to be seen on the new American flag that flew so merrily over all this wretchedness.

'If I were the general,' Gilles observed in an undertone, 'I shouldn't be so uppity about the gold I was given. It seems to me he needs it badly. In all fairness, he should have hugged me.'

'He smiled at you,' said Colonel Hamilton, who had overheard this. 'With him, that's a sign of delirious happiness. As for our men, they may not look much, but they can fight. And wait until you see our cavalry! Your La Fayette says he's rarely seen anything to touch it.'

'I meant no aspersion on your troops, Colonel. Indeed, it would ill become me since you, for your part, might judge the King of France's men by my appearance, which is scarcely brilliant.'

Rochambeau's emissaries had in fact taken less than five days to cover the forty-odd leagues of forest, intersected with lakes and swamps, which lay between Rhode Island and the Hudson River. They were hideously dirty and the smell of them would have put off a badger, while they were having a perpetual struggle to stay awake. Or at least Gilles was, for Tim, inured by long usage to extensive journeys over difficult ground, had calmly hoisted Igrak over his shoulder as they left the General's tent without even waking him. The Indian boy had fallen straight into the sleep of exhaustion at the feet of the sentry into whose care they had given him on their arrival.

Hamilton led his general's guests as far as the wooden palisades bordering the river. There, by the entrance to the camp, stood a collection of buildings, part tents, part Indian huts, about which moved a number of persons recognizable by their sunbonnets as women. These were the 'Molly Pitchers', the camp followers who carried water to the men in battle, assisted the surgeons and did what they could to improve the soldiers' fare by such means as came to hand, notably by quiet depredations on the neighbouring farmyards. They got their name from the heroic woman who, at the battle of Monmouth courthouse, had taken her wounded husband's place in the firing line and had kept the whole regiment supplied with water. It was, indeed, a very affectionate nickname.

The young colonel went up to one of the women, a little dark creature, as wizened as a prune and barely half as tall as her companions but who nevertheless appeared to be a person of authority among them.

'Janet Mulligan,' he said, 'the General sends you these two boys. They are his guests and he would have you look after them until the morning. They need food and rest.'

Without a word, Janet left her tub and the washing in it, dried her hands on her hips and stalked across to Tim. She gazed at his burden with a jaundiced eye and sniffed.

'And that?' she said, pointing a soapy finger at Igrak. 'Do I have to take care of that as well?'

'More than of the other two,' Hamilton assured her imperturbably. 'He's the General's hostage.'

'Then let him look to him himself! He's an Iroquois. And I want none of them here. My man Harvey was scalped and burned alive at German Flats by those devils belonging to the Mohawk chief Joseph Brant. I'd rather starve than give a pinch of maize to one of those brigands! Be off with you! Get him out of here! Take the creature away and if the General doesn't like it he can come and ask me why himself. Isn't that right, girls?'

The group of women that had gathered round the washtub as round an altar, chorused their agreement.

Such unanimity drew a beaming smile from Janet.

'We're all agreed, you see, Colonel Hamilton. So you can put your Indian where you like so long as you get him out of here. As to the other two—'

'Madam,' Gilles interposed, bowing as deeply as to a great lady, 'all we ask of you is some quiet corner where this child may go on sleeping. We ourselves will find food for him. As

188

the colonel has told you, he is of great importance to your general.'

Janet's eyes widened in surprise as they took in the young man, from muddied moccasins to tangled fair hair.

'What have we here? He's as dirty as a pot, as beautiful as a god and he talks like a lord. Except that no lord ever spoke to me like that . . . Madam, he says! Madam! To me!'

Gilles laughed. 'I am a Frenchman,' he said, 'and you are a woman. To us, all women are – are ladies. I came here with the King of France's army, to fight alongside you, and it was I who captured this child. The General holds him to be valuable. I beseech you – madam – give us a corner to put him in. My friend cannot carry him over his shoulder all night long.'

Quite unexpectedly, Janet Mulligan was blushing like a girl, eyelashes aflutter. She broke into a sudden smile and even sketched a curtsy.

'Don't you be giving me those looks, young sir! Such eyes as you've got! Such eyes! There then, just you come this way.'

Without further explanation, she herself led the travellers to a tent and began kicking out of it various cooking pots and other implements. That done, she begged them to make themselves at home, adding that whatever they wished for they had only to ask.

Nor did the kindness of Janet and her friends end there. Clearly much taken with the young Frenchman, they bustled round him, miraculously producing bread, not too stale, meat that was edible and cool beer. Then, when Gilles made known his intention of washing in the river, they generously presented him with a piece of soap, which they made themselves.

'This isn't the place for you,' Tim teased him, as they splashed together in the sun-warmed waters of the Hudson River. 'You ought to be in the Indies. You'd have made a fine sultan. All these women are in love with you already.'

'What do you expect?. There can't be many Frenchmen here. I am a curiosity to them, that's all.'

'The curiosity is all on their side. Take a look over by those bushes. They're all there, watching us take our dip. I guess they want to see if a Frenchman strips like an American.'

Tim executed a neat dive, his buttocks gleamed for an instant in the sunshine and then he vanished under water,

swimming out into the stream like a great otter, while Gilles
lay back idly and let the great river carry him along on its
green waters, flowing majestically between wooded banks. At
that moment it was hard to remember that they were at war, for
all that rich countryside basked in an almost divine peace. Only,
here and there, were wooden forts whose obvious newness
gave them away and downstream some suspicious smoke was
dissolving in the blue sky. And when Gilles swam across to the
far bank, he caught a glimpse of distant black points : the spars
of the English vessels anchored in the Hudson River. New York
was not much more than thirty miles away.

The true face of war showed itself once more in the blaze
of the setting sun, when, with a thunderous noise of hoofbeats
raising echoes in the countryside, three troops of cavalry
loomed up through the dust and swept in through the wide-
open gates of the camp, yelling a savage song of victory at the
tops of their voices. They were led by a kind of centaur in rent
and bloodstained garments, white teeth bared in laughter and
flourishing a reddened sword. He was guiding his splendid
devil of a horse with his knees alone.

'Colonel Delancey,' Tim remarked. 'And part of the famous
Virginia cavalry. What do you think of them?'

'Nothing at all,' Gilles said, his eyes devouring the amazing
display of horsemanship, the magnificent animals and the
infectious enthusiasm emanating from the men. 'I'm lost in
admiration! I think I'm going to enjoy fighting alongside men
like that.'

Lying on the bare ground under a blanket, lent by Janet,
which was very nearly clean, Gilles lay awake late into the
night, listening to the noises of the camp and the cries of the
seabirds, so reminiscent of Brittany. Tired as he was, excitement drove out sleep. He was impatient for the morning,
impatient to find out what it was that this amazing General
Washington, of whom even the English said that there was
not a king in Europe but would look like a lackey next to him,
wanted them to do for him. So far he had seen nothing of the
war but the interminable preparations for it, a distant encounter
with the English fleet at sea and the routine of camp life,
manoeuvres, discussions and politics, and the joys of the com-
missariat. But the men around him had been fighting for

months and every day brought its quota of arms and bloodshed. Gilles wanted his share in all this, and he wanted it now.

All at once, in spite of the din of Tim's snores filling the tent, he was aware of a slight rustle. The canvas flap across the entrance was raised noiselessly, then the rustling was resumed. Someone was crawling inside.

Gilles' hand slid to his side, touched the handle of the hunting knife at his belt and closed upon it firmly. At the same time, he eased the folds of blanket gently aside, preparing to defend himself against attack . . . But as he did so he felt groping hands and a smell of soap and wet grass filled his nostrils.

Quickly, he grasped one of the hands and knew, from the faint squeak she gave, that it was a woman.

'Who are you?' he whispered. 'What do you want?'

'Hush! ,You'll wake your friend. Janet Mulligan sent me. I'm her niece, Betty. As to what I want—'

'Well?'

She gave a stifled giggle and he was suddenly aware of warm hands parting the front of his deerskin shirt and sliding over his chest.

'Janet wants me to welcome you on behalf of the girls of America,' Betty whispered teasingly. 'She said you ought to be pleased because that's all Frenchmen think of!' And with that, she was on him. Warm, hard breasts, firm thighs, hot belly and moist lips all moulded themselves to the young man's body and instinctively he closed his arms on them.

As his fingers touched the soft skin of her bare back, he felt a long shiver run through the girl, like an electric shock which passed irresistibly into his own body. The great hunger for love which he had felt in Manon's arms returned to him and gladly he embraced the unexpected gift. The honour of Frenchmen was at stake. Ripping off the remainder of his clothes, he crushed the yielding body to him fiercely and gave free rein to the accumulated desires of many months.

Dawn was approaching when the tent flap was raised once more to let out the woman whom he knew only by touch and Gilles at last allowed sleep to flow over him like a beneficent wave, with no thought in his head but that America was a wonderful country and the soldier's life the finest in the world.

As for Tim, the storm of passion which had been unleashed a couple of yards away from him had disturbed him not at all. He had snored on through it all.

General Washington waved the end of his telescope towards the far bank of the Hudson River.

'Less than ten miles from here is West Point, our best defended position on the river and the key to our strategy. The fortifications, for which, like nearly all those in these parts, we are indebted to a young Polish colonel of engineers, Colonel Kosciusko, are built on an inaccessible rock and covered by shore-level batteries placed on a low island. The Hudson is also blocked at that point by a great chain. The position is impregnable . . . except by treachery. That is the place where I have ordered General Allen's company of militia, which is to take delivery of the gold, to deposit it. In that way I can be certain that not one penny of it will be diverted to causes other than the needs of the army. So you see,' he added, with the half smile that gave him such charm, 'I do value the French loan at its true worth.'

'I never doubted it, General,' Gilles answered. 'Or that, for the moment, you are sure of the place and its keeper. But did you not say that it might fall by treachery?'

Washington's face resumed its earlier sternness.

'You are not an American, sir, or you would never dare to voice any such suspicion. General Benedict Arnold, who commands West Point, is one of our real heroes, the victor of our greatest battle, Saratoga—'

'But his style of life is ruinous and he is always short of money,' put in another voice, an unmistakably American one this time. Washington spun round as though stung.

'I know you do not like Arnold, Hamilton, and that you disapproved of his marriage to Miss Shippen because she comes from one of the most influential tory families, but to go from there to believing him capable of treachery— Must I remind you that he is my friend and I trust him?'

There was the faintest tremor of anger in his voice but his face, thanks to the exceptional degree of self-control that characterized him, remained expressionless. Hamilton stiffened at the rebuke but took it without flinching.

'I beg your pardon, General. But I maintain that West Point is not the ideal place in which to put what amounts to our total war resources. Your friendship has saved General Arnold once already, when he was called upon at the Council of War to account for the finances of his army during the Quebec expedition. Aren't you tempting providence a little?'

'That will do, Colonel Hamilton. We will not discuss the matter any further. Come, gentlemen. Now that your first mission has been so successfully completed, we must talk about the task I have for you.'

Turning on his heel, Washington made off rapidly in the direction of his headquarters. Gilles followed him, somewhat startled at hearing a junior officer so openly disputing his superior's orders. Tim, at his side, gave a chuckle.

'With us, anyone may give his opinion, even on the gravest matters. That is what we call democracy—'

'Democracy,' Gilles echoed, liking the new sound of the classical word on his friend's lips. 'Have we gone back two thousand years and are you the new Athenians?'

'I don't know if we're the new – whatever it was you said, but I do know one thing, and that is that we've had more than enough of the King of England and his henchmen. We simply want to be ourselves! We are grown big enough! And now, shall we go and see what the great white chief wants of us?'

An hour later, Tim and Gilles left the camp at Peekskill on horseback, having been mounted by the General, and with Igrak up behind. They were followed by the noisy farewells of the Molly Pitchers who crowded to the river bank to watch them go. Gilles' eyes lingered for a moment on a tall, fair girl standing next to Janet Mulligan who blew him a kiss as he passed. That must be Betty and he was glad to see that her eyes were clear and the sun played prettily on her hair. He returned her kiss with a surge of gratitude for the soft body which had given him so much pleasure.

'We'll meet again, Betty,' he called into the light southerly breeze. She broke into a laugh that showed her strong, white teeth.

'God and the redcoats willing, handsome cavalier – whenever you like!'

193

'She'd do better to say the Senecas willing,' Tim growled. His cheerful face had grown somewhat grimmer since they had been given their orders. 'If we come out of this adventure with a whole skin we can think it a miracle. We'll be lucky if it costs us no more than our scalps.'

But the agreeable recollections of the past night had put Gilles in too good a humour to be disturbed by his friend's pessimistic forecasts.

'If I hadn't heard you snoring all night long, I'd say you'd not slept well, my lad! Or didn't you hear what Washington said? We are envoys of peace. We are going to return to Sagoyewatha a brother he probably thinks lost and whom, in the greatness of his heart, the great white chief is restoring to him, even though he had been taken prisoner. That's a friendly gesture, surely? In a way, we're holding out the hand of friendship from the Rebels to their free red brothers. I can't see why Sagoyewatha should take our scalps for that!'

'Damn me if he doesn't believe it!' Tim burst out. 'He talks as though it were gospel true! Messengers of peace! More like seeds of discord, if you ask me! You forget the second half of our commission, to insinuate to the chief of the Wolf clan that his brother in Gitche Manito the god of thunder, the Iroquois chief Cornplanter, is actually a base villain with no thought but to break the alliance of the Six Nations so as to seize his possessions and rob him of his wife into the bargain. Well, let me tell you, if Sagoyewatha spares our scalps, Cornplanter won't, because he'll very soon find out what's afoot. That man has spies everywhere – and he is a wild beast to make a cougar look like a tame kitten.'

'Then why did you agree? You say you have the right to dispute your general's orders. You should have refused.'

Tim Thocker seemed to swell up suddenly and his face grew so red that Gilles half-expected him to breathe fire from his nostrils.

'Because I'm a damned fool. And because I rather like the idea of spreading trouble among the Six Nations who are doing such good work for the English. It's just that it's only my mind likes the idea. My body would rather stay in one piece for Miss Martha Carpenter, on the day she lets me lead her to the altar.'

Gilles laughed.

194

'Well, since there's no going back, the best thing is to get it over with as soon as possible. In a case like this, there is nothing worse than indecision. Come on!'

He spurred his horse to a gallop along the easy road beside the river. They were to cross by the ferry at Stony Point and then make their way north-west through the Catskills to the Seneca chief's new camp on the bank of the Susquehanna. Igrak was to show them the exact location.

'Since he went on the warpath, Sagoyewatha has had to leave his grounds by Lake Cayuga, because they have been ravaged by the Rebels, and find other maizefields,' Igrak had told them.

The distance covered by the youthful scalp hunter in his quest for glory – not far off a hundred leagues – was not the least cause of amazement to Gilles. For a child of that age, it was a considerable exploit, but Tim had seemed much less surprised.

'The initiation rites of the Iroquois can be mighty tough,' was all he said. 'Distance is nothing to them, nor is time when it comes to winning fame. As the son and brother of chiefs, Igrak is hoping one day to be the kind of warrior whose deeds are handed down for generations.'

'I shouldn't be surprised if he were.'

The boy was certainly proud, noble and brave. They had learned that by living with him. His whole behaviour, the silence he maintained for most of the time, were far in advance of his age and often, as they journeyed, they had seen him go apart by himself, not to try and escape but simply to be alone beside a swamp or in a hollow cave, and he might crouch there, motionless, for hours, as though listening to the immensity of nature all around. Sometimes he would pick up a stone, or the fallen feather of a bird, sometimes a plant, and put it carefully into the little leather bag he wore round his neck.

'He is making his own medicine,' Tim would say then, watching him out of the corner of his eye. 'Which means that he is collecting things he thinks might bring him luck.'

'But how does he choose them?'

'He doesn't. The things must be linked to a dream that he has had or to some premonition. Warriors usually do it later, but Igrak's uncle, Hiakin, Bear Face, is the Senecas' medicine

195

man – a great wizard. Perhaps the boy hopes to succeed him. If that is so, he must be precious to the tribe and we may have a hope of saving our scalps.'

The idea seemed to reassure him and he faced up to the remainder of their journey with less nervousness.

Some days after leaving Peekskill, the three travellers reached the crest of the last rocky slope before the Susquehanna.

'You're in such a hurry to find out how they'll serve us up for dinner. Well, you won't have to wait much longer,' Tim announced, pointing to the winding ribbon of the river. 'If the kid has told us right, his brother's camp can't be more than half an hour's march away.'

But Gilles made no answer. For some moments he had been watching the evolutions of a bird, obviously a bird of prey, which had caught his eye. It was a splendid creature, a little smaller than an eagle but no less regal and startlingly white.

Wings outspread, it glided along invisible columns of air in wide, planing circles, high, high above the wooded shoulders of the mountain. It sailed against the blue sky, hieratic and formidable, the whiteness of its feathers in no way detracting from the power of its beak and claws. The young man stopped, fascinated.

'Well?' Tim said. 'Are you coming?'

'Look! What is it? An eagle?'

Tim narrowed his eyes against the light.

'No. It looks a little like one but I don't think it is. I think it's a gyrfalcon.'

Gilles' heart missed a beat.

'A gyrfalcon? Are you sure?'

'As sure as one can be of a bird that's not often seen in these parts, for most of its kind live farther north. This one is a splendid specimen.'

With the instinctive movement of the hunter, Tim was already raising his gun but Gilles stopped him with a cry.

'No!' More quietly, he added : 'It would be a shame.'

Tim restored his weapon to its holster without protest.

'You're right. And stupid, too. We are too near the Indian camp and they identify those birds with their tutelary god, the thunderbird.'

They went on. The path ran downhill through trees but it

was broad enough for Gilles to keep an eye on the gyrfalcon which was still flying in wide circles, as though in search of something. Then, without warning, the woodlands fell away on either hand, the path skirted the shoulder of the hill and plunged steeply down to the valley. There lay the Indian camp.

The huts, made of wattle, bark and yellowed reeds, dotted the river bank between the sparkling water and two fields of maize planted in the Indian fashion which gave them an unfamiliar look. For it was the Iroquois custom to plant four grains of maize and two beans in every hole. The result was a mottled greenery very pleasing to the eye, but a ring of sharpened pine stakes surrounded the camp and its plantations and hid the view.

The huts were shaped like boxes with rounded lids and most were covered with deerskin painted in bright colours. Female figures with long black plaits were busy about the cooking fires, pounding grain in stone mortars and plucking the game the hunters had killed. Some of these, half-naked men with shaven heads, except for one long black lock of hair entwined with feathers, were gathered about the largest of the huts, before which stood a pole bushed like a poplar tree with the scalps that hung from it. Down by the waterside, where lay several canoes which could be reached by a wide opening in the surrounding fence, near-naked children were playing among the chickens and skinny dogs.

Gilles' eyes took in the unfamiliar sight eagerly. The camp was enormous. The violent colours of the huts and the women's clothes gave it an air of richness. As for the tall warriors with their gleaming dark skins, they looked powerful and dangerous.

'What do you think of it?' Tim murmured. 'Still in a hurry to get a closer look at a tribe of Iroquois?'

'More than ever! It's just as you described, and everything I dreamed of! Whatever happens, I'll never regret coming. The land, the people and the animals are all equally splendid and proud.' He glanced up for a last look at the gyrfalcon. 'Good God!'

The bird of prey had suddenly ceased its graceful planing flight and with a beat of its powerful wings was stooping on something moving in one of the two fields – something which, though vague in detail, was unquestionably human. From where they stood, the two young men could see light hair showing above the hump of a sack the figure was carrying on its back.

'It's a woman,' Tim said tonelessly. 'A white woman! The bird must have been attracted by her hair. He's going for her—'

His words were drowned in a scream, as the gyrfalcon bore down on the fair head. Gilles' gun was already in his hand. He had moved as swiftly as the striking bird. He put it to his shoulder and fired, almost without taking aim. The sound of the shot, thrown back by the mountains, was deafening but the gyrfalcon released its victim and fell to the ground.

'Nice shot,' Tim said appreciatively. 'But this is where the trouble starts. We may as well give up any idea of sneaking in quietly. The whole camp is already on the warpath.'

But Gilles was not listening. He had set spurs to his horse and, at the risk of his neck, was clattering down the steep slope to the maizefield. Seconds later, he descended thunderously on the crowd that was collecting round the dead bird and its victim. Strangely, however, he spared little attention for the latter. He had a vague impression of a bundle of rags with a grimy face emerging from it, blue eyes still wide with terror and a faded head of yellow hair streaked with blood.

'No great harm done?' he inquired merely.

The creature shook her head but already Gilles had forgotten her. He had gone down on one knee and, bending, lifted the gyrfalcon tenderly. The bird had been killed outright but its limp body was still warm and the touch of the soft, bloodied feathers filled Gilles with a mixture of grief and rage. It seemed to him that in attacking this beautiful white killer he had turned against all those of his own kind, had somehow broken faith with them. They had all been birds of prey, magnificently impervious to pity or to anything else but their own will, and he had ranged himself alongside the featureless herd of their victims. For the sake of a dirty, shapeless being he had been told was a woman, he had slaughtered one of God's most glorious creatures, the sign of destiny which only a short while before had been sailing proudly in the skies that now spread above him, the shade, it might be, of Taran himself . . .

198

Tim's big hand on his arm brought him back to reality.

'I think you've just signed our death warrant,' the American said softly. 'Look.'

Slowly, but without laying down the bird in his hands, Gilles rose to his feet. Lost in his own remorse, he had not noticed the circle of Indian warriors drawing closer about them. With their gleaming skins and the black and white designs painted on them, they looked like frescoes done on Spanish leather, but they were armed with bows and feathered spears and every eye was alight with hatred and anger.

'Let's try what talking can do, at any rate,' Tim sighed.

Drawing himself up to his full height, he advanced upon an elderly man who, from the sort of crown of crimson-dyed deerskin and the necklace of bear's teeth which he wore, seemed to be the leader. He raised his right hand to shoulder level and moved it in a circle, palm outwards, then, half closing it so that only the index and middle fingers remained upright in the form of a V, he brought it down slowly until it was on a level with his waist before beginning on a speech which, except for occasional mentions of the names of Igrak and Sagoyewatha, was perfectly unintelligible to Gilles.

This went on for some while and not for a moment did the Senecas abandon their attitudes of scornful immobility. Then, all at once, while Tim Thocker was still speaking, the man in the red crown stretched out his arm, pointing imperiously to the two white men. Instantly, several pairs of hands seized and overpowered them, binding their hands behind their backs with ropes of plaited hemp.

'Your speech doesn't seem to have gone down too well,' Gilles remarked. 'Have we got the wrong tribe, or do these people not care much for their children? It's nice to bring one back to them—'

Igrak, who had remained silent throughout Tim's speech, had now slipped off the horse and was running to the old Indian, trying to get between the warriors and his new friends and pouring out a stream of explanations to which the man listened with a smile. He laid his hand affectionately on the boy's head and spoke a few words to him, but, despite his protests, would not allow him to rejoin those whom he was evidently trying to defend. Instead, he handed him over to two of his companions who bore him off to the camp, shouting and struggling for all he was worth. Tim shrugged.

'I was ready to bet this was how it would be. You can't argue with the Iroquois. They're like wild animals.'

'I thought Sagoyewatha was a young man?' Gilles said, with a jerk of his head towards the man with the crown.

'He is a young man, and a wise and cautious one, too. This is his uncle, Hiakin, otherwise known as Bear Face, the Senecas' chief medicine man. He takes the chief's place when he is away – and that means that Sagoyewatha is not here and we are lost. He was our only chance.'

Pushed and jostled by men who seemed to feel a fierce hatred for them, the two young men passed through the palisade into the Indian village, whither Igrak and the gyrfalcon's victim had already preceded them. She, in fact, had been unceremoniously driven away with contemptuous kicks that made her lowly status in the tribe sufficiently clear.

'A slave!' Tim growled. 'Some poor creature taken in a raid, I suppose, and, as ill luck will have it, one of ours! You saw her fair hair? She's a white woman—'

As to the bird, it had been wrenched from Gilles' grasp and Hiakin himself now bore it, laid on his two hands which were raised before his face towards the setting sun.

Some moments later, Gilles and Tim were thrust by their captors into harsh contact with the floor of a dark, cramped hut that reeked unbearably of rotten fish. Even so, they greeted it with a kind of relief because their passage through the village, between a double row of women transformed into a horde of furies hurling everything that came to hand, had been far from pleasant.

Gilles had landed face down and so managed to scramble up without too much difficulty, in spite of his bound hands, and seat himself with his back against a post. His eyes soon grew accustomed to the gloom and he looked for his friend, who was crawling about like a huge snail in his efforts to get up.

'What do you think they'll do with us?'

'Nothing pleasant. Not for us, at any rate, because we can always comfort ourselves with the knowledge that we shall provide them with some excellent entertainment. There's nothing the Iroquois enjoy more than putting a prisoner to death in due form. And two prisoners!'

Gilles looked at it from every angle and decided that their situation was very far from enviable, but discovered to his satisfaction that he was not unduly perturbed.

'I see,' he said coolly. 'Will it – take long?'

Tim, who had managed to hoist himself up alongside his friend, uttered a short, mirthless laugh.

'I should think so. We are white warriors and as such have a right to every consideration.'

'Meaning?'

'That they will be pleased to honour us with their most re-fined tortures. And you can't think how imaginative they can be.'

For all his courage, Gilles could not help feeling an un-pleasant prickle up his spine. Staring death in the face was one thing, but watching it creep up on you inch by inch through an eternity of suffering was quite another.

'Oh well – I may as well make up my mind to it,' he sighed. 'In the meantime, move round until your hands are touching mine. I'm going to try and untie you. I hate the idea of sitting here like a fowl trussed for the spit.'

The cords were tight but his fingers managed to find the knot and set to work.

'Do you think it will be tonight?' he asked after a moment. 'Because if so, I'm wasting my time.'

'No. It will probably be tomorrow, at sunrise. Go on. If you can't do it, I'll have a try at yours.'

It was not an easy task and took a long time, and after all he did not have time to finish it, for just as the first knot gave way men came to fetch them from their prison.

Darkness had fallen but the whole village was out of doors and a huge fire had been lighted in the centre, with two garishly painted posts beside it, casting a bright glow over the whole area, as far as the wooded slopes across the river. Round this open space, the Senecas stood in a wide, silent circle. This time, no one stirred as the prisoners passed but an almost voluptuous sigh went up, like a signal.

'They are already gloating over the thought of watching us die,' Gilles thought in a cold anger.

As they tied him to one of the posts, his mind went back a few years to a time when, in the course of one of his boyhood rambles, he had lost himself in the deep forest that stretched to the north of Hennebont. As it got dark, he had seen the eyes of a pack of wolves gleaming in the shadows and had owed his safety only to a tall tree in which he had taken refuge. A party of peasants, led by the Chevalier de Langle, had come in the morning and rescued him – but tonight no stout Bretons or bold hunter would come and scatter the circle of bright eyes waiting avidly for the first blood.

Pride drew him up to his full height. His cold, contemptuous blue gaze travelled over the onlookers, most of whom were old men, women and children. It seemed that Tim was right and most of the warriors were away. Only those absolutely necessary to guard the camp had been left behind. A mere handful. He turned his head towards Tim.

'They are in a mighty hurry to see us die,' he said bitterly. 'They aren't even going to leave us until tomorrow.'

The woodsman shook his head.

'I still think it will not be right away. On the other hand, I think we stand a good chance of spending the night in this uncomfortable position, so that fatigue may increase our sufferings and sap our courage.'

He broke off at the sound of a number of drums being beaten rapidly. Some young boys were crouching on either side of the entrance to one of the largest huts, holding small drums between their knees and pounding away at them. Almost at once, the deerskin curtain across the hut doorway was flung aside and Hiakin appeared. The red designs painted on his body and the shaggy headdress on his shaven crown, joined to his height and the peculiar set of his features, which did indeed have some resemblance to a bear's, all made him look like some malevolent deity. He paced slowly up to the prisoners until he stood before them, arms folded high on his chest.

'Men of the salt,'[1] he said in excellent English. 'You come to us with false hearts, intending evil—'

'You lie!' Gilles interrupted him. 'We come to you in peace, bearing words of friendship from the great chief who commands the American army.'

[1] i.e. from over the sea.

202

'Words of friendship from an enemy are always false. We have made a treaty with our friends, the Redcoats. We cannot listen to words of peace from their enemies, the men of the coast.'

A harsh chuckle sounded incongruously at Gilles' side. Tim was indulging in a crack of sardonic laughter.

'You, Hiakin, the great medicine man of the Senecas, the one who speaks with the Great Spirit and for whom the veil of the future is no more than a fine mist, do you proclaim yourself the slave of the Redcoats? Do you confess that you serve them? Moreover you lie, as my friend said. You lie like a frightened old woman. He is no man of the salt but a soldier of the mighty King of France who reigns on the other side of the water, in a palace so splendid that beside it those of your redcoat masters are like the lodges of beavers! Have you forgotten that we have made a long journey in order to return to your camp fires the younger brother of your chief, Sagoyewatha, the wisest of the wise, "he who speaks that others may remain awake" – and he to whom we have been sent?'

The medicine man's blue lips stretched into a broad, contemptuous grin.

'It is not hard to capture a child who takes himself for a man, and easier still to win his innocent young heart. After that the two faces of the spy may readily put on the smile of friendship in order to infiltrate our council fires. But Hiakin is not deceived. As you yourself said, the Great Spirit is his guide – and the Great Spirit calls for the blood of those who have dared to strike down his favourite messenger, the great white bird which was coming to me. Therefore I, Hiakin, say that tomorrow, when the sun quits his bed of darkness, you, men of the salt, shall enter into the kingdom of death, slowly, as befits the warriors you claim to be.'

Gilles' eyes, coolly ironic, rested on those of the sorcerer.

'You reason ill, Bear Face. You speak of warriors, yet you do not seem to understand what that word means. The laws of war are noble laws and you know nothing of them, for you do not respect a parley. With God's help – the help of my God, to whom your Great Spirit is merely an apprentice – I shall show you how a soldier of the King of France can die. You shall see—'

He broke off, all the breath suddenly taken from him. The Indian village, the rushing river tumbling by, the background of mountains and even the hedge of cruel eyes that stood between him and life, all these vanished from Gilles' sight as though by magic. Rising out of the darkness like a new dawn, a young woman had come to stand at Hiakin's side, a young woman of such beauty as he had never known was possible.

Tall, slender and graceful, she had a face to dream about, with a wonderful golden skin and huge eyes that shone like pools of pale gold between thick lashes, highlighting the warmer colour of her skin and the red rosebud lips, parted slightly to show a gleam of white teeth, which were the very image of sensuality. Her white dress, ornamented with garlands of black and green leaves, clung so closely to her body that it might have been painted on. It was as if it had been moulded to her, a second skin making unseemly revelations about the length of her thighs, the soft shadows at her groin and unashamed perfection of her breasts. Below the narrow white band that confined it, her midnight hair fell in a shining stream to her knees. She bore herself like a queen, but her slightest movement was a poem of sensual delight.

She stood for a moment in silence, contemplating the prisoner, who was devouring her with his eyes. His face was suddenly much older and she read in it such evident desire that heat flamed in her cheeks and it was with difficulty that she turned her eyes away.

'Why such haste, Hiakin?' she said, and she too spoke in English. 'The crime these men have committed is very grave but it was Sagoyewatha they came to see. You might at least wait for his return before putting them to death . . . or have you forgotten that you are not the chief?'

Her voice was low and grave with a husky note in it which gave it a peculiar charm, while at the same time in no way detracting from the faintly contemptuous irony of her tone.

'I am sole ruler in his absence,' the other reported. 'Sagoyewatha has declared it, Sitapanoki! And no one should know it better than you, his beloved wife. Moreover these men have killed the bird which strikes like lightning. None of these people would understand it if they should not be put to death with no more delay than that required by our custom.'

The lovely Indian girl's small teeth gleamed in a mocking smile.

'They would understand it very well if you were to take the trouble to explain it to them, Hiakin. They believe every word that falls from your lips, for they think that they are all inspired by the Great Spirit – even when it is not so! In any case, I have no need of the Great Spirit to predict that my valiant husband will be greatly displeased to find only rotting corpses where there might have been ambassadors—'

'Your valiant husband is a weak man too much inclined to listen to the honeyed words of his enemies. It is best that these two should die. Nor do I fear his anger. Go back to your house, woman! Tomorrow, if you wish, you may take part in the festival with the other squaws.'

The great liquid golden eyes flamed with sudden anger.

'I am no squaw as others are, Hiakin. Nor will I permit you to forget it. This man is a Frenchman and his people and mine were linked by long friendship in the past, before they were massacred by the Iroquois. Moreover, he has brought Igrak back to us. If he dies tomorrow, my husband will listen to my voice as well as to yours – and more, perhaps!'

They were confronting one another now, the man with the face of a bear and the woman with the sun in her eyes, and although neither abated one jot of their dignity, the hatred between them was almost palpable. It was like the eternal challenge of the forces of light to the power of darkness, angel and devil – but the angel had a body which set Gilles' blood on fire. He strained unconsciously at his bonds, like a captive wolf, in an involuntary movement towards the woman who had turned, with a gracefully disdainful lift of her shoulders, and was walking easily away. She vanished inside the chief's hut and Hiakin's loud voice followed her before the deerskin curtain dropped behind her.

'Yet he shall die like the other, for the Great Spirit demands it and I, Hiakin, say it is my will—'

But Sitapanoki did not reappear. All was over for that night. The drums began beating again and, after a last threatening gesture towards the prisoners, Hiakin too made his way back to his hut and the Indians dispersed in all directions. The prisoners were left alone, bound to their posts beside the fire

205

which was slowly dying down. The gateways to the camp were barred and the Senecas turned to their evening meal. But Gilles' eyes remained fixed on the big hut with its closed doorway, as though he were still hoping for another glimpse of the miraculous vision.

His muscles were growing cramped from the agonizing grip of the ropes and he was beginning to be very tired, but he did not notice it. He had even ceased to remember the hideous death awaiting him when the night was over. Instead, he was suffering unbearably from a curious feeling of frustration and of desolation now that she was no longer there. And he knew that when death came to him he would not be thinking of his lost dreams of glory, or of his blighted hopes, or of the battles he had so longed for and now would never see – nor even of Judith de Saint-Mélaine who would wait for him in vain. He would take with him only one regret, that he had never lived to hold in his arms an Indian girl of whose very existence he had been unaware an hour before.

He heard Tim's lazy voice at his side, sounding strangely unlike himself.

'What a woman!' He sighed. 'I'd heard that she was beautiful but I never imagined anything like that. I can understand why Cornplanter's crazy about her and has sworn to snatch her from her husband. General Washington is damned well informed – though I think Hiakin is going to save us having to carry out our distressing mission. The Six Nations are going to stay united. Sagoyewatha will never know that Cornplanter covets his wife – and the Trojan War will not take place.'

But Gilles' mind was not on Greek history.

'Sitapanoki,' he murmured. 'What a strange name!'

'It means "She whose feet sing when she walks". And not only her feet, either. It's enough to make any man sing to see her, and any woman weep—'

'What was that she was saying about her people?'

'That before France lost Canada they were allies. Sitapanoki is the granddaughter of the last Sagamore of the Algonquins, who were defeated by the Iroquois. She could have been no better than a captive, like that wretched girl you saved from the gyrfalcon, but for her beauty, which is so great that she won the heart of the Seneca chief—'

206

Beside them, the fire had sunk to a few glowing embers. Slowly, the darkness was gathering round them. Yet the night was clear and, looking up, the two prisoners could see the sky riddled with stars. The night wind brought with it all the scents of the mountain.

'It may be our last night,' Gilles murmured, 'but it's very beautiful . . .'

'Maybe, but I'd rather it poured with rain if I could have a good draught of rum.'

They fell silent. Each wrapped in his own thoughts, trying to get some rest by supporting their weight on the ropes that held them, but already their numbed limbs were becoming an agony.

Time passed. The wind freshened. One by one, the noises of the Indian village died away and soon there was nothing to be heard but the distant cries of night birds – and a snoring which told Gilles that Tim had somehow succeeded in falling asleep.

All at once, he was aware of a presence close beside him. Clouds had covered the stars and the night was darker now but he could still make out a crouching human figure. It stood up as he peered at it.

'I am going to cut your bonds,' whispered a voice. 'Then I'll free your friend.'

The voice was a woman's but it was almost impossible to distinguish any other details of the shadowy bundle. Hands searched for the ropes, slid a knife under them and began to cut . . .

'Who are you?' Gilles breathed. 'I had not looked for any help among these savages—'

'I am she you saved from the bird and for whose sake you are to die. I do not want that. A slave—'

'A captive,' the young man corrected her. 'And you belong to my own people. What is your name?'

'Before I became less than a dog, I was called Gunilla.'

9

Cicero and Attila

Gunilla's knife was sharp. In a few seconds, Gilles and Tim were both free. It took a little longer for them to regain the use of their limbs.

'What do we do now?' whispered the hunter. 'How are we to get out of the village?'

'There is a broken stake in the palisade. It is possible to shift it – possible for a man, that is. I've never been able to do it myself, or I should have run away long ago.'

'Well,' Gilles promised, 'you shall run away with us. Show us the way.'

As noiselessly as cats, they crossed the open centre of the village in single file. Tim went first, followed by the slave girl and then Gilles. But when they came to the huts, the route pointed out by Gunilla led past the chief's house and Gilles slowed down, held by a power stronger than his will. There, close by, breathed the woman who still burned in his memory.

It was dark inside the hut. The deerskin curtain drawn across the entrance was not securely fastened and stirred a little in the night air, as though inviting a hand to lift it. Gilles' heart began thudding loudly in his chest and at the same time he was seized again by the same ferment of desire, fierce, demanding and irresistible, which only a little while before, when he was bound to the stake, had made him oblivious even of his own imminent death.

Sitapanoki was there, within two yards of him. He had only to make the slightest move to be with her, to touch her – or merely to watch her as she slept.

'This is madness!' the terrified voice of caution was telling him inwardly. 'Fly! Don't tempt providence . . .'

But Gilles' feet were rooted to the spot. If he went now, he would never see again that divine loveliness which made the Indian girl a living goddess of love, and the thought was more than he could bear. He must see her again! He must see her, even if he died for it.

Someone took his hand and was trying to pull him away.

'What are you doing?' Gunilla hissed. 'There is no time—'

'Just a moment— Leave me.'

'Leave you? Are you mad?'

'Go on! Go with Tim. I'll catch you up in a moment. Go and help him move the post and leave it open.'

But she still clung to him and he saw her eyes flash angrily in the darkness.

'Are you out of your mind? That is the chief's hut. If you go in there, nothing can save you.'

'I know,' Gilles answered impatiently. 'Go on, I tell you—'

He started to prise the clinging hand off his arm but at that moment, with a moan of terror, Gunilla stepped back. The deerskin curtain had been raised and a pale figure stood there. Dark as it was, it seemed to Gilles that the sun had risen.

For an instant, Sitapanoki stood quite still, facing the young man. She was so close that he could hear her breathing. She did not glance at the slave but at a movement of her arm Gunilla faded into the shadows.

'Why do you not escape?' the Indian whispered furiously. 'I have been watching "the stone girl". I knew that she would try to free you. But what are you doing here? Fly!'

But Gilles was past all coherent thought. Seizing hold of the girl, he thrust her back into the hut so that no one could hear them. A mad idea had germinated suddenly in his brain.

'I came to find you,' he said. 'I know all about you. These people are the enemies of your people as they are of mine. Let me take you with me—'

He clasped her to him in the darkness and the touch of her body woke a demon in him. She did not struggle and he heard a soft laugh against his cheek.

'You are as mad as you are young, although your eyes are

like a glacier under the moon. But I do not want to go away. Sagoyewatha loves me – and he is a great chief.'

'And do you love him? Oh come, I beseech you! If you will come with me, I will love you as no other man could ever do—'

'Love me? You love me and yet only yesterday you did not know me?'

'I am not trying to explain it. Look, I ought to have been only too glad to escape, to avoid the death that awaited me, and yet I could not go away from you. I had to see you again, at least one more time. I know you think that I am mad but you have set me on fire, Sitapanoki—'

'And you will be set on fire in good earnest if you do not go away at once! You know my name,' she added with feeling, 'but do you know the eternity of pain Hiakin has in store for you? You will scream for days, perhaps, before death takes you and I shall see you destroyed slowly before my eyes and be powerless even to shorten your sufferings! If "the stone girl" had not released you, I swear by the Great Spirit that I should have done so, but now go—'

'Not without you.' And before she could even stir, he had swept her up in his arms and was carrying her out of the hut. He was beyond all logical thought. The blood of his forefathers, masterful and demanding, with its leaning towards rapine and violence, had risen in him. Whatever the peril, he wanted this woman and could not bear the thought of being parted from her.

Sitapanoki uttered no cry, not so much as a sigh escaped her, and yet the inevitable happened. Before Gilles had gone three steps from the hut, a tall figure barred his way. From somewhere a lighted torch appeared, and then a second and a third. Gilles' intoxication left him abruptly as he came face to face with Hiakin and three other men. The Indian girl wriggled lithely from his arms and vanished like a snake into the night.

'The spirits of darkness must be your friends, since they have succeeded in setting you free,' the sorcerer said harshly. 'And you have dared to steal away one of our women! But you shall not escape your fate a second time. Behold, here comes the dawn!'

It was true. Eastwards, beyond the mountains, the sky was

210

growing lighter. A cock crowed somewhere and suddenly the whole village was stirring, like a wasps' nest kicked open. Gilles was seized by a score of hands and dragged to the stake. His clothes were stripped from him and he was bound to it firmly once again while women stacked wood to relight the fire.

Hiakin, arms folded on his chest, considered his prisoner with savage joy.

'Your brother, the man with red hair has escaped. So much the worse for you. You shall suffer for both.'

He went on to describe with satisfaction all the sufferings that would be his as soon as the first rays of sunlight struck the village. His whole body would be burned slowly with the aid of a variety of instruments, armfuls of which were being brought to the fire by women and old men, until it was raw. His face would be mutilated beyond recognition. The skin would be stripped from his skull and replaced with a bed of burning coals. His bones would be broken one by one . . .

Throughout this catalogue of horrors, Gilles kept his eyes fixed, wide open, on the mountain tops and tried not to listen, clinging to the one consolation that was left to him : Tim was safe. Tim was out of these savages' reach. He might even have managed to steal a musket with which to put an end to his friend's agony from a distance.

Two men approached the condemned man carrying jars filled with red and black paint and with this they proceeded to anoint his body, according to the custom of the Iroquois.

The fire was burning up now, giving off a thick smoke. The hatchets, spikes and iron bars that had been placed in it were beginning to glow red.

'Will you not beg for mercy?' Hiakin jeered. 'Why do you not plead with us?'

'When you put men of your own race to the torture, do they beg for mercy?' Gilles asked scornfully.

'Indians are brave men, whatever their tribe. Not only do they not weep, but they sing as the instruments of their death are prepared. The bravest sing even under torture.'

'They sing, do they?'

Gilles drew in his breath with the energy of despair. Miraculously, a song came to his lips. It was one which the soldiers of the regiment of Saintonge had often sung in the evenings in the camp at Newport.

> 'Dans les jardins d'mon père
> Les lilas sont fleuris
> Dans les jardins d'mon père
> Les lilas sont fleuris
> Tous les oiseaux du monde
> Viennent y faire leur nid
> Auprès de ma blonde
> Qu'il fait bon, fait bon, fait bon
> Auprès de ma blonde
> Qu'il fait bon dormi ...

The hubbub in the Indian village had given way to complete silence. The women and old men bringing their tools to the fire slowed their pace. The hatred in their eyes had softened a little to something like respect. The prisoner was singing . . . His voice rang out in the silence of that mountainous place like a cry of victory and suddenly, in the doorway of the largest hut, Gilles saw a pale figure that set his heart beating faster. His voice died away on the last words. It was the angel of death coming to him in the shape of the woman who had so made him lose his head.

Then, all at once, the sun leaped up into the sky like a ball of fire and the whole valley was illumined. It was the signal. An old man, nearly bald except for one thin grey lock hanging from his scalp, grasped a long brand of red hot iron and approached the stake. Gilles began to sing again, with a kind of desperate fury.

> La caille, la tourterelle et la jolie perdrix
> Et ma jolie colombe qui chante jour et nuit ...

The last word rose to a shrill pitch of agony, as the end of the iron was set to his thigh. In an instant he was drenched with sweat. The pain was agonizing and it went on and on, while a sickening smell of burned flesh rose into the air. Gilles clenched his teeth and gasped for breath, straining his whole will to go on with his song. Now it was an old woman coming towards him, armed with a glowing claw.

> Qui chante ... pour les filles ... qui n'ont pas de mari ...

The old woman smiled like a grinning skull and waved her horrible implement before the prisoner's face so that he could feel the heat of it. Then there was a sudden commotion. An Indian in one of the observation posts overlooking the river was shouting something and gesturing wildly. Another voice echoed him. It belonged to Sitapanoki.

'Sagoyewatha! He has come back!'

Instantly, all attention was turned from the prisoner to the great gateway leading down to the water, which was thrown wide open. From where he stood, Gilles could see the bend of the river literally covered with canoes, all full of warriors. A tall, thin man of imposing presence was standing, arms folded, at the prow of the leading canoe. He wore a head-dress of eagle's feathers and rose above the trails of mist upon the water like a tall statue of bronze, representing some savage river god.

The whole village burst out into a roar of welcome. Some of the women tore off their garments and plunged in, naked, to swim to meet the new arrivals. Once again, the drums began to beat.

Gilles, still bound fast to his stake, tried not to let hope invade him. Tim had certainly insisted that in Sagoyewatha's presence lay their only hope of safety, but how would he view a man who, that very night, had attempted to carry off his wife?

The canoes were grounding now. The naked swimmers were emerging from the water. Some of them held their husbands' war trophies gripped between their teeth : severed heads, held by the hair to enable them to swim. Those who had none gazed on their sisters with a dreadful envy. Only then did Gilles close his eyes, overcome by a wave of nausea which, fortunately, was quick to pass. The bloody heads were those of white men.

When he looked again, the chief had stepped ashore and entered the village compound. And, with a sudden surge of mingled joy and thankfulness, Gilles realized why Sagoyewatha had returned unexpectedly. For his hand was resting on the shoulder of a boy, and the boy was Igrak. Having failed to persuade Hiakin to release his new friends, he must have stolen away from the village secretly in the night and gone to find his brother. Fortunately, the Seneca chief could not have been far off but, at the same time, that explained the sorcerer's haste to be rid of the intruders.

213

Led by the child, Sagoyewatha walked straight to the prisoner, regally brushing aside Bear Face's voluble explanations. As their eyes met, Gilles thought that he had rarely seen a prouder face than this Indian's. His hook nose and thin, disdainfully curved lips gave him a kind of resemblance to the bird whose plumage he wore and made him look older than he was. But the smooth copper skin and the brilliance of his deep-set dark eyes, the balance of his lean, well-muscled body showed him to be a young man. There was no anger in his expression, only a good deal of curiosity.

'My brother, "The eagle who never sleeps", told me that two strangers had come to my camp. Where is your companion, O man of the salt?'

'He fled in the night. Pardon him,' Gilles added with an attempt at a smile, 'that he did not avail himself of the hospitality of your people.'

'Our hospitality should not have been stinted to one who, though he might have kept my brother as a hostage, yet, in his magnanimity, took the trouble to return him to us. But you broke our most sacred laws in killing the white bird which strikes like lightning. Moreover, you were about to fly yourself – taking with you one of our women.'

One of our women? Could it be that in the darkness Hiakin had not recognized Sitapanoki? If that were so, then luck might still be on the side of Washington's emissaries. With some difficulty, on account of his bonds, Gilles managed a shrug of magnificent disdain.

'It is true. General Washington had entrusted us, Tim Thocker and I, with messages to you. My own stupidity and the anger of your people prevented us from discharging our errand and I thought, by taking a hostage, to force you to talk to me none the less.'

As an excuse, it was perhaps a trifle threadbare but Sagoyewatha seemed satisfied. His eyes dwelt gravely for a moment on his prisoner's calm face. What he saw there must have pleased him. The long burn on his thigh showed that the prisoner had already suffered pain, yet the Seneca chief had heard him singing. His eyes, the cold, pale blue of a wintry sky, looked straight at him, proud but not arrogant. Sagoyewatha nodded.

'The Great Spirit is our father but the Earth is our mother, as she is the mother of the pale faces who beseech her for their food, even as we do. But they do not know the Great Spirit and they believe that all living things on the earth were created for their use. They do not know that the white bird is of a divine essence . . .'

Gilles listened in fascination. The Indian chief had a hypnotically musical voice, warm, dark and velvety, against which the words stood out in startling relief. Gilles realized why it was that this young man carried such weight that even the haughty Washington desired to win him over. Even so, he tried to shake off the spell.

'Even had I known your laws,' he said daringly, 'I should have fired none the less. Your divine bird was on the point of killing a woman.'

'A slave—'

'My skin is the same colour as that slave's. Suppose that the victim had been a girl of your own race, Sagoyewatha. Would you have let her die?'

'Perhaps. We never cross the will of the Great Spirit when he has chosen his victim. But you could not understand that – and that is why I am releasing you.'

Drawing a long knife from his belt, the chief sliced swiftly through the cords binding the young man to the stake. That they had also been holding him up appeared when Gilles tried to take a step forward. He reeled giddily. He had not eaten or drunk since the previous day and now the effects of the night's agony were beginning to make themselves felt. He swayed on his feet and groped blindly for a support. Igrak darted forward and held him, calling out something as he did so. Sagoyewatha smiled.

'The child is right, you need food and rest. Come. You are the messenger of the great white chief and so from now on you are my guest.'

He made a lordly gesture and two of the Indians, who a moment before had been preparing to cut the Frenchman to ribbons and listen to his screams as to the sweetest music, now carried him with all the tenderness of a mother to a hut close by the chief's own.

Before very much longer Gilles, fed on maize and grilled

215

fish, with a plaster of herbs on his injured thigh, was wrapped in a warm blanket and dropping into a sound sleep that should repair the ravages of the most harrowing twenty-four hours of his life.

The two women who crouched on either side of Gilles' couch offered a striking contrast. The light of the small wood fire heightened Sitapanoki's beauty and emphasized the wizened age of her companion, a shrivelled-up, mummified creature who sat puffing at her pipe with all the gravity of an old pirate on the bridge of his ship. Gilles kept his eyes averted from her.

He hoisted himself on one elbow and smiled at the younger woman.

'If your husband has given me into your keeping, he has made me the happiest man in the world,' the former pupil of St Yves murmured softly, the graceful compliment, wholly French, springing instinctively to his lips. 'The other is not so desirable, though,' he added, jerking his head faintly in the direction of the pipe-smoking crone, 'and I could well do without her.'

'Sagoyewatha is too wise not to know that one should never light a fire in a pine forest at the end of a dry summer. As for the old woman, it is not you she is guarding, but me. She is my mother-in-law. Her name is Nemissa. This land belongs to her, according to the custom of the Iroquois.'

Gilles, impressed, sketched a vague bow in the direction of the old woman who responded with a chilly stare and then went on puffing at her pipe as though he had never been.

'She doesn't seem to like me very much,' he said with a sigh. 'In any case, it's time I got up. I must see your husband.'

He threw back the blanket, remembered just in time that he was stark naked except for the paint which they had smeared over him at the stake and did his best to drape his body in the rough cloth. The aged Nemissa rose at once and moved as though to bar his way, at the same time uttering something incomprehensible.

'You are not to go out,' Sitapanoki translated. 'In fact, we are here to stop you doing just that. Sagoyewatha is entertaining another chief at the council fire and he does not wish him to know of your presence here.'

216

'Who is this other chief?'

'Kiontwocki, who is called the Planter of Maize—'

'I have heard of Cornplanter,' Gilles said, recalling with no great enthusiasm the curious mission with which he had been entrusted. 'It is said that he covets you and is jealous of your husband. What is he doing here?'

'You have heard truly. Twice already I have escaped attempts to carry me off which could only have been made by him, although Sagoyewatha refuses to believe it because he himself is noble and upright.'

'Have the Iroquois no respect for their brothers' wives, then?'

'Yes. When they are of the same tribe. But I am of an enemy tribe, a kind of captive. As to what Cornplanter is doing here, I think he is trying to persuade Sagoyewatha into joining a foray against the colonists of Schoharie, farther up the valley.'

Gilles took a step towards the doorway of the hut. Nemissa placed herself before him with folded arms, fiercely forbidding. Gilles gently but firmly put her aside.

'Tell her I am not going outside. But I want to have a look at this Cornplanter. I must know what he is like.'

He had no need to move the deerskin across the doorway very far. The Seneca council was taking place just within his field of vision. Darkness had fallen again and the Indians were clearly visible in the light of the fire. It seemed to Gilles that there were a great many of them. Most were young men, with strong bodies under the fierce warpaint which made them look so ferocious. He saw Sagoyewatha, still wearing his eagle head-dress but clad now, for the occasion, in the magnificent red coat of an English officer. The effect was certainly startling. Finally, facing him like a fighting cock, Gilles saw a tall man with a pale copper-coloured skin who wore a kind of silver coronet on his shaven head. The thick black lock hanging from the top of his head was plaited with multi-coloured feathers. Heavy silver ornaments hung from the deeply pierced lobes of his ears and were set in his arrogant nostrils. His eyes were flashing and a stream of angry words was pouring from his scornful lips.

'He is saying that the harvest round Schoharie has never

217

been so good,' Sitapanoki whispered, 'and that now or never is the moment to teach the people of the valley that the Iroquois have not forgotten their brethren massacred by General Sullivan, that they are still here and thirsting for vengeance. He wants to burn the whole valley.'

'And what does your husband say?'

'That we should respect the fruits of the earth who is our mother, that soon winter will come and we shall be hungry, and also that while it is very well to attack soldiers, the farmers of Schoharie have few warriors amongst them. But these are reasons beyond Cornplanter's understanding. He cares only for blood and for the screams of the dying. The Iroquois are cruel but he is the worst of all. I have heard it said that there is white blood in his veins and that is the reason for his frenzied hatred of your people.'

The discussion round the fire went on for a long time with no apparent conclusion. Cornplanter breathed fire and slaughter, in which he was seconded by Hiakin, while Sagoyewatha opposed him with every argument of real wisdom. Then, suddenly, the voices were lowered and nothing more could be heard until Sagoyewatha finally said something in a strong voice.

'My husband wishes to have the night to think the matter over,' Sitapanoki translated. 'Cornplanter and his followers are to withdraw. He will return tomorrow for his answer. But I fear he will win. It is never pleasant to hear oneself called a coward. Yet I cannot understand why Cornplanter is so insistent. He and Sagoyewatha have never fought together and he has warriors enough to overrun Schoharie without help from us.'

Gilles felt a shiver run through him at these last words and he recalled Washington's warning which he and Tim had been charged to deliver to the chief of the Wolf clan. If he allowed himself to be drawn into going with Cornplanter, then the village would be left in charge of Hiakin, as it had been when the two envoys were captured, Hiakin who now seemed to be urging the Iroquois' cause so eagerly, Hiakin who hated Sitapanoki . . .'

Old Nemissa caught the young woman's arm and pointed imperiously to the doorway.

Outside, the warriors were dispersing. Only Sagoyewatha was still standing by the fire, staring down thoughtfully into the embers.

'I must go to my husband,' Sitapanoki said quietly. 'Nemissa will stay with you until a man comes to watch over you in her place. I am sorry,' she added, with the shadow of a smile.

'Not as sorry as I am,' Gilles muttered. 'But please tell your husband that I want to speak to him, and tonight. He must hear what I have to say before he makes up his mind.'

The great golden eyes dwelled for a moment on the young man's troubled face. He realized that she was anxious, even though she did not know all that was in his mind, and so he smiled at her.

'Please, Sitapanoki, tell him I need to see him. It is important – for all of us.'

He would say no more, feeling that it was pointless to alarm her by revealing what was in his mind and the growing suspicion he had that the third attempt to carry her off might be successful, when the Iroquois knew that the village had been emptied of its warriors and was held by his ally, Hiakin.

He said as much to the sachem when he bent his head to enter the hut, from which Nemissa promptly effaced herself. The chief had doffed his red coat but his face was stern.

'Cornplanter only wants you to go with him so as to get you away from your camp,' Gilles told him boldly. 'You will be with him, under his eye. Your village will contain none but women and old men and he will be able to send some of his warriors to seize the thing he covets most. You should beware of him, Sagoyewatha, for he is jealous and he hates you.'

The face of the Seneca chief showed nothing of the turmoil within him but Gilles' sharp eyes did not miss the almost imperceptible clenching of his hands while the beautiful, grave voice murmured evenly, almost uninterestedly:

'Is this what General Washington has sent you to tell me? What are the possessions, or even the honour of an enemy to him? I am an Indian and he is a Virginian gentleman.'

'One may respect, even admire an enemy as noble as you are. The General regrets that you and yours should stand against him when he is fighting for the liberty of the land where both of you were born. For myself, coming from a country traditionally at odds with England, it is hard to understand how you Americans can fight one another, whatever the colour of your skins. What made you choose to ally yourself with the English – to the point of even wearing their uniform?'

'The redcoats treat us as allies and as equals. Those who are called colonists regard us like wild beasts. Yet when their ancestors crossed the great waters to land in this country they found us their friends and not their enemies. They told us they had left their own lands a prey to wicked men and that they came here to practise their religion in peace. We took pity on them. We gave them what they asked and they settled amongst us. We gave them maize and meat – in return they gave us poison – the fire water that burns and which turned us into beasts. When you return to your own people – if I set you free – tell your general that Sagoyewatha has no need of his counsels, that he knows how to protect himself and he scorns the soft voices that murmur artfully, seeking to divide brother from brother.'

'So you have decided to go with Cornplanter?'

'I have just said that he is my brother.'

'That is not true! Any more than he is a true Indian. Do you know that he is the son of a settler? That his father is still living in Fort Plain and that his name is John O'Bail? You may not know that but the General knows it and that is why he sent me to you, to say to you, Great Chief, beware of the man you think is of your own blood but who is only on one side for, although he has no right to it, he dreams of ruling the Six Nations of the Iroquois. In order to achieve that, he is willing to crush all the other chiefs, and you first of all.'

For the first time, a flash of anger showed in Sagoyewatha's eyes and his voice shook.

'Your tongue speaks with the hissing of a snake! However ambitious, Cornplanter could not hope to vanquish the greatest of us all, the Mohawk chief Thayendanega. So what has he to do with me, who am less powerful than he?'

'Does your Mohawk chief possess the most beautiful of wives . . .?'

For a moment, Gilles thought the Seneca chief was going to fly at his throat, but the man's self-control was phenomenal. The dark eyes and the light met and held, as they had done earlier at the stake, then, with a magnificent shrug of the shoulders, the sachem turned away.

'Our words go with the wind which shall soon sweep away the colonial army. It is riven with treachery and in a little while their chief will no longer think of making offers of friendship even to the poorest of us. As for you, I will decide tomorrow whether you shall live or die.'

Disregarding the threat, Gilles pounced on one word the chief had uttered.

'Treachery? What do you mean?'

But Sagoyewatha did not answer. He left the hut and as Gilles darted after him, a pair of spears crossed instantly before his face. He realized that his status in the Indian camp had undergone another change. From a potential martyr, he had become an honoured guest and now, for some unknown reason, he had been transformed into prisoner again.

Any slight doubts he may have entertained on this score were removed when two men burst into his hut. One carried a bowl of maize porridge mixed with a little fish and a pitcher of water, the other had pegs, rope and a mallet. They made him understand by gestures that he was to eat quickly, which he did without enjoyment and simply to keep up his strength, for the Indian stew was far from tasty. The two Indians watched him impassively and as soon as he had swallowed the last mouthful they fell upon him simultaneously and without warning. They laid him down spreadeagled on the ground and fastened his wrists and ankles to pegs driven into the floor of the hut, taking no notice whatever of his furious protests. Sagoyewatha, it seemed, placed no faith in the security of his huts and meant to make sure that his guest could not use the hours of darkness to make a hole in the wall and escape. Gilles had, in fact, been planning to do precisely that.

Helpless, angry and humiliated, as well as apprehensive, the young man passed a trying and uncomfortable night. His head was full of questions. What could the Iroquois have said to Sagoyewatha? What was the treachery that threatened Washington and would lead to such an overwhelming defeat for him? Where the devil could Tim and the girl called Gunilla have got to!

He managed to doze off towards morning but was dragged

221

from his uneasy sleep by the din that broke out in the village with the first rays of the sun. He tried to move, uttered a groan of anguish and then began swearing like an old trooper. His body was as stiff as a board, his mouth was dry and he felt as if he smelt as badly as the whole camp put together. What was more, the paint which had dried on his body was making him itch frantically.

At the cost of another twinge, he managed to raise his head a little to listen. There could be no doubt as to the cause of all the row. The Seneca warriors were leaving their village again to go with Cornplanter on his deadly raid against the peaceful settlers of Schoharie. The red devils were going to fall like lightning on some village where the harvest was ripening in the summer sun and put it to fire and slaughter, leaving nothing but scorched earth and piles of scalped bodies. And there was nothing anyone could do to prevent it.

Such faint hope as he had cherished of persuading Sagoyewatha when he came to tell him what he had decided vanished when a tall shadow came between him and the pale square of the opened doorway. He knew from the shape of the head-dress that it was Hiakin and privately commended his soul to God. The fact that the sorcerer had come himself told him that the news was bad. They were going to drag him back to that damned stake for sure, and carry on with the festivities from where they had left off.

He was too young to endure the medicine man's sardonic scrutiny in silence and burst out angrily :

'Well, Hiakin, what have you come for? To hear the end of my song?'

Bear Face shrugged the bunched muscles which passed for his shoulders.

'If it were for me to decide, you could begin it here and now,' he snarled in the same tone. 'But Sagoyewatha thinks you'll be more useful to him as a hostage, for when the Virginian is defeated and has slunk back to his earth, the warriors from across the great waters may be generous in buying back their prisoners to take them home again.'

'And you,' Gilles retorted, 'what do you think? Do you believe in this crazy tale of Cornplanter's, this unlikely story of treachery which he says is going to deliver the American army up to the redcoats? I thought you had more sense. Not one of Washington's men would do such a thing!'

'Save one who burns with the thirst for gold! An unlikely story, do you say?' Hiakin cried, letting his rage lead him into the trap laid for his pride. 'Know, then, that the man with the pale hair, the warrior who commands West Point, the valiant General Benedict Arnold, has been for many weeks in contact with his former masters in order to give pleasure to his squaw. Before the new moon he will have yielded the fortress on the Hudson in return for much gold. Your great white chief will vanish like the morning mist.'

The last words were lost in a burst of laughter from Gilles, laughter which was all the louder because of the anxiety it concealed, for Bear Face's revelation held a sinister ring of truth. It fitted too well with the doubts which Colonel Hamilton had expressed at Peekskill about the trust which could be placed in the hero of Saratoga. If Arnold yielded up West Point, not only would Washington lose his strongest position but the French gold would go straight into the pockets of his enemies. What could Rochambeau and his five thousand men do then, perched on their island with the English fleet on one side and on the other this vast continent where they would no longer have any support at all?

'Why do you laugh?' Hiakin said sulkily.

'Because you are even crazier than I thought. So this was why Sagoyewatha refuses to listen to the words of my master? You poor fools! Do you think that West Point is Washington's only stronghold? Go and tell your chief to ask his young brother. Igrak could tell him about the warriors of the King of France, their weapons and their ships! And those warriors are only the advance guard, for soon others will come, with yet more arms and more guns and more ships. Your friends the redcoats will be swept away like leaves in a storm, and you with them. Kill me now, if you like – but do not forget my words when the time comes.'

The medicine man's only answer was a furious kick aimed at his ribs as he departed, much faster than he had come.

The noise outside had risen to a hellish din. A savage chanting broken by hysterical shrieks rose above the frenzied beating of the war drums. The very earth was trembling beneath the

223

rhythmic pounding of hundreds of feet stamping out the war dance. Clouds of dust poured in through the open door-flap. Gilles was covered with it, it rasped his throat and set him coughing, which made him still more angry. Attila had defeated Cicero and was setting forth with his barbarian hordes to spread death and desolation through the midst of this fair land, while the vile greed of a man without honour dealt a stab in the back to one of the greatest men ever born on this earth, and moreover a man who was his friend.

Half-mad with anger, Gilles began tugging fiercely at the ropes which bound him to the pegs, trying to loosen them at least, in the hope of managing to pull them out. But they held firm. His skin was raw and bleeding but the pegs had not even shifted. Yet at all costs he had to get out of there, he had to escape from that accursed village. The peril of abduction facing the lovely Sitapanoki paled before the deadly peril of the Rebels, faced with treachery by one of their own side.

'O Lord,' he prayed aloud, 'and you, Our Lady and defender of just causes, help me! Get me out of here so that I can save them! Send help – or tell me what that blockhead Tim Thocker is up to!'

He had shouted his strange prayer to the heavens but his voice was lost in the din outside, to which the neighing of horses had now been added.

Then he felt a warm breath on his face. A small voice whispered: 'Sssh!' and Gilles, who had closed his eyes, opened them again to see the anxious face of Igrak kneeling by him, a finger to his lips. Gilles smiled but the boy was already tugging with all his strength at one of the pegs. He shook it fiercely, the youthful muscles standing out under his coppery skin which was soon covered in sweat. But, in a little while, the peg did move enough to permit the hope of pulling it out at last. With a triumphant grin, the small warrior flung himself on the next piece of wood but at that moment someone outside called his name.

The boy shivered and Gilles saw the fear in his strained face. 'Go quickly!' he whispered. 'I'll manage the rest by myself. Thank you, thank you a hundred times—'

Igrak's eyes shone and as he rose he slipped a knife quickly under Gilles' shoulders.

'Friend,' he said and then, with a wriggle like an eel, he slid through a hole which he must have made in the bottom of one wall without Gilles seeing him. Gilles, left alone, first listened intently. The noise was beginning to die down. The footsteps of men and horses were undoubtedly moving away. Probably no one would come to look at him for some time yet, but it might be better to wait for nightfall before freeing himself finally. On the other hand, if anyone came to bring him food they might notice the damaged peg, in which case it would all be to do again, without the help of Igrak. After all, for the child to have chosen that moment to try and free him, must mean that there was a chance to be taken. So Gilles bunched his muscles and began to pull with all his might. He could feel the blade of the knife beneath his back and its touch gave him a fresh spurt of energy. He pulled and pulled – and bit back a shout of triumph as the peg came out suddenly.

With his right hand free, he wriggled until he could feel the knife and manage to close his numbed fingers on it. His whole aching body was crying out with pain but he was borne up by the excitement of feeling that freedom was near. The blade bit through the ropes that bound his left hand. Igrak had done his work well, the blade was razor sharp. The strands of hemp parted in seconds. After that, to free his feet was a simple exercise.

Once on his feet, he stretched himself several times and flexed his knees. Painfully at first, but then more easily, the circulation began to flow once more. Then he took a cautious look outside.

There was no one to be seen. All those who were not going were crowded at the gateway to the river where the canoes were being launched. Those Indians who were mounted had already set out on horseback, the rest were getting into the long painted war canoes. No one was paying any attention to what might be happening in the village, all were concentrated on bidding farewell to the warriors. His heart thudding, Gilles saw that there was no one at the gate giving on to the maize fields. Grabbing the blanket which was lying in a corner, so as to make himself some sort of a garment when he had time, he darted out, stark naked, and ran until his heart was bursting, praying that no one would see him. Then he was through the

225

palisade and plunging into the maize field, which swallowed him up like the sea.

He paused only for an instant. His flight might be discovered at any moment. He must lose no time. He used his knife to cut a broad strip off the blanket and make himself a kind of loin-cloth, stuck the invaluable blade into it and rolled up the rest and carried it under his arm to put over himself at night. Then he set off across the green sea, making for the woods that flowed down almost to the valley bottom.

The sun was glaring hot and he was grateful for the coolness when he reached the wood. It was thick and dark with dense thickets of blueberries and brambles which scratched him but from which he was able to glean a little nourishment as he passed. The wild fruit was sour and indigestible but it stayed his thirst.

The wooded slope was steep and Gilles' heart was pounding in his chest like a drum. His breath came in noisy gasps. It crossed his mind that if the Senecas gave chase he would very soon be overtaken and recaptured. It might be better not to go too far but to look for a hiding place where he could wait until nightfall. His pursuers would probably not expect him to stay so close to the camp but the chief difficulty lay in con-cealing his tracks. Tim had told him a hundred times of the Indians' incredible skill as trackers.

The sound of a stream caught his ears, one of the hundreds that flowed down into the river. Thinking that this was the best way to cover his tracks, Gilles stepped into it and went on climbing, rather enjoying it because the cool water was pleasant to the sores on his bare feet.

The sound of shouting reached him, still much too close. It came from the village where his flight must certainly have been discovered. Now the hunt was up and if he did not find himself a hiding place very quickly, his chances of escape would be very slim indeed.

He looked about him. His glance rested on a huge tree, obviously of immense age, that stood beside the stream. One branch overhung the water, so low that it might just be possible to reach it . . .

Gilles scrambled on to a rock whose surface was just under water, stretched out his arms and poised himself for a spring, then he leaped upwards, praying that he would make it, for he could never regain his foothold on the slippery rock. His fingers touched wood and clung. For an instant he hung suspended between the tree and the water, while he got his breath for the final effort, then he had succeeded and was sitting astride the branch. From there he studied the tree.

It was an ancient beech, like the great trees he was familiar with in his own Breton woods, and he thought that heaven must be on his side for often, when these trees were very old, there was a hollow in the main fork big enough for a man to hide in. Gilles wasted no more time. He started to climb.

The beech was tall but Gilles climbed it in record time, spurred on by his danger, for his pursuers must be getting perilously close although he could hear no sounds of pursuit. With a sigh of relief he saw that there was, as he had hoped, a deep, cradle-shaped hollow at the top of the trunk and he settled into it contentedly. From below, he must be quite invisible and the cool moss that lined his refuge was particularly pleasant to his sore back, where the skin was still tender from his recent flogging. Nor had he vanished from the face of the earth a moment too soon ...

No additional sound made itself heard, but silent forms had appeared between the trees, gliding like ghosts in their light deerskin moccasins. The Senecas had picked up the fugitive's trail all too easily.

They were moving up the stream, just as he had done, and were evidently studying the banks for signs that he had left it. Tall as it was, the great beech barely earned a glance from them as they passed beneath its shade. Not for a moment did it occur to them that their quarry was holding his breath in the giant's crown. In a minute or two they were gone, making no more disturbance than a ripple on the water.

For a long time after they had gone, Gilles stayed huddled in his mossy haven, alert for the slightest rustle of leaves, the softest cry, staring into the green depths of the forest, waiting for the Indians to come back before he moved. But nothing came, nothing but sleep which took his tired body without warning, so that he lost all sense of time as of all else in the world.

He woke shivering with cold and fever. The sun had gone

and moisture was creeping up from the bottom of the valley. The heat of the day had given way to the breeze of evening. Gilles stretched his cramped limbs cautiously. He must find another hiding place at once for the nights were getting colder as the year wore on and to spend one half-naked at the top of a tree with nothing but a bit of blanket for covering was sheer madness. Moreover, it was becoming urgent to find something to eat. Never had his stomach felt so empty.

He began to make his way down carefully. It was infinitely more difficult than the ascent had been because of his aching muscles and the shivering which made him clumsy. But once on the ground he began to run to try and warm himself a little. His intention was to head back to the river, since he could not hope to cross the mountains by night with no other weapon than his knife, at the mercy of the first wild beast he met. Better the vicinity of the camp – and its maize fields – in spite of the danger. There might be a cave to shelter in where the feet of the mountains ran right down to the Susquehanna.

He did not have to look for long before he made out a dark crack in the gathering darkness. He approached it as cautiously as any Indian, entered and was felled unconscious by a blow from an unseen hand.

When he surfaced again, it was to feel himself in paradise, despite the thunderous ringing in his head, for the voice cursing so fluently beside him was Tim's.

'God damn it all! That was a pretty fright you gave us! What the devil possessed you to go into the hut, you crazy fool, instead of taking to your heels along with us? We'd have been miles away by now! And instead of that, here's me and this brave little gal here been racking our brains for two days to think of a way to save your skin. And all for the sake of some damned dusky maiden—'

Gilles had never seen him so angry. He was literally foaming at the mouth and his voice rang harshly in the small cave into which he had dragged his friend's helpless body. It made Gilles' head ache. He felt it gingerly. There was a respectable lump forming. Meanwhile his eyes took in his surroundings. He was in a small cave which must run back a long way because the entrance was out of sight. Moreover a fire of brushwood was burning there, warming his chilled body pleasantly. The escaped slave, Gunilla, was crouching by it, paying no more heed to the two men than if they had not existed. Her arms were wrapped round her knees and with her dirty hair straggling over her face, she looked more than ever like a drab, grey bundle. She was too dirty to arouse much human sympathy but Gilles was too happy to have found Tim again to bother with such minor details. With his friend's quiet strength all things were possible.

'Bawl at me as much as you like,' he said, laughing. 'You're right all along the line. But why the devil did you knock me on the head?'

'I took you for a Seneca. I saw a naked figure in the shadows. And with that paint on you, you must admit you look just like one! What happened to you? I could see from up there—' he jerked his head towards the mountain above them, 'what was going on in the village. I saw Sagoyewatha come back – just as I was beginning to wonder whether I shouldn't try and put a bullet through your head, even at this distance. I saw Cornplanter and those red devils of his arrive as well and then I saw the whole lot of them set off arm in arm this morning – but I didn't see you escape. So I was preparing to make a little raid on the village on my own account tonight, since you seemed disposed to stay there.'

'I was a fool, I know,' Gilles said gruffly. 'But I couldn't help myself. It was stronger than I was. I just had to speak to her. But you'll see that I've not done quite as badly as it seems.'

As faithfully as he could, he repeated the strange news that Cornplanter had brought to Sagoyewatha's camp, then waited for an explosion of rage and an indignant outburst from Tim. But he waited in vain. Instead, Tim's usually cheerful face turned a curious greenish colour and assumed a rigid expression. For a moment he looked like a man who had received his death blow and Gilles wondered in alarm whether he might not be going to faint dead away. But it was only for a moment. Then Tim turned away from his friend and let out a great sigh which showed how greatly he was upset.

'You're right,' he said at last. 'It was worth staying a bit longer to learn that. Only we've wasted enough time. We must get away from here, quickly! Washington must be warned.

But you'll have to make do with your paint and your blanket to cover you until we reach civilization. I'll just try—'

He broke off, for Gunilla, who had slipped out when Gilles began speaking, came running back then and began hurriedly stamping out the fire.

'Hey!' Tim protested. 'What's the matter? What are you up to? You've left us in the dark!'

'Would you rather they spotted us? There is a canoe on the river with four Iroquois in it, making for the village. They are making no noise and seem to be keeping in the shadows, for the night is not very dark. I don't understand what they can be after.'

'I can,' Gilles said, already on his feet and feeling his way to the entrance while his eyes grew accustomed to the dark. 'They have been sent by Cornplanter to carry off Sitapanoki, and Hiakin is certainly not going to stop them. I'll wager the water gate to the camp has been left open. Damned scoundrels!'

The river was clearly visible in the light of countless stars but it needed a good pair of eyes to make out the shape of the canoe, close up against the far bank, gliding along on the current with no help from the paddles. In a few more seconds it would be out of sight behind the palisade round the village.

'They are going to take her,' Gilles raged. 'We can't let them—'

'Why not?' Tim said flatly. 'Let them take her, if that's what they want. What difference does it make to us? Sagoyewatha wouldn't heed our warnings, he'll only get what he deserves. Besides, Cornplanter will be doing us a good turn by confirming what he said. Our mission will have succeeded, thanks to him – and beyond all our hopes. It's time we took advantage of it to be off! In a little while, the Iroquois will be tearing each other apart. It will be the Trojan war all over again—'

'Are you quite sure Sagoyewatha is going to blame his brother in arms? Hiakin is too cunning for that. I'm beginning to wonder whether my escape wasn't just a little too easy. How do you know they won't blame me for abducting her and that, through me, Sagoyewatha won't hold Washington responsible? You go and tell him what's in store for him at West Point! It doesn't need the two of us for that. I'm staying here.'

'You fool, what are you going to do? Launch an attack on a whole battalion of Iroquois singlehanded, with nothing but a knife and your good intentions? Get yourself stupidly killed, just for a squaw?'

'It's my problem and it's my life! I'm not letting those savages carry off Sitapanoki.'

'And what is she but a savage herself?'

The whispered argument flung to and fro. The two young men faced one another, friendship and common goals forgotten, ready to come to blows each on behalf of his own point of view. Gunilla came between them.

'Are you both mad? Why not shout aloud? The valley has an echo and the Iroquois have ears like wolves! Just because you can't see them any more, that doesn't mean they won't hear you.'

Tim and Gilles came back to earth and held their breath. The canoe had indeed disappeared and all around them was only silence, the heavy silence that falls when all nature seems to hold its breath before some great calamity.

'Let's go,' Tim muttered. 'It's none of our business.'

But he stayed where he was, held by the ex-slave's grip upon his arm, which had grown suddenly urgent.

'Sitapanoki is good,' she said, 'and Cornplanter is nothing but a brute.'

Startled, Gilles turned to look at her, seeing his new ally for the first time. The moon had sailed out from behind the mountain and in another moment it would be behind a pale cloud, but in its light he saw two grey eyes smiling timidly.

'I'll help you, if you like,' Gunilla said simply.

Tim sighed deeply enough to fill the sails of a man-of-war but he did not hesitate. He began stripping off his clothes.

'And of course I'm going to let you walk right into the frightful business,' he grumbled. 'I've always said one should choose one's friends carefully and keep clear of fools. It will serve me right! Come on! Into the water! They'll be back soon, I shouldn't wonder. In any case, you could do with a bath—'

A moment later, the two young men had slipped noiselessly into the cold waters of the Susquehanna, taking care to keep close to the bank, for the moon had come out from behind the clouds. From where they were, they could see the canoe waiting close by the gateway into the Indian village. One man was still sitting in it, keeping watch, although there was probably no need, for Sagoyewatha's camp seemed unusually silent. Even the guards had disappeared.

'I told you that scoundrel Hiakin was in league with them,' Gilles muttered. 'I'm willing to wager he's already drugged the poor woman unconscious so that her screams won't give the alarm. Wait, look!'

The Iroquois were coming back. One of them was carrying an apparently motionless white figure over his shoulder.

'It'll be up to us,' Tim breathed. 'Can you swim under water?'

'I'm a Breton,' came the retort. 'That means I'm half a fish!'

A swift word or two decided the plan they were to follow, then, taking a deep breath, the two boys dived as one and disappeared beneath the surface, each holding a knife between his teeth. Meanwhile Gunilla crouched among the long grass on the bank and resigned herself to waiting.

The canoe came fast, even against the current, propelled by strong arms. The Iroquois were in a hurry. Very soon they came level with Gunilla's look-out post. After that, it all happened very quickly. The fragile craft tipped suddenly, overturned by unseen hands, throwing its occupants into the river. The surprise was complete. One of the Indians toppled almost into Gilles' arms. He raised his knife and struck, then wrenched the weapon free just in time to meet another adversary. This time, he had to fight for it. The Iroquois was evidently a big man and this did not seem to be the first time he had fought in the water. But Gilles was in his element and he had speed and agility on his side. He slid out of the grip that was seeking his throat, turned and struck with all his strength. The blade sank up to the hilt in the man's stomach and he uttered a brief grunt which was immediately stifled by the water. Gilles shot up to the surface and looked about him. They had done it. Four bodies were drifting with the current and over by the bank Tim was towing something that showed as a white shape beneath the water.

Gilles grabbed hastily at one of the dead Indians and began pulling him ashore. The man's scanty clothing, and especially

232

his moccasins, were what he needed, to say nothing of his weapons.

When he reached the bank, Gunilla was helping Tim to pull Sitapanoki's still body out of the water and stretch it on the grass. It lay quite still.

'You were right,' Tim said to his friend. 'The thing was planned. This woman is unconscious. She's been drugged.'

'You're quite sure? She's not—?'

'Not a bit of it! She's breathing. But it's no help to us. I had hoped to persuade her to go back to the camp as though nothing had—'

'Go back? Are you out of your senses? So that Hiakin can do tomorrow what he has failed in today? Our only chance of saving Sitapanoki from Cornplanter is to take her with us.'

'Take her with us? Carry her, you mean. Because God knows how long she'll sleep for.'

'Very well. I'll carry her.'

Gilles had forgotten his weariness, his wounds and the hunger which had been gnawing at him all afternoon. All clothed in silver by the moon, the slim white figure which lay at his feet, the sweet face with its closed eyelids and the thought of the hours of her company which lay ahead all acted on him like a salve, or like a wonderful tonic. He felt in himself the strength of ten and a heart great enough to fight an army single-handed, like the warriors of the Venetiae, his forebears, for whom to be matched against an equal number of foes was almost a dishonour.

It took him a few seconds only to strip the man he had killed of his deerskin trousers, moccasins and belt. This last still had a long knife and a heavy tomahawk thrust into it. All these, Gilles put on, then he bent his back.

'Put her over my shoulders,' he said simply. 'And then we'll be on our way. We'll need to have gone some distance already before dawn.'

The girl was no light weight but Gilles' heart was light and full of joy as he began the long climb up the mountainside.

10

The House of the Mennonite

The storm broke with unexpected violence. The rain flailed down upon the fugitives in almost horizontal squalls, adding to the exhaustion of nearly forty-eight hours' uninterrupted march. For, in their anxiety to put as much distance as possible between them and their probable pursuers and their equally strong desire to reach the banks of the Hudson River as soon as possible, Tim and Gilles had set their companions a killing pace, allowing them only an occasional hour or two of rest. Not that either had uttered a single word of protest.

Gunilla walked with bent back and eyes on the ground, in an attitude more reminiscent of a pack animal than a human being. It was as though she could not help it and it was a poignant reminder of the grinding servitude the girl (she had told them her age was sixteen) had endured in the four long years since her parents' small farm by the Allegheny had been sacked and burned by the Senecas. She belonged to one of the Swedish families that had originally founded Fort Christina, on the banks of the Delaware. In order to escape from the domination of William Penn's Quakers, who left them defenceless against the Atlantic pirates, they had preferred to retreat inland when the hand of authority grew too heavy, and live a lonely but at least a peaceful life.

When Tim had asked her if she wanted to go back to her home, Gunilla had regarded him with something like horror.

'There is nothing there, nothing but ashes. I never want to see it again. But I think I have an aunt in New York. I might go to her, perhaps . . .'

No more had been said on the subject and since then the girl had behaved as though her presence with the young men was a matter of course. She was brave and hardy and not a single word of complaint ever passed her lips. For Gilles, at least, she had become a kind of familiar shadow, not absolutely indispensable but pleasant to have on hand.

Sitapanoki's attitude was quite different. When the effects of the drug with which Hiakin had dosed her food wore off, she had been deceived by appearances into a violent display of anger. She had reproached them bitterly for conspiring to abduct her, a fate which in her view both dishonoured her and laid her open to a frightful retribution.

'Sagoyewatha is great and powerful,' she cried. 'He will never bear such an insult. He will not rest until he has found me. And then nothing, least of all you, you young madman, for you he will put to death in torment, nothing can save me from the punishment meted out to unfaithful wives. They will slit my nostrils, they will slash my face and I shall be nothing but an object of revulsion to all men, condemned to the most menial labour.'

She began to cry at the thought, like a child in disgrace, already mourning her vanished beauty. Gilles was distressed, recalling that he had seen two or three women who had been treated in such a way about the camp, and he tried to comfort her and reassure her by promising that his intention was to place her under the protection of General Washington, but he was wasting his breath, Sitapanoki did not mean to be soothed.

At this point, Gunilla broke silence and took matters in hand.

'The daughter of the Algonquin squeals like a stuck turkey, which gives one no great opinion of her breeding,' she said contemptuously. 'If you would rather become Cornplanter's concubine, you can easily go to him, since that was the fate which awaited you before we intervened. Go to Schoharie. There, by the smoking walls and the bodies of the farmers, you will find the man who can save your face.'

The deliberate roughness of her tone got through to the other woman and, as she looked up at her in sudden doubt, the one-time slave continued quietly :

'Do you think it was so that you might fly with the man he

meant to kill that Hiakin took the trouble to put into your food a herb which should make you fall deeply asleep? He handed you over to Cornplanter's people and these did but snatch you from them – but you are quite free to go back to them!'

'I might even say that would suit us fine,' Tim added, 'because then your husband would have good cause to seek a reckoning with Cornplanter and break the alliance between them. And, what is more, little lady, I'm wondering what General Washington is going to say when he sees you step ashore. I'll be mighty surprised if he's best pleased, because it's not quite what he asked us to do. Besides, you're slowing us down and we are in a hurry.'

Gilles, for his part, said nothing. Sitapanoki's tirade had wounded him too deeply for excuses or explanations. Ever since he had first seen her, he had lived in a kind of waking dream. He was Tristan setting down the empty cup which had contained the philtre given him by Yseult, he was Merlin held captive by the enchantments of the fairy Vivian, and never for a moment had it occurred to him that his spontaneous passion could fail to be returned with a tenderness at least as natural. Like a fool, he had believed that the goddess with the golden eyes had needed him, he had believed that she was unhappy – in exactly the same way that he had believed that Judith was drowning.

The thought of Judith, set abruptly alongside that of Sita- panoki, had the effect of giving him a painful jolt but was not otherwise unpleasant. Her image lay hidden somewhere deep in the recesses of his heart and he knew that whenever he chose to look for it, he would find his love for her intact, though quite different from the love he felt for the Indian girl. It was his body, much more than his heart, that called for Sitapanoki. He hungered for her and he knew it, but what he could not guess was what would become of his passion when once that hunger was assuaged.

A hand touched his arm and a timid voice said softly: 'Forgive me! I – I did not know.'

Perhaps because at that moment Judith was uppermost in his mind, she got no more from him than a cool look. Gently detaching the hand that lingered on his bare arm so that he

236

could feel its warmth, he bowed slightly and murmured in polite, cold tones :

'I have nothing to forgive. Gunilla is right. You are free to go wherever you like, Sitapanoki. I am only sorry to have displeased you. Perhaps, after all, you knew that your food had been drugged.'

She drew herself up, her eyes flashing.

'What do you mean?'

'No more than I said. Cornplanter, too, is a great chief . . . and a very handsome man.'

Even before the word was out, her hand had smacked across his cheek. He accepted the blow with a disdainful smile and a shrug.

'As you wish,' he said and turned back to Tim. 'But that proves nothing.'

After that, he and the Indian girl appeared to ignore one another and did not speak. She walked in front of him, behind Gunilla who was following Tim, and never once turned round. When the storm caught them among the wooded hills of Pennsylvania, it was more than twenty-four hours since the start of their quarrel. Not that any of them had talked much and all day long there was little to be heard except Tim muttering through his teeth from time to time: 'We're losing time! If only we could get along faster—'

Possessed by the same haste, Gilles kept silent, but the thought of what could be happening at West Point at any moment was always with him.

The path they were following was climbing through the woods when, with no other warning than the increasing heat, a fierce clap of thunder broke over their heads. As if that were the signal, a perfect torrent of water descended with such violence that it penetrated the light covering of branches in an instant and drenched the four travellers ruthlessly. Almost before they could draw breath, they were soaked to the skin.

'We must find shelter,' Tim yelled above the storm. 'The wind is in the east and when the clouds build up in the mountains along the Hudson like this, it generally lasts at least two days.'

'Shelter?' Gilles echoed. 'Where do you think we'll find any? We're right in the middle of nowhere.'

'No, we're not. Someone made this path. And just now, as we came round the shoulder of the hill, I thought I saw some smoke ahead. Let's run, before the path turns into a swamp. We'll have to stop in any case. It's getting dark and we can't go on in this weather.'

He set them an example. Gunilla followed him like clockwork but Sitapanoki was less hardened to fatigue than her one-time slave. Far from copying, she seemed to collapse inwardly. Her legs buckled and in an instant Gilles was at her side.

'You are tired out. I'll help you.'

She started as though bitten by a snake and glared at him.

'No! I do not need you.'

She tried to move faster but she could not. Gilles grinned harshly, drawing back his lips in his tanned face.

'And we don't need you to delay us further.'

With that he picked her up bodily and began to run after his friend, and such was his pleasure in his small triumph that he did not even notice the extra weight he carried. Even so, it was a considerable achievement, for Sitapanoki, with an offended air, refused to put her arms round his neck but kept them folded firmly across her breast. Luckily, the smoke that Tim had seen proved to be not far off.

A small farmhouse with its back against a high rock stood at the corner of the wood and not far away a hole cut in the mountain and lined with pine logs proclaimed the presence of a mine.

The house was low, squat and grey, with a small wooden veranda. Seen through the rain it looked almost ghostly but for the small column of smoke rising gallantly from the chimney. As the fugitives approached, a dog barked somewhere and almost at the same time a man with a sack over his head emerged from the mine and started towards the house. At the sight of them he turned and stood staring at them.

His features were half-hidden under his improvised umbrella but he was evidently cast in the same mould as Tim. The voice that came from underneath the sack was deep and cavernous.

'Peace be with you,' he said, rather as if the phrase were a declaration of war. 'What brings you here?'

'The heavens' opening,' Tim answered him. 'If this house

238

belongs to you, allow us to shelter here for a while. We have women with us.'

'And Indians also, by what I see,' the man said. He had not moved from where he stood and seemed to be rooted in the mud until Judgment day.

'When did you ever see a fair-haired Indian?' Gilles asked shortly. 'There are times when one wears what one can get. I am a Frenchman – and a Breton. As for this woman – oh, what more do you want! We'll take shelter whether you will or no.'

He leaped for the veranda where he set down his burden and shook himself like a spaniel.

'My name is Tim Thocker,' Tim said, giving him a disapproving glance. 'I'm the son of the minister of Stillborough, on the Pawtucket River. We need help. Will you give us hospitality?'

A granite eye appeared from under the sack, framed in a fringe of grey hair and a long beard of the same colour.

'Hospitality is God's commandment, brother,' their owner pronounced solemnly. 'Enter into my house and do not fear. It is open to you, but your friend, the fair-haired Indian, might have allowed me to make my own decision.'

'I am not an Indian,' Gilles protested. 'I am—'

'You've said that already,' Tim whispered, digging him hard but discreetly in the ribs.

Before they went inside, however, they were obliged to submit to a curious kind of ceremony. The man with the sack stood on the threshold and kissed them, one by one, upon the lips before turning to the interior and calling :

'Wife, here are guests! Heat some water so that we may wash their feet according to our law.'

Gilles' eyes widened but Tim knew at once with whom he had to deal.

'You are an Amish, brother?' he asked, casting a swift glance over the plain black clothes and austere hair-cut revealed as the sack was shrugged off.

'I am indeed a follower of Menno Simonsz,' was the reply. 'It means that you will find naught but peace here. Enter, brother, and have no fear. My name is Jakob Van Baren and this is my wife, Mariekje,' he added, indicating a figure of indeterminate age, as thin and solemn as himself. She differed

239

from her husband only in her full skirts and the head-dress of coarse, unbleached cloth which marked her sex.

Inside, the little house was extremely simple but its cleanliness was wholly Flemish and did credit to Mariekje's talents. It was surely something of a record for a woman whose husband must have spent most of his time down a mine and who probably worked the small cultivated patch before the house with her own hands.

The walls and floor and what few furnishings there were were of pine, so well scrubbed that they looked as though they had been painted white. The only luxuries were a big black book upon the mantelshelf, a pair of brass candlesticks and a few Bible texts done in red and black cross stitch and hung here and there about the walls. Above the chimney piece was *O give thanks unto the Lord for He is good; for His mercy endureth for ever.* The wall on one side proclaimed *And He said to me: Son of man, stand upon thy feet and I will speak to thee,* and on the other: *Happy is he that hath the God of Jacob for his help, whose hope is in the Lord his God.* There was a similar inscription over the door but that was so faded and so profusely ornamented with flowers that it was quite impossible to read it.

At a sign from the master of the house, the four guests sat down in a row on a bench beside the hearth and had to dip their feet in turn in Mariekje's basin. It was an odd experience but Gilles found himself rather enjoying it and was only sorry he could not plunge his whole body in. But it seemed that Van Baren's kindness did not stop there. As soon as they were on their feet again, Jakob presented Gilles with a black cloth bundle.

'It is not fitting that you remain so immodestly clad under my roof, brother,' he told him, with a disparaging glance at the soiled Indian trousers Gilles had inherited from the dead Iroquois and which, except for his blanket, were his only covering. 'These garments are worn but serviceable and we must be much of a size. You will find a pump and a lean-to behind the house. Go and dress yourself.'

Abandoning the problem of why they had washed his feet only to send him wading out into the mud again, Gilles took the clothes and went out. He put them on without much relish.

His body was beginning to get used to the feel of the fresh air, in the Indian way, and the clothes themselves, while clean, seemed to him to have an unpleasant odour. But he could not refuse them without giving offence to his host who appeared, all things considered, rather well disposed towards his uninvited guests.

He washed himself quickly, partly under the pump and partly in the rain, and got back just in time to take his place at the end of the table assigned to the men. At the other end, seated on either side of Mariekje, Sitapanoki and Gunilla were struggling to keep their eyes open and to fend off sleep. Jakob Van Baren noticed it.

'Feed these poor souls, wife,' he commanded, 'and then put them to sleep in the loft. They can hardly stay upright. The men can sleep in the barn.'

He muttered a prayer of which Gilles, trying vainly to pick up some familiar phrase, could disentangle not one single word, and then, as it was rapidly getting dark, set about lighting a reeking oil lamp which he hung from a hook over the table.

His wife, meanwhile, was trying to get Sitapanoki and Gunilla to eat something but they were too exhausted to have any appetite. They took a little milk and some small rolls made of maize flour straight out of the oven and then begged permission to retire. At that, Mariekje put the men's supper on the table and then led them away.

Somewhat to the two young men's surprise, the supper was excellent. It consisted of some pickled cucumbers, big river trout rolled in maize flour and fried over the fire and a vast blueberry pie which had presumably been cooking along with the maize bread. There was cool beer and then hot tea to wash it down with.

The three men ate in silence. Gilles was so hungry that he felt he could have eaten everything in sight, the table included, but he had a formidable rival in Tim. The young American ate as if it were his last meal before crossing the desert but all the time he continued to absorb vast quantities of food, his friend noticed, his brow remained furrowed and Gilles wondered why. When Tim looked like that, it meant that something was bothering him and Gilles could not guess what it could be.

241

When they had swallowed the last mouthful, Jakob Van Baren muttered another, equally unintelligible grace, wiped his beard and, rising from the table, invited his guests to be seated on the bench by the fire while he fetched a long clay pipe and began to fill it with tobacco.

'Now that the needs of our bodies have been satisfied,' he said with the same unctuous gravity which informed his every word and gesture, 'we must gratify our souls, brothers, by becoming better acquainted. A Frenchman is a rare visitor to our mountains. Tell me something of how you and your friend came here. Who are the women you have with you? The Indian, especially, does not have the air of a common squaw.'

The granite eye was fixed on Gilles and he was just opening his mouth to answer when Tim broke in first.

'We are escaped prisoners. We were on a hunting trip in the Catskills when we were captured by Senecas. They were going to put us to death but we managed to escape with the help of the fair girl who is with us. She was their slave. She managed to cut through our bonds when we were tied to the stake for the night.'

'And the other? The Indian?'

Tim shrugged with an air of resignation.

'She saw it all. She asked us to take her with us, or she threatened to rouse the whole camp. She, too, was a captive in a way.'

'But not a slave. She is far too beautiful and—'

'I know nothing of her reasons,' Tim interrupted him, a hint of irritation in his voice. 'She wanted to come, that's all I know.'

Gilles' eyes narrowed, looking from one to the other, from Tim, seated on the bench and also apparently fighting a losing battle with sleep, to Jakob Van Baren standing looking down at the hearth, with the flames reddening his long nose and his beard. There was a kind of tension between them. Tim had succeeded in wiping away the furrow from his brow but Gilles could feel that his suspicions were awake and he determined to be on his guard. There must be something wrong about this man, for all his generous welcome to them.

There was a silence, unbroken by anything save the drumming of the rain on the roof and the noise made by the woman washing the dishes. Gilles glanced across at her. Seen from behind, her figure in her black dress looked almost as athletic as her husband's. They could hear her cough from time to time but they had not yet heard her voice, for from the moment the travellers arrived she had never once opened her mouth except to eat.

'Really very beautiful that Indian girl is,' Van Baren went on, almost as though talking to himself. 'I wonder who she is, for with such beauty she must be famous among the Six Nations . . . It's a fact that the four of you make a curious party : a woodsman, an escaped slave, a – Frenchman, dressed as an Indian – and then her. It certainly does make one wonder.'

'You're right there,' Tim said, flushing visibly without any help from the fire. 'There's always plenty to wonder about when you've a mind to it. Take yourself, for instance. I've always heard that the Mennonites live entirely off the produce of the earth they till. Yet there is a mine close by your house—'

Jakob raised his curiously dull eyes to the ceiling, as though calling it to witness.

'And is coal not the produce of the earth? I found that little mine abandoned when I settled here. It was a gift of God,' he added, wagging a finger sententiously. 'I take from it no more than is needed to assist the poorest of our small community scattered about the mountain. And we ourselves live, according to the law, only on what we grow. But you have not yet told me—'

Gilles stood up suddenly and began to yawn, with more ostentation than politeness. He had had enough of this fellow's questions and, in particular, he was irritated by the man's continued harping on Sitapanoki's beauty. He was even beginning to think quite kindly of the rain-sodden woods.

'Your pardon, brother,' he said, 'but we have still a long way to go before we reach Stillborough. We must start at daybreak. Will you be good enough to show us where we are to sleep?'

'Of course, of course . . . but you should not be in such a hurry because you will have great trouble in reaching the Hudson River without me to guide you – and I cannot do so tomorrow, for it is the Lord's Day.'

Tim started and frowned.

'Why? What should stop us?'

Jakob shrugged, fetching a second lamp and making something of a business of lighting it before he answered.

'A gang of Cowboys has been seen in the area. It is strong and well-armed and led by a man who calls himself The Avenger, and it is made up of lawless, brutal men who will rob and burn – and kill all those who do not share their views. And it's my belief that you don't fit into that category – or else the French have changed a good deal?'

Tim stiffened and his eyebrows drew into a single thick, red line across the bridge of his nose.

'Cowboys – here? But surely we are in Pennsylvania, the first of all the Independent States?'

'That does not mean that everyone is of the same mind. There are still plenty of tories even in Philadelphia. But they say the night brings counsel. We'll speak more of this in the morning. Follow me.'

They bowed to the mistress of the house but she was busy with the fire and took no notice of them, and then followed Van Baren out of the house. It was pitch black outside but the rain had eased. They followed the flickering light of the lantern and reached the barn which stood behind the house, not far from the entrance to the mine.

The door creaked open and Jakob raised his lantern.

'There's not much room,' he said, 'but you'll be quite comfortable. Good night. I'll come and wake you before daybreak.'

The barn was three parts filled with great bales of dried bracken which smelled nice and promised a soft enough bed. They looked at it contentedly enough but, just as Jakob was about to leave them, Gilles asked him whether he would mind leaving the lantern. When the man expressed some surprise that they should need a light to sleep by, Gilles explained in a quavering tone, taking care not to look at Tim, that he had never been able to sleep in the dark ever since, as a child, the ceiling in his bedchamber had collapsed on him. It was a nervous complaint, he added.

'And what if you set fire to all this?' Jakob growled.

'Oh, don't worry about that! Tim will put the light out as soon as I'm asleep. He's used to it.'

Van Baren mumbled something impolite, to the effect that the King of France had probably seized the opportunity to rid himself of all the cowards in his kingdom by sending them off to join the gallant fighters for Independence, but he left the lantern on the ground.

'Sleep well,' he said ironically, pulling the door to behind him. It creaked more loudly than ever. Then the bar fell with a crash – but not loud enough to cover another, more sinister sound, the sound of a key turning in a lock.

Snatching up the lantern, Gilles sprang forward and bent down. There was, in fact, a lock on the outside of the door. It could be seen quite clearly just below the bar. Cursing under his breath, he turned back to Tim.

'You didn't trust him, did you? Well, you were right. We've been caught in some sort of a trap. He's locked us in.'

'So I heard,' his friend said gruffly, and then he grinned. 'What's more, I guess I wasn't the only one who was suspicious, or else why should a gallant soldier of France suddenly see fit to make himself look a fool?'

The Breton's cool eyes met the American's and the same gleam of laughter lurked in both.

'When you have an oil lamp, and a creaking door and a strong mistrust of your host, then there are some things you must resign yourself to,' he said. 'But I fear I covered myself with shame to no avail. We've been caught like rats.'

'Maybe,' Tim said.

Without another word, he took his knife from his pocket and began poking about at the door, although more from a sense of duty than from any real conviction, since it seemed to have been stoutly made and the wood was sound.

'All this to protect a load of bracken seems rather overdoing it,' he murmured as he worked.

Gilles, meanwhile, was pacing out the space allotted to them, searching for a hole in the walls or a shaky board that might offer them a way out.

'By the way,' he said, giving up with a sigh and coming back to sit beside his friend, 'what put you on your guard?'

'A whole lot of things. I happen to know a good deal about the Mennonites. We've some at Stillborough. They are so peace-loving and so hospitable they'd never let themselves ask

245

a benighted traveller any questions, not even if he came with a knife in his teeth.'

'These are troubled times. That could explain his mistrust—'

'Yes, but not his appearance. Here's a man who digs out coal in his spare time, a thing which no Amish would ever do, and spends the rest of his life tilling the soil, and yet there's not the smallest trace of dirt in his hands or under his finger-nails? And finally, if you want to know, I thought he had too good a cook. It doesn't fit in with the austerity of that sect! But after all, there's nothing to be done. Yet I'd like to find a way of getting out of here without our host's permission. I've an idea he's got something in store for us . . . Besides, we're wasting time.'

'I know, but even if we do get out, what good will it do us? It's still raining. The women are both inside the house. What's more, they are too tired to go another step, especially in weather like this. Can you see us abandoning them to the mercy of this fellow?'

'Yes.'

It was said fiercely, almost savagely, and Gilles shivered as he looked again at his friend and scarcely knew him. The tracker's normally cheerful face was set like stone.

'You're not thinking what you're saying!'

Tim thrust his long nose close to Gilles' and looked him straight in the eyes.

'I'm thinking exactly that! We have to face facts, old lad. The girls are holding us up. If it had not been for them, we'd never have got into this hornet's nest and every minute's delay might have the gravest consequences. How do we know that Arnold isn't handing West Point over to the English at this very moment? We are soldiers first and foremost and we have a mission to fulfil. It is our duty to get away from here as fast as possible, women or no women! And don't try telling me to go alone. If we've a gang of Cowboys to face, two of us will be none too many, for at least one of us must get through at all costs! So do me a favour and leave your high-flown chivalry out of it.'

'But what will become of them?'

'As Van Baren would say. "God will provide". Besides, even if he's not what he pretends to be, he can hardly murder them.

The worst that can happen to them is to be made into servants to Mariekje. And now let's try and find a hole.'

He got up to show that the subject was closed and began exploring the place as Gilles had done, but keeping his nose close to the ground, like a dog on a scent.

'You're wasting your time,' Gilles told him crossly. 'There's not room for a pin between those boards. This barn was well built.' Angrily brushing away a drip of water from his nose, he added : 'Well built but very badly roofed. The rain is coming in—'

Both in the same instant looked up at the boarded roof and measured its slope with their eyes.

'Tim—' Gilles whispered. 'There may be a way ! Look. The bracken is piled right up to the top. Perhaps we could climb up and try to wrench out one of the boards. If the wind has managed to shift one, there's no reason why—'

He had no need to finish. Tim was already surveying the height of the barn with a brightening eye. Then, without more ado, he took a run at the pile of bracken.

'Let's go !' he said.

It was no easy task to scale the big, unsteady bales. They were obliged to check their enthusiasm and go more carefully. Then, when they reached the top, they needed to go higher still and had to move several of the bales without dislodging them and ending up on the floor again amid an avalanche.

With Tim braced against three of the bales of bracken on which he stood and doing his best to hold them steady, Gilles reached precariously up to the roof and endeavoured to push up one of the boards. To his delight he found that, although heavy, it would shift a little. Some of the nails had come away.

'I'm afraid I can't do it alone,' he panted. 'There will have to be two of us up here to push.'

'Let's try, then. Come down—'

They added more bales to the topmost layer and made them as firm as possible. When, at last, the two of them were standing just beneath the roof, Tim tested it with his hand.

'It should do it with the two of us,' he said with satisfaction. 'Let's push.'

'Wait a moment !'

Quickly peeling off the kind of black gown which Jakob had

247

bestowed on him, Gilles cast it over the lantern. The barn was plunged into darkness.

'You crazy?' Tim said mildly.

'Not a bit! What do you think will happen if Van Baren takes a look out of the window and sees light coming out of the roof of his barn? We don't need to see much for what we're going to do.'

One side of the board gave slightly before the united efforts of the two of them. The other end held firm. They pushed harder, regardless of the rain which was now pouring in to mingle with the sweat that drenched their bodies. The board gave way at last. They heard it slither away and then land with a dull thud on the ground. They were left standing in the rain, but in the free air.

In another moment, they were on the roof and beginning a cautious descent of the long slope made slippery by the rain. It was especially awkward for Gilles because he had refused to be parted from the lantern, despite Tim's vigorous objections. At last they reached the gutter and a downpipe ending in an already overflowing water butt brought them to the ground. Joyfully, they felt their feet touch the soaking earth.

They were in the small yard between the barn and the house which rose before them, so ominously dark and silent that Gilles felt a tightening of the heart.

'Tim—' he whispered. 'We must try and take them with us. We can't just desert them like this, it would be too—'

He broke off, half-stifled, as Tim's great paw was clamped over his mouth and stayed there, like a limpet, while in his ear the American's voice whispered remorselessly :

'Not another word about that! And now, my lad, listen carefully to what I'm going to say, for I shan't say it again. The outcome of the war and the liberty of a whole nation may depend on our survival. So, even if I knew that those two women were in danger of being put to death at dawn, I should still do exactly what we are going to do. And since they're certainly not in any danger of the kind, that's enough of that and let's be on our way!'

Gilles thrust his friend's hand away angrily, but he uttered no further protest. Tim's argument was incontestable because the secret they had stumbled upon was one, in fact, which went beyond all ordinary feelings. They were no longer free to act as they would. What were two young women compared to the vast struggle which the Rebels had undertaken? As though in answer to his thoughts, Tim spoke again, but this time with an unexpected gentleness.

'If my own mother were shut up in that house, I would not hesitate to leave her there.'

'Very well,' Gilles said with a sigh. 'I'm coming.'

In order to avoid having to pass in front of the house, they went on along the side of the hill, past the mine entrance – and both stopped suddenly at the same moment. Somewhere, far down inside the black opening, they had heard a whinney.

'Well, well!' Tim said. 'I'm beginning to think there may be something in that famous Breton stubbornness of yours. It looks as though your lantern is going to prove useful.'

In single file, the two friends made their way into the mine tunnel. Gilles uncovered the lantern just enough to keep them from breaking their necks. Once past the entrance, it was high enough and the wooden props looked to be in good condition, but there was little trace of any work being done. If Van Baren were extracting coal, he could not have been doing so for some time.

'And yet,' Gilles said, 'he was certainly coming out of this tunnel when we arrived.'

'That doesn't mean he had been working here. Listen—'

They could hear the whinneying again, closer now, guiding their steps. A moment later they discovered what they had probably been hoping for unconsciously ever since they had entered the mine: a largish cave, its entrance half-concealed behind an outcrop of rock, had been turned into a very fair stable, for light must surely penetrate it during the day from the numerous cracks in the rock, well overgrown with vegetation.

'Do you see what I see?' Tim asked delightedly.

There were two horses, standing docilely in improvised stalls, two horses that were evidently well cared for, for their litter of dry bracken was clean and their coats shone. The saddles and harness hanging on the nearest wall gleamed with polishing.

'If these nags are for working on the farm I'll eat my hat,' Gilles said.

249

'Then you've no need to worry – and nor have I, since you've no hat of your own! These horses belong to the British army – see where they're marked.' Tim held the lantern up close to one of the beasts. 'It's strange, to say the least – and I'm beginning to wonder whether Van Baren's a rogue or a good patriot—'

'We can ask questions later. Heaven has sent us horses. Let's saddle up and be off.'

It was done in a trice. Then, leading the animals with one hand and holding their noses with the other to keep them from whinneying, they made their way out of the improvised stable and along the mine tunnel back to the open air. All at once Tim, who was leading the way with the lantern, stopped dead in his tracks.

'Well?' Gilles said impatiently. 'Go on!'

Tim said: yes, yes, absently and then, in a different voice, he went on : 'All in all, I guess he is an abominable rogue.' Then he put out the light abruptly and they were plunged in darkness. But they were near enough to the entrance and Gilles merely put it down to caution on his part. He was glad to be in the open air again.

The night seemed light after the stifling darkness of the mine and the smell of the forest unusually fragrant. Gilles took a deep breath full of enjoyment and then, eager to feel the warm, familiar power of a horse between his knees, he leaped into the saddle.

Without a backward glance at the house of Jakob Van Baren to tempt them to second thoughts, the two friends reached the cover of the trees, and the sound of their departing hoofs was muffled by the moss. It had stopped raining at last.

11

West Point

Daylight came like a thief, creeping in a grey mist between the tall trunks of the wet pine trees, giving out a meagre ration of light from an overcast sky, still swollen with rain. The two men had travelled all night in silence, guided by Tim's sure instinct, and despite the hazards of the way they must have covered a fair distance but even so, they were not yet done with the forest and its swamps.

'I'd give a lot to be able to gallop for a while,' Gilles groaned. 'This damned path seems to go on for ever. Do you know where we are?'

'I've a vague idea,' Tim muttered without turning round. 'We're in Sullivan county. That little stream down there is Ten Mile River. We've come a good way.'

'We haven't met Van Baren's famous bugbears, at any rate! Not a sign of the terrible Cowboys.'

Almost before the words were out of his mouth, there was a shrill whistle high above their heads and the forest around them was suddenly full of people. Fierce-looking men, dressed for the most part like countrymen, emerged from behind the trees. Three of them stationed themselves across the path, guns at the ready. The one who seemed to be their leader was wearing Hessian uniform.

'Well,' Tim said. 'Talk of the devil. But you'd have done better to have held your tongue. Here are your Cowboys.'

'Good day to you, honourable travellers,' the man in Hessian uniform declaimed. 'It's a pleasure to meet you, and those

251

splendid animals you're riding. Will you be good enough to dismount—'

'So that you can more readily rifle our pockets?' Tim finished sardonically. 'Well, Cowboys, you're going to be disappointed. Our pockets are empty. You won't find a brass farthing, however hard you look.'

'A pity. In that case, I'll make do with your horses.'

'Is that all? And what will that leave us, Cowboy?'

'Your lives – so long as you stop calling me Cowboy. I don't like being insulted.'

Gilles and Tim exchanged glances and it was the Breton who answered.

'Your pardon, friend. We were warned that we might well encounter a large gang of these Cowboys. We took you for the one known as the Avenger.'

The man lowered his gun and came closer, leaving his two companions still standing in the same attitude. He was frowning.

'Where did you hear of the Avenger? It's three months since he disappeared and I've been searching for him. We have an account to settle, he and I.'

'Then,' Tim broke in, 'if you are not him, and not a Cowboy, who are you? A Skinner?'

'And proud of it,' the man cried, thumping his chest. 'It's in the family. My name's Sam Paulding and no Paulding ever served King George, not willingly at first. We serve the cause of Independence – and it is in the name of that cause that I require your horses, for unfortunately we are short of them. So will you now dismount. I should be sorry to be obliged to kill you,' he added, pointing his gun at Tim's chest. Tim remained unmoved.

'So should we,' he agreed mildly. 'But you ought to look twice before you kill us, if you serve the cause of liberty, or leave us our horses and let us go on our way, because we're in a hurry to get back to General Washington who is waiting for a report on our mission. He doesn't care to be kept waiting, and if he has to wait too long and gets to hear that it was Sam Paulding who delayed us by stealing our horses, I don't think he'll be grateful. And he has a heavy hand, our general.'

The man smiled broadly, showing a splendid set of teeth.

Under his military coat, he was remarkably dirty but neither coarse nor particularly ill-looking, and there was a directness in his keen eyes.

'Is that so? You look like staff officers, I must say! In another minute you'll be telling me those beasts you're riding belong to the Virginia cavalry. Still, I'd better make sure. Don't want to look a fool!' Then he snapped out suddenly: 'Hey! I know horses! I'll be hanged if these don't belong to the Redcoats!'

His eyes narrowed. Tossing his gun to one of his men, he went quickly to Gilles' horse's head and, holding it still with a practised hand, began rubbing the creature's forehead.

'Here!' Gilles protested. 'What are you up to?'

'You must have had some heavy rain in the mountains,' he said. 'This animal is soaking wet – and the dye is coming off him.' He held up his hands, showing chocolate-coloured finger-tips. Still holding the horse's head, he felt in his pocket and produced a faded rag which might have been a handkerchief. He spat on it and began to rub harder, then stood back, like a painter judging the effect of his work. Light dawned in his face.

'Well, I'll be damned!' he said, grinning all over his face. 'If it ain't Winner! The Avenger's own horse! It's too rich!' He swung round to his men. 'Here, you fellows, fetch these two sweet-talking rogues along with us! I'm willing to wager they belong to that son of a bitch's gang and we're going to have a little chat.'

Tim and Gilles, heavily outnumbered, were hauled from their horses despite their protests and made to go with the ragged band down towards the valley. In a short while they came to what was evidently their lair, a half-ruined hovel on the Ten Mile River which might once have been a mill. They were dragged inside, into the one habitable room which was crowded with men and women of all ages and descriptions.

Sam Paulding seated himself on an upturned cask and prepared to hold a kind of trial. Several of his men ranged themselves behind him, weapons at the slope.

'Gentlemen,' he said gazing round him with an autocratic stare, 'we are about to pass judgment upon these two suspects but, before we do, it is right that we should ask them some questions, to which they would be well advised to answer freely if they wish to spare themselves – and us, for we are civilized people – some extremely unpleasant measures. And the first of these questions, is where is the Avenger?'

The exaggerated dignity of his tone and attitude gave Gilles an idea. Clearly, the man took himself for a great personage. So, drawing himself up to his full height, Gilles stepped forward and bowed with the respectful courtesy of an ambassador presenting his credentials.

'I fear, sir, that there has been a regrettable misunderstanding. There is indeed no reason why I should withhold from you information which I should be the first to wish for, since this Avenger is as much an enemy of mine as of yours. My name is Gilles Goëlo. I am a Frenchman and private secretary to His Excellency General Count de Rochambeau, who commands the expeditionary force sent by His Most Gracious Majesty Louis the Sixteenth, by the Grace of God King of France and of Navarre, to aid the Rebels. And, since we have come to this land in friendship, I am confident, Mr Paulding, that my best security lies in the courtesy and hospitality of a true American gentleman.'

The 'American gentleman' flushed with pleasure and bowed in a dignified fashion as the younger man continued coolly :

'As for our horses, with which you seem to be so well acquainted, I will confess in all honesty that we stole them in the mountains, from one Jakob Van Baren who had them concealed in a disused coal mine.'

Sam Paulding stared at him with honest amazement.

'Van Baren? Horses hidden in the old mine? What is this? Old Jakob is so bent from working his land that he could not so much as get his leg up to the stirrup. As for the mine, it's long since anyone went down there! What would he be doing with horses, poor fellow?'

'Just a moment!' Tim broke in sharply and then continued in a fair imitation of Gilles' courtly manner:

'Mr Paulding, may I ask you to tell us how long it is since you set eyes on Jakob Van Baren, and what he looks like?'

'Why, he is the strictest and most pious of all the Mennonites of my acquaintance! A little old man like a wizened apple, with a square-cut grey beard and long hair to his shoulders.

He's as solemn as the Bible, which he quotes all the time, and his only weakness is his wife Mariekje, a little round old Dutchwoman, fresh-faced still and as quick as a mouse. She's probably the best housewife in the whole county. It must be six months since I saw them. But, here! I thought I was supposed to be asking the questions!'

'Only one more! Is the Avenger a tall man, thin but somewhat of my build, with reddish grey hair and eyes like grey granite?'

'If you are one of his men, you ought to know that's just exactly what he looks like,' Sam Paulding retorted with a sneer. 'But I don't see—'

'But I do,' Tim said coolly. 'And now we will answer the question you asked earlier. If you want to find the man you're seeking, go to look for Jakob Van Baren and there you'll find your enemy, using his name and living in his house. As for the old couple you described to us, seek them in the main tunnel of the mine, on the left side about a hundred feet from the entrance. That's where the Avenger buried them.'

A total silence followed Tim's words. Sam Paulding had turned very pale and, all around him, every eye was bright with suppressed anger. Gilles turned on his friend indignantly.

'Is that what you saw in the mine when you put out the light? Why didn't you tell me?'

'Because I wasn't sure then – and because we had to get away from there at all costs.'

'A robber? A murderer! And we left those two poor women there?'

'There was nothing else we could do.'

'I know that and I'm not blaming you. But now you can go to Washington by yourself.'

'And you?'

'I?' Gilles turned to Paulding. 'Give me back my horse and let me have weapons and I'll promise to bring you back your enemy's head.'

'I'm quite capable of getting it for myself,' the other man said grimly. 'It's not a pleasure I'm willing to leave to anyone else. But I am beginning to believe your story. Tell me what happened at Van Baren's house and we shall see.'

Gilles told him, as clearly and concisely as he could, of the events which had brought them, with Sitapanoki and Gunilla, to the Mennonite's small farm. He described honestly all that they had seen and all that had been said and done. He told finally how, in order to reach Washington and warn him of a grave danger threatening him, they had been obliged to desert their companions. Without quite understanding why he did it, he obeyed his instinct and kept nothing back, taking the leader of the Skinners very much into his confidence. There was something about him which was different from the ordinary brigand, if only the way he had of looking people straight in the eyes.

Sam heard him in silence. At the end, he seemed to consult the faces of the men who stood about him and even to look over the heads of his prisoners at the remainder of the band. From all he got the same response, a silent nod of approval. Then the Skinner rose from his cask and came towards the two young men.

'Where were you to rejoin Washington?' he asked.

'We were expecting to find him where we left him, at Peekskill,' Gilles said.

'He is no longer there. He has pushed on and set up his new headquarters at Tappan, some twenty miles farther south, on the right bank of the Hudson, right on the border of New Jersey. But you may not find him there. I heard that he was preparing to march to Hartford, Connecticut, so as to link up with the French commanders, General Rochambeau and Admiral de Ternay, and confer with them.'

'You're very well informed,' Gilles said admiringly.

Paulding smiled and became a different man.

'This country is packed with spies,' he said, 'but our information is no worse than the Redcoats'. As for yourselves, I collect that it is truly urgent for you to reach the Virginian as soon as may be?'

'The fate of the war may depend on it,' Tim said gravely.

'Then you can't go running all over the country after him, and he moves like lightning . . . I must think. In the meanwhile, we'll have some beer and a bite to eat.'

'We are no longer prisoners, then?' Gilles asked.

'When men are fighting for the same cause, they should learn to know and help one another. Even a Skinner knows that! You will go where your duty calls you. I'll settle my account with the Avenger, and I'll take care of your friends.'

Gilles did not hesitate. He put out his hand.

'How can we thank you?'

'By speaking up for me to the General when he's had enough of my peculiar methods of warfare. None of us wants to finish at a rope's end.'

'I swear it, by all the saints in Brittany—'

Their hands met and clasped for a moment, with a firmness which said more than words. It expressed the feelings of both men and all around them the rest of the band broke into applause. Tim, in turn, shook Paulding by the hand and then they all seated themselves round a roast which appeared as though by magic and took counsel together, while two of the Skinners set about broaching the cask on which their leader had just been sitting.

As dusk was falling, Gilles and Tim left the mill on Ten Mile River and were escorted down to the valley by Sam Paulding himself with two of his lieutenants. They carried guns, a rifle for Tim, since that was his favourite weapon, and a pair of pistols for Gilles. They had also been given precise directions and their horses had of course been restored to them.

'But only as a loan, mind,' Sam had insisted. 'I've had my eye on that Winner for too long now. When you're through with your mission, you need only seek out my brother Ned. He leads another band of Skinners, north of White Plains, over by the Croton River. Give the horses to him and he'll see they get back to me. Good luck!'

Once they got over his ruffianly side, Sam Paulding had shown himself a sensible man, so sensible, in fact, that his new friends had not hesitated to confide in him the real reason for their haste to rejoin Washington. And since their greatest problem was to find out where the General was at that time, Paulding sent them to the house of his cousin, a farmer by the name of Joshua Smith who lived near Tellers Point on the right bank of the Hudson, not far from the fort of West Point.

'Go and see Josh,' he told them. 'You'll gain by it in several ways. First, if you keep going straight ahead, it will bring you almost to Tellers Point, and then my cousin is surely the best-informed man for a hundred miles round. Finally, if there is

257

anything suspicious going on at West Point, he'll be the first to spot it and give you a helping hand in trying to keep the damage to the minimum, if only by calling in my brother Ned to the rescue!'

So that Gilles and Tim went on their way thanking providence for putting a brigand named Sam Paulding in their path and determined not to halt again for anything except to rest their horses.

Forty-eight hours later, just as dusk was falling, they caught their first sight of the Hudson River. The last rays of sunset were gleaming on the water and, tired as they were, the sight drew from them both a deep sigh of relief, which Tim was the first to put into words.

'We're not far from Tellers Point. Now all we have to do is find Joshua Smith's house. I hope he'll have a bed, or at least a bale of straw for us.'

'A bed? And what if he tells us Washington is prancing about a hundred miles away? Although, I must say, we'd have to go on foot because our horses could never hold out. Though we could always steal some more, of course,' he added nonchalantly, as an afterthought.

'Well, for one who was going to be a priest, you're certainly making progress,' Tim observed. 'Come on, then. It's getting dark infernally fast.'

They set off up river, having struck it somewhat downstream of the place they wanted. Gilles, who was bringing up the rear, reined in his horse suddenly and called softly to his friend.

'Look!' he whispered. 'What's that?'

It was a warship, moving silently in the same direction as themselves, coming up the Hudson under shortened sail, gliding like a great ghost, a darker shadow among the shadows of the twilight.

'A corvette,' Gilles murmured. 'A real miniature ship of the line. Look at the two pretty carronades on the foredeck. Add to them the twenty more guns she's hiding modestly under her lowered ports and you'll have an idea of what she can do. I wonder what she's doing here?' he added, trying to throw off the uneasy feeling that it gave him.

'We used to see them often enough in the past,' Tim said slowly. 'They used to ply between New York and Albany, carrying supplies for the forts on Lake Champlain, Ticonderoga and Crown Point. But no English vessel has sailed up here since the war began, and especially not since the new defences were erected at West Point and the big chain stretched across the river.'

'You think that is an English vessel?'

'Why yes! I'm sure of it. There's still light enough for me to know her, even though she's not showing her colours. She's the *Vulture*, the ship Sir Henry Clinton is accustomed to use for his tours of inspection round New York.'

There was something ominous in Tim's level voice. The two friends stayed quite still in the shadow of a large tree, watching the dainty vessel, each gripped by a dread which neither could bring himself to utter. Could it be that they were too late? That the West Point forts had already been yielded up by their unworthy defender? Where else could the *Vulture* be heading but for West Point, even if the passage through to Albany were not yet open?

'We must know!' Gilles said flatly. 'Let's seek out Joshua – or even go on to West Point—'

'Just a moment! I suggest we go down to the bank first, to get a closer view of the river. What we want to know is whether the *Vulture* is alone or if she is the first of a flotilla, in which case it could be the landing party making for West Point—'

'Or, if the fort has already fallen, for Ticonderoga or Crown Point. But if that's so, it seems to me that vessel is keeping pretty quiet. She looks as if she's trying to avoid notice.'

'We'll do the same. And above all, no noise! Sounds carry over water.'

They left their horses tied to the tree, which gave them good concealment, and descended the short slope, keeping in the shelter of the bushes. Then they wormed their way through the reeds and long grass to the edge of the water. From there, they could see the stern of the corvette which was in complete darkness, with not even a riding light. They could also see the whole of that reach of the river downstream and their question was answered. The river was empty. The *Vulture* was quite alone.

Suddenly, the ship seemed to melt even more completely into the darkness. All her sails had been struck. At the same time, the rattle of an anchor chain being paid out floated over the still water.

'They're dropping anchor!' Gilles whispered.

'Hush! Listen!'

As though echoing the anchor, they heard another, fainter sound: the cautious splash of oars. In a little while the outline of a boat appeared, making for the corvette. It was growing darker minute by minute but at the same time their eyes were getting accustomed. The watchers were able to see the boat pull alongside and a man get to his feet, while someone else wrapped in a cloak came down a rope ladder over the ship's side into the boat. Then it moved off again into the darkness but the sound of oars continued for some time, though growing fainter. Meanwhile, on board the corvette, all was still and silent again, except for the gentle creaking of her timbers.

Gilles wriggled backwards into the bushes and got up.

'That's odd! Shall we go and see?'

'Good idea, but on foot if we don't want to be spotted.'

Abandoning the path, where they would have been too conspicuous, Tim and Gilles followed the river upstream as fast as they could with safety. They soon heard the sound of the oars again and slowed down as the small boat came in sight, being content simply to keep it within a reasonable distance.

All at once it turned in towards the bank and disappeared. A moment later, the sound of oars gave way to the rasp of wood on stones.

'They seem to have arrived,' Gilles whispered. 'But I can't see anything but blackness.'

'It's a fir wood! It fills a gulley in between two hills. I know the place. It's called Long Cove. Follow me. We're going into that wood, as well. But don't make a noise.'

It was not the first time Gilles had had reason to admire the tracker's easy, noiseless progress through the trees, but this time he excelled himself. His big body might have weighed nothing at all as he advanced through the dark undergrowth without the crack of a twig or the rustle of a leaf. Gilles endeavoured to copy him and succeeded tolerably well, thanks to his Indian moccasins.

Suddenly Tim stopped and groped for his friend's arm. A light had sprung up a few yards away from them. In the glow of a lantern which had been set down on a fallen tree trunk, they saw three men. One, by his rough clothes, was evidently the boatman. He it was who had been carrying the lantern and he was already retiring into the shadows to leave the other two alone. That both of these were officers was clear from the uniforms they wore beneath their identical black cloaks, but there the resemblance ended, for one was British and the other American. The Englishman was young, fair and good-looking, with the clear eyes, gentle features and winning smile that would attract immediate liking. The American was very different, short and fortyish, with a tense, nervous manner which made it impossible for him to keep still, in spite of a lame leg. The yellow light accentuated his beaky profile and the regular twitch in his thin features.

Beside him, Gilles heard Tim catch his breath.

'Good God!' he gasped. 'The little one is Benedict Arnold! The damned—'

Eager patriot as he was, young Thocker had seemed to accept the possible defection of the hero of Saratoga readily enough but Gilles knew now, from the real distress in his voice, that he had not wholly credited it until now. The proof was very grievous to him.

'Yours is a big country,' he whispered back. 'For every traitor, how many heroes are there? Let's try and creep a bit nearer. We can't hear anything.'

A sudden gust of wind whirled noisily through the trees and covered their movements. They were able to get close enough to hear that the two men had got no farther than the preliminaries. Then the American hugged his cloak around him and put up his head and sniffed the wind.

'We're in for a storm. Better not linger here. Did you tell them when to expect you back on board, Major?'

'No, General. Colonel Beverley, who is waiting for me there, knows that we may take some time. All night perhaps.'

'Good. In that case, there's no need to stay here. Joshua!'

There was a pause and then the boatman reappeared. In the light it could be seen that, although his clothes were those of a labourer, his manner was not. He was a cool, active-looking individual with well-cut features and an air of distinction.

'General?'

261

'The weather is worsening and, as you may guess, we have much of a delicate nature to discuss. Can you give us shelter for the night without too much risk? Your house is close at hand.'

'My house is ready. I guessed it was going to be a bad night and I made my arrangements accordingly. Everyone is asleep, or else from home.'

'Excellent! Take the lantern, then, and be our guide.' Turning to the English officer, Arnold went on: 'You can put complete confidence in Joshua Smith and his house, Major. He's an honest man and hospitality is a sacred trust to him.'

The Englishman bowed and smiled pleasantly.

'I don't doubt it for an instant, General, and I will gladly go with you.'

The three men began walking into the wind, which got up again just as the first drops of rain began to fall. Gilles and Tim let them get some way ahead. Apart from anything else, they needed time to assimilate what they had just heard. Gilles said, thinking aloud: 'Is there only one Joshua Smith in these parts?'

'I'm sure, and I must say I don't understand much, except that Arnold is not the only rogue round here. We'll work out what to do about it later. For the present, we can only follow them.'

'And try and find out more. I suppose the thing that is going to take them so long to discuss must be the handing over of West Point. It's a good thing in a way. It proves that nothing has happened yet and we are still in time.'

The yellow light flitted among the trees, farther and farther off. It went out abruptly, once it left the wood, but the two following were able to make out some low roofs behind a hedge and a number of farm buildings through the rainy night. Everywhere was in darkness but as they reached the hedge they saw lights go up in two downstairs windows.

'There!' Tim said softly. 'Let's take a look, and pray God there are no dogs!'

The farmhouse was connected to a little lane by means of a narrow gate in the hedge which, on the other side, went on down to the river. They passed through it easily, making no noise to give away their presence, and then stood poised for barking dogs, or even an attack.

'This is absurd,' Gilles said. 'If Smith has a dog, he must have shut it up to keep it from betraying that there are strangers here.'

In the event, they reached the lighted windows without incident and settled themselves in a gooseberry bed beneath it, from where they could see the two officers in the act of removing their cloaks. Smith stood waiting to take them.

Two rocking chairs were standing one on either side of a broad hearth in which a good fire was burning. A pot was steaming on an iron trivet and on a small table by the fire was a large tray laden with pewter mugs, an odd-shaped bottle of venerable appearance, a basin of dazzling white sugar and several spice jars. On another table, a little farther off, where Josh Smith had just finished lighting the lamp, was a supply of writing materials. Arnold laid a roll of white paper on it, which might well have been a map.

The two officers sat down and Josh Smith, without the slightest loss of his cool dignity, set about preparing a hot punch for them. Then, with a slight bow, he withdrew, as discreetly as a good servant, closing the door behind him.

'Well,' Tim said gloomily, 'we can sit here getting soaked to the skin and watch them all we like, but we shan't be much the wiser. We'd have to break the window—'

'I may have an idea,' Gilles said and he disappeared into the darkness without waiting for an answer, leaving Tim crouching among the gooseberries and cursing inwardly. The vision of the traitor sitting there at his ease before a good fire and drinking rum punch with his confederate, while he himself squatted in the bushes with rain pouring on his head, was more than his good American soul could endure. But he had great faith in his French friend's ingenuity and so he bore his discomfort patiently.

Soon, however, the peaceful scene within was somewhat disturbed. The fire, instead of burning properly, began to smoke, slightly to begin with and then more and more thickly. The room filled with smoke and the two men started to cough. Tim had just time to duck down among the gooseberries before General Arnold was at the window, throwing it up.

'We'll choke to death!' Tim heard him say. 'I'll call Smith—'

'Don't trouble,' came the young Englishman's voice hoarsely. 'It's this dreadful weather. The water must be coming down the chimney. Leave the window up a little and don't call anyone, or it could go on for ever. What does it matter if it is a little cool? Let's get down to business . . . Acting on behalf of the British government, Sir Henry Clinton is willing to accept your return to a proper way of thinking and to grant you the rank of brigadier-general in the British army, as well as the sum of £20,000. The *Vulture* will, of course, remain within call to take you and Mrs Arnold to New York as soon as matters are in hand at the fort. She has an excellent anchorage. In fact we spent last night there, while waiting for your signal.'

Just then, Gilles, wetter than ever, rejoined his friend among the gooseberries. He was dripping but cheerful.

'Well?' he asked in a whisper, indicating the chimney, which was still smoking heavily. 'What do you think of it?'

'How did you do it? Throw water down?'

'No. Put a big flat stone across the top of the chimney. It will go on smoking until Smith goes up there to see what's the trouble. Interesting?'

'Even more than you think. Listen—'

Inside, the two men had got to the point of discussing the price, and somewhat acrimoniously. Arnold considered £20,000 rather too little, in view of the enormous advantage he was giving to the English by delivering up to them the plans of the fort's defences, the size of the garrison and the strength of the guns, even down to identifying defective pieces.

'I can even give you,' he went on, 'the text of Washington's last speech at the council of war held on the sixth of this month and the overall situation of our forces.'

Tim turned away suddenly, retched and vomited. Gilles was very pale and there were beads of sweat on his brow, but he could not take his eyes off the figure of the man who, for money, was prepared to sell his friends, his brothers, his own land whose only crime lay in wanting to be itself and not a colony. But inside the room the voice of the young English major rose scathingly.

'Sir,' he said, 'we are not unaware that a short while ago General Washington transferred to your cellars a large sum in gold, brought from France by Admiral de Ternay. There is no objection to your carrying away with you as much as you can take. The *Vulture*'s holds are capacious and empty. But I am not empowered to argue further about the conditions which are offered you. Take it – or I must go back and defer the whole matter until some later date.'

Arnold's beaky profile was etched darkly against the smoke-red glare of the hearth as he stood with his eyes closed in thought and his hands clasped behind his back. Gilles felt Tim tugging him back and he eased himself carefully out of his bush into the denser shadow of an old apple tree that stood at the entrance to the vegetable garden. Until then, the silence of the night had been broken only by the patter of the rain and the moaning of the wind, but now another sound had been added, the distant rattle of musket fire and, farther off, the rumble of the guns.

'What is it?' Gilles whispered.

'The English and American positions are still somewhat confused. There are plenty of places between here and New York where there's nearly always some firing going on. But that's not why I called you away. There was something I had to say. Look, you go back to the gooseberry bushes and stay there until they've finished their damned talk. Then, when it's over, or when it's getting light, come back and join me where we left the horses.'

'But what about you?'

'It's my turn to have an idea! And since we must find out all we can about this devil Arnold, we must go our separate ways. See you later.'

With that, Tim vanished into the darkness in his customary fashion, making no more noise than a cat, and Gilles went back stoically to his post beneath the window. He remained there for hours, listening as hard as he could. Arnold and the Englishman let the fire go out. The room was no longer full of smoke but they were so absorbed in their plans that they did not think to close the window. From where he crouched, Gilles could see them both bent over the big map spread out on the table, marking roads and taking notes. Arnold's features shone with a frightening intelligence which had the young Breton torn between admiration and disgust. The traitor had the stuff of greatness in him and yet he chose to debase himself, to

265

destroy his own legend, for the sake of worldly gain. He worked with a fierce concentration, quite unconscious of the sad, contemptuous looks which came over his young companion's face from time to time as he glanced at him. Clearly, the British major had a very different concept of a soldier's honour.

An asthmatic cockerel crowed somewhere not far off, rousing the one in Smith's fowlhouse to retaliate with a triumphant *cockadoodledoo*! As if in answer, a cannon went off close by, rousing the two men bent over the map abruptly. It was followed by another.

'Who's that firing?' the Englishman asked. 'And at whom?'

'I don't know. I didn't know there were any big guns near here.'

Just then, Josh Smith reappeared. He held a telescope in one hand. His glance took in the cold room, the dead fire and the open window.

'It was such a warm night,' the Englishman said, smiling. 'We wanted to make the most of it.'

'That damned chimney of yours started smoking like a hundred Indian chiefs,' Arnold growled.

Gilles took advantage of Smith's entrance to quit his post in the gooseberries at last. It was nearly light and he was in danger of being caught. Running quickly, keeping his head down, he reached the gate and cleared it in a bound, despite his stiffened muscles, but then crept back along the hedge until he was level with the window. Joshua Smith was standing at it, his telescope to his eye and an officer on either side of him. His startled voice came clearly to Gilles.

'The *Vulture*! They're firing at the *Vulture*!'

'Who? Who?' Arnold cried, beside himself and oblivious of caution.

'The only gun we have between here and West Point is the one at Colonel Lamb's post. But he's too far away,' Smith said. 'That sounds as if it's coming from Colonel Livingston's, but he has none! Oh, my God! The ship is weighing anchor – she's going!'

Clear on the morning breeze which had followed last night's storm came the sound of the young Englishman's laughter and his voice saying coolly: 'And without me! It looks as though I'm going to have to walk back to New York.'

'I'll find you a horse, sir, and I'll take you myself if need be,' Josh Smith declared. 'I'll not have it said that any man came to parley from the enemy and I didn't see him safely back. It's a matter of honour with me.'

Then the window was closed again at last and Gilles heard nothing more. But the farmer's last words had made him think. He had used the phrase 'to parley from the enemy'. Was it possible that he was not in league with Arnold, or at least not wittingly? Could he have been another of the lame devil's dupes? He could well have been blinded by hints about a possible truce, in view of the onset of bad weather making operations difficult.

His thoughts were interrupted by noise of galloping hooves and he flattened himself as best he could against the hedge. A troop of American horse with an officer in command came down the lane at the back of Smith's house and clattered to a halt. The officer dismounted and went inside, to return a moment later escorting General Arnold. A horse was brought to him and he paused with one foot in the stirrup to speak to Josh Smith.

'Goodbye for the present, Smith,' he said, perhaps a shade too loudly. 'Do nothing without orders, do you understand? Nothing!'

'I understand, General. I'll wait for orders.'

It seemed to Gilles that it was high time he rejoined Tim and told him what had passed. The traitor's last words were clear enough. The Englishman was to remain hidden in Smith's house until a way could be found for him to return to his own lines. Indeed, it could hardly have been possible for him to show himself in broad daylight in his red coat in the very midst of the American positions.

Keeping in the shelter of the hedge, Gilles made his way down to the river under cover of the bustle of Arnold's noisy departure on the road above. Once there, he took to his heels and sprinted all the way back to the tree where they had left the horses tethered. There he found Tim rubbing the beasts down. He had already fed them and they seemed none the worse for their night out in the wet. The American was apparently in the best of humours and was whistling as he

267

worked. He greeted his friend as cheerfully as if they had both just risen from a good night's sleep in comfortable beds.

'And suppose you tell me all about that gun,' Gilles suggested, half-laughing. 'It sounds extraordinarily interesting.'

Tim's smile broadened until it seemed to split his face in two.

'Good, eh? I knew that Colonel Lamb, whose post is farther up the river, had a very pretty cannon that was quite easy to move. I persuaded him to lend it to the commander of a small fort up there, where you can hardly see it, a certain Captain Livingston. It wasn't altogether easy. Lamb cherishes his piece of artillery like an heirloom. Livingston had to promise him to get it back to him by midday, in case of an inspection. But it worked, you see. The *Vulture* thought herself so well hidden, and now she's upped and gone. Now let's hear from you. How do things stand?'

Gilles gave a brief account of his night and of the effects of the gunfire and then, full of enthusiasm, he went on: 'Arnold has gone. The Englishman is all alone at Josh Smith's house. Why don't we go and take him prisoner and carry him off to General Washington?'

'We might do that if Josh Smith really were a traitor but from what you've told me I do believe he thinks that by helping to bring about a meeting between an emissary of the British and the commander of West Point he has been serving the cause of Independence. He would not understand and we should get no help from anyone, either from Livingston's men or those at West Point. Do you want me to tell you what would happen?'

'Don't bother. I know. They would think we were either spies or madmen and hang us on the spot—'

'For the very good reason that we should be taken straight to Arnold himself. So that's that. We'll have to think of something else. Don't forget that we look much more like highway robbers than like honest soldiers fighting for a just cause. What we want is to be able to lay hands on the little English major, but out of Arnold's reach. Only then could we take him to Washington and there at least we should have more in the way of proof than a vague tale told by an Indian.'

'It sounds wonderfully simple,' Gilles said, with heavy irony.

'All we have to do is put it into practice. So what are we going to do now?'

'The horses are ready. We'll have something to eat – Livingston, bless his heart, not only gave me oats for the horses but took pity on my hungry looks as well and gave me enough for a substantial breakfast – and after that, we'll be on our way.'

'On our way to where? Wouldn't it be better to go on keeping watch on Smith's house? What if he puts the Englishman over the river tonight in his boat?'

'He won't. For then the major would have to pass Peekskill and our lines. If he wants to reach the English outposts at White Plains, he will have to keep on this side of the river all the way down to King's Ferry. That is the first place he can cross. He'll be disguised, of course, but you got a good enough look at him last night. You would know him again, surely?'

'Without a moment's doubt. Even disguised as a woodsman or a parson!'

'There you are then! Rather than risk getting caught round here, we'll go ahead to King's Ferry and wait quietly for him on the other side of the river.'

Tim's confidence was infectious, and yet Gilles could not wholly bring himself to share it. The uneasiness which was to come upon him so often in after days that he would learn to recognize it as a kind of sixth sense, warned him against it. Who could say that Arnold, whose brains were not in doubt, would not find some other way of getting his accomplice back to his own side, even if it meant procuring an American uniform for him to enable him to pass securely through their lines, while his pursuers waited for him in vain at King's Ferry?

For all that Tim Thocker was not fond of hearing his companion dispute his opinions, Gilles felt so strongly that they would be taking too great a risk that he said so roundly. To his surprise, Tim readily admitted his objection.

'Anything is possible with that devil! But in that case, there's only one place to wait for the Englishman, one place he'll have to pass on his way back, and that's the ford at Croton River. If we miss him at King's Ferry, we'll have him there. Now let's have done with talking and be on our way!'

Gilles' answer was to hoist himself into the saddle.

The rain caught up with them again long before they reached the crossing and beat down on them as though it had a personal grudge against them. In the grey daylight, masses of thick cloud raced along the valley, releasing an icy deluge which no clothing could keep out.

'I wonder if I'll ever be quite dry again?' Gilles muttered through clenched teeth. 'I think I'm turning into a fish!'

Shoulders hunched against the downpour, the two riders cantered along the wooded skirts of the valley, oblivious of cold, weariness and even the wet. Their minds and bodies were bent ruthlessly to one end only, to stop the English emissary and bring Washington the proof of Arnold's betrayal, the written proof which Gilles had seen passed over before his eyes. This object they must achieve at all costs, whatever obstacles might stand in their way.

The first of these presented itself at King's Ferry in the persons of two militiamen, recognizable by the pine sprig they wore in their battered cocked hats. The ferry was not to go. They had orders from above. This was to prevent the necessity of firing upon it in the event of any more English ships attempting to sail up to West Point.

Tim was already opening his mouth in furious protest when a frosty look from Gilles made him shut it again. Meanwhile, the Breton was saying cheerfully : 'Oh, well then, let's wait. If we can't cross, we can comfort ourselves with the thought that no one else can either. And I see a tavern over there.'

'Are you out of your mind?' Tim asked roughly. 'Taverns cost money and we haven't a bean !'

'Quite right! Not a bean – but a few dollars, all the same, thanks to our understanding friend, Sam Paulding. He slipped them to me quietly and I never remembered to tell you. I shall repay him, naturally—'

'He gave you money? I'd never have thought he would be so generous,' Tim said in astonishment.

'Nor should I,' Gilles retorted with a chuckle. 'But I heard his pocket chinking and saw the great bulge in it. We can send it back to him later – if we're alive to do it !'

Tim's eyes were as round as the coins which emerged so miraculously from his friend's sodden gown.

'Well, well, well!' he said again. 'I'd never have thought that someone who was going to be a priest could turn out so neat-fingered when it came to picking a rogue's pocket!'

'If you knew what my family had been capable of a few hundred years ago, you'd not be so surprised. And it wasn't always a matter of life and death, either,' the last scion of the lords of La Hunaudaye remarked in a self-satisfied tone. 'Well, are we going to the inn?'

'I'm right behind you!'

A few minutes later, the two young men were sitting with their wet feet steaming on the fender of the inn and savouring a hot punch, with the prospect of a nourishing onion broth to follow. But Gilles had taken care to seat himself where he could keep an eye on the road and the approach to the ferry.

'We ought to get some sleep,' Tim said, as he finished his soup. 'I shouldn't think they'd be likely to come before the evening, and I for one am feeling pretty sleepy.'

'I'm not. You sleep if you want to. I'll wake you if I see anything—'

'You'll be tired out by tonight.'

'Then I'll sleep on my horse, and you can lead me. Besides, who knows if we will be going farther tonight?'

Propped against the chimney piece, his body warm and relaxed but his brain wide awake and his eyes alert, Gilles whiled away the time with drinking endless cups of tea and now and then chatting to the militiamen when one or other of them came in to warm himself, or to the landlady of the inn, who was a thin, chirpy little woman, dressed in black as became a widow but with a lively eye for men in general.

The tall, fair youth who wore his disgraceful garments with such an air of elegance clearly attracted her, perhaps because of his light blue eyes which, in a face tanned almost as dark as an Indian's, were like windows opening on to a pale, morning sky. She kept hovering about him in a way that he began to find extremely trying, since her black dress was continually coming between him and the window he was watching.

She had told him all about the heroic death of her husband, the late Mr Sullivan, at Monmouth Courthouse and was embarking on the tale of their courtship beneath the blossoming apple

271

trees of Northcastle, when some instinct brought Gilles to his feet.

Excusing himself, he strode over to the window and leaned out, feeling the blood beat faster in his veins. Two horsemen were standing at the ferry landing, talking to the militiamen.

They were dressed alike in brown suits with silver buttons under their long, dark cloaks, but the faces beneath their black cocked hats were those which Gilles had been watching for so persistently. They were Josh Smith and the English major, disguised as good American citizens.

They talked for a moment longer. Then Gilles saw the Englishman take a piece of white paper from under his cloak and hold it out to the militiaman who took it with a bored expression, read it, shrugged helplessly and then turned away to the ferryman's hut, while the two travellers made their way slowly down to the ferryboat and stepped aboard.

Cursing volubly, Gilles flung himself on Tim, dragged him off his bench still half awake and hauled him over to the window.

'Look! They've managed to get across!'

Tim's dazed eyes focused abruptly and he let out a volley of oaths which would have shocked his father, the minister. Then he made a dash for the door, wrenched it open and plunged towards the militia post, with Gilles at his heels. But quick as they were, they were still too late. The ferry had left the bank and was well out in the stream.

'What is the meaning of this?' Tim yelled furiously. 'Here have we been sitting in the inn for hours because you said your damned ferry wasn't running! Orders from above, you said! Will you tell me what it is doing now, for those two?'

The militiaman shrugged phlegmatically, pulled his pipe out of his pocket and began methodically filling it.

'Couldn't say no to them, cully! Their orders come from even higher up. A pass signed by General Arnold himself! No good saying no to him. No good you getting yourself in such a state about it, either,' he added with a touch of alarm as Tim's rage showed signs of becoming uncontrollable.

Gilles, on the other hand, began to laugh.

'He's right, Tim! It can't do any good. There are some injustices even in a democracy. Never mind,' he added, turning to the militiaman. 'They must be members of Congress at least, to have such passes. Do you know where they were bound?'

Grateful for this unexpected support, the man grinned broadly at Gilles and spat majestically on the ground.

'Congress? No such thing! One of them is Joshua Smith, a big farmer and well known in these parts, and the other's a cousin of his from Albany. They are expected at the house of Smith's brother-in-law, Mr Pendleton at Long Grove, some two miles from here. Seems there's trouble there.'

The militiaman moved away, leaving the two friends staring at the river which seemed to mock them. The ferryboat was already nearly at the other side.

'We must get across!' Tim muttered, gritting his teeth.

'We can't get the horses across without the ferry. I can see only one solution.'

'What is it?'

'To wait until well after nightfall when there's no one around and steal the boat.'

'Always supposing it comes back, which I doubt. The ferry-man lives on the other side. He must have been delighted to be obliged to go back home!'

Gilles' calmness was beginning to desert him.

'Then we must go farther on and find another ferry. The main thing is to get ahead of him before—'

'The river gets a lot wider after this. We'd have to go all the way down to Tappan and cross at Dobbs Ferry, then come back to the Croton River.'

They went back glumly to the inn, to be met by Mrs Sullivan with broad smiles, for she had feared that the handsome young gentleman was about to depart without paying his shot.

'I'll have your suppers ready in a trice,' she promised gaily. 'I don't like to boast, mind, but I think you'll be pleased. And then a good room shall be made ready for you. This is a modest house but my bedchambers want for nothing. Unless you gentlemen are in haste to continue your journey and would wish to cross the river after you have supped?'

'We are indeed in haste,' Gilles said, 'but it is not kind in you to mock us, ma'am. You know that no one may cross the river tonight.'

'But I am not mocking you. I know that you are in haste. You have spent the whole day watching the ferry and then when it takes others across, you both go rushing out like madmen! Yet you can cross none the less, for I have a boat.'

She was taking pewter plates down from a dresser and setting them on the table as she spoke. Gilles sighed wretchedly.

'We cannot take our horses across in a boat, and we cannot go without them.'

The landlady laughed. 'As to your horses, let me tell you that not only do I have a boat, I also have a son that is a farrier in the village across the river, and he has horses for hire. You have only to leave your beasts with me and I will give you a note for Nat in exchange, and he will give you two more, fresh horses. You can bring them back when you come to collect your own from here. Oh! There, now, young man! That will do!'

In his excitement, Gilles had caught up the old woman in his arms and deposited a smacking kiss on either cheek, an expression of a gratitude infinitely more sincere than was the indignation of its recipient. She promptly disappeared into her store room in a whirl of petticoats to bring out her best preserves, looking ten years younger.

Tim sat with his elbows on the table and regarded his friend with admiration.

'Being attractive to women can cause complications, but you must admit there are times when it comes in confoundedly handy!'

There were no other guests at the inn that night and supper, presided over by Mrs Sullivan herself, was a merry meal. They heard the rest of the story of the hero of Monmouth Courthouse and his bride, Gilles talked of Brittany and Tim of his travels to Paris. They finished by toasting General Washington in the late Mr Sullivan's best brandy. At last, towards nine o'clock, they began to think of departing.

While the two young men checked their weapons, Mrs Sullivan left the room and reappeared with a heavy sleeveless jacket, sheepskin lined, which she put round Gilles' shoulders.

'It belonged to my late husband,' she said, smiling a trifle moistly. 'He doesn't need it now, poor man, and you could do with something to keep you warm.'

'Mrs Sullivan, you are the best of women,' Gilles told her,

deeply touched. 'I look forward to coming back to see you again.'

He kissed her once more, as he might have kissed Rozenn or his mother, always supposing she would have allowed it. Tim shook her warmly by the hand and then the two of them stepped out into the night and made for the little boathouse she had shown them.

Five minutes later, they were rowing for the scattering of lights on the far bank.

There was a strong current but the weather had moderated and the two friends pulled on their oars with such a will that they were very soon across the river.

'Now all we have to do is to find the farrier,' Tim said as he sprang on to the little landing stage.

Dawn found them at the Croton River ford. The welcome they had received from Mrs Sullivan's son, after knocking him up in the middle of the night, had been in every way the equal of his mother's. In addition to the promised horses, he provided them with a few hours' sleep and a valuable piece of information. The two travellers had indeed gone to Mr Pendleton's house, arriving there at nightfall. And now Gilles and Tim were sitting their horses behind a thin screen of trees, keeping a watch on the line of stakes across the river which marked the ford. They themselves had crossed without difficulty.

They did not have to wait long. A pair of kingfishers skimmed the surface of the water and rose skywards and in the same instant, a horseman appeared and rode quietly into the ford. Gilles' keen eyes knew him at once. It was the Englishman.

'There he is,' he said softly. 'Strange, though . . . he is alone.'

'Not so strange. It is not far now to the English lines. Smith must have decided there was no more to fear and turned back.'

The officer certainly appeared tranquil enough. He was guiding his horse carelessly with one hand, the other hanging loosely at his side, and gazing about him, smiling slightly, at the green countryside, washed clean by the heavy rains of the previous day. It was a beautiful, peaceful morning in which war seemed to have no place and he was clearly far from imagining any danger.

'Let's go,' Gilles said, as the Englishman reached dry ground. He levelled his pistol and rode out from behind the screen of trees, with Tim at his heels, and blocked the traveller's path. Having no hat to doff, he contented himself with a slight inclination of his head.

'Sir,' he said, with perfect politeness, 'be so good as to consider yourself our prisoner and to hand over the papers you received from General Arnold.'

If he were surprised, the young officer did not show it.

'Who are you, sir?' he asked mildly.

'Although you might not think it from our dress, we belong to the United States Army.'

'You do not speak like an American.'

'I serve the King of France but you must know that at the present time that comes to the same thing. Come, sir, the papers! We know precisely what you have been doing in the house of Josh Smith.'

The Englishman's smile was a miracle of quiet charm. He shook his head gently.

'Indeed, sir, I fear your wits have gone a-begging. I have no idea what papers you are referring to. Unless, perhaps, to this?'

He drew a folded paper from his breast. It did indeed carry the signature of General Arnold and contain his clear and unmistakable order to whom it might concern to facilitate the journey of one John Anderson, Esquire, of Albany, travelling to Norwalk.

'Not that, as you well know. Will you be good enough to dismount?'

'As you wish.'

While Tim kept the Englishman carefully covered with his rifle, Gilles searched him thoroughly, but found nothing.

'This is too much!' he exclaimed. 'I saw with my own eyes that traitor Arnold hand you a description of the fort's defences and the strength of the garrison.'

The Englishman laughed and, completely ignoring Tim, went to catch his horse which had begun to move away.

'Then your eyes were playing tricks on you,' he said. 'Now may I continue my journey?'

But something about him had put Gilles on his guard.

'I see that you are walking with a limp?' he observed sardonically.

276

'A slight sprain. I slipped in the mud when dismounting yesterday.'

'Indeed? Then would you mind removing your boot?'

Gilles knew by the Englishman's sudden pallor that he had guessed correctly. The papers he was looking for were there, carefully folded, in between his stocking and his foot.

'We have them now, Tim,' he said happily, holding the papers towards his friend. 'Look!'

In his delight, he failed to notice the change which had come over his prisoner's face and he started as he heard a drawling voice behind him say : 'I'd like a look at those papers you seem to find so interesting, young man.'

A number of men had appeared from nowhere, villainous-looking fellows clad in an assortment of military tunics and rough jackets and breeches. They were drawn up around the group on the path in a wide semi-circle based on the river. The Englishman cried out gladly.

'This is a godsend! Surely, you must be Cowboys? I was told there were some hereabouts. These men are Americans. Get me away from them.'

The one who seemed to be their leader, and whose appearance was, if possible, even more villainous than his men's, came forward, twitching the papers out of Gilles' hands as he did so.

'And who are you?'

'One of you – more or less. I am a British officer. On a special mission for General Clinton.'

The other man pushed back the greasy cocked hat with a flamboyant feather in it, which served him for headgear, and laughed. Something about his laughter struck a chord in Gilles' mind.

'A British officer, eh? Well, if you're the best friend Clinton can show by way of secret agents, he's in a poor way. You're out in your reckoning, my boy. We're not Cowboys. Skinners is what we are.'

'More of them!' Gilles could not help exclaiming. He felt as if he had been here before. But then Tim broke in.

'Your name wouldn't be Ned Paulding, by any chance?'

The face that turned towards him had a red nose and eyes to match, but it bore a gratified expression.

'That's the ticket! My fame's spread, has it?'

'No, but we know your brother Sam. In fact he told us to look for you round about the Croton River. You gave us a nasty turn. We've been following this man, who is a British spy, for two days and we thought he was going to give us the slip. If you'll return those papers to us, we'll be on our way with him.'

'Not so fast! What you say may well be true, but Sam and me, that's not altogether the same thing.'

He peered at the papers, turning them over in stubby, tobacco-stained fingers.

'These could be worth a mint of money, I guess,' he said, as if to himself.

'If it's money you want,' the Englishman cried, snatching at a possible means of escape, 'I can give it to you. I have five hundred dollars on me, and a gold watch – take them and let me go.'

'Interesting. Hand them over.'

'You call yourself an American and you are going to let him get away!' Gilles cried angrily, watching the Skinner pocket the money and the watch. 'This is high treason and you deserve hanging for it!'

Ned Paulding sniffed, wiped his nose on his sleeve and favoured him with what was clearly intended to be a winning smile.

'Calm down, young feller-me-lad, calm down! We Pauldings are no traitors, as Sam must have told you. But we're not fools, either. So it's we are going to take this prisoner of yours to the proper place for him. I've a notion the Colonel Jameson, who commands the cavalry post at North Castle, might give a few more dollars for him.'

'That is unworthy! You have taken the man's money! Either let him go or give it back to him. As for the papers—'

'I'm very glad to have them,' the other said, putting them in his pocket. 'But since you seem to me to be a trifle too inclined to meddle in other men's affairs, you'll oblige me by staying here. You, there! Lay hold of these pullets and tie them each to a tree! We'll have time enough to finish our business before they manage to free themselves – and we'll get two more horses into the bargain.'

Almost before he had finished speaking, Gilles and Tim were set upon by a score of men and trussed helplessly although they both put up a spirited defence. Gilles bellowed like an ox, beside himself with rage. The tears started from his eyes as he saw the English officer's bound wrists roped to the saddle of his own horse and Ned Paulding bestriding it.

'Sir,' he cried. 'I ask your pardon. It was my duty to intercept you, but I would rather you had gone free than have seen you in the hands of these wretches. They are a disgrace to an honourable cause!'

The Englishman gave him the charming smile which Gilles, had been struck by in Josh Smith's house.

'I know that, sir. In all the time that we have been fighting the French, we have always known that honour to them was more than an empty word. But have no fear. I should not think of confusing these men with General Washington's, for he is a perfect gentleman. Goodbye to you, sir, and thank you for what you tried to do.'

The party rode off in a cloud of dust. When it subsided, the banks of the Croton River were as peaceful as before. The two young men, lashed to their separate trees, had, perforce, become a part of the scene and Gilles' temper gradually grew calm again.

'It remains to be seen how long we shall be obliged to stay here,' he said with a sigh, tugging at his bonds to test their strength.

'We're not far from the ford. Someone will be bound to come sooner or later. And after all, why should we worry? Arnold's trick has failed in any case. Colonel Jameson, whoever he is, must be able to read. He'll do what's needed.'

'If those damned Skinners don't run into the Cowboys or an English patrol on the way to North Castle.'

'Trust Paulding for that. He's a natural-born bandit, that one! He'll guard his prisoner like a dog its bone. Besides, it may not be long before we're free. Someone will surely come along—'

But the hours passed and no one crossed the ford. They had to wait until nearly nightfall for their release, which came to them in the shape of a strong troop of regular horse.

The officer with them was the second-in-command at the North Castle post. His name was Colonel Benjamin Tallmadge and he was a man of middle age, cool, deliberate and somewhat taciturn. His rigid features were quite devoid of expression but his gaze was direct and uncompromising and his speech forthright. The questions he put to them were short and to the point, and he listened carefully to what they told him in reply. He seemed to feel no great surprise at the adventures of these two villainously dressed strangers, or at their story of the night at Josh Smith's house. But he frowned when Gilles told him of the Skinners' intention to sell their prisoner to Colonel Jameson.

'Get up behind two of my men,' he told them. 'We are going back to North Castle.' And he added, as though to himself: 'Colonel Jameson is a good soldier but he is also a particular friend of General Arnold and deeply indebted to him.'

They found the post in a state of ferment and Colonel Jameson standing in the yard with two of his officers. But there was no sign of the Skinners or their prisoner. They soon discovered, however, that they had been there and that Colonel Tallmadge's half-expressed fears had been fully justified. Much incensed by what he regarded as a base attack on his beloved General Arnold, Colonel Jameson's reaction had been to despatch the prisoner to West Point with an escort commanded by a Lieutenant Allen.

Tallmadge went straight in to the attack. He spoke calmly and without raising his voice, but every one of his words went home.

'Colonel Jameson, unless you have a fancy to find yourself answering a charge of high treason before General Washington and the United States Congress, you had better send after Allen and get that prisoner back here at once. He is a member of General Clinton's staff.'

'What gave you that idea, Tallmadge? He's a man called John Anderson and he carries a pass signed by General Arnold and other papers which confirm him as a spy.'

'He is not a spy, and Arnold is a traitor. Question these men here. They are on their way back from a mission on Washington's behalf.'

Two hours later, when the night was far advanced, Lieutenant Allen and his party returned to North Castle. At the sight of the prisoner, who looked tired and discouraged under this fresh blow of fate which had brought him back when he had thought himself within sight of freedom, Tallmadge turned to Gilles.

'You were right. This man is certainly an English officer. That much is clear from his bearing.'

The Englishman shrugged and gave them a weary smile.

'There's no point in concealing it now. I am Major John André of the British Army, on a mission for General Clinton.'

As he was led off to Colonel Jameson, Gilles turned to Tallmadge.

'What will happen to him?'

'The usual fate of spies. If he had been taken in uniform, he would have been treated as a prisoner of war, and shot at need. But thanks to his civilian dress, he will be hanged.'

'But he is not a spy! He came in response to a summons from Arnold, to talk to him, and I can swear that he was wearing uniform then. It was circumstances forced him to dress like that.'

For the life of him, Gilles could not have said what it was that made him spring to the young Englishman's defence like this. His own sense of justice and honour were part of it, but there was also an instinctive liking which he could not help. He felt attracted to the good-looking young man, scarcely older than himself. He would have liked him for a friend. And in fact it was as a friend that John André had greeted him as he entered the post, with a smile and a lift of his hand.

Tallmadge shrugged. 'Well,' he said, 'you can always speak for him at his trial.'

With the prisoner under lock and key, there was some discussion about what to do with him. It was decided that, in view of the urgency of the situation, he should be delivered to Washington as soon as possible. But where was the General to be found? Was he still at Hartford, where he had been meeting Rochambeau and de Ternay, or had he already moved on from there to West Point, which had been his intention?

'There's only one thing to do,' Tallmadge said. 'We must send messages to both places.'

Jameson looked gloomily from Gilles to Tim.

'Washington knows you both. Could you undertake to do it? One of you would go to Hartford with a letter from me, and the other to West Point, with these damned papers. You'd be given horses and could start at dawn.'

'We are at your service, Colonel,' they replied with one voice.

So, as dawn was breaking the next day, Gilles and Tim rode out of North Castle, bade each other a cheerful farewell and went their separate ways. Tim headed north-west for Hartford and Gilles sped back the way they had come the day before, making for King's Ferry and West Point. It was he who carried the proof of Arnold's treachery. He was also the bearer of a letter which Major André had asked should be given to General Washington. In it, the major bravely admitted to the charges laid against him. He went on :

'Unhappy as I am, I have nothing to be ashamed of. I have had no other object than to serve my King. I engaged in this subterfuge willingly. I ask your permission to write an open letter to Sir Henry Clinton and another to a friend to ask for fresh linen and clothes. I take the liberty of reminding you of the situation of several persons who, being prisoners on parole at Charleston, engaged in a conspiracy against us. Perhaps they might be exchanged for me. It is my trust in your generosity no less than my respect for your high office which encourages me to importune you in this fashion. I am, etc.'

In handing this letter to the young Breton, the prisoner had insisted that he read it.

'Since you have the General's confidence, perhaps, sir, you would tell him what you know of this sad business and—'

'Plead an honest man's cause? You may rely on me, Major. I cannot promise you success but I will do all I can to see that you do not suffer for another's crime.'

Bending low over the neck of his galloping horse, Gilles felt as though on wings. It was a long time since he had felt such inner content. Against all the odds, he and Tim had succeeded in forestalling treachery, the Rebels were saved and he himself was on his way back to rejoin the man he admired more than any other. Then, too, he had the hope of being able to save the life of the young Englishman who had been caught in the toils of treason and was now under threat of a shameful death. The thought of André dangling at a rope's end was one he did not like to contemplate. It was absurd and unjust and thoroughly distasteful. Lastly, he was back in uniform once more, for the first time in many days. Tallmadge had equipped him with a cavalryman's dress and Gilles had felt a thrill of excitement as he put on the white breeches, boots and black coat with gilt buttons worn by every soldier of Congress, from the latest recruit up to Washington himself. When he placed the black tricorn with its black cockade on his head, it was as if those few yards of cloth and scraps of leather had bestowed upon him a kind of baptism into this great country which was growing dearer to him with every passing minute. Given victory and promotion, he would be able to go boldly knocking on the door of the convent at Hennebont, snatch Judith away and bring her back to America so that they might found a family together.

The thought of Judith came into his mind quite naturally. It may have been his wild ride and the salt tang of the not far distant sea borne on the wind which had torn away the soft veil of mist that covered her in his memory, or perhaps the hope of a worthier future which was beginning to take shape in his mind, but Gilles found his love for her and his need to win her and to make her his for ever still unchanged. The fierce desire he had felt for Sitapanoki had faded as soon as he was no longer with her. She drew him as a magnet would draw iron, but the attraction could not survive separation. And now he was glad of a parting which had seemed painful only for a moment. God knew what folly he might have been driven to by his imperative need for her body!

'She would have made an idiot of you, my friend,' he told himself, clapping spurs to his horse. 'And that is no fit state for a Tournemine.'

It was just after one o'clock in the afternoon when the messenger came in sight of West Point. He reined in for a second, gazing in admiration at what La Fayette was to call America's Gibraltar. The site was very impressive. The fortress stood on a rocky hill on the right bank of the Hudson. The river at that point was as broad as a lake and flowed between steep, thickly wooded banks covered in a mixture of oaks and conifers. The outer fortifications, partly carved out of the living rock and partly built of stout logs covered the surrounding slopes. As for the citadel itself, it housed at that time four thousand men and a score of guns, and the flag with the thirteen stars of the new Republic flew proudly from the topmost pinnacle. Several well-armed schooners lay at anchor in the river.

There was a good deal of activity in the narrow field that lay between the fortress and the river. A company of foot, dressed in assorted garments but each with a splendid red and black plume in his hat and a gilt sword at his side, were drawn up there.

Not quite sure what he was going to find, Gilles rode forward cautiously and addressed the nearest man.

'Despatches from North Castle,' he said briefly. 'Our information is that General Washington is expected here?'

The man looked at him oddly and then roared with laughter.

'Well I'm blest!' he said, speaking in French with a strong accent of the Auvergne. 'You've an accent that doesn't go with your fine uniform, my friend! You wouldn't be one of us, by any chance?'

'Why, of course I'm French! And a Breton, what's more,' Gilles responded gaily, leaning down to shake the soldier's hand. 'But what is your regiment? I don't recognize your colours.'

'You may well say that! And there are none too many Frenchmen among us, I must admit. This is General La Fayette's division.'

'La Fayette is here?'

'He is indeed! He arrived a good hour since, with Colonel Hamilton, sent from General Washington to accompany him. We've been on escort duty ever since Litchfield. All three of them must be up there still.'

'And General Arnold?'

'Ah, him! No one knows where he is. Seems he went off on a tour of inspection across the river.'

But Gilles was no longer listening. Calling out his thanks, he set his horse at a gallop up the ramp leading to the gate and thundered into West Point. He cleared the sentries' crossed weapons like a hedge, with a cry of: 'Urgent despatches for General Washington!'

284

A moment later, he was dismounting almost at the feet of the Virginian who had appeared in the doorway of a casemate like Lazarus summoned by Jesus from the tomb. He knew Gilles at once, but showed a good deal of surprise at seeing him.

'You, sir? And in this uniform?'

'I bring grave news, General. Colonel Jameson, who sent me, thought that this would give me the best chance of delivering it.'

Saluting formally, he held out the packet containing the papers as well as André's letter and another from Jameson himself explaining matters.

It came as an even greater blow to the commander-in-chief than he had feared. For all his legendary self-control, Washington turned pale, swayed and closed his eyes. Gilles heard him murmur softly: 'Twenty thousand pounds! . . . The rank of brigadier general! Oh, God!'

For a moment it seemed that he would swoon, overcome by the perfidy of the man he loved and trusted. Gilles scarcely dared to breathe, much less stretch out a hand to support him. Guessing that the best way to respect his feelings was to pretend not to notice, he remained standing straight as a ramrod, his eyes fixed on the wall of the casemate. There was a silence which seemed to him to last a thousand years but which was not in fact more than a few seconds. At last, Washington opened his eyes. They rested on the military dummy before him and Gilles heard him draw a breath.

'I am told that it is to you and your friend Tim Thocker that we owe the discovery of this plot?' he said dully, keeping his voice steady with an effort.

Gilles nerved himself to look at him.

'We are at your service, General,' he said with a fervour that brought a touch of colour back to the commander's face. 'We have done no more than our duty.'

Washington stepped forward and laid a hand on his shoulder and gripped it, saying simply: 'Thank you.'

Gilles felt himself more royally rewarded by that word and the gesture that accompanied it than if he had been made a full colonel and presented with a fortune. But already the momentary show of feeling was over. Washington blenched suddenly and a startled look came into his eyes.

'My God! The gold?' he said. 'Follow me!'

One after the other, they ran across the courtyard to where a low door in the far corner was guarded by a soldier with a musket.

'Get me the keys!' the General snapped. 'They are in General Arnold's office. Ask Major Grant for them.'

The man was soon back and Major Grant with him.

'We have not got the keys,' the officer said. 'General Arnold carried them with him at all times.'

'Then break down the door.'

It took ten men and a stout ram to accomplish it. It gave at last, with a thunderous crash, revealing the beginning of a flight of steps leading down into the ground.

'A lantern! Hurry!'

With Gilles going ahead to light the way and Major Grant bringing up the rear, Washington descended the steps. They ended in a narrow passage at the far end of which were more steps leading deeper still. It was miserably cold and damp. At last they came to another door, so formidably barred with iron that Gilles wondered how they were ever going to get it open without blowing up the entire fortress. But, strangely enough, it opened without difficulty once they had withdrawn the bar.

Before them lay a long cellar. It was empty except for a row of small casks ranged neatly in order. They did not seem to have been tampered with, for the impressive seal on each one was unbroken.

'Thank God! I think we are in time,' Washington said grimly. 'All the same, we had best make sure. The man is cunning. Major, get one of these barrels open—'

The major selected one at random and prised the lid off with the point of his sword, while Gilles held the lantern up for him. What he found inside wrenched an exclamation from him.

'Stones! Nothing but stones!'

Swearing like a trooper, the General tipped the barrel over and then, in a kind of fury, drew his own sword and began ripping the lids out of the remaining ones. With the exception of two which stood a little removed from the rest, they were all filled with stones. Most of the French gold had gone.

White to the lips, Washington stared from one to the other of his companions. Both were equally pale and Gilles was trembling.

'He did not have time to complete his wicked work,' he said bitterly, 'but this winter also my men will die of hunger. Damn him! The coward!'

He looked at Grant. 'Have the two remaining barrels taken to the fortress's strong room and tell them to saddle my horse, and a fresh mount for this man here. We are going to Robinson House. That is where Arnold lives,' he added for Gilles' benefit. 'General La Fayette and Colonel Hamilton have gone there ahead of me, so as not to keep Mrs Arnold's dinner waiting. Her – her husband should be there, since he has not come to me here . . . Oh, how could I be mad enough to trust him with such a fortune? It was tempting providence. But then how could I have foreseen this catastrophe?'

Once mounted, they left the fortress and rode like the wind towards a substantial house built at some small distance away and set in a neat garden planted with coniferous trees. The setting, with the noble river flowing by, was both splendid and serene, which was more than could be said for the house itself, for a state of total confusion reigned within. A black footman, speeding towards the stables, passed the two riders with no more than a glance. Grouped about the doorway were La Fayette and Hamilton, apparently conferring together, with two more footmen and a mulatto woman weeping copiously into her apron. At the sight of the General, the two officers sprang forward with evident relief.

'Ah, General!' La Fayette cried. 'You come in the nick of time! We are in great distress of mind. General Arnold has gone and—'

'Arnold is a traitor,' Washington broke in curtly. 'My God! Who can one trust! I have just received this, Marquis. Read it.'

One peering over the other's shoulder, the two men scanned the documents, unable to restrain their cries of indignation. When they had done, each turned his appalled gaze on Gilles, standing three paces behind the General.

'Yes,' Washington said, his teeth clenched on a scrap of bark torn from a tree which he was chewing to calm his nerves.

'We have to thank this young man for the discovery of what was planned. He has acted with great courage.'

'Why, but surely it's our great catcher of Indians?' La Fayette cried, his anxious face suddenly illumined by a youthful smile. 'Put it there, sir! To find a Frenchman equally devoted to our dear General and to the American cause makes it doubly a pleasure to shake you by the hand. General Rochambeau speaks very highly of you.'

With a thrill of pleasure, Gilles did as he was bid, reflecting that this was indeed a land of miracles, where a great lord of Auvergne offered his hand to a Breton bastard. But Washington called a halt to the exchange.

'Now tell me what has happened here.'

It was Colonel Hamilton who undertook the tale. In a few words, he told how on arriving unexpectedly for dinner at the Robinson House with the news that the commander-in-chief was on their heels, they had found Arnold just getting off his horse after coming from across the river. Rather than keep his wife waiting or risk passing Washington on the way from West Point, he had sat down to dinner with the two young men. The meal had begun pleasantly enough when a messenger had arrived with a letter.

Arnold had read it with no change of expression and begged his guests in the most natural way to excuse him as he was called away on urgent business. He got up and left the dining-room, giving a sign to his wife who presently rose and followed him to his own room. Shortly afterwards, La Fayette and Hamilton had seen him mount his horse and ride away southwards.

Left alone at the table, they soon found themselves growing restless, for Mrs Arnold did not reappear. Eventually they questioned the servant who returned after a moment, bringing the lady's maid. She seemed to be in near hysterics and was weeping copiously.

The girl had told them through her sobs that her mistress was in strong convulsions and, since she was also in an interesting condition, her symptoms had become so alarming that a physician had been sent for.

'We presumed upon our friendship,' La Fayette said, 'to go up to her. She was a pitiable sight. The poor woman is quite

288

out of her mind. She is throwing herself about and you would hear her screams from here if we had not shut the window. She is saying – forgive me, General, but I think it right to tell you the whole – she is saying that you are coming here to kill her child—'

Gilles never forgot the murderous flash of Washington's blue eyes.

'So that is what they think of me here!' he said. 'That is what we may expect from those we love. Peggy Arnold is no fool. If she is acting like one, it is because she knows her husband has fled.'

'Will you not see her?' Hamilton asked.

'No. Stay here, both of you, just in case the traitor should try to return for his wife. I and the Frenchman will return to West Point. I have things to do before I leave here.'

Throughout the remainder of that day, Washington carried out a detailed inspection of the defences of West Point, sent out scouts and read despatches, surrounded by his silent and shamefaced staff. Gilles, promoted to the rank of temporary aide-de-camp, trotted after him, ready to ride to the ends of the earth at the snap of his fingers.

Towards evening, when they were all assembled in what had been Arnold's office for something like a council of war, a black slave appeared as though from nowhere bringing a letter. It was from Arnold and Washington read it aloud:

'When a man has the consciousness of having acted for the best,' the traitor dared to write, 'he does not seek to excuse his actions because the world might censure them. I have always been guided by the love of my country from the beginning of this fatal struggle between Great Britain and her colonies. The same love of my country dictates my present conduct, however contradictory that may seem to the public, which rarely judges us with justice. I have too often experienced the ingratitude of my native land to expect anything of her. But I know enough of Your Excellency's humanity not to fear to solicit your protection for Mistress Arnold against the injustices and insults to which she may be exposed by the desire of revenge. I alone must be its object. She is as innocent as an angel and incapable of the slightest wrong. I ask you to permit her to return to her friends in Philadelphia or to come to me, whichever she prefers. I have no fears for her where Your Excellency is concerned, but may she not be in danger from the unbridled rage of the citizens? I entreat you to be good enough to have the accompanying letter delivered to her and to permit her to write to me. I must also request you to send to me my clothes and baggage which is of little value. If necessary, I will account for their value.

P.S. I owe it to the officers of my staff to make it clear that they had no knowledge of these events which they would have considered fatal to the public good. The same is true of Joshua Smith, on whom suspicion may also rest . . .

Washington finished the letter to a shocked murmur from the officers. He folded it and put it into his pocket, while his eyes travelled coldly from one to another of the assembled men.

'Calm yourselves, gentlemen! This is all very sad. Who can say for sure that this man is cynical or conscienceless? Truly, it is past understanding.' He turned to Gilles.

'Go back to the Robinson House, Mr Goëlo. Tell General La Fayette and Colonel Hamilton to come here. But first of all, deliver Mrs Arnold's letter to her and assure her that her husband is quite certainly safe behind the English lines and that I will send her to her father in Philadelphia whenever she wishes. Say also that her – husband's personal effects are to be got together and brought here to me. You shall bring them, but see that it does not take you too long. We are leaving again in the morning for Tappan for the trial of the English spy who will have been sent there by Colonel Tallmadge.'

The tone in which Washington uttered the two words 'English spy' drove Gilles to break the silence he had preserved upon that subject all day, rather than exacerbate the General's anger.

'Forgive me, General, but have you read Major André's letter?'

'I have. Why do you ask?'

'Because that letter must have told you that the major was no spy. He is a brave and loyal officer who was merely carrying

290

out Sir Henry Clinton's orders, although much against the grain.'

'I do not doubt it. Yet he was taken out of uniform.'

'But through no wish of his own. Necessity alone——'

Washington struck the table with his fist.

'Do not trifle with me. The law is the law. Any officer or man taken in civilian clothes upon enemy soil shall be regarded as a spy and so treated. He shall be hanged, as our man, Nathan Hale by name, was hanged as a spy by General Howe.'

'I daresay, but if the law is the law, you are General Washington,' Gilles pleaded, throwing caution to the winds. 'You are the law, the law for all of us, even for me, a foreigner. Can you not be merciful?'

He was encouraged by a general murmur of approval, but Washington cut it short with a lift of his hand. However, his voice softened a little as he said:

'Whatever you may think, I have not the right to take the law into my own hands, or to pardon anyone, for our supreme authority is vested in Congress. I am commander of the army merely – and whether you like it or not, Major André must face a court martial. From its verdict there is no appeal, and you must not count on me to try to influence it. The danger to those fighting for liberty has been too great. Go now and remember only that you are a soldier.'

No sleep came to Gilles that night. Washington's quiet anger troubled him infinitely more than an outburst of rage would have done. The General's disappointment had struck deep, into the regions where grief becomes unbearable. Arnold's unwitting accomplice had everything to fear from a man who had been so cruelly wounded.

291

12

Between Love and War

Standing stiffly to attention with a straight back and eyes gazing fixedly in front of him, Gilles Goëlo tried not to see the gallows which had been erected not far from the farm where Washington had his headquarters. It was the second of October and the troops were drawn up about the field at Tappan where Major André was to die by hanging, like the rogue he was not.

Gilles was appalled at what was coming. Not because a man was going to die, for this was war and hanging was a familiar penalty in his native Brittany, but because the Englishman did not deserve to die by the rope. If they had shot him, Gilles would have accepted it as in the nature of things. A firing squad was a soldier's death, carried out by soldiers. The gallows meant death by the hand of an executioner, who today would be a Cowboy prisoner with his face masked by soot.

They had no right to do it, he felt. They had no right to do this to the prisoner, or to himself. It gave a sour taste to the pleasure of the reward he had received, to his new rank of lieutenant and the silver medal engraved with a shield and the word 'Fidelity'. The same medal had gone to Tim, together with the sum of two hundred dollars because he had preferred to remain a free tracker, and they owed it to the man who was now about to die upon this shameful scaffold.

He had told Washington so, with his usual bluntness, when the General had informed him that he had written to Rochambeau requesting him to release his former secretary for service on his own headquarters staff.

'I am as sorry as you are,' Washington had replied. 'But the tribunal has pronounced sentence and its president, General Greene, is quite inflexible. An example must be made. I did all I could. I even made Clinton an offer to exchange André for Arnold. I had my answer from Arnold himself.'

'And that was?'

Washington shrugged his shoulders.

'Just what one might expect from such a man. If we shoot André, he will execute the American prisoners they hold in New York. We cannot draw back now. I have just explained all this to General La Fayette,' he added sadly. 'Like you, he was interceding for André. War is a terrible thing but for us, who have chosen rebellion, it is the only possible way and we must wage it to the end. If it is any comfort to you, I shall mourn the poor young man as much as you, for I have rarely found an enemy so sympathetic.'

Certainly an execution could rarely have been carried out in an atmosphere of greater gloom. The courage and charm of the young Englishman had won all hearts. Even Tim, standing a few yards away from Gilles, in the forefront of a group of the local inhabitants, wore his most bearlike expression and a suspicious brightness in his eyes. The 'English spy' was going to his death amid the tears of his enemies.

At the first stroke of noon, the drums began to roll and the military bands drawn up along the road the condemned man was to follow broke into the the tune of *Blue Bird*. Then Major André, escorted by a platoon of soldiers, appeared in the doorway of the house where he had been held. He was dressed in the clothes in which he had been captured, and which were the justification for his sentence, but his hands were free and his eyes steady. He even smiled at the musicians and congratulated them pleasantly on the excellence of their playing. Then, all at once, his eye fell on the gallows and the cart which had been placed beneath it to serve as a scaffold. He bowed his head a little and bit his lip, stamping his foot in anger as he was heard to ask with a sigh : 'Must I really die like that?'

But it was only for a moment. Then he recovered himself and walked firmly to the cart and climbed up on to it without assistance, although he could not refrain from a slight grimace of revulsion as he came face to face with the executioner with his blackened face. He turned his back to him, so that he need not see the running noose, and stood with arms akimbo studying the troops drawn up around. His eyes met Gilles' and he greeted him with a little nod and a half-smile.

Then the officer in command of the escort party mounted his horse and said in a loud voice : 'Major André, if you have anything to say, you may speak now, having only a short time to live.'

The condemned man shrugged his shoulders.

'Concerning my sentence, I have nothing to say, but only regarding the manner of execution. All I ask of you, gentlemen, is to bear witness that I die bravely.'

Just then, the executioner would have placed the rope around his neck but he repulsed him, saying that his hands were dirty. Then he took the rope and put it over his own head and gallantly tightened the knot himself. After that he took out a handkerchief and passed it to the executioner so that he might tie his hands behind his back, with another to bind his eyes.

Again, the drums rolled. The officer raised his sword. The executioner whipped up his horse and at the same time a soldier swarmed up on to the gallows. The cart moved away, leaving the victim's body swinging briefly in the air. As it began to writhe and jerk, the soldier on the gallows flung himself on the man's shoulders, bearing down with all his weight to shorten the death throes. The body was still.

Unable to remain longer gazing at the corpse for which he felt partly responsible, Gilles turned and ran. He wanted to hit something or someone, preferably the executioner who had earned his own release by putting to death one of his own side – or even General Greene who had presided over the court martial and refused the firing squad, but instead had stood by and let an honourable man die wretchedly. But it was better to plunge deep into the woods, as he used to do at home, and let their unbroken peace sink into him.

He had not gone far when a young soldier came galloping after him, calling his name hoarsely.

'Well?' Gilles snapped, turning his rage against the harmless lad. 'What are you yelling about? You wanted me?'

'I? No, sir!' the boy gasped out. 'It's the General, General Washington is asking for you. He's in a hurry, sir.'

Gilles turned and strode back towards the small, shuttered brick house where Washington had chosen to immure himself all day, which was his way of showing his disapproval of an execution he liked no better than his men did. The militiaman on guard saluted and opened the door, without moving from his post. Washington's voice spoke icily as he entered.

'These two women have just been brought in from our outposts. They are asking for you. Will you tell me what is the meaning of it?'

Seated side by side, like two birds on one twig, Gunilla and Sitapanoki gazed up at the young man with wide, apprehensive eyes. He flushed scarlet but Washington gave him no time to decide whether this reunion was agreeable to him or not.

'The only thing we can get out of them is that they come from Sagoyewatha's camp and that they insist upon seeing you. Apart from that, they don't seem to have a thought in their heads. Will you kindly tell me who they are? The Indian especially. I have frequently heard that the French are devout ladies' men but you appear to me to hold some kind of record.'

The drama of West Point and the death of Major André had driven the Seneca tribes out of the forefront of the commander's mind. Gilles had certainly given him a rapid summary of the events which had taken place by the Susquehanna but he had listened somewhat abstractedly. And just as Gilles was recounting how he and Tim had rescued Sitapanoki from Cornplanter's men the door had opened and caused a diversion.

'Excellent, excellent!' Washington had murmured, without seeming altogether aware of what he was saying, and had turned at once to Colonel Hamilton who had come into the room. A little resentfully, Gilles had let the matter drop.

'You are mistaken, General,' he answered abruptly now. 'I did not seduce these women and if you had been good enough to hear me out the other day, you would know precisely who they are. This young lady's name is Gunilla Söderstrom. She has been held captive by the Senecas for a number of years. She helped us to escape and now her wish is to join her aunt in New York, who is the only family she has left. This other is a great lady, the wife of Sagoyewatha himself, who would have been abducted by the Iroquois but that we prevented it. You may recall that you charged us to warn the

Seneca chief of Cornplanter's treacherous intentions towards her—'

Washington's face changed colour and his fist crashed down on the table, making the papers on it jump.

'And you encouraged her to go with you? Are you utterly insane? Does it not occur to you that Sagoyewatha will promptly accuse us of stealing her away and that Cornplanter will be only too happy to back him up? Far from dividing the nations of the Iroquois, you will have united them more firmly than ever.'

'There was nothing else we could do, General. If the woman had gone back to the Indian village, she would not have been safe while her husband was still away. The medicine man, Hiakin, was in league with the abductors. They would have repeated their attempt in a day or two.'

'Why should we care for that? Would it not have been the living proof that my warning was genuine? The two chiefs would have fought to the death—'

The Indian girl's great golden eyes had been going from one to the other of the two men in growing indignation. At this, she rose up.

'So this is what is hidden behind the white men's words of friendship?' she said scornfully. 'Secretly, they wish to see the Indian tribes rend one another, to increase their own power. My husband speaks truly when he says that the red man's sorrows began when the white man came to him. And I, I believed the words of this, your messenger, when he urged me to place myself under your protection! I looked to be received with honour, as is fitting for the wife of a great chief, but here I have only insults. You dare to express your sorrow that they failed to drag me like a slave to Cornplanter's bed? And you dare to say it in my hearing?'

Her low, rather husky voice was shaking with grief and anger. Washington turned, without a word, and went to the window, where he pushed the closed shutters back a little. A ray of sunshine entered through the gap and clothed the girl's figure in its warm light. She did not flinch. The General looked at her for a few moments in silence.

For all her obvious weariness and wretched clothes and dirt, the Indian girl's beauty illumined the room. Gilles devoured her with his eyes, feeling all her old fascination for him tighten its grip on his heart and his brain already reeling and ripe for any folly.

The silence that followed Sitapanoki's outburst lasted for no more than a moment. Then, ever the perfect gentleman, Washington was bowing gracefully before her.

'Forgive me,' he said quietly. 'I said more than I meant. I was angry at the thought of losing for ever the friendship of Sagoyewatha, which I had hoped to win, for they say that he is wisest of the wise. As long as you remain in my camp, you shall be treated according to your rank, but that will not be for long. As soon as I can learn that your husband has returned to his own camp fires, I shall send you back to him with a proper escort and a letter from me to tell him what really happened. For the present, I beg you will consider yourself my guest, and this young lady also. For as long as the siege continues, it will be impossible for her to reach New York. In a moment, you shall be taken to a house where they will look after you.'

He ushered the two women courteously into the neighbouring room and then returned to Gilles who, feeling his usefulness to be at an end, was on the point of leaving the room.

'I have not yet done with you,' Washington said curtly.

He selected a letter from among the maps and papers littering the table and the Breton's keen eyes recognized the seal at once. It came from Newport.

'I have news from General Rochambeau which will be of interest to you,' Washington said. 'He is happy to know of the large part you played in unmasking the plans of the traitor, Arnold, and readily consents to lend you to me. He declares himself delighted that a soldier of the Royal Deux-Ponts should become an American officer. He is sure that you will prove worthy of your appointment. Here, also, is a letter from him addressed to yourself. Take it, and then be off with you.'

Gilles took the letter and tucked it into his belt but stood his ground.

'May I say one more thing, General?'

'Yes. But be quick.'

'I should like to ask a favour. May I make one of the escort party to accompany Sagoyewatha's wife back to her camp?'

'A strange request. Why, may I ask?'

'Simply that it was I who took her away and consequently

297

I who stand accused of having abducted her. So it seems only natural that I should be the one to return her. If only to give Sagoyewatha satisfaction if he should demand it.'

For a moment, the Virginian studied the young man standing stiffly to attention before him without speaking. He even walked round him once, his hands clasped behind his back, before coming back to look him straight in the eye. His expression was very serious.

'Hmm! . . . I see. A very prickly sense of honour, haven't you? Very French! But – will you swear to me on your honour that this great urge of yours to exonerate yourself in the eyes of the Seneca chief is the sole reason for your request?'

'N-no, General.'

'I thought not. Stop gazing at the shutters and look at me, if you please. And now, listen carefully to what I say. You will not make one of the Indian princess's escort because I have no wish to lose a brave man. She will be leaving Tappan within a fortnight, with an escort of men I can trust to remain impervious to her charms, a minister of religion and men who are veterans of the Indian war. You are much too young for that task – and she is by far too lovely.'

Washington's decision was a wise one. Yet, once outside, Gilles was conscious that the dissatisfaction which had come upon him during the execution had returned more strongly than before. It had done him no good to see Sitapanoki again. He had thought himself recovered from his infatuation but once in her presence he had been as weak as a child. One look from those great golden eyes had set the fire raging in his blood again and now he had only one idea, which was to see her.

Consequently, it was with only half his mind that he read Rochambeau's letter. Yet what it said was interesting enough, for it constituted something like a rehabilitation of himself and Tim. The French commander wrote to tell his former secretary that he had been cleared of the charge of murder levelled against him.

'The trooper of Lauzun's regiment who goes by the name of Samson was apprehended in the act of attempting, with three companions, to intercept the consignment of gold shortly after its leaving Newport. Two of the rogues were slain. Unhappily,

298

those who fell into our hands afterwards succeeded in making their escape. Samson was one of these and we have so far been unable to recapture him. I have to tell you, therefore, that you are restored to the good esteem of your comrades and to the good graces of the Duc de Lauzun, and that whenever, by God's will, we return to France, you shall return to occupy the place of which it was never my intention to deprive you . . .'

Gilles crumpled the letter convulsively between his fingers. He did not feel particularly gratified, but rather the reverse. Of course, it was agreeable to know that he was no longer an outcast, but his pride was injured. Washington had made him an officer. Yet when he returned to the French ranks it seemed that it would be to take up his pen again. Well, if America wanted to adopt him, she could have him all the way.

The part of the letter which gave him the greatest satisfaction was undoubtedly the news of Morvan's escape. Morvan's death was not a matter for a court martial, it belonged to Gilles Goëlo. Not even the king had the right to take that from him. The hatred between them had grown too fierce to end so senselessly, without at least another confrontation.

'Those damned fools of the provost's couldn't catch him!' he muttered to himself, chewing nervously on a blade of grass. 'But I know that I shall do it, sooner or later, wherever he may be.'

The people who had followed the unfortunate Major André's body to the little cemetery of Tappan were beginning to return. Gilles caught sight of Tim holding forth to three or four men a head shorter than himself and called out to him to join him in a glass or two of rum at the inn. Rochambeau's letter certainly called for some sort of celebration and coming on top of the execution and Sitapanoki's unexpected reappearance it gaves Gilles a raging impulse to go and get drunk.

He set himself conscientiously to achieving this end, with full encouragement from Tim who viewed the Indian girl's arrival with a good deal less than enthusiasm.

'I'd be a lot happier if only you could stay drunk until that confounded woman has left this village altogether,' he declared, pouring his friend a generous measure. 'You've risked your neck for her sake quite enough and I wouldn't put it past you to do it again.'

'It's not death I want – it's her! I feel as though, if I could only have her – just once – I'd be cured.'

'Or hooked worse than ever! Some women are like drink. When you've once tasted them, you want them again. You'd do better to try and think of something else. Here's to you!'

But, curiously enough, Gilles was unable to get drunk at all. It was Tim who succumbed, letting his head sink on to the table and starting to snore. Gilles looked at him gloomily for a moment. It was no fun drinking alone and if Tim had deserted him there was no point in remaining any longer at the inn. Tossing a few coins on to the table, he made his way a trifle unsteadily outside and saw that it was already dark.

A few deep breaths of the cold air soon drove the fumes from his brain. The night was illumined by the glow of the various watch fires that ringed Tappan but everything was quiet, although they were no more than a few miles from the besieged city of New York. The guns were silent and the occasional shot in the distance might have been no more than a belated hunter. Autumn had come and the war, like the land itself, was growing sleepy. Both sides were preparing to hold their present positions until spring. And what would that bring? New ways of carrying the city, more guns, more men, more money? The men on both sides must become farmers again if the fields were to be tilled and this year would see no solution.

Sighing, Gilles set out to walk back to his billet but without paying much heed to his direction. He was in no hurry to get back. He was not sleepy and in fact he did not really know quite what he wanted, except perhaps to be rid of the throbbing in his head. He bumped into something and cursed and then apologized at once when he saw that it was a woman.

'I was looking for you.' The quiet voice was Gunilla's. 'Only don't shout so. You'll wake the whole village.'

He gaped at her incredulously as she stood in the yellow light from the windows of a nearby house.

'I should never have known you,' he said, amazed.

'Perhaps because you have never looked at me.'

That was true. From the moment when he had saved her from the gyrfalcon, she had been no more to him than a grey shadow, a bundle of dirty clothes surmounted by a grimy

300

yellow thatch, a miserable object midway between a goat and a midden, supposing that either were endowed with the power of speech. But what stood before him now was a slim young girl, the slenderness of her waist emphasized by the black dress she wore. The hands emerging from her white linen cuffs and the face beneath the goffered cap were a trifle browned perhaps by long exposure to the sun and wind, but the eyes had the blue of flax flowers and the hair drawn up into a heavy knot upon her neck was like pale silk. The picture she presented was so pretty that Gilles smiled involuntarily.

'That was unforgivable of me, Gunilla,' he said. 'You are truly charming.'

The compliment did not win an answering smile from her. She even gave a tiny shrug of annoyance.

'Keep your compliments. It was not for them I came in search of you, but because she asked me to. She wants to see you.'

'She?'

'Don't be stupid. Who do you think? Sitapanoki, of course. She cannot come out herself. General Washington has asked her not to show herself in the village. And she made me promise to fetch you to her. Will you come?'

'I'm coming. Where are we going?'

'They have lodged us with the minister's wife. She is a kindly person, although her ideas are strict. She welcomed me as though I were her own daughter, but she is not best pleased to be entertaining an Indian beneath her roof.'

'And now you want to take a man into the house? Why, she'll throw me out!'

'She won't know. Mrs Gibson is the kind of woman who has an answer for everything. She has put Sitapanoki in an outbuilding where she has her sewing room. She pretends it is out of respect for her rank. In any case, Sitapanoki would not live under the same roof as the priest of the great spirit from over the sea. It is at the bottom of the orchard. No one will see you.'

'What does Sitapanoki want with me?'

Gunilla had walked on a little ahead of him. Gilles' question had been harmless enough and yet he saw the girl's slender back stiffen and she turned on him suddenly, her eyes blazing with anger.

301

'I don't know and I don't want to know! I came to find you because she threatened to go herself if I did not. But I wish she were in hell, for my part! She's a devil, that Indian, like all the rest of them!'

And without another word of explanation, Gunilla picked up her skirts and ran towards the far end of the village. Gilles was forced to follow at the same pace. He knew the house of Mr Gibson, the minister, but he did not know whereabouts his guide meant to take him. In fact, she skirted the garden, pushed through a hedge of dogwood and stopped at last by a flight of narrow wooden steps.

'Up there,' she said, jerking her head towards a lighted window. 'You can leave the same way. Good night.'

She melted into the darkness of the orchard and Gilles raced up the rickety stairway with a thudding heart. The door seemed to open of its own accord beneath his impatient hand, revealing a bright, simple room furnished in a plain, country style with frilled muslin curtains which gave it a touchingly virginal air. It was lit only by the fire burning in the hearth and he did not at first see Sitapanoki. It was not until he looked at the bed which stood in the farthest corner from the fire, that he saw her. She was in bed, the covers drawn up to her chin and she seemed to be asleep.

He moved towards her softly, cursing the pine floor boards that creaked beneath his weight, and stood for a moment looking at her, holding his breath and revelling in her beauty.

The tumbled mass of her hair made a dark halo within which her face glowed like a golden flower. Her long lashes threw soft shadows on cheeks that were flushed with warmth and her moist lips were slightly parted as though, in her sleep, she were awaiting a kiss. Marvelling, Gilles could scarcely believe that he had stepped from the cold night outside into this feminine paradise.

He was almost on the point of bending over her when, without opening her eyes, the sleeper murmured: 'You came quickly. Even before I could go to sleep. It's very nice of you . . .'

The irony of her tone broke the spell. Gilles drew himself up.

'You asked for me. I had no cause to keep you waiting. What do you want of me?'

'Only to know something. When I return to my noble husband, Sagoyewatha, will you be my escort?'

'No. General Washington does not wish it.'

Suddenly, she opened her eyes, enveloping him in their warm light with the glint of mockery in it.

'You asked him, then?'

'I did. I thought it my duty to escort you back myself, so as to clear myself, in your husband's eyes, of the charge of abduction which Hiakin has no doubt put upon me.'

The Indian girl smiled, half-closed her eyes and studied the young man covertly through her lashes. She was acknowledging to herself that no man had ever pleased her as this one did. War suited him. The past weeks had hardened his face, removing for ever the last traces of boyhood, and Sitapanoki did not. have to tax her memory very far to recall the perfect physique that lay beneath the dark uniform coat. And then there was that ice-blue glance, and the little sardonic curl at the corner of his firm mouth. A fine figure of a man indeed, as handsome as Cornplanter but infinitely more attractive.

'Was that the only reason? Had you truly no other wish but to restore me to my husband, or—?'

'Or what?' His voice was defensive.

'Oh, nothing . . . I must have dreamed it, but I thought that one night, in my dwelling, you besought me to fly with you— Dreams are a strange thing, you know, because it seems to me that I can still hear your words. "If you will come with me," you said, "I will love you as no other man could ever do." '

'You were not dreaming. I said those words and I do not deny them, but—'

'But? That is not a word that women like to hear.'

'Forgive me. I meant what I said then but so many things are different now. I am no longer my own man. I am one of General Washington's officers.'

'You mean that you no longer love me? A pity. For you see, I was ready to love you—'

Abruptly, she flung back the covers and stood before him, naked as truth, tossing back the dark mass of her hair with a movement that emphasized the proud hillocks of her breasts. But she made no move towards him. Instead, she walked past him as though he had all at once ceased to exist, crossing over to the fire, swaying on her long legs and affording him glimpses of high, firm buttocks through the shining curtain of her hair.

Gilles watched her stroll over to the hearth, the perfection of her body outlined against the ruddy glow, and his throat felt suddenly drier than a summer desert while the blood beat in his temples. He heard himself saying hoarsely, in a voice that seemed dredged out of the earth : 'What are you playing at? You say that you were ready to love me?'

'Why else should I have come here to find you when it would have been easy for me to go back to my own place after the Skinners had slowly killed the Avenger and burned the farm?'

She turned slowly, so that he could see her sideways-on against the flames. The bold curve of her breasts was enough to drive a man to madness and below it the exquisitely gentle line of the flat stomach and the softly rising mount of Venus . . . Her voice deepened, rasping his quivering nerves.

'I desired you in my husband's camp and I desire you now. Oh, I know what is holding you back! You are afraid of displeasing the man you have chosen to serve – but that is not enough. Perhaps, after all, I was mistaken. Perhaps you are not truly a man?'

He took her then. Brutally and completely. As completely as she melted into his embrace. The floor, with good Mrs Gibson's home-made rag rug upon it, rose up to meet them, warm from the fire. The girl's flesh was hot but Gilles' hands were icy cold. She nibbled his lips gently, like a little animal, then thrust him away and knelt beside him.

'Let me take those absurd clothes off you! You are so much more beautiful without them.'

Impatient to have her in his arms again, he tore off his coat and the long white waistcoat and was attacking his cravat when she stopped him.

'No. I want to do it myself. We daughters of the great woods are taught how to draw out the pleasure of our chosen master, to make it last.'

Gilles laughed. 'Just as you learn how to spin out your torments?' he asked. But she did not smile.

'It is the same thing. Love is a slow death from which one is reborn continually. Pleasure, like pain, should be a climax.'

The play that their two bodies engaged in, there in front of the dying fire, was agonizingly subtle and delicious. Before she yielded to him at last, in an ecstasy of defeat, Sitapanoki teased her partner's desire to the limits of endurance, from which he was released at last with a growl like a wild beast. It was echoed by a gasping cry from her. Then came oblivion.

Gilles was the first to awake from that blessed swoon of love. He eased himself away gently. The fire had sunk to embers. He put a few logs on and blew them into life. Tall yellow flames sprang up, bathing the sleeping woman in their light. Bright threads of sweat showed on her smooth skin. Gilles traced one of them lightly with his finger until it disappeared into the shadow of her parted thighs. Sitapanoki, dozing, felt the caress and moaned and turned towards him without opening her eyes.

Once again desire swelled in the young man's loins, but for some moments yet, he remained kneeling by her, playing her woman's body like a harp, feeling it writhing and panting under his touch, revelling in the moans she made, until at last she rose up and fell on him, enfolding him in her flesh and in the warm, spicy scent of her hair and all but tipping both of them into the fire. Then Gilles carried her over to the bed to lose himself with her amid the white sheets.

Three times more they made love and still they could not tire of one another. Their bodies seemed to have been created from all time to fit close and never part. But Sitapanoki seemed at last to want to rest. She nestled her head against her lover's neck and wrapped her arms round him.

She was so silent for a while that he thought she must have fallen asleep, but then he felt soft kisses on his skin and heard her whisper : 'Take me away—'

'Where do you want me to take you? To your own place? I have already told you—'

'To my own place, yes – but not to my husband.'

She raised herself on her elbow and kissed him, a long kiss, while her fingers travelled softly through the downy hair upon his chest, tracing the pattern of muscle.

'Listen – after many days' journeying up the river that flows by here, you come to a still greater river, the river the French called St Lawrence. Once, my people owned vast territories

305

north of that river. They were slaughtered by the Iroquois and those few who escaped fled westwards. My father's tribe managed to survive longer than the rest, owing to a refuge of which, now, only I and some few others know the secret. One day, alas, they had to come out and were lured into a trap. Not many escaped the arrows of the Iroquois, and I was taken captive. But the enemy never discovered our refuge and I think that some still live there. Come with me. You shall be their chief and I will be your wife and give you sons.'

Gently, Gilles unwound her arms and laid her down and gazed long into her eyes.

'This is madness, Sita . . . You are daydreaming. How could your people take a paleface for their chief? Nor do I wish to become a deserter, for that is what I should be if I fled with you.'

'You say you love me,' she said bitterly, 'and when I offer to give my life to you, you say it is madness. I was mad indeed to give myself to you – you, who can coolly accept that I return to my husband.'

Quick as a snake, she slipped out of the bed and stretched herself like a cat in the failing light of the fire.

'Who says I accept it?' Gilles said, watching her from the pillows. 'But I can see no way of avoiding it with honour.'

She did not answer and seemed even not to hear his words. She was staring wide-eyed into the fire, as though seeing strange pictures there, and she murmured as if to herself: 'Sagoyewatha will not punish me because he will believe the words of the great white chief, but perhaps he will no longer wish to keep me for his wife? My life then will be wretched indeed. It may be that I can win him back, but only by giving him more love even than I have given to you.'

And softly, intimately, as though to herself, she began to describe, in frightening detail, the caresses she would lavish on him. It was done in a gentle, murmuring voice, like a kind of sensual incantation, a monologue so full of the poetry of physical passion that it charged the very air with electricity, as though she had been quite alone. And all the while, her long hands were dreamily stroking her body from her hips up to her breasts and cupping them in her palms.

Suddenly, Gilles seemed to see her in the Indian's arms and

he sprang out of bed and tried to take her in his own. But she repulsed him angrily.

'Are you still here? Why don't you go? I was wrong to welcome you tonight and you have taught me my error. I must think only of my husband from now on. Go away—'

'Why are you so angry? Can't you understand?'

'No! All I can understand is that the man to whom I belong must also belong to me also. You will not have it so, and therefore I am yours no longer.'

'But only think! The thing you ask is very serious and you should understand that. What man of your people would agree, all in a moment like this, to abandon his brothers in arms, his duty and his people to fly with another man's wife? There may be a way out but you must give me time to think of it. You are not leaving tomorrow.'

He had been drawing gradually nearer to her, now he pulled her to him and this time she did not try very hard to drive him away. After a moment, she started to laugh and put her lips up to his.

'You are right – only, you see, I love you so much already that I cannot face the prospect of ever having to part from you again.'

'I love you too. Don't you know that yet? How could I live without you?'

She pressed herself against him, moulding every inch of her body to his, and very gently, her hips began to sway.

'Then prove it to me once more,' she breathed. 'Soon it will be dawn, and the hours will be long until tonight.'

When, an hour later, he left the warm room and plunged into the damp chill of the early morning, Gilles felt like a conqueror and all sensible thought had been driven from his head. It had cost him untold anguish to wrest himself from Sitapanoki's arms. Her final capitulation had left him swollen with pride for she had been infinitely tender and even humble, begging him to forgive her for presuming to try and deflect him from his duty as a warrior. In that last hour, she had lavished such kisses and caresses on him that the memory of them still clung about him as he walked back to the centre of the village, whistling a martial air and feeling a trifle weak about the knees but radiant in his mind. The night that had passed had finally effaced the last traces of his boyhood, for no man who was the lover of such a woman as Sitapanoki could be other than a man indeed.

He never even guessed at the slim white figure standing motionless and desolate behind one of the dark windows of the Gibsons' house, watching him with eyes full of tears as he cleared the hedge in a single bound.

All that day, Lieutenant Goëlo performed his duties with an absent mind and a remarkable lack of enthusiasm. Remembering his new staff officer's previous experience with Rochambeau, General Washington had requested him, with great practical good sense but a certain absence of psychological insight, to see if he could make some sense of his administrative records and estimate how much in the way of stores – scanty enough – they would have for the winter. The young man himself disliked this clerking very much and his eye kept turning to the clock on the mantelpiece as he sat with his pen in the air and his mind a long way away, contemplating prospects that were far removed from gallons of beer and bags of flour.

The only time he really emerged from his sensual daydreams was when he bade a half-hearted farewell to Tim, who was going back to Newport, bearing messages from Washington to the French commanders and glad enough in his heart to be renewing his courtship of Martha Carpenter, whom he was conscious of having somewhat neglected of late.

The last stroke of nine o'clock found Gilles making his way through the dogwoods with one eye on the glow in the window behind which his mistress was waiting for him. The door was no sooner closed behind him than she was in his arms, and all was as it had been the night before.

The nights that followed were filled with the same blazing madness. Sitapanoki loved making love. She was familiar with all the devious refinements whose powerful effect she had proved on her husband, though he was a man of great wisdom and good sense. With this handsome youth, full of strength and ardour, she attained sublimity. In between snatches of sleep, in which even then they were not divided, the lovers made love with a passion which only increased their infatuation night by night.

The Indian had not renewed her proposal that Gilles should fly with her and when he broached the subject amid the ravages of their bed she closed his lips with a long kiss.

'Let be. It will all come right . . . we shall find a way.'

But, little by little, she was binding him in the invisible web of her embraces. Her beauty, heightened still more by passion, slowly became a powerful drug which he craved more and more. Sitapanoki knew how to make herself ardent, commanding and submissive by turns, abasing herself like a magnificent black panther, purring with contentment, stretching herself in his arms with little moans of happiness. And with every dawn the parting became more difficult and his mood more sombre. The little room had become a world for him, like a heavenly paradise in which the lovely Indian reigned in her glorious nakedness, Eve and the serpent in one, the lovely Indian who had sworn to have him all to herself for always.

She knew that she had won one morning when, as they were kissing goodbye, he crushed her to him more passionately even than usual. All night long, he had made love to her with a kind of desperation which he would not explain. Then, just as he was about to leave her, he murmured with his lips against her neck: 'The General has decided it is time you went, Sita. In three days you are to return to your husband's camp.'

She shuddered and went rigid.

'In three days?' she said, her voice suddenly small and sad. 'Only three days?'

But he only hugged her closer, as though trying to draw her into himself.

'Yes – but I will come for you, tomorrow night! We will fly together, wherever you wish – to the great river you told me of.'

It was so sudden, so unexpected that it almost frightened her. She held him from her gently, looking anxiously into his face which was drawn with worry and fatigue.

'You – you really want to take me? To abandon your whole life?'

'You are my life! I cling to you more with every hour that passes. I love you, Sita. I love you to distraction. I cannot stay here, endlessly scratching away at pieces of paper, while you go away for ever. You cannot know how much I love you!'

'I love you, too,' she said gravely. 'I did not think that I

309

would come to love you so much. I liked you and I wanted you, but now I can no longer imagine life without you. You are my master. But will you not regret the things that you are leaving? Can you bear—?'

'There is only one thing I could not bear, Sita, and that is to know that you were with someone else, in another man's arms, in another man's bed.'

'But your country, your family – your career?'

'I have no family now, if I ever had one. In my own country, I am nothing and it is long now since I have wished to become an adopted son of this land. As for my career – Washington has given me a commission but the only weapons I wield are a pen and inkwell. Once the war is over, I shall be nothing again. No, Sita, I shall leave without regret if I have you. I will come tonight at the usual time, but I will bring with me a suit of men's clothes for you to put on. Then we will make our escape.'

She longed too deeply to believe him to doubt her victory any longer.

'I will spend my whole life trying to make you happy. You shall see how good it is to live a free life in the forest where the great rapids leap down the rocks. One day, the war will be over and then we will become colonists, we will have children and lands of our own to till, and a house where I will try to be a good wife according to the manner of your people. We will have an empire, perhaps . . . This land of ours is vast and all things are possible. And I will love you, I will love you as no man was ever loved by woman before!'

Gilles took the beautiful face with its great, lambent eyes, between his hands and gazed at it with infinite tenderness.

'Perhaps none of that will happen. Perhaps we shall find death at the end of the road, if your husband should catch up with us. But perhaps that is the supreme happiness, to die together, for then there can be no regrets and no remorse. Until tonight, then.'

The kiss that passed between them then was wholly chaste, the kiss of a true betrothal, driving out all calculation and all fleshly lust. There was no longer either victor or vanquished in that passionate contest in which both had been striving un-consciously to bend the other to their will, there was nothing

310

but two beings who had chosen to set aside all that stood between them, all that, in the last resort, counted for less than their love, who had chosen to belong only to one another. She had ceased to be an Indian princess as he had ceased to be a Breton, a soldier of King Louis and an officer in the rebel army of the young United States. They were two brand new beings in the dawn of the world. Their bodies, welded together by desire, had drawn their hearts after, even when their owners had least expected it.

For once, the day passed like a dream. Gilles applied himself to the task which only twenty-four hours previously had been the bane of his life as he had never done before. Then he got together a few things, including a suit of man's clothing for Sitapanoki, some provisions and the weapons necessary to anyone bent on travelling through the virgin forest. After that, he wrote three letters to leave behind. One was for Washington, one for Rochambeau and one for Tim, whose help, he knew, would always be his to command. Finally, instead of dining in the company of the other officers of the headquarters staff, he ate alone in a corner of the inn's common room and smoked a leisurely pipe until it was time to go to meet his mistress.

He felt curiously lighthearted, with the sense of release that often comes when a difficult decision has been made. Everything had suddenly become so simple. He had only to say no to ambition, to ordinary life, to the old world which, bound in its ancient, rigid, monarchical framework, could offer him nothing but a narrow, limited existence, and, finally, to Judith who, supposing that her challenging tryst had been genuine, would wait for him in vain. The little red-haired siren of the Blavet had faded like the early morning dreams that fade with the first ray of the sun. She was tucked away in his memory as a whiteness with little of the flesh about it, a scentless flower, a fleeting image in the water . . . She, too, had been vanquished.

As darkness fell and the trumpets sounded for lights out, he left the inn, bowing carelessly to the company in general on his way out, and made for the churchyard where he had hidden his baggage in a hollow under a hedge. Hoisting it on to his shoulder, he turned his steps towards the minister's house. He felt as light as a bird. In fact, it had made things a great deal easier for him that he had not seen Washington all day. The commander-in-chief had left on a tour of inspection with Colonel Hamilton and Gilles was glad of it because he was not at all sure how he could have sustained the General's direct gaze.

He saw the window shining in the distance, like a gold star in the night, and passing through the hedge ascended the stair as noiselessly as a cat. As he pushed the door open in the familiar way, he was already smiling at the scene he knew that he would find within. Sita would be waiting for him, as she did every night, reclining in front of the fire, like a siren on the edge of the waves, although tonight, no doubt, she would still be wearing her clothes, for lovemaking formed no part of their plans in the hours ahead.

He threw the door wide open, ready to take her in his arms.

'Come in,' said a cold voice.

The little room seemed suddenly to have shrunk. Sitapanoki had mysteriously vanished. In her stead, the tall figure of General Washington stood framed against the firelight. His back was turned and he was stirring up the fire.

The familiar crackle of the logs filled the sudden silence. Everything was as usual. The warm, resinous scent of burning pine logs, the white curtains with their silly frills and the rag rug which was no longer quite the same when adorned by nothing more than the General's buckled shoes. And yet the world seemed to have turned upside down and paradise without Eve was like a narrow purgatory.

'Shut the door,' Washington commanded. 'There's an icy draught. And you may put that bundle in the corner.'

He laid down the poker and brushed his hands together to get rid of the dust. They were long and beautiful below their immaculate cuffs of white lawn and he took the greatest care of them.

'Where is she?' Gilles demanded, wasting no pains on unnecessary politeness.

'The wife of Chief Sagoyewatha is on her way back to her husband. I sent her off unobtrusively very early this morning and as a mark of respect I went with her myself for the first few miles. Have you anything against it? Or have you quite forgotten what the woman stands for, to say nothing of the fact that we are at war and you are a soldier? What is your

312

commanding officer to call what you were about to do with the baggage you were carrying?'

'Desertion,' Gilles retorted boldly.

'And what does that deserve?'

'Death. Shoot me, then. Or hang me, since that seems to be the current fate of soldiers.'

'I do not advise you to be insolent. What have you to say for yourself?'

'Nothing. Except that I love the woman and she loves me.'

'So? Who are you to interfere with my plans? The last thing we need in our present situation is another Trojan War to set the whole of the Six Nations in arms against us. You are no Paris, nor she a Helen! Why in the name of damnation must you French always be putting love before all else? You brandish it like a flag, you wear it like a medal – I have no time for love! Liberty is what interests me and I had thought it was the same with you, or I should not have given a Don Juan a commission in my army. But then, perhaps, in spite of appearances, you may be a coward after all—'

Gilles whitened and clenched his fists as though he would have fallen upon Washington.

'Kill me, General, but do not insult me.'

'You may stop badgering me to make away with you. I've too much need of living men to see any use in making one more corpse. Now, just you listen to me. No one but myself knows that you were on the point of giving us the slip. It proves that I was right not to let you form one of the woman's escort, for you would not have returned, but I was wrong to put you to work with me. You were made for action. In a fight you think straight and do not play the fool. Would you like to see some fighting?'

'It's all I've ever wanted, that and—'

'I forbid you to think of her more! Go home and make your preparations. We have discovered through a spy, a man named Champ, exactly where Arnold is to be found. General La Fayette who, like yourself, cannot get over André's death, is leaving at dawn with a detachment of riflemen to try and capture him. You shall go with them.'

When Washington used a certain tone of voice and a certain turn of phrase he could be irresistible, for his knowledge of men was unequalled. Beaten but unreconciled, Gilles drew himself up, clicked his heels and bowed correctly.

'Your servant, General, and thank you for being good enough to overlook what has passed. If I can prove my gratitude with my life, I will. Now I have only to return to my billet and there burn certain letters which are of no further interest.'

Washington laughed suddenly and strolling over to the younger man gave him an easy buffet on the arm.

'Stubborn mule of a Breton! I've just been exerting myself to explain to you why I want you alive. Besides—' His voice softened but took on a graver note, although the smile still lurked in his eyes. 'Besides, no man of talent should destroy his future for the sake of any woman, however beautiful, believe me. They are not worth it. Ask Arnold, if you find him. But for his excessive devotion to his wife, the fair Peggy, he might still be an honest man and a hero.'

13

Pongo

With the brave red feather of La Fayette's troops stuck in his hat, Lieutenant Goëlo plunged into war like a prisoner plunging into a shark-infested sea, to emerge a free man or not at all. With the spy, Champ, as their guide, they succeeded, after facing a host of perils, in approaching Fort Constitution, on the bay of New York, where the traitor was said to be living, only to discover that the bird had flown. In a raging temper and thirsting for vengeance, Arnold had been unable to face the thought of spending the winter shut up in another fortress. He had obtained Sir Henry Clinton's permission to join the English army in the south and had just left for Virginia, determined to make Washington's countrymen pay dearly for the humiliating position in which he found himself through no fault but his own.

The expedition returned to Tappan empty-handed and all the more angry on that account. La Fayette and Gilles both fell on Washington, demanding his permission to pursue the traitor into Virginia. But the General would not hear of it.

'We are besieging New York, gentlemen, which you seem to have forgotten, and I have no troops to spare. Do me the favour of remaining here and carrying out my orders to the letter.'

There was a still more searing disappointment awaiting Gilles, for Mr Gibson and the escort deputed to accompany Sitapanoki back to the Susquehanna had returned during his absence, much sooner than expected, having failed to complete their journey. The Indian girl had slipped away one night while they were encamped near Dingman's Ferry on the Delaware. She had simply vanished without trace.

At first, the young lieutenant was secretly thrilled by the news, which he learned from the commander's own lips.

'She did not want to go back to Sagoyewatha,' he said, unable quite to conceal his delight. 'She wanted us to go and live together far away in the north, in the secret place which was the refuge of her father's tribe before the massacre.'

'And you think, do you, that she has gone there alone – that she may be waiting for you there?'

'Why not? She was as sure of me as I am of her.'

'Sure of her? Oh, youth! It gives me no pleasure to tell you what I am about to, my poor friend, but I owe it to myself to help you erase even the shadow of regret from your heart. Do you know what my spies in Indian territory have told me? The wife of Sagoyewatha the wise, the woman for whom you would have renounced everything, even your own blood, has not gone to the great northern forests where the Algonquin once lived but only as far as the Mohawk valley – and Cornplanter's camp fires!'

Gilles was speechless, too stricken to do or say a thing. Never for one moment did it occur to him to doubt the General's word. The name of the Iroquois chief had struck him like a death blow and made him dumb. He could only shake his head and then, turning without even a bow, rush from the room, almost knocking over La Fayette and General Knox who were just entering.

'Good God!' the Frenchman exclaimed. 'Was that Lieutenant Goëlo? Where is he off to so fast? He looked as though he'd seen a ghost.'

Washington, who had followed him to the threshold, shrugged his shoulders and smiled sadly.

'The ghost of his last illusion, my dear Marquis. I have just severed him from a woman he held dear.'

'Aha! The famous Indian princess you had in keeping at the minister's house and whom he managed to make his mistress none the less?'

'Now, how do you know that?'

The marquis laughed. 'When there's a pretty woman in the case I always make it my business to know everything. A little talent, if you like, General, that belongs very much to my country. Unfortunately, I never so much as set eyes on her.'

'I'm sorry for your sake, for she is remarkably lovely. Like a magnificent wild cat. But the boy is a thoroughbred also and I should not like him to do anything foolish.'

'I shouldn't think he would. I saw him fight when we were nearly taken by the English. He's a real brave! All the same, I'll go in search of him after we've had our orders from you.'

Gilles had not in fact gone very far. He had run out without looking where he was going, like the wounded deer relying on the undergrowth to drag the arrow from its side, but when he came to the inn with its sign illustrating the name, the *Grand Washington*, he pulled up short. His first thought had been to dash down to the Hudson and plunge in once and for all. But the brightly coloured inn sign with its idealized portrait of his chief made him change his mind. The thought of Sita-panoki going straight from his arms to those of Cornplanter made him feel sick with disgust but even so he was not going to destroy himself for that, like a pregnant housemaid abandoned by her lover.

'Women!' he spat out, grinding his teeth. 'Like a bitch on heat! Surely no Tournemine ever killed himself for such a cause! If you mean to drown yourself, my boy, you might as well do it in rum.'

With that he wheeled round and, rushing headlong through the door, plonked himself down at a table and, roaring loudly for a bottle, set himself to get thoroughly and systematically drunk.

It was there that General La Fayette and one of his adjutants, Colonel Poor, found him a couple of hours later. He was magnificently drunk and standing on a table surrounded by a hilarious circle of infantrymen who were clapping their hands to mark time while he sang, at the top of his voice, one of the sea shanties that all Bretons knew from infancy.

> *Chantons, pour passer le temps*
> *Les amours jolies d'une belle fille*
> *Chantons pour passer le temps*
> *Les amours jolies d'une fille de quinze ans . . .'*

317

The soldiers were trying to pick up the choruses but could make nothing of the French words and since liberal potations of rum had done nothing to improve their leader's voice the resulting cacophony was enough to make La Fayette screw up his face in anguish.

He was too well known not to be able to obtain an instant silence but persuading Gilles to descend from his table proved somewhat more difficult. The Breton announced that he was going to stay there in order to deliver a bitter tirade against the faithlessness of women. With the help of Poor and two of the men, the marquis got him down soon enough only to have the unaccustomed tope cast himself into his arms weeping like a fountain and calling him his 'dear, po-faced, little General', which left the last descendant of the La Fayettes deeply puzzled but highly amused.

There was nothing more for him to do but to have the lieutenant conveyed to his tent and put to bed, where he began to snore at once.

'Well, he'll do there until morning,' the marquis said with a sigh. 'But what the devil possessed the boy to go falling in love with a redskin?'

'I caught a glimpse of her as she was leaving,' Colonel Poor said, 'and, if you want my opinion, I think General Washington was wise to keep her out of sight of the men. She would have set the whole army on fire.'

'Whew! You'll make me sorry I didn't see her myself. I'm beginning to understand young Goëlo – and envy him!'

Gilles, when he woke, felt that there was no one in the world less to be envied than himself. He had a throat like wood and a distinct impression that the end of the world was at hand. What was more, when he ventured to put his head outside his tent, he saw that it was raining hard and the whole camp had become a sea of mud. He had, however, sense enough not to allow the memory of Sitapanoki's treachery to return to haunt him. For though the emotional side of his love might be foundering in scorn and disgust, that did not make him forget the nights of passion he had spent with her. He still had to get over his desire for her.

When he had stopped feeling quite so sick and the sun seemed to be standing more or less still again, he went, very properly, to render thanks to La Fayette for his solicitude, which he had been aware of even through the fumes of alcohol. He was able to do this without the slightest embarrassment, for undertaking the New York expedition in his company had given him a juster estimate of the young general who had been such a figure of romance to him in Vannes and such a disappointment at Rhode Island. For all his squeaky voice and the element of complacency in his character, the Marquis from Auvergne was not without charm. Gifted with exquisite manners and an unfailing courage, he was also wholly without false pride. In addition, he had the knack of winning people to him and, apart from Washington who treated him like a son, he had acquired the blind devotion of the two thousand-odd men, regular soldiers and half-wild militiamen, who made up his brigade. He certainly looked after them like a mother, spending his own money without stint – he was one of the richest men in France – to keep them properly equipped. Madame La Fayette was continually receiving letters full of endearments and requests for money. As for the fine ladies of Philadelphia, where Washington was always sending him to practise his cajolery, he had talked them into sewing endless shirts and knitting mountains of stockings for his 'legion'. He made no secret of his fondness for women in general, but this in no way interfered with his love for his own wife in particular.

'Don't apologize,' he told his lieutenant when that young gentleman presented himself before him. 'I did exactly the same thing myself before I left France. I was madly in love with a very beautiful lady but I was not the only one and so she spurned me. I downed many a bottle of old burgundy in the effort to forget her. How do you feel this morning?'

'Ashamed, angry – and itching for a fight. Preferably against the Iroquois.'

'Excellent! But I can't myself feel much interest in the Iroquois when there is this splendid collection of British and Hessians just waiting for us to make mincemeat of them. If I may say so, sir, I begin to like you more and more.'

'And I you, General. Only permit me to remind you that I never knew my father and that the name I bear is my mother's.'

'Why should I be nicer in that respect than General Washington? In this country, one man is as good as another.

Besides, we each of us come of an ancient race very far from the Frankish invaders who gave their name to our country. You are a Breton, which is to say a Celt, and I am an Auvergnat and so a Gaul.'

'A Gaul?'

'So I devoutly hope and believe because there were very few Franks who settled in the mountains of Auvergne. I prefer Vercingetorix, defending his mountain fastnesses, to the brigand Clovis and his abominable successors.'

'But—' Gilles said, startled, 'but those abominable successors were—'

'The kings of France and most of their associates? I know. I do not care for kings, sir, and what I came here for was a lesson in liberty. And I will tell you this as well. My grandfather, the Marquis de la Riviére, is one hundred per cent Breton. So let us shake hands and then go and see what kind of task we can talk General Washington into giving us. I am like you, I want to be away from here.'

But although La Fayette, supported by his staff, urged and pleaded with him, Washington refused steadfastly to let himself be drawn into ill-timed attacks on the outer defences of New York. In vain did the Marquis insist that vigorous action would spur the French King's ministers to further generosity; the American had no desire to get his men killed when he had been at such pains to keep them alive.

'If we can hold the positions we have already won all winter, that will be very well. In any case, we need fresh reinforcements. The Comte de Rochambeau has told me that his son has returned to Versailles on board the *Amazone*, under the command of M. de La Pérouse, to ask for another fleet to be sent. The English have sailed from Newport at last but the Chevalier de Ternay still has too few ships to guard the main river outlets and complete the blockade of New York. We must wait.'

Wait! Wait! It was not a word that either La Fayette or his new lieutenant liked to hear. They did, however, succeed at last in obtaining permission to launch a night attack on two of the Hessians' camps and left them badly mauled.

But before long, they had to face a new enemy. Winter fell on them suddenly, half-way through the autumn, and set in for good. It buried the whole continent at a stroke, and the usual, marvellous respite of Indian summer was not granted to them this year. Whirling snowstorms hid the great forests, smothered towns and villages and laid a heavy silence over all, while the rivers froze over all the way to the sea where the waters in the great bays of Chesapeake and New York were white and crusted.

Then, as Washington had foreseen, both armies began to suffer, but the Rebels especially. They had few reserves and no money to buy what was needed. Officers and men alike ate bread made of a mixture of buckwheat, rye, wheat and maize, when there was any and the time soon came when they might go three days, not only without meat, for there was little enough of that except when the hunting was good, but even without bread. Their clothes were no better and a flourishing black market grew up.

The French, established behind the newly rebuilt defences of Newport, were slightly better off, but the provisions which had been brought from France were all gone by now and the generals were obliged to buy in food for the troops at exorbitant prices. They were waiting impatiently for news from France, for Rochambeau had asked, not merely for more men and the twenty-five millions needed by Washington, but for an unbelievable quantity of other things, from six thousand shirts, ten thousand pairs of shoes to three thousand sacks of flour, two dozen copper stoves and six dozen enema syringes. But Versailles seemed to have forgotten all about the army on the other side of the world and answers were infrequent.

Both armies passed the time as best they could, solidly entrenched in their own positions and making no attempts at hostile demonstrations which were, in any case, rendered impossible by the weather. Only La Fayette made frequent journeys to Philadelphia to prevail upon congressmen and their wives to contribute, willy nilly, to the war effort. In this way he successfully acquired much that was needed.

On Christmas Eve, Tim Thocker arrived at headquarters, gliding in on his snow shoes like a gull on the water. But he brought sad news. At daybreak on the fifteenth of December the French flagship, the *Duc de Bourgogne*, had hauled her flags to half mast and braced her yards in sign of mourning, while her guns began to sound under the grey sky. Soon the other ships of the fleet had followed suit. The high and puissant seigneur Charles-Henri-Louis d'Arsac, Chevalier de Ternay, Chevalier de Malte, Admiral of the King's Fleet had died at half past five in the morning, two hours before dawn.

The news came as a shock to Washington who had conceived a great admiration for the greatness of the gallant, taciturn little admiral, who was so often the butt for his junior officers.

'Is it known how he died?' he asked the messenger.

'I was told of a putrid fever but there was some talk of an inflammation of the lungs.'

'I'll tell you what he died of,' burst out La Fayette, who had listened to the news with evident distress. 'He died of grief at the way those at Versailles have abandoned the army. He knew this winter was going to prove disastrous and it wore him out. Monsieur de Sartines is three parts to blame for his death, for I know that he encouraged his junior officers from a distance to conspire against him. What do those gilded imbeciles in their ministries know about war – and those who command in it?'

'Who will take his place as commander of the fleet?' Gilles asked, equally saddened, as though by the death of a friend. 'Will we have to wait for another appointment from Versailles?'

'That would be the last straw! The command should go by rights to the *Neptune*'s captain, the Chevalier Destouches, who is a fine man.'

'And it is he who has succeeded to the command at present,' Tim replied. 'But I must say, the funeral very nearly caused a riot. The anabaptists of Newport are not used to the ceremonies of your Romish Church and General Rochambeau managed it very well. They haven't got over it yet.'

For Tim, the news he brought was first and foremost an opportunity to see his friend again and Gilles was glad of his presence at the modest Christmas festivities that Washington made a point of laying on for his officers and men. The enforced inaction of camp life was having its effect on his character. He was becoming more reserved, more taciturn and losing some of his earlier spontaneity. When not roving the camp like a sick wolf, he could be found at one of the outposts, standing for hours on end upon some eminence, his service

322

cloak pulled up to his eyes, staring out at the hummocky white-ness of the forest and the snow-covered hills as though he could see into the distance to the exact spot where stood the woman he had believed in and who had betrayed him. Over and over again, he asked himself what Sita could have hoped to gain from it all. Why, if she had really wanted the Iroquois, had she encouraged him to desert to go with her? Unless it was to make a gift of him to Cornplanter's executioners, as the man who had prevented her from coming to him before? It was an appalling and discouraging thought, but he could see no other explanation.

But although, by slow degrees and almost without his realizing it, contempt was extinguishing love in him, it could do nothing to combat the imperious demands of his senses. Continence began to be a torture to him, for which he sought such relief as he could. Not that it was difficult. His steel blue eyes, the sardonic curl to his lips and his air of careless arro-gance attracted women as larks to a mirror. His charm and the skill he had developed in all the arts of love held them to him afterwards.

But he formed no new attachments. His desire satisfied, he went on his way to the next conquest, careless of the tears and lamentations that followed his going.

In this way, he passed from the wealthiest woman farmer in New Windsor, a red-haired Juno of ample proportions who would have married him, to the minister's niece, a fragile, secretive girl who would beat her breast between embraces and wail that she would go to hell for it, but was none the less able to turn on all the arts of a courtesan to bring him back when he showed signs of tiring of her. There was the wife of an inn-keeper and a Molly Pitcher, passive and purring, in whose great, vacant eyes he sought in vain for some resemblance to the delightful Betty who had crept into his tent that night at Peekskill. In any case, Sitapanoki's memory was still too keen and poisoned all these fleeting fancies with its too ready comparisons.

Only once did he meet with a rebuff. It was one evening when he had gone in search of wood to revive the dying fire in his tent and returned in time to see a woman enveloped in a long cloak come quickly out and walk off in the direction of

323

the village. Dropping his faggots, he ran after her and caught her up.

'When the master of a house is not at home,' he cried, his arms tightening round the thick woollen stuff that seemed more solid than the slender form within, 'it is not polite to enter and then leave again without waiting.'

'Let me go, Lieutenant,' Gunilla's cool voice answered him. 'What cause would I have to remain in your tent since you were absent?'

Gilles let go his hold, drew back and bowed courteously.

'Forgive me, Gunilla. I had not recognized you in that cloak. But please, don't go away now.'

'I have no time. Mrs Gibson is waiting for me and she will be anxious if I stay longer. I only came to bring you a pot of jam.'

'Jam? That was good of you. But do come in, if only for a moment – so that I can at least tell you honestly how good it is!'

She followed him in silence, just as she had once done in the mountains of Pennsylvania. Inside the tent a lantern was burning and it was almost cosy. The pot of jam was standing next to the lantern and Gilles picked it up and opened it, inhaling the fruity smell of it yet at the same time never taking his eyes off the girl. It was some while since he had seen her for, ever since her arrival at headquarters, Gunilla had been living very much under the wing of Mrs Gibson who had loved her at once for her courage and gentleness and treated her like the daughter she had never had. In her house, Gunilla led a life that was tranquil to the point of austerity but she adapted to it happily. She scarcely ever left the house and garden, with the farther end of which Gilles was so well acquainted.

He looked at her now with surprise and curiosity. Standing there in the yellow light of the lantern, her serious small face framed in the whiteness of her goffered cap from which a few strands of pale silky hair escaped, she was the very picture of freshness and tranquillity. Her skin had lost the tanned roughness brought about by toil and slavery and was now smooth and fair, and the eyes beneath the heavy fringe of her lashes were bluer than ever.

Gilles caught himself thinking that she had grown very

pretty. She was looking at him, yet there was a kind of timidity, almost an apprehensiveness in the way she met his gaze. He dug one finger into the jam and licked it like a schoolboy, grinning at her.

'It's a long time since I tasted anything so good,' he exclaimed. 'Thank you, Gunilla!'

'It is not me you should thank, but Mrs Gibson.'

'Come, come! You'll not persuade me that good lady has suddenly taken it into her head to worry about me. If I were General Washington, perhaps! No, I think the idea came from you – and very charming it was, too.'

He set down the jampot and moved closer to her, looking down on her from his greater height. She watched him but did not move. Her eyes were very wide and stared back into his like those of a mesmerized bird. He smiled into the limpid gaze.

'As charming as yourself, Gunilla. How could I have been such a fool as not to notice that before?'

He reproached himself sincerely, although he could not have said what drove him to pay court to the child. Perhaps it was the sense of cleanliness and purity which emanated from her, in spite of all she must have been through at the hands of the Senecas. She could not be a virgin, since no slave who wished to live would dare oppose the wishes of her masters, and the poor girl must have been forced to endure the warrior who had captured her many times over. But once restored to the life she had been bred to, she had resumed her old personality again and it still fitted her like a glove. It was as though she had resumed her virginity at the same time.

Gilles bent his head a little lower and his lips touched hers. They were cool and smelled of apples. For an instant, he felt them come alive, yielding responsively to his kiss. But when he tried to fold his arms round the slight figure, it was all at once like trying to embrace a thorn bush. Gunilla struggled like a wildcat, tore herself out of his grasp and delivered a stinging blow to his face.

'How dare you!' she cried. 'What do you take me for? I am not your Indian woman! No, nor second best, either!'

She had struck him with all her strength. One hand to his burning cheek, Gilles put the other out to her but she was already out of the tent and running like a hunted rabbit through the snow. Gilles gave a shrug.

'A pity,' he murmured, with a fair assumption of carelessness. In fact, he was furious and, to get over it, went to spend the remainder of the night with his red-haired Juno who exerted herself to her utmost to please a lover she had never known to be so exacting.

Hating to admit defeat, Gilles tried to see Gunilla again but without success. Whenever he chanced to catch sight of her about the village, she fled out of reach, nor was there any repetition of the pot of jam.

However he soon had other things to think about. January was a terrible month. There was unrest among the troops in Pennsylvania. Groups of the ill-clad, ill-fed and unpaid men mutinied. Then Washington struck back. Dreadful punishments were meted out to the mutineers, and men were flogged until their backs were raw. Day by day, the General's brow grew darker.

Yet there was one item of good news. Sagoyewatha had taken the warpath against his former ally, Cornplanter. The clans were at one another's throats over a woman and the blood reddening the snow to the south of Lake Ontario and in the Mohawk valley came not only from slaughtered game or wolves. Washington and those few Indian tribes who had not sided with the English, such as the Cakawangas, were able to breathe again. The nations of the Iroquois had other things on their mind. Which did not prevent Gilles, still thirsting to dip his sword in the blood of the man Sitapanoki had preferred to himself, from badgering his superiors to let him put on snowshoes like Tim's and go with him to 'observe' the Indian's war. But permission was always refused.

'You are here to serve the United States,' Colonel Hamilton told him, 'and not your own inclinations.'

He might have gone, permission or no, but for La Fayette who, returning one night from Philadelphia where he was whiling away his enforced leisure, at Washington's request, by having his portrait painted by the artist Charles Peale, brought shocking news. The traitor Arnold had gone to join the fighting in Virginia. With the British forces, he was ravaging and burning everything that fell into his hands and General Greene, who had replaced General Gates in the south, and his much weakened army could do nothing to stop him, for he was turning against his former friends the very method of warfare which they had employed with such miraculous success in the past, a guerrilla war of ambuscades and surprise attacks. Greene was asking for help, the more so since he was obliged to push on down to Carolina to try and stop Cornwallis.

This was La Fayette's opportunity and on February 20th he set out for Virginia with several thousand men, making for Hampton on the Chesapeake. The Chevalier Destouches was to meet him there with ships to take them across the huge estuary. Lieutenant Goëlo went with him, feeling happy for the first time in weeks. Failing Cornplanter, Arnold was just the quarry he felt like hunting.

La Fayette, on his part, was only half satisfied. He was certainly glad to be going after Arnold but he was chiefly afraid that the great battle of the spring, which would undoubtedly be fought around New York, might take place without him. Washington had to promise to recall him in time before he would consent to go. But he was overjoyed when one of his greatest friends came from Newport to fight at his side. This was the Comte de Charlus, second in command of the Saintonge regiment, whose father, the Maréchal de Castries had, since October 13th, replaced the odious Monsieur de Sartines at the head of their navy, at the same time as the Comte de Ségur had taken over from the Prince de Montbarrey at the war ministry. The King had been doing some spring cleaning. Finally, Colonel Hamilton, tired of putting up with Washington's moods, had resigned from his post as aide-de-camp and joined La Fayette's legion. He wanted space and a change of air. The expeditionary force was going to be an army to be reckoned with.

The months that followed were, for Gilles, at once the happiest and most wretched of his whole life. They were short of practically everything : money, food, shirts, sometimes even shoes. Horses were a thing of the past and even cavalrymen like Gilles were obliged to go on foot. What was more, the snow had given way to floods. The swollen rivers made quagmires of the ground and feet had to be dragged squelching out of the mud at every step. Yet never was there a more united army than that motley assortment of French and Americans, many of them unable to communicate except by signs, but amongst whom all notions of class had been practically abolished.

Partly to be with his friend and partly to please his beloved Martha who had favoured him with a pithy account of her feelings at the prospect of finding herself married to a mere woodsman, Tim Thocker had brought himself to enlist in one of the five companies from Connecticut which, with a number of others from New Hampshire, Rhode Island and New Jersey made up La Fayette's little army. His woodcraft and marksmanship made him more than welcome.

While still on the march, they received a new addition to their force. They were looking for a way across the Delaware which the floods had swollen to twice its normal breadth, when Gilles heard pitiable cries coming from the water. He at once dived in and returned to the small hillock which was all that was visible of the bank dragging triumphantly with him an emaciated Indian trussed like a chicken who no sooner recovered from his fright than he fell down and embraced his knees, pouring out a flood of speech which soon had Tim grinning all over his face.

'He says that you are the son of the Great Spirit, the brother of the thunderbird, his father, his mother, all his nearest relations and a host of other less important characters. He adds that from now on he is your slave, your dog, your left arm and your best friend – but you may as well throw him back in the water.'

'Oh, yes?' Gilles said, busy pulling on his coat and boots which he had flung off hastily before entering the water. 'And why should I do that?'

'Because he's an Onondaga, which is to say an Iroquois, and you swore weeks ago to exterminate the whole tribe. What is more, he is a medicine man in trouble, which means he is a bad medicine man.'

The soldiers who had gathered round the three of them expressed vociferous approval of Tim's words, but Gilles was in no mood to be trifled with.

'When I save a man, I think I have the right to decide what

shall be done with him,' he snapped. 'When I want your advice, I'll ask for it. As for this fellow—'

He looked down at the man still kneeling before him and felt not the slightest wish to make him the victim of any unseasonable ideas of revenge. He was, in fact, a curious creature, having nothing in common with the gigantic Hiakin of evil memory. He had a broad chest supported on unusually short legs and very long arms which gave him something of the look of a chimpanzee. His little eyes, as round and bright as beads of jet, lit a face whose most remarkable features were a long nose, a notable absence of chin and two long white teeth, like piano keys, protruding below his upper lip and producing a startling resemblance to a rabbit.

'Tell him he can go,' Gilles said. 'He is free. And now let us go and join the others and try and see if we can find that damned ferry!'

But the Indian had no wish for liberty. Launching into an improbable gibberish with odd English words mixed up in it, he expressed his earnest desire to follow in his rescuer's footsteps and make himself his living shield in the combats which surely lay before so valiant a warrior. Then, drawing the knife that hung from his belt, he cut his arm and let a few drops of blood fall on the young man.

'He says that his blood is yours,' Tim explained, 'and I'm beginning to think he means what he says. Will you have him as a servant? As far as he's concerned, I rather think you are something of a life raft.'

While they searched for the ferryboat which had been carried away by the swollen river, the rescued Indian told them his story. He was the medicine man of a small tribe of Onondagas that dwelt in the neighbourhood and rejoiced in a completely unpronounceable name which meant 'The Beaver who found the magic eagle's feather' and, as Tim had said, he had not been altogether happy in the exercise of his calling. When, for example, the aged mother of his chief was suffering from a brain fever, he had been able to think of nothing better to do than to make a hole in the poor woman's head to let the bad spirits out, a treatment from which his patient had promptly died. Whereupon he had been blamed, not for causing the old woman's death, but for employing forbidden methods, since the Indians had no use for surgery. Then, when, immediately after the chief's mother's departure for the kingdom of the dead, the river had risen in spate, carrying away half their wigwams and all that they contained, the survivors had decided that their sorcerer was not worth having and simply cast him into the river, thus depriving him of the funeral ceremonies without which the soul of a dead warrior can never find rest. It was this latter circumstance in particular which had earned Gilles the man's desperate gratitude, for, like all good Indians, he was not particularly afraid of death.

'Well,' Gilles decided, 'with the General's permission, I will keep him in my service, but only on condition that he never tries to cure me if I am hurt or wounded.'

Since he found the ex-medicine man's name quite impossible to pronounce, he took a part of it and rechristened him Pongo, whereat the man appeared delighted. And Pongo at once began to prove himself astonishingly useful. He might not have been a very good medicine man but he was a matchless hunter and warrior. He knew how to make a host of things, from bark canoes to huts made of branches, and including making the greatest possible use of the game they killed and discovering edible roots. Moreover, in spite of his short legs, he was remarkably strong, very agile and extremely clever, so that whenever he failed to find what was needed, he could be relied upon to steal it without being suspected. Finally, he was a better tracker than the finest bloodhound.

'Brother Fox and Pongo on the trail, Pongo win!' he would declare with his broad grin.

Gradually, Gilles grew accustomed to the copper-coloured shadow which clung to him as closely as his own and almost as soundlessly. Pongo ate little, seemed permanently enchanted with his lot, spoke hardly at all (it was a good six months before Gilles managed to achieve any kind of conversation with him) and smiled a great deal, showing the huge front teeth which before long were almost as well known to the army as the plume in La Fayette's hat.

They took so long to reach Virginia that it began to seem to them something like the promised land. At Elk Point they waited in vain for the Chevalier Destouches and his little fleet who had found their way blocked by the whole naval might of the English admiral Arbuthnot and had been obliged to turn back. From there they withdrew into Maryland, around Baltimore, where La Fayette again set all the ladies to work sewing, and skirting the immense shore of Chesapeake Bay, crossed the Potomac and came at last to Richmond which Arnold was busy burning.

They spent the whole of that spring in skirmishing and playing games of hide and seek, in which each side was alternately the hunter and the hunted, but still the traitor Arnold eluded them. He had replaced General Phillips, who had died suddenly, and was protected by a solid phalanx of troops. La Fayette's small force raced back and forth across Virginia which had otherwise been left virtually defenceless since General Greene had gone to the Carolinas to deal with Lord Cornwallis, one of the finest English generals.

In May, they had disquieting news. Cornwallis had practically wiped out Greene and was moving up to join Arnold. He was making no secret of how he meant to deal with La Fayette's army.

'I'll not let that boy get away from me,' was how he contemptuously expressed it.

They waited uneasily. For all his unquenchable optimism, La Fayette had no illusions and on May 22nd he wrote to the French ambassador to Congress, La Luzerne :

'We are still alive and the fell visitation has not yet fallen on our little force . . .'

But he need not have worried. The approach of the most formidable of his enemies galvanized his men. The company which Lieutenant Goëlo commanded as acting captain was in high fettle. For it was being said that Cornwallis was only on his way north to strengthen New York, where Clinton could not do without him in the final battle.

'He may say that the boy shall not escape him,' Gilles declared to his men, 'but all he means to do is to sweep us aside like chaff. So it is for us to bar the way and show him what we are made of. Without Cornwallis, Clinton will not be able to hold New York for long once the reinforcements which the King of France has promised have arrived. So at all costs we must prevent Cornwallis from reaching New York.'

The reinforcements were in fact on their way. Under the

urgings of de Castries, Vergennes and Louis XVI had finally made up their minds to commit a good half of France's considerable naval strength to aid the Rebels. Admiral de Barres de Saint-Laurent had reached Newfoundland with several ships and was at that moment cruising off Newport. Furthermore, at daybreak on March 22nd, the guns of Brest had fired a parting salute for the huge fleet under Admiral de Grasse which was sailing up the American coast from the West Indies. It could be bringing victory and an end to the war.

'We must stand firm, stand firm at all costs,' Gilles cried, echoing La Fayette. 'We must hold out to the last man.'

Theirs was no easy task. They numbered only fifteen hundred men and the small bodies of local troops in conjunction with whom they were operating were mainly irregulars, though their leaders bore names like Lee and Sumter. They had also absorbed Baron de Steuben's force. It came to at most fifteen hundred men all told, but deployed in such a way that the English, with a strength of something like ten thousand, should believe them much more numerous.

Taught by Pongo, Gilles had become an adept in all the subtleties of Indian warfare. He was without equal in the art of worming his way up to an objective without giving away his presence and could then strike like lightning, quick and hard, and melt away again leaving men dead behind him who had never known what hit them. Dressed in deerskin garments manufactured by the Indian to replace the smart uniform, long since in rags, and which provided an infinitely better protection against mosquitoes, he had acquired a considerable reputation at his deadly game, as well as a fierce and formidable appearance which often made Tim look thoughtful.

Tim said to him one day : 'Do you remember that bird you killed by the Susquehanna? The one that nearly cost us our scalps?'

'The gyrfalcon? Of course I remember,' Gilles replied easily, though his heart missed a beat.

'Well, I was thinking that you are like that. He dropped out of the sky, struck and was away again. You drop out of trees, but the end is the same.'

'Don't take it too far. I don't carry my victims off and tear them with my beak.'

332

He was laughing, but it pleased him all the same. Tim, in his friendship, had hit instinctively on the one comparison that could touch his frozen heart. It was as though the intangible links with his forebears had all at once taken form and substance. And since Tim did not keep his thought to himself and would describe the incident with the Senecas to back it up, the nickname soon began to stick. His men even held a weird ceremony in which they identified him with the totem in Indian fashion and in which Pongo reverted for once to his role of medicine man.

'Did you know,' he asked, when the young man jibbed at taking part in a ritual that seemed to him vaguely absurd, 'that your own general himself received a name from my people? By them, La Fayette is called Kayewla, "wonderful horseman". You will be "the ruthless gyrfalcon that strikes in the mist".'

With the whole company looking on approvingly, Pongo, his body ritually painted, lit a fire and strewed herbs upon it to produce a thick smoke, then danced in a tight circle round Gilles and the fire, chanting aloud. After a final invocation of the Great Spirit, he traced black and white marks upon him to represent his new name and that was that. La Fayette congratulated his lieutenant and presented the company with a cask of rum and the occasion ended in a cloud of tobacco smoke, this being the only thing that had not been in short supply since their entry into the country of George Washington and the Princess Pocahontas. But on the following night, the Gyrfalcon's men justified their leader's new name by surprising a party of Cornwallis' scouts who, under the persuasive influence of the one-time medicine man, revealed some astonishing facts. The English General, after abandoning the state capital of Richmond to La Fayette the previous year, somewhat to the latter's mystification, had now evacuated Williamsburg.

This time, La Fayette understood well enough. Cornwallis, tired of pursuing him, was leaving him to his fate and returning to his first aim which was to make a forced march on New York in order to help Clinton to win a decisive victory, or rather to win it for him, for the two men disliked one another extremely and were as jealous as they could possibly be.

In desperation, the Marquis flung his whole force after the

English, forcing them to entrench themselves in Yorktown, at the mouth of the river York which flowed at that point into the vast Chesapeake estuary. At the same time, he sent a letter to Washington, begging to be allowed to rejoin him, or at least to be told what to do. The heat was overpowering, the mosquitoes unbearable and, despite the arrival of a battalion from Pennsylvania, La Fayette was at his wits' end. Cornwallis was fortifying Yorktown as though he meant to remain there for the rest of his life. It was already midway through August and still no decisive battle had been fought.

The answer came like a thunderclap, brought by a French officer, General du Portail. Washington's orders to his dear marquis were to stay where he was and keep an eye on Cornwallis because he had finally given in to the arguments of Rochambeau, who was against a battle for New York, and had decided that the much-heralded decisive battle should take place in Virginia.

Almost beside himself with delight, the young General called his officers together and tossed the latest news at them piece-meal, like a bunch of flowers. Rochambeau's troops had left Newport, had joined up with Washington at Philipsburg and were now marching, in an excellent order that was to excite the admiration of the Americans, down into Virginia. Admiral de Grasse's fleet, meanwhile, was to drop anchor at the mouth of the Chesapeake, while Barras remained off New York to keep Clinton guessing about the American's intentions.

'Gentlemen,' La Fayette cried, in his squeaky voice, 'at all costs, we must keep Cornwallis bottled up in Yorktown until our friends arrive. Get yourselves killed to the last man, but do not let a single Englishman escape. Long live the United States of America! Long live General Washington! Long live France!'

He was rewarded with a vociferous cry of 'Long live La Fayette!' Hope being the best of tonics, all those wretched men who for months had been fighting their way blindly across a ravaged countryside, had ceased even to believe that it would ever come to an end. They believed themselves forgotten, relegated to the duties of a guard dog, and now they were going to be in the very heart of the action, they had become indispensable and now they were sure that their deaths would not be in vain. That night, the sick were less feverish and the dying closed their eyes with a smile.

'What I can't understand,' Tim said, scratching his head, 'is what Cornwallis hopes to gain by shutting himself up in a small place like Yorktown. It's not even as though it was important. So why waste time fortifying it rather than going on?'

'Because, unless he goes the long way round as we did, he has to cross the estuary. And for that, he is waiting for Admiral Rodney's fleet to take his men all the way to New York painlessly. We can only hope that Admiral Grasse will get here first.'

The die was cast now. The winter's slow manoeuvring, the exchange of letters, the councils, the patient work of spies, was all coming together at last and the clock of America was about to strike the hour of destiny. They must be victorious at Yorktown, or else renounce the marvellous dream of Independence for ever.

14

Destiny

Yorktown . . . The red and blue folds of the union jack flapping over a timber fort, bristling with guns, perched on a headland far up the York river and flanked by two strong redoubts. Low houses built of weathered wood, watchtowers and the delicate spire of a little church. And all around, marshes, reedbeds, sea pines, yellow hills, well-wooded and ideally suited for observation, with, away to the east, the great bight of Chesapeake Bay and the immense ocean beyond.

Lieutenant Goëlo leaned his back against one of the trees that overhung his quarters, arms folded on his chest, gazing meditatively at the broad landscape where fate had decreed that the fate of a nation would be decided. All was ready for the final act. The commanders, united as never before, had drawn a tight cordon of steel from the river bank on either side around the promontory on which the town stood. Starting at Wormeley's Creek, there were the troops which General Greene had brought up from the Carolinas, then La Fayette's and Lincoln's, drawn up below the heavy guns of the American artillery, next door to which was Rochambeau's with Washington's position immediately behind and a part of the French artillery in front of them. Between this and the river were the French regiments of Baron Viomenil and the Vicomte, his brother and then the three thousand men of the Agenais, Touraine and Gâtinais regiments under the command of the Marquis de Saint-Simon, landed by Admiral de Grasse coming up from the West Indies.

And on the other side, blocking the estuary from Cape Henry

336

to Cape Charles, were the tall white pyramids of the French fleet under shortened sail and keeping station on the huge, 104-gun *Ville de Paris*, the Comte de Grasse's flagship. The fleet was resting comfortably on its laurels after its recent victory over Admirals Graves and Hood, who had now gone off to New York to lick their wounds, although without abating one jot of its vigilance notwithstanding. There was no telling whether the formidable Rodney might not come down on them in an attempt to force an entry into the Chesapeake and relieve Cornwallis. In the meanwhile, the giant de Grasse was standing guard, made glorious not merely by his victory but by the enormous popularity he had acquired with the army at his first encounter with Washington by embracing him warmly and calling him 'my little general'.

'It's nice to have a full-scale battle after all that skirmishing,' Tim said, coming to join his friend. 'It certainly looks impressive, I must say.'

'A battle? But it hasn't begun yet.'

'What?' Tim cried, yelling to make himself heard above the roar of the guns. 'I could have sworn—'

The bombardment had in fact been going on for four days and nights now, covering the fields and marshes in a pall of white smoke and opening breaches which were as quickly filled. Meanwhile, for a fortnight past, General de Portail's sappers had been crawling methodically and inexorably nearer to the besieged town, digging saps and trenches. It was true that the real battle would only begin when the signal was given for the general advance, but there were some dead already and many wounded lying in the field hospital which had been set up to the westward on the road to Williamsburg and was already too small.

Gilles shrugged and sighed.

'It won't be today, at any rate.'

The day, in fact, was almost over. The sun had gone behind the hills, swallowed up into the trees. A trumpet was sounding somewhere and all over the camp the fires were being lighted. A party of horsemen was riding back to headquarters, led by two tall figures instantly recognizable as Washington and Rochambeau, returning from their daily inspection of the ground. In a little while, it would be growing cold.

Tim had moved off, but there was someone else approaching. 'What is it, Pongo?' Gilles asked, without turning. From living in the wild, his ear had grown keen enough to catch and identify the smallest sounds. Moreover, on this occasion, the Indian's quickened breathing indicated that he had been running.

'An ambush!'

His master swung round instantly.

'Where?'

'Over there – in the woods. The Hampton road.' He spread out his fingers to indicate half a score of men.

'Who are they? French, or Americans?'

'Americans – but not soldiers. They hide in trees. They men of this country – wait for white officer.'

'I don't know what you're talking about, but we'll go and see.'

Gilles borrowed a horse from Colonel de Gimat and, taking Pongo up behind him, rode towards the woods through which ran the road to Hampton. The road itself he carefully avoided. When he came to the edge of the trees, he dismounted, tethering the animal to a tree, and signed to Pongo to lead the way. Darkness had fallen but there was still light enough for these two, who had eyes like cats. Not the smallest rustle of leaves betrayed their presence, moving on into the wood.

It was very quiet. From time to time there came the quick scamper of a rabbit or the cry of some nocturnal creature, but that was all. All at once, Pongo, who had been crouching low, stopped dead. They had reached the Hampton road.

The Indian raised his arm cautiously, pointing to a spot among the trees. Autumn had already begun to thin out the leaves and some darker patches showed where a number of men were in hiding, waiting for something, or someone. Gilles made a sign that he had understood and crept forward slowly, keeping his eye on the treetops, until there was only a bramble bush between him and the road. Once there, he drew the two loaded pistols which, with his sword, comprised his whole armament. That done, he froze, leaving Pongo to his own devices. In an affair of this kind it was never necessary to give him any orders. He seemed to know instinctively what to do.

They did not have to wait long. They heard the light clop

338

of a horse's hooves and, echoing them, a voice that whispered :
'Here he comes!'

Gilles peered out and made out the light splash of a white
horse, surmounted by the dark figure of its rider, against the
ribbon of the road.

A flash of the white cockade in the black cocked hat had
told Gilles that the officer was French and, what was more,
someone he was quite certainly acquainted with. The man's
figure, enveloped in its great black cloak, was vague but there
was something about his way of sitting a horse and the shortened reins which reminded him of someone.

It all happened very quickly. The rider passed in under the
trees and then, a few yards beyond Gilles, he pulled up short
with an angry shout. A large fishing net had descended on him
from the trees above, enveloping him and his horse which
stumbled and fell with a whinney of pain. In the same instant,
the waiting men swarmed out of the trees.

Someone shouted: 'Don't kill him! I want him alive! It
would be too easy otherwise!'

The next moment there were two yells of anguish as Gilles
discharged both pistols at the legs of the supposed bandits.
Then he had his sword out and charged straight at them, with
a fiendish cry which was echoed by a howl from Pongo, who
had elected to emulate the first party and drop from the trees.

His sword met no opposition beyond some long knives and
a few strokes were enough to put two men out of action, Pongo
just striking down his second victim. The rest fled, leaving the
place to the wounded and the rider on his fallen horse, still
tangled in the net. Gilles went to kneel beside him.

'Are you hurt, sir?'

'Not at all, thanks to you. But I fear my horse's leg is
broken.'

The stranger spoke French with an accent which Gilles had
not the slightest difficulty in recognizing. He started to laugh.

'Why, Monsieur de Fersen! What the devil have you been
up to, Count, to make these fellows try to net you in the woods
like this?'

The prisoner in the net struggled furiously.

'And who the devil are you?' he snarled. 'A Frenchman I
take it, and your voice is somewhat familiar, but I can't see a

339

thing and you'd be better employed in getting me out of this.'

'We're trying to. If you'd only keep still. Pongo's knife is as sharp as a razor. I'd hate to get you out piecemeal.'

The Indian cut swiftly through the meshes and Fersen was able to free himself but his first action was to bend over his horse, which was still lying on its side and twitching spasmodically, and examine it carefully.

'I'm afraid there's nothing to be done,' Gilles said. 'His leg is broken.'

The Swede, cursing softly, stroked the animal's neck with tenderness and it turned its head towards him, but he did not hesitate. Taking his pistol from his belt, he put the barrel close to the long, silky ear, then turned his eyes away and pulled the trigger. The horse's body jerked once and then lay still.

Gilles had watched its death in a tense silence. Every fibre of his being responded to the feelings of the man forced to shoot his companion. War had taught him to kill with a measure of indifference and yet he would never be able to see a horse or a dog die without grieving.

Fersen, meanwhile, had found a dry pine branch and set light to it. The glare illuminated the scene, revealing, stark against the surrounding dark, the great white body of the horse, the red-brown figure of Pongo standing over the two wounded men whose eyes glittered furiously in their soot-blackened faces, and, finally, Gilles himself. At the sight of his face, Fersen let out an exclamation of delight.

'Monsieur de Goëlo! Good God! It is a pleasure to have been saved by you! Your reputation has travelled a long way. It stands as high with the French as with the Rebels. You are a credit to your country.'

'I thank you,' Gilles said, laughing. 'But however high the reputation you would bestow on me, it cannot ennoble me, you know. The "de" is superfluous.'

'And no one could be sorrier than I! But it may not always be so. I have some credit at court and when we return to France you may count on me to do my best to see my rescuer honoured as he deserves. You have my word for that. And now, give me your hand to seal the bargain and our friendship after the manner of this country.'

A groan, half of pain and half of sheer fury recalled them

to the existence of their wounded prisoners. One had fainted after trying to rise but the other was champing with helpless rage.

'Why don't you stop congratulating yourselves and finish us off?' he roared. 'I'm suffering the agonies of the damned!'

'If it comes to that,' Gilles said, 'will you tell me the reason for this ambush? You were ten against one, and that one a man who came here out of his generosity to serve your country—'

'To serve our country?' The man sneered, his young face looking like an angry faun. 'We never asked you to. And, for another thing, if your way of serving us is to assault our womenfolk, you'd have done better to have stayed at home.'

'Suppose you tell me just what happened?' Gilles said, bending down to look at the man's injured leg. It was not a pretty sight. The tibia had been fractured and a long splinter of white bone protruded through the mangled flesh. The man would always walk with a limp.

'My name is Arthur Collins. I'm a fisherman and I have a small house not far from here. I live there with my young sister, Margaret . . . She is pretty enough to have caught this gentleman's eye and he has often come to her in the night while I have been at sea. Yesterday morning, I was just in time to see him jump out of the window and make off.

'I thought I would go mad. My sister! That wretch dared to debauch my sister! As though she were some common strumpet—'

'He did not rape her, I imagine?'

'No. Poor fool, she let him bewitch her with his fine words. He told her she was like a European lady – a great lady of the court. She told me that through her tears, and now she takes herself for a princess. She raved at me and I had to lock her up to stop her going after him. What have you to say to that? I think he deserves to die – and worse than that. I'd like to see him eaten by sharks!'

Gilles' shoulders lifted a little in disgust. The hatred of the man was almost palpable.

'I have nothing to say. Except that people will always make fools of themselves for love, that you are as bloodthirsty as an Iroquois – and that your leg badly needs attention. We're

341

going to put you up on my horse and take you to the army hospital.'

'And let them murder us? No thank you! Besides, I don't want your help. If you don't want to finish us off, just leave us here and go away. Someone will come and see to us as soon as you've taken that savage of yours away.'

'Just as you like. But next time you have a score of this kind to settle, go and ask for satisfaction in daylight, and don't behave like highway robbers. Come, sir.'

He took the Swede by the arm and would have drawn him off but Fersen, freeing himself gently, went back to where the man lay and took out his purse and laid it by him.

'Find a good physician to tend you and your friend. As for Margaret, tell her I was not deceiving her and that I shall always remember her.'

'You can go to hell! I don't want your money.'

But Fersen had already rejoined the others and together they made their way back to the place where Gilles had left his horse.

'Take this to get you home,' he told the Swede. 'You have farther to go than I. Only send him back to us when you have done. I borrowed him from Colonel de Gimat.'

The moon was rising and its light fell on the Swede's cool, handsome face and tousled fair hair. He had lost his wig in the affray and it had had the misfortune to fall in a puddle and was quite unwearable, but this only made him look younger. The cloak thrown back from one shoulder gave a glimpse of his exquisite blue and yellow uniform coat and immaculate white cuffs and leathers. He had emerged from his fishing net looking as neat as if he were going to a ball. But he declined the horse.

'Good lord, no! I can walk.'

'In boots?'

'Yes, in boots! I have deserved some punishment for my sins and there is no reason why you should do penance for me. Besides, walking is good for thinking, and it is a beautiful night. I shall have my dreams.'

'Of the great lady who is so beautiful that you seek her memory, even among the fishermen's sisters in Virginia?' Gilles asked boldly.

A shiver ran through Fersen. His eyes, which always had a tendency to gaze into some invisible distances, returned gravely to his interlocutor.

'Do not say memory – say rather her image, my friend. For to me she is only a dream – an unattainable dream. But better still, do not speak of her at all.' Then he laughed suddenly and went on: 'Now tell me something. I thought you had your commission?'

'I have. I am a lieutenant in the Marquis de La Fayette's legion. I know I don't look like it, but I left my fine black uniform coat somewhere in a thicket near Richmond. I had to fall back on my Indian's tailoring. You may not know it, but we Americans are practically penniless.'

'I see. Well, I shall see to it that you do not remain so! France will have much to offer you. I am told, by the by, that your men have given you a nickname – some bird, I think?'

'That's it. They call me the Gyrfalcon,' Gilles said with a laugh, 'and you can't think how proud I am of it. It's the best name I've ever had.'

Fersen studied the younger man for a moment, his tall, slim figure moulded by the crude deerskin, the firm, tanned features, hawk nose and hard eyes, which the moonlight turned to steel.

'You are right,' he said thoughtfully. 'It suits you better than any. The gyrfalcon makes his home in my country and I have cause to know that you can strike as fast as he. He is a great hunter. Only, I do not care much for your present plumage, Sir Gyrfalcon. It's more suited to an owl than to a king of the skies. Good night.'

With that, the Swede wrapped himself in his cloak and set off resolutely down the rutted track somewhat pretentiously styled the Hampton road, his elegant, highly polished boots protesting at every step.

'Oh well,' Gilles murmured, grinning, 'his dreams are likely to be painful ones. He'll have some blisters on his feet before he gets there. Come on, Pongo. Let's go.'

When Gilles woke the next morning to the sound of reveille, he saw the Indian entering his tent, solemnly bearing a large parcel done up in strong grey canvas. There was a note pinned to it.

'Soldier bring this for you,' Pongo said, laying his burden down upon Gilles' lap.

The letter was from Fersen :

'Just in case you should have forgotten it, my friend, I will remind you that your name still figures on the roll of the Royal Deux-Ponts Regiment and that our Colonel-in-Chief, the Comte de Deux-Ponts, has not yet released you. He commands me to tell you that it will be inscribed there in future with the rank of lieutenant which General Washington conferred upon you. You will also make it plain to General Washington, as also to the Marquis de La Fayette, that you are merely on loan from us.

'You will find enclosed the wherewithal to appear fittingly in the battle or in the hour of victory. The sword is my own, a family heirloom, and I know that you will make good use of it. It and the rest come to you in token of the friendship of Axel de Fersen. P.S. The assault will be for today.'

The parcel contained the uniform, brand new, of an officer in the Royal Deux-Ponts. It was all there, the blue coat with the yellow facings, the brass gorget with the arms of the regiment upon it, the gold epaulettes and the tricorn hat with the yellow plume. With it was a magnificent gold-hilted sword. Engraved upon the blued steel blade with which Gilles was already making delighted passes through the air, was the one word *Semper*.

Gilles' first impulse was to put on all this brilliant plumage at once. He was already shaking out the shirt of fine lawn, when he chanced to look up and see one of his men, Sergeant Parker, pass by the opening of his tent. Parker's dress was a haphazard combination of a pair of striped trousers, much patched and too short for him, faded stockings wrinkling round his ankles, one shoe gaping like an oyster and a waistcoat, green with age, that lacked both buttons and facings but was possessed of a grand assortment of rents and holes.

Carefully, Gilles put the smart uniform back into its grey canvas wrappings. Then he dressed himself in his old, battered deerskins. If the assault was to be for today, he would not lead his men into the English fire clad in a way that should set him apart from them. Compared with the magnificent blue and white of the French regiments and the brilliant red coats of the English, which sometimes made the besieged town look like an outsized strawberry, the American troops had a shoddy appearance, but if the sun of glory would only shine for them, then it would turn their poverty to splendour.

'These poor garments have been through so much,' he murmured to himself, 'they have earned the right to go on to honour – or to death. Fersen would understand.'

The sword, however, he took with him gratefully, for this was no dress sword but a real soldier's weapon, a strong and formidable blade, much better than his own which had a damaged guard. He hung it proudly from his old, plain, leather sword belt, then knelt and said a rapid prayer, commending his soul to God if death should come to him that day. That done, he went out to get his orders from the General, feeling happy and at peace with himself for the first time for many months. Perhaps it was because the supreme moment had come when nothing mattered any more, except the fact that they were going into battle.

Outside, it seemed to him as though a curtain had been lifted on the last act of a great tragedy and he was looking for the first time on the landscape which had grown more ruined with every day that passed.

Before him, across a vast plain crawling with troops and scored with trenches, with the grey splashes of marshland scattered over it as traps for the unwary, he saw the smoking heap of rubble that was Yorktown. No citizens remained there now, only the stubborn swarms of red ants, moving to the shrill, unending music of the pipes of the Scots 71st Foot. And beyond it, on the river, the black hulks of the still blazing frigates *Loyalist* and *Guadeloupe* and the half-submerged *Charon* alongside them. The artillery of the Comte de Choisy and General Knox had done its work well and had not finished yet, for the guns on both sides were still pounding. The town was fighting back furiously, despite the shells ceaselessly eating into its walls. The two redoubts held firm. But as Rochambeau slowly tightened his patient grip, so the mines went up one by one, taking men with them, so that the shrieks of the wounded and dying mingled with the continuous roar of the guns. The sun shone, the sea was blue and the gaily coloured flags streamed in the morning breeze, and yet the scene was like an inferno, but an inferno from which no man sought to escape. Gilles himself was burning to plunge into it.

The officers of La Fayette's staff were assembled in his tent. There were Hamilton, Barber, Laurens, Poor and Gimat. But the General himself was absent. No one was speaking. They sat, each in his own corner, wrapped in his own silent thoughts and nursing his own impatience. The word had gone round that the assault would be that day, but no one dared believe it. Hamilton, who had received the rough edge of Washington's tongue yet again when he went to inquire, was biting his nails and brooding near the doorway. When Gilles came in, he literally fell on him.

'Well? Have you heard anything? Is it today or tomorrow—?'

'If I can believe a note I had from one of Rochambeau's aides, it is today.'

Hamilton's face lit up and he flung his arms round him.

'God send you may be right! It's enough to drive one mad, sitting here watching men shot down and doing nothing. If this goes on, Yorktown will fall to the sappers and the gunners, without our striking a single blow.'

At that moment, La Fayette sprang from his horse outside the tent and swept inside. His eyes were sparkling and his wig askew and he was evidently in the grip of some strong excitement, but whether of joy or anger none of them could have said. It seemed to Lieutenant Goëlo that it was something of both.

'Gentlemen,' La Fayette cried, casting his hat into a corner, 'today we are to have the honour of attacking one of the two redoubts. We shall be on the right while the French attack on the left.'

'We?' Hamilton said. 'Who do you mean by *we*? Our whole force?'

'No, sir. When I say *we*, I mean ourselves – La Fayette's division. And the same with the French. Their assault will be led by Baron Viomenil with a regiment or two—' He stopped, his face suddenly suffused a dull brick red, and the unpleasantly high-pitched voice which grated so painfully on the ears rose to a shout : 'And if I have my way, we shall have taken that redoubt before that nincompoop Viomenil has even reached the

346

parapet! Do you know – do you know what he dared to say just now, when Washington and Rochambeau gave out the orders for the day?'

He glared round at them, his whole body trembling from head to foot.

'He dared to cast doubts on the gallantry of my men! He dared to suggest that we could not fight well enough to take the redoubt from the English! So, gentlemen, you may tell your men. I'll have the hide off any man who even looks like hesitating. I am determined to make an end before them, do you hear? Determined! Go, now, and make your preparations. We attack before nightfall. We will be told the exact time in due course.'

The officers filed out in silence. Gilles was about to follow when the young General held him back.

'One moment, if you please,' he said curtly. 'It seems I have to congratulate you, lieutenant. General Rochambeau's aides can talk of nothing but your exploits. You saved Count Fersen's life, I believe?'

'It is not worth talking of, General.'

There had been a truculence in La Fayette's tone which Gilles did not understand and did not like.

'You think not? On the contrary, I feel sure that you accomplished an excellent piece of work. The best, perhaps, that you have ever done in your life, for now your future is assured. The Queen will be able to refuse you nothing.'

'The Qu—'

'Do not look at me with that bewildered expression. Yes, the Queen. Count Fersen is a great friend of hers – and our ravishing sovereign lady does not like people to harm her friends. So, I congratulate you. That young sprig is very dear to her.'

So that was the Swede's secret! Just two short words, a mere eight letters in all: the Queen! He was in love with the Queen and, suddenly, Gilles found himself wanting to see what Margaret Collins looked like, that for her sake the Swede had nearly ended in a shark's belly.

Yet whether or not Fersen was in love with the wife of his king, it still did not explain La Fayette's vicious tone, the contemptuous curl to his lip or the bitterness in his eyes. What was the nature of his own feelings for Marie-Antoinette? Gilles wondered. He was well aware of his opinions regarding kings in general, but he considered his impassioned tirades rather as the expression of idealistic views engendered by their present adventures. Brought up on the encyclopedists and a practising freemason, La Fayette could scarcely be expected to sound like a staunch monarchist. But the Queen was a woman . . .

'My lord Marquis,' Gilles said, stressing the title deliberately, 'Her Majesty is not acquainted with me and most probably never will be. Yet permit me to say I am amazed to hear her spoken of disrespectfully, in a foreign land, by a gentleman of France.'

For a moment, he thought the General would burst. The blood rushed to his face.

'Respect, you talk of? You poor provincial fool! Go to court once, only once, and look about you at the Queen's circle, and then come and tell me how many of the fine gentlemen who surround her are thinking of her as their queen, and how many are simply dreaming of getting her into their beds.'

Eyes like blue ice swept over La Fayette, now frothing with anger, then, from his greater height, the Gyrfalcon spoke scornfully.

'I have heard enough. I may be a provincial, though I'll take leave to tell you that my province is as good as yours, but by your words you give me cause to think that you yourself have made one of the gentlemen you speak of, and that you are merely jealous of Count Fersen. For, if I understand you, you seem to blame me for saving a fellow-officer's life.'

He withdrew in time to avoid the inkwell which came flying after him, though its contents left a few more stains on the much-abused deerskin, and emerged into the sunshine with a sense of actual physical relief. The scene had upset him because he was conscious of a growing attachment to his chief, whom he admired for his courage, and he did not want to have to change his opinion.

'What's going on?' Tim demanded, coming to meet him. 'I heard the shouting from the bottom of the hill. What have you done to him?'

Gilles smiled at him enigmatically. He took off his battered hat and studied the red plume nonchalantly.

'Nothing at all. We disagreed upon a point of etiquette. You know, I think that General La Fayette has become too good an American to remain a proper Frenchman . . . I had thought better of him.'

And carelessly, as though by accident, he opened his fingers and let the wind take the red feather and carry it lightly away down the hill.

The assault began just before five o'clock that evening. Covered by a continuous bombardment from the guns of Knox and Choisy, the two waves advanced on the redoubts. The French troops moved forward as though on parade, in impressive order, led by Baron Viomenil and the Comte de Deux-Ponts. There were two regiments only, the Royal Deux-Ponts and the Saintonge, two solid walls of white and red and blue and yellow, marching straight into the English fire with pipes and drums playing, and not a man out of step to spoil the magnificent array.

On the American side, things were somewhat different.

'Forward!' La Fayette yelled. 'Charge!'

He dashed straight ahead, waving his sword, followed by Hamilton, de Gimat and the rest. The men charged like lions, in a furious rush to scale the parapets. For the first time, Gilles felt the elation of a pitched battle. While Tim flailed away, alternately using his bayonet and the butt of his gun as a club, he raced up the slope with Pongo hard on his heels wielding his tomahawk like a master, regardless of the bullets whistling around him. Once upon the parapet, Gilles plunged with a yell of triumph into what seemed like a seething mass of pointed hats, the Hessians of von Bose's regiment. The lust of battle that was in his blood had taken possession of him wholly now, surging up out of the deeps of time, carrying him beyond reason and sweeping away the basic instinct of self-preservation. He drove forward irresistibly, cutting his way through the mass of bodies which gave way before him, caught sight of the standard, shot through with bullet holes but still erect upon a heap of rubble, and in a wild dash reached and grabbed it.

His cry of triumph was answered by a rousing cheer and it was only then he saw that the fighting had ceased suddenly. The redoubt had fallen. All its defenders were either dead or taken prisoner. It was all over – so soon!

With a sense of disappointment at the brevity of the thing, he leaped down from his pile of rubble, the flag still in his hand, and found himself face to face with La Fayette. The General was smiling, although the smile did not reach his eyes.

'Good work, lieutenant. I am sorry, though, that in the heat of battle you appear to have lost the plume from your hat.'

'I did not lose it, General. I took it off.'

'I see.' He paused and then resumed: 'Well, lieutenant, since you are evidently burning to distinguish yourself, and in view of your keen interest in the French army, I have a task for you.'

'Yes, sir?'

La Fayette turned and crossed over to the parapet, whence it was possible to see the other redoubt. It was still keeping up a sustained fire and consequently the French troops were making little headway.

'As you see, they are not yet inside.'

'It looks to be more strongly defended.'

'Possibly. Nevertheless, you will carry my compliments to Baron Viomenil and say that should he happen to require any assistance we shall be most happy to render it.'

Gilles bowed, coolly smiling.

'I shall do it with pleasure, General. Not so much for the enjoyment of giving the Baron a facer as because I could do with some more action.'

With that, he leapt over the parapet and plunged eagerly back into the fighting, the Indian still on his heels. But, hard as he tried, he was still too late. The second redoubt had just fallen in its turn. Both outposts of the besieged town were now gone and its fall was only a matter of time. For the first time for many days, the guns were silent and the long lines of wounded were making their way towards the overloaded wagons.

Gilles found Baron Viomenil, surrounded by his staff, and delivered La Fayette's insolent message with a straight face, without altering a syllable. Among the officers present, he saw Fersen, black with powder and supporting one arm which had suffered a cut from a bayonet. The Swede flashed him a grin.

'Still in your old feathers? What have you done with my gift?'

'Kept it for the sun of victory to shine on. I couldn't wear it today. My men would not have understood. They too, you see, look more like night owls than like soldiers.'

'It's not often you find an officer with so much consideration for his men, but I cannot but agree with you.'

Fersen's smile changed to a grimace as he altered his grip on his wounded arm.

'You cannot stay like that,' Gilles said. 'Let me get you to a surgeon.'

'By no means. My servants can take care of me. There's no ball to be extracted and the surgeons are overworked already. I'll do better with my own people. Besides, La Fayette would never forgive you if you left the field without his permission. We'll meet again soon.'

Once back with his own men, Gilles stood looking out over the marshy plain with a jaundiced eye. The noise of the guns had given way to the groans of the injured, shamelessly revealing the other hideous face of war. Now that the excitement of the battle was gone, all that remained was pain and wretchedness. Men mown down by the musket fire from the forts lay everywhere, their eyes staring and hands clutching at places where the congealing blood stuck the rags of tattered uniforms to gaping wounds. Others, on whom death had not yet laid his hand, were striving to drag themselves along, their own weight too much for their failing strength, and crying like lost children or pouring out a string of blasphemous oaths. Now they had to contend with swarms of flies and with the mosquitoes that haunted the marshy ground. The smell of blood mingled with the odours of the mire and here and there a figure could be seen moving helplessly among the wounded, engaged in God alone knew what tragic and futile task of selection.

'My God!' Gilles murmured in shock and horror. 'How is it possible?'

'Never seen a battlefield before, eh?' Colonel Hamilton said. 'You've seen men die before, but cleanly, in a manner of speaking – by shot or steel? Grape-shot and shells do an altogether nastier job, crushing and tearing. No – it's not a pleasant sight.'

Dusk was falling. Everywhere, fires were being lit and the plain was dotted with points of light. The victors were manning the conquered redoubts and the last of the wounded were being moved out. Colonel de Gimat was carried off on a stretcher, along with the Chevalier de Lameth who was gravely wounded in the legs. Out on the water, the ships were lowering sail and on board the *Ville de Paris*, burly Admiral de Grasse was folding his telescope and hobbling back on two sticks to his armchair, cursing the gout in his toes. Silence hung over Yorktown and in both camps the exhausted men prepared for sleep. Darkness would bring its own blessed truce.

In the middle of the night, however, hostilities flared up again, like a flame from a badly smothered fire. Under cover of darkness Lord Cornwallis, having reached the end of his food and munitions, tried a desperate stroke. A handful of volunteers succeeded in quitting Yorktown secretly and reaching the French lines. They got through the first row of guns by passing themselves off as Americans and fell without warning on the second line. But even before orders could come from above, the Chevalier de Chastellux had flown to the support of the guns with half of the Bourbonnais regiment and some of Lauzun's hussars. It was all over in the twinkling of an eye. The volunteers were dead or captured and the last hope for the besieged was gone. No help could reach them now. The surrender could not be long postponed.

Sunrise found Lieutenant Goëlo and his Indian shadow on the way to the French camp. A servant of Fersen's had come to him just before daybreak to say that his master had sent for him urgently.

He found the Swede drinking coffee with his arm in a sling. His wound did not appear to be troubling him overmuch for, except for his empty coat sleeve, he was dressed with his usual care and elegance. He greeted the Frenchman with his characteristic melancholy smile.

'I apologize for calling you so early,' he said, pouring out, unasked, a large cup of coffee for his visitor. 'But I think you will forgive me when you know what it is I have to show you, and you will see that we have not much time. Drink this, all the same, for the morning is a cold one.'

Gilles swallowed the coffee gratefully. The warm, fragrant drink did him good, for he had not managed to sleep again after the disturbance in the night. But he wondered why the Swede was looking at him so earnestly. It was almost as though he had never seen him before and were trying to fix his features in his memory.

'Why do you look at me like that?' he could not help asking as he set down his empty cup.

'I think you will soon know why. Come with me.'

Gilles followed him into the other half of the tent which, like all those belonging to senior officers of the French regiments, was very large and a great deal more comfortable than its American counterparts. A wounded man was lying on a camp bed, watched over by another, dressed in black, who wiped his brow with a damp cloth from time to time.

It was dark in this part of the tent, the only light coming from a large lantern, and the head of the injured man was in shadow. His painful breathing filled the confined space but he uttered no complaint. Only, now and then, his hand clenched on the covers. A torn and bloodstained white uniform lay in a corner.

'On my way back here yesterday,' Axel explained in an undertone, 'I found this man dragging himself out of a reed-bed. He fell unconscious almost at my feet, so I could hardly help looking at him. What I saw so startled me that I had him brought here. Look—'

Motioning his servant to stand aside, he grasped the lantern and held it up over the bed so that the light fell on the man's face with its closed eyes.

For all his practised self-control, it seemed to Gilles as if the ground had been removed from under his feet, for what he saw was almost incredible. Allowing for a difference in age of some twenty or twenty-five years, the face that emerged from the shadows was his own.

The skin was grey and the face hollow with suffering and there were sinister shadows in it which seemed a very foretaste of the grave, but still the similarity was startling. There were the same strong jaw, the same clear-cut features, though the skin was tannned by much exposure to the sun, the same hawk nose, curved like the beak of a bird of prey, the same sardonic twist to the shapely mouth and the same straight brows that lifted slightly towards the temples – only the youth was lacking and the disillusionment much greater. Gilles had the frightening feeling that he was looking at himself as he would be after twenty or thirty years' hard living. It was like looking in some evil magician's mirror.

'Do you know who – who he is?' he stammered.

Fersen's shoulders lifted slightly.

'A man of the Touraine regiment, one of those belonging to the Marquis de Saint-Simon that the fleet picked up in the West Indies. But he is none the less a Breton – as you are. All that I have been able to learn about him is that his name is Pierre Barac'h, and that he comes from Retz.'

Gilles said nothing. He was remembering, as though it were before his eyes, a page of the old book which he had read once in his godfather's house at Hennebont, a page of Breton armorial bearings.

'Lord of Botloy, of Lézardrieux, of Plessis-Eon, of Kermeno, of Coetmeur, of Barac'h . . .' And at the same time he seemed to hear the Abbé de Talhouët's voice saying: 'He was called Pierre . . .'

Was it possible that fate had brought him face to face at last with the one man who, all his short life, had haunted his dreams like an unattainable mirage? In a daze, he bent over the still form, eagerly studying the reflection of his own face, a reflection which did so much to explain his mother's unrelenting hatred. How that hatred must have grown year by year as he, Gilles, had grown and as his resemblance to the man whose memory she loathed became more unmistakable.

Gazing at the still face, his feelings were a mixture of joy and despair, and that despair told him that his heart was not mistaken. He had longed so deeply for this man, longed so to give him all the love which Marie-Jeanne rejected, that his longing had come true. And now he was going to die, without knowing he left anyone to grieve for him, without so much as a sign of affection between them.

Axel's voice came to him as though through a mist.

'When we fought, that time in Brest, you told me you have never known your father, that—'

'That I was a bastard. You need not be afraid to say it, Count. I'm used to it.'

'I am not afraid of it. There have been famous bastards. What was your father's name?'

'Pierre – Pierre de Tournemine.'

'Do you know – what were his arms?'

'A simple shield quartered or and azure, with the device *Aultre n'auray*.'

Without a word, the Swede put something into his hand. Gilles' fingers closed themselves round it instinctively. It was a heavy gold ring, a signet with an enamelled seal depicting precisely the heraldic device he had just described. His eyes blurred with tears as he gazed down without surprise at the blue and gold circle in his hand and after a moment he lifted it and touched it very reverently with his lips. Then he gave it back to Fersen.

'Where did you find it? On his finger?'

'No. He carried this ring in a little leather bag worn on a thong round his neck. I'll put it back now.'

He did so, so deftly that the wounded man seemed scarcely aware of him. But a moment afterwards he stirred and uttered a faint moan.

'He is gravely injured, is he not?' Gilles said, his heart wrung. 'He is going to die—'

'Yes. A shell has shattered his left hip, but he may live for a few hours yet – or even days. At present he is under the influence of a sedative drug which my faithful Sven, who has some skill in medicines, has given to him.'

Gilles looked for the first time at the man they had found seated by the bed. Unlike the Count's other servants, he was not in livery but wore a plain black suit which told Gilles nothing.

'You have not seen him before,' the Count said. 'He joined me only in the spring. My sister Sophie sent him because she worried about me. He's a clever fellow. Your father could not be in better hands.'

Gilles' heart leapt at the word, yet even so he demurred, a little sadly.

355

'Do not call him so. It may be that he would not care for it.'
The Swede's eyes met his steadily.

'It would surprise me, seeing what you are. Or else we are both wrong and he is not your father, for in that case he would not deserve to be.'

The wounded man was growing increasingly restless and Sven urged the two of them gently to the other side of the tent.

'You must let him rest,' he said. 'I will give him something to make him sleep until this evening.'

'Can't I stay with him?' Gilles begged. 'I will keep very still. I won't—'

'No. He is a little better and I think that by this evening he may recover consciousness. Come back then.'

'Come and sup with me,' Fersen said. 'And do not worry. I'll call you if anything should happen. Leave that Indian of yours with me and I will send him to you at need. And trust me, my friend. I believe that it was God's hand set this man in my path. You may rely on me to do all I can to help. For one thing, I am going to send for one of the army chaplains – if one can be found willing to set foot inside a protestant's tent.'

He put his arm affectionately round the younger man and gave him a brotherly hug, then steered him outside to where Pongo waited, arms folded across his chest, as motionless as a statue carved out of mahogany. He received the order to remain at Count Fersen's bidding with his customary impassivity, merely seating himself, cross-legged, outside the tent, prepared to stay there without food or drink, without so much as twitching an eyebrow, for as long as it might please the man he had chosen to call master.

Gilles went back to his own quarters like a man walking in his sleep. He neither saw nor heard anything, although he passed through an army wild with joy because of the scrap of white cloth which now fluttered above the besieged town where before the British flag had flown. It was surrender. Cornwallis was giving up and asking for a parley. This might well be the end of five years' struggle and wretchedness but for the first time, Gilles did not feel involved. Nothing mattered to him just then but his own inner turmoil.

He walked blindly straight into the arms of Tim who barred his way exuberantly.

'Well! Where are you off to, looking like a death's head on a mopstick? We've won! Everyone's rejoicing, and you look as though you've just come back from the dead!'

'I think perhaps I have. I'm even beginning to think I may be mad – or dreaming. Something unbelievable has happened to me this past hour.'

Tim's laughter died on his lips. Without taking his arm from the other's shoulders, he looked closely into his strained face.

'That's what friends are for,' he said seriously. 'To believe the unbelievable. And I'm your friend. So let's have it.'

He steered Gilles into his tent and fed him a stiff measure of rum, of which he seemed to possess an inexhaustible supply, and watched with satisfaction as the colour crept back into his friend's wan face.

'I heard that the Swedish colonel had sent word for you,' he said. 'La Fayette is furious, and with reason, perhaps, if he is the cause of your being in this state.'

'Damn La Fayette and his warped ideas!' Gilles said violently. 'Except for you, I can't think of anyone in the world who would have done for me what Fersen has. Listen.'

Tim listened without interruption to his halting account. Even when he had done, his expression did not change but he took Gilles by the hand and led him over to the rough little wooden cross which, like a good Christian, the Breton had hung on his tent pole.

'The Swede is right,' he said at last. 'There is God's hand in this. Let's pray together that He may spare your father long enough to know he has a son.'

'How do you know he hasn't others? How do you know it will please him?'

'I don't,' Tim admitted frankly. 'But a man who has a regular home and family doesn't go about under a false name. So we'll pray.'

Gilles knelt meekly beside his friend and together they prayed in the words of their different religions. He felt better for it, although he still held himself aloof from the general rejoicings. He could not keep his thoughts from that fragile canvas shelter in which a life was flickering on the verge of extinction, a life which had suddenly become amazingly precious to him.

'Stay in your tent,' Tim advised him. 'I'll say you have a fever. The fighting is all over. You will not be needed.'

When Pongo made his appearance, at about five o'clock, Gilles' heart sank but, before he could open his mouth, the Indian reassured him with a gesture.

'Man not yet gone to join his ancestors,' he said. He held out a folded sheet of paper. 'Your friend gave me the paper which talks to bring you.'

The note consisted of a single line only.

'Come,' Fersen had written, 'and have the goodness to wear the uniform I sent you.'

Half an hour later, washed, shaved, brushed, combed and bewigged, Gilles quitted his tent like a butterfly emerging from the chrysalis, transformed as if by magic into a brilliant officer of the king's army. Tim, smoking his pipe in the shade of a ragged pine, greeted his appearance with an oath of admiration.

'By Abraham and all the prophets,' he exclaimed, 'you outshine the sun! Here,' he added, 'Colonel Hamilton told me to bring you his horse, thinking you were bound to be in a hurry.' He led the animal out from behind the tree, where it had been waiting, ready saddled.

'How did he know? Did someone tell him?'

'Not I, at all events. I've just seen him for the first time today and he looked to be in even greater haste than you. He practically thrust the creature into my arms and ran.'

But Gilles was already in the saddle. It was no use trying to understand. Today was evidently a day of miracles. A few minutes' gallop brought him to the tent. The flaps were wide open but he hesitated in the doorway, a prey to an unwonted nervousness. He had taken off his hat and tucked it under his arm when Fersen's familiar voice reached him, calling encouragingly: 'Come in, my friend. We have been waiting for you.'

Gilles walked a couple of steps, then pulled up short, feeling his brass gorget suddenly uncomfortably tight. Propped on a pile of pillows and rolled overcoats, the wounded man was watching him.

The bed had been carried into the main part of the tent and set down in the centre of it, like a throne or an altar. A clean white shirt rose and fell with the dying man's panting breath. For dying he was, beyond a doubt. Pierre de Tournemine was paler even than he had been in the morning and the shadows round his eyes were darker, but his eyes, the same clear blue as Gilles' own, were wide open and looked straight at him.

They fastened on the young man with a kind of eagerness, taking silent note of his face, of his athletic figure, the slightly arrogant tilt of his head, his hands and the whitened knuckles of the one that gripped the brim of his black hat. It was no more than a few seconds but to Gilles it seemed a lifetime. He was caught between hope and fear of what those dry lips, which Sven moistened from time to time, would say. When the words came at last, the voice was so low and weak that they seemed to emerge from the depths of the earth itself.

'So – you are Marie-Jeanne's child? Count Fersen told me— My God! If I had only known – so many things might have been different – so many things— And now I have so little time— Come here— Come here – my son.'

Gilles took one faltering step and fell on his knees beside the bed, his eyes filled with tears.

'Father!' he cried, overwhelmed by the sound of that one short word which it was his to utter for the first time in his life. 'Father, I have thought of you so often. I have called you—'

The dying man's hand groped feebly for his and held it. It felt as cold and dry as a bird's claw.

'You did not hate me, then? Your mother did not teach you to hate me? She – she was so bitter against me.'

'She never spoke of you at all.'

'Then who – who? Oh God, I want to know. Tell me! Tell me about yourself – about your childhood. A bastard – that's what you were. And it was my fault, I suppose. But hers too. I loved her, you see, and she loved me. Oh, not for long! Only for a moment – for a single night. The night she came to me. But afterwards – she took it all back. She drew away from me and when I begged her to leave everything – to come with me to Africa to be my wife, she spurned me with horror. She called me the devil. Talk to me, my son. Tell me about yourself. I have so little time to know you.'

Axel appeared, a pale figure on the far side of the bed, and bent over him.

'May I ask you to postpone your talk for a moment, sir,' he said gently. 'Those you were expecting are here. Everything is ready.'

The grey lips parted in a faint smile.

'You are very right. I must use the minutes I have left as best I may. Ask them to come in. Lift me up, my son.'

The tent filled silently with a brilliant throng. Standing with his hand still locked in his father's, Gilles stared in amazement as there entered the Vicomte de Noailles, the Comte de Charlus, the Duc de Lauzun, resplendent in his red dolman, the Marquis de Saint-Simon, the Comte de Deux-Ponts and, finally, General Rochambeau in person. The others grouped themselves on either side of him and a monk appeared, his brown robe a striking contrast to their splendid uniforms. The dying man greeted them with a smile and a nod.

'I have to thank you, gentlemen, for coming here – to help me to right the gravest of the wrongs I have done before – before I meet my Maker. God has been good to me. He has seen to it that my line shall not die out with my own miserable life. Unknown to myself, I left a son behind me in France, to be brought up by his mother under her own name. That son stands before you now, gentlemen, and I ask you to witness the solemn declaration which I shall make now, in my last hour.'

He paused and watched as Fersen unrolled a sheet of paper in front of him.

'By this deed, which, in the absence of a lawyer, the chaplain of the Touraine regiment, Father Verdier here, has been good enough to draw up for me, I duly recognize and legitimize my son Gilles Goëlo, born out of wedlock, as the sole heir of the house of Tournemine de la Hunaudaye, so that he may in future, subject to the King's approval, bear the name and the arms which are his by right of birth. You, Count—' he looked at Rochambeau. 'I think you knew him before I. Will you honour us both by being the first to append your signature?'

'The honour is mine, sir. All of us here, in our own ways, have come to know and value this young man. Not so much, perhaps, as our American friends, to whom he is already a legend, but enough to congratulate you on having such a son to carry on your name. You may die in peace for I give you my word, you leave it in good hands.'

With that, the General took the pen which Sven was holding out to him and quickly signed his name. The rest followed. When it was done, the dying man asked them to lift him up so that he too might add his name. The effort cost him a great deal of agony but he completed it before the pen slipped from his fingers and left a trail of ink across the page. They laid him back gently.

'Thank you—' he gasped. 'Thank you, all of you. May God – who gave you victory – be with you and keep you—'

One by one, the officers bowed and left the tent, until only Fersen and his servant remained. Gilles knelt once more beside the bed and softly carried the wounded man's hand to his lips, not even trying to hide the tears that were streaming down his cheeks.

'Father,' he said brokenly. 'What can I say—'

'Nothing. There is nothing you need say. It is only justice – and it makes me very happy. And now, talk to me – I know my life is running out. I have held on to it as long as I can. Now the night is coming. It will take me, but with you here I shall fall asleep more easily. Talk to me – tell me. I want to hear it all—'

Gilles talked for a long time. He talked about his mother, about his childhood, about the people he had known, about Brittany and about America. His quiet voice filled the tent while the candlelight threw dancing shadows on the walls. He would have liked to question his father in his turn and learn what his life had been up to that moment, and about the tragedy of his leaving France and the love which had come too late in a life already vitiated by self-indulgence, a life which Marie-Jeanne had rejected with loathing. But Pierre de Tourne-mine scarcely stirred now. His eyes had closed and there were moments when he almost ceased to breathe. Then Gilles would fall silent but always the hand which still clasped his would tighten faintly.

'Go on,' the dying man would whisper.

And Gilles went on, his voice sinking to a quieter and quieter note, until at last the grip of the cold fingers relaxed completely. The man breathed out and did not breathe in again. There was silence in the tent. Pierre de Tournemine had ceased to live.

Somewhere a cock crowed. It was nearly dawn. Already, in the east, the sky was growing pale.

Fersen, who had watched throughout the night, said huskily: 'In a little while, the English will be coming out of Yorktown to lay down their arms to Washington and General Rochambeau, but this evening we will bury your father with all the honours due to a soldier. Go and rest now, Monsieur de Tournemine.'

Gilles looked up and met the Swede's eyes. He opened his mouth to say something but found himself unable to speak. He looked down again at the still figure in the bloodstained sheets. A sudden pang of grief stabbed at his heart and, with a harsh cry, he fell forward sobbing on the body of the man he had never had the time to love.

PART THREE

The Bride of Trecesson

15

The Inn at Ploermel

The last light of a wet February evening was falling on the vast, solitary waste which had once been the forest of Broceliande. The rider on the raking bay horse emerged from a hollow in the hills, crossed a stretch of open ground, leaping easily over the faded clumps of bracken, grey whin bushes and purplish-coloured rocks in his way, crossed a stream, sending the water splashing under his horse's hooves, and paused for a moment to look around him. A great blue cloak of a military cut fell in stiff folds over his horse's crupper, allowing a glimpse of two long-barrelled pistols in the saddle holsters and the brass tip of a sword sheath.

'What shall we do, boy?' the man said, smiling as he patted the animal's neck. 'You'd like to stay here, I daresay, but you must remember that Viviane departed long ago.'

The blue pepper-pot towers of a small château showed above the trees and welcoming coils of smoke were rising from it. Gilles hesitated for a moment. He had ridden Merlin a long way and no gentleman would be likely to refuse hospitality to the Chevalier de Tournemine of the Queen's Dragoons. But he did not feel like meeting new people tonight. Even though it was still a good two leagues to Ploermel, it would be better to go on. A good inn might be found there for horse and rider where a welcome would not have to be paid for in conversation.

'Courage, old lad,' he said finally. 'We're going on. But I promise you a good ration of oats.'

He had no need to use the spurs. Merlin was off like an arrow, and actually pulling as he raced through wood and heathland to the gates of the little town that crouched shivering beneath its mantle of sleet. He was obviously in a hurry to reach the promised oats. He thundered in among the houses and at the crossroads his master was obliged to rein him in with a firm hand.

The place was deserted. The only signs of life came from a few flickering lights and clacking sabots of an old woman drawing water from the well. Gilles called out to her.

'My good woman, can you tell me the way to the inn?'

'A little farther down, sir. Just by the church. You'll have no trouble finding it. It's a posting house.'

She was right. A square tower loomed massively against the evening sky and next to it some gothic gables. A dim light alongside illumined an arched entry and fell faintly on a sign proclaiming that the *Duchesse Anne* was able to supply post horses.

The horseman rode under the archway. The clatter of hooves and the horse's glad whinney brought a stable boy running. He cast a knowledgeable eye over man and beast.

'Shall I find good lodging here?' the man asked.

'Yes, indeed, sir. And a good dinner also. See, here comes the landlord now.'

A short man, somewhat oddly dressed in boots and a postilion's jacket under his large white apron, came hurrying out to greet his customer, who had finally made up his mind to dismount.

'Have my saddle and my baggage brought up,' he said to the boy, 'and see to it that my horse has good fodder. And above all, no wet straw! And don't forget to rub him down well. And plenty of good litter, eh?'

A coin flicked from Gilles' hand to the boy's, who caught it deftly.

'Have no fear, sir,' the landlord said. 'We know how to care for horses here. Will your honour please to step this way.'

A moment later, the traveller was taking possession of a large, whitewashed room in which the only decorative items were a black wooden crucifix, a portrait of the graceless features of his majesty, King Louis XVI and an immense red eiderdown perched like a swollen strawberry on the white bed. It was cold and distinctly clammy but the landlord hastened to light the fire which was ready laid on the hearth, and in another minute the room was looking almost festive.

'Will your honour dine downstairs, or will you have it brought up to you here?'

'No, no. I will come down. Tell me, my friend, do you know of an estate in these parts called Le Frêne?'

The landlord's naturally cheerful countenance shut up like an oyster.

'Some five or six leagues from here, on the road to Dinan, on the verge of the forest.'

The man spoke with evident reluctance and only after some hesitation.

'You do not seem to care for the place?' Gilles remarked idly.

'It's not for me to be saying one way or the other, sir. Le Frêne is a great house and I am only the landlord of a posting inn. But you'd not catch me going out there after dark – or even in broad daylight – not for any money. It's a bad place.'

'Why? Is—?'

But the landlord was already bowing his way to the door.

'You'll excuse me, sir, but I'm stayed for below. You'll not be best pleased if your dinner's spoilt, and no more shall I.'

He departed, leaving Gilles to his own speculations which were far from pleasant. Clearly, time had done nothing to improve the Saint-Mélaines' unsavoury reputation. He drew a chair up to the fire of dried bracken and whin which gave the room a scent of outdoors and, settling himself in it, stretched out his long, booted legs and got out Judith's letter once again. He sat there, staring at the eager, sprawling hand. He had no need to read it. In the week since it had reached him, he had got its contents by heart.

'Why have you gone so far away?' it ran. 'I feel as though I am casting this letter into the sea, to drift for ever on the face of the waters and never find you. Whatever happens, it will come too late to save me. I promised to wait for you for three years, and to myself, I swore it. Alas! I am forced to break my word to both of us. How could my father have believed for a moment that a convent walls and his sovereign will would be enough to restrain my brothers when their own interests were involved? They have decided to take me back with them and they have informed our lady abbess, Madame de la Bourdonnaye, that they are coming for me tomorrow. Tomorrow! Only a few more hours, and I shall be on my way back to the manor of Le Frêne. It frightens me so much. There is no way out. They have the law on their side and have threatened to call in the constables. I think they are quite capable of violating the sanctuary of the chapel even, if I should try to take refuge there. But I shall not do that because I do not wish to make myself an object of scandal and trouble here.

'Tomorrow, therefore, I shall go with them. I know that they are determined to marry me to a Monsieur de Vauferrier, who is an old man and a companion in their debauches, but he is rich and owns ships. It seems that Morvan has been to America and that he met him in the West Indies and came home on one of his vessels.

'I shall go with them, as I said, but I shall not let them give me to this man, for one of my companions here is related to him and has drawn a dreadful picture of him. I am not a slave to be sold for money. And for so long now I have dreamed of being yours. I think from that very first day when you pulled me from the river. Now that we are about to be parted and there is little hope that we shall ever meet again, I can tell you that I have loved you from the first moment. I loved you at first sight and if I was odious and horrid to you later, it was only because my pride would not give in to my love.

'Oh God, how could I have been so stupid, so idiotically arrogant! I called you "the little priest", my love, and yet in my heart I was yours even then. I would have gone with you, followed you anywhere – even if it meant living in a charcoal burner's hut in the woods, so long as we could be together. That time you brought me back to the convent, I think I would have gone with you without a second thought if you had asked me. I could have fled to America disguised as a boy, anything – but that might have been to hinder you in your destiny. And now it is all over. Now there is no one I can cling to, for not even God can do anything to help me!

'Farewell. I do not know where I shall be by the time you

read this letter. If you ever read it. Perhaps, if there is nothing else for it, I shall be no longer on this earth. But I know that as long as my heart beats and there is breath in my body, I shall love you— Judith.'

Gilles smoothed the worn paper very gently with the tips of his fingers. In places, the ink was smudged with tears. He would never forget the moment when that letter had hit him like a thunderclap, at the very moment when it seemed to him that he held the world in his hands. It had wrenched him from his long love affair with America and at the sight of that desolate scrawl he had found out that, underneath the successful warrior, he was still the same youth who had fished a siren from the water, although his dreams had grown still faster than himself. How could he ever for a moment have perhaps not forgotten Judith but pictured her as something born out of the mist and his own romantic imagination and his need for love? How could he ever have been mad for love of another woman?

Over there, across the ocean, he had become another person, a real man. He had known friendship, privation, danger, war and a certain taste for liberty, and finally passion and betrayal, all in that gigantic melting pot, that fabulous witches' cauldron from which he had emerged a new man. Of his love for Sitapanoki nothing remained but a vague nostalgia, a stirring of his loins whenever he happened to think of the beautiful Indian, coupled with a somewhat selfish sense of relief at having escaped from a fatal temptation. Had he gone into the forest with her, he would have turned his back on the supreme gift which fate had offered him on the battlefield at Yorktown. He would be living by some lakeside an existence not far removed from that of the beasts, or else his bones would be whitening on Indian soil, beside the stake where he had died.

He drove the unpleasant thought out of his mind with an impatient little shiver, pulled out his pipe and filled it with the Virginian tobacco he had come to like and of which he had brought a good supply home with him. He lit it with a brand from the fire and then, resuming his relaxed attitude, began smoking away earnestly while he tried to sort out the problem before him and, to some extent, to clarify his mind.

369

As far as he himself was concerned, fate had been wonderfully kind to him in the four months since he had left the Chesapeake. And it had all happened so fast.

First there had been his sudden return home, in company with Lauzun. Rochambeau had entrusted the young duke with the task of carrying the news of the victory back to Versailles and with what was, considering what their past relations had been, quite unlooked-for generosity, Lauzun had promptly engaged Lieutenant Goëlo to go with him.

'You must strike while the iron is hot,' he told him. 'Your father acknowledged you as far as it lay in his power, but now you need the King's word on it. And also, even before it I should say, that of Monsieur Chérin. You do not know Monsieur Chérin?'

'Good lord, no! Versailles is another world to me, Duke. It's like another planet. I know nothing about it at all, or about this gentleman either.'

'Well, you are not alone there. He shuns the company of men and keeps his favours for the old parchments, seals, blasons, labels, quarterings, mottoes and all the rest of the tangled web of armorial descents. He is the official Genealogist and Historiographer Royal. His integrity is fanatical and the scrupulous care with which he goes into claims to nobility has made him many enemies. He is completely incorruptible and if he decides that your claim will not stand, then not even the King himself can do anything about it. So you must make haste and present that document of yours at Versailles while all the signatories are still happily alive. You can always come back afterwards if you like. The way may not be quite over.'

That was true. The surrender of Yorktown was a major victory for the United States, and one that might well prove decisive, but the English still had considerable forces at their disposal and might think it worth while to continue the struggle until one or other side was wiped out.

And so, with the willing consent of his superior officers, Gilles shook Fersen by the hand, receiving quantities of advice as he did so, embraced his friend Tim and entrusted Pongo to him until his return. Persuading the Indian to part, even temporarily, from the master he worshipped, had been by no means the least of his troubles.

'What if you never come back?' Pongo had asked, his face expressing a mixture of grief and offence.

'There's no reason why I should not come back but if that should happen, then I promise you that I will send for you. Although I'm not at all sure that you'd like it in Europe.'

'Pongo cannot be happy except where you are. If you abandon him, then he will die.'

'You are my brother in arms. I will never abandon you. Trust me, and wait for me.'

Three days after Cornwallis surrendered, Lauzun and Gilles went aboard the swift *Surveillante*, commanded by Monsieur de Cillard, and reached Brest in three weeks, a journey which had taken more than two months on the way out. From there, before Gilles had more than time enough to breathe his native air, they had posted straight to Versailles, where they arrived in the midst of general rejoicings. On October 22nd, a few days after the battle of Yorktown, the Queen had given birth to a dauphin. Paris was wild with joy. Versailles was swarming with fireworks, banners and pealing organs.

Gilles, whose only experience of kingly magnificence had been in ships and weapons, was dazzled by the ramifications of the palace. The town, the gardens, the vast, luxurious palace, peopled with men and women dressed in silks and cloth of gold, filled him with an admiration which his pride forbade him to show. Alongside all this, Brest was no better than a village and Hennebont a molehill.

But he would never forget his presentation to the King. He had been expecting the crushing splendours of a throne room. Instead, they led him up to the attics under the roof of the palace and into a workshop. A forge fire was burning and the place rang with the sound of hammering. He had expected a haughty ruler, decked out in brocade and diamonds. He found himself face to face with a nervous, shortsighted man of some twenty-eight years of age, but already grown a trifle stout, with hair receding from a high forehead, lacklustre eyes and very ordinary clothes which were covered by a large leather apron. But for a certain natural dignity, he could easily have been mistaken for any of his subjects. Nevertheless, the royal locksmith greeted him with the greatest kindness.

'I have heard of your history and of your exploits, sir,' he said, carefully refraining from looking at Lauzun, for whom he seemed to have no great affection. 'They make you a most interesting person and we should beware of opposing God's will when it is made as clearly manifest as it is in your reunion with your father. The Comte de Tournemine de la Hunaudaye has acknowledged you publicly as his son and ·we shall do likewise.'

'Sire,' Lauzun ventured to say, the irony in his voice too slight wholly to conceal its insolence, 'does your majesty think your genealogist will be of the same opinion?'

The King, who was washing his hands in the basin a page was holding for him, looked up sharply. His short-sighted eyes looked stonily at the young duke, who reddened in spite of himself.

'Need I remind you, Duke, that Monsieur Chérin is here to serve me and that a good servant does not flout his master's orders?' he said coldly. 'Here is no case for researches into genealogy, or for proving a title to nobility which is among the most ancient in the realm of France. Monsieur Chérin will see to it that this young man's affiliation is properly registered, and when that is done I trust that I shall find a good servant in him also. Is that not so, sir?'

'Sire,' Gilles murmured, deeply moved, 'I have been your majesty's subject and servant from my birth and I am ashamed that I have nothing better to offer you than that which has been yours all along, my life!'

Louis XVI smiled benevolently. Then he extended his hand to the young man and said, unconsciously echoing Washington: 'Take good care of it, Monsieur de Tournemine. A dead servant may deserve my respect, but he is not much use to me.'

Gilles knelt and kissed the hand which smelled agreeably of verbena soap, and then backed out, bowing deeply. The King's voice followed him:

'They tell me you are a formidable woodsman and a fine shot, and that you learned to hunt from the American Indians? We must hunt together one of these days. You shall instruct me. Monsieur de Lauzun, when the time comes, you will present this young man to the Queen.'

'Damnation!' Lauzun exclaimed, as soon as they had left the royal presence. 'You have made a success! You are not merely recognized, you are high in favour. He must have liked you a lot. I make you my compliments, for it is not easily done.'

And indeed, only two days later, Gilles had received from the chancellery the documents which conferred on him the hereditary title of chevalier. It was accompanied by a lieutenant's commission in the Queen's Dragoons, commanded by the Chevalier de Coigny, and also a note to be presented to the regimental paymaster to enable him to draw his first quarter's pay at once. For Gilles, it meant both fame and fortune.

Beside himself with joy, the new chevalier seized his pen upon the instant to impart to the Abbé de Talhouët the news of his return and of the astonishing good fortune which had come to him as a result of his providential meeting with Pierre de Tournemine. It was several months since he had written and so the letter was an unusually long one. He concluded with the hope that he would soon be able to revisit his home and embrace those dear to him, if only on his way back to America, supposing he were granted permission to return there.

The response to this was threefold, in the shape of a boy, a horse and a letter, the second bearing the other two. The boy's name was Pierrot and he was a son of Guillaume Briant. The horse was none other than Fersen's one-time Magnus, whom Gilles himself had rechristened Merlin. The letter was from the rector of Hennebont, and Gilles could not read the superscription without a thrill of pleasure, for it was addressed to the Chevalier de Tournemine de la Hunaudaye, at the house of the Duc de Lauzun in the rue des Réservoirs.

In it, the good abbé wrote at length of his joy and loving kindness in receiving the good news. He explained that Count Fersen had himself written to Guillaume Briant, telling him of his intention to make a present of the horse to his young friend. Finally, he enclosed the letter which Judith de Saint-Mélaine had sent to him by the extern sister of the convent on the day of her departure for Le Frêne.

'It is already three months' old,' the rector wrote, 'and it grieves me to send it to you, for you missed one another by so little. As I understand it, Judith was taken away by her brothers on, or near, the very day that you landed in France. But in this, as in all things, we must bow to God's will, and He has already done much for you. We cannot look for every happiness in this vile world and a wise man will content himself with what he has. Farewell, my dear chevalier. I will see to it that your mother is informed of what has befallen you. Remember that you are always in my prayers and in my heart . . .'

The fire was dying down. Gilles refolded Judith's letter and replaced it over his heart. Then he rose and stretched himself with a sigh. The poor, unhappy tearstained epistle had overwhelmed him. As for resigning himself to the tyrannical decrees of the Saint-Mélaine brothers, he would do nothing of the kind. Perhaps, if he were to make haste, he might still be in time to snatch Judith from her fate.

Heaven, moreover, seemed to be on his side because the Queen's Dragoons were at that moment quartered at Pontivy. Gilles had gone to find Lauzun and asked him to postpone his presentation to the Queen, telling him of his desire to reach Brittany as soon as possible. Then he had packed Pierrot into the coach for Brest, buckled his valise and, bestriding Merlin, set off full tilt for the land of his birth.

He had no very clear idea of what he meant to do. He only knew that life would mean nothing to him unless he knew what had become of Judith. If he found that she had chosen death in preference to a marriage she hated, then at least he would have the satisfaction of sticking several inches of steel into Morvan's guts, and spitting his elder brother Tudal at the same time. That alone would be worth the journey.

Gilles took out his watch, a present from Washington, and saw that it was time he went down to his dinner. His stomach, in fact, was already telling him so in no uncertain terms. He washed his hands, straightened his wig and after giving a final brush to his dark blue coat of somewhat military cut, went down to the common room with the fixed idea in his mind of getting his host to talk about the Saint-Mélaines, however reluctant that worthy man might prove to be. Perhaps if he plied him with drink . . . But then the capacity of a man who kept an inn was likely to be prodigious.

A table had been laid for him in the corner nearest to the great granite hearth and a not particularly trim maidservant was busy tossing pancakes. Gilles sniffed the familiar fragrance. It was such a long time since he had eaten them. He seated himself at the table, with its check tablecloth, colourful pottery and pewter tankard. A decorated pat of butter, a crusty loaf and a jug of the sparkling cider which was the pride of Ploermel completed the spread.

He settled down to eat with all the appetite of a man who had been all day in the saddle and knew the value of keeping his bodily needs well satisfied.

When the last pancake had been finished, Gilles uttered a sigh of satisfaction, took out his pipe and began to fill it, looking around him for the landlord as he did so. He found him a short way off, leaning both fists on a table and deep in conversation with two postilions while he waited for the Rennes coach. Gilles beckoned him over.

'Where there's such good cider, there must be a brandy to go with it,' he said.

The man smiled, his pride and joy evidently gratified.

'To be sure, your honour. And the very best.'

'Bring it then – and two glasses! We'll drink together.'

The landlord obeyed with alacrity and returned with a small cask.

Gilles sipped and smacked his lips, then he pushed his tobacco pouch towards his host who was savouring his brandy with his gaze fixed raptly on the ceiling with the expression of a man in bliss.

'Sit down for a moment and try this tobacco, if you like to smoke. I want to ask you something. By the way, what is your name?'

The blissful landlord came down to earth abruptly. The corners of his mouth, curved upwards in a beatific smile, drooped at once.

'Le Coz – Yvon Le Coz. But if your question has anything to do with Le Frêne, then I'd as lief not answer it, by your leave.'

'You obviously don't like the place! No, I only wanted to ask you whether you'd heard anything of a great wedding taking place in these parts – in the last two months, say?'

Le Coz stared at him in a way that made Gilles think for a moment he was about to burst into tears. He sat down rather suddenly on the stool opposite his guest and, pulling the cask towards him, poured himself another glass and swallowed it at a gulp.

'Well,' Gilles said. 'I didn't know it would have that effect on you. Yet a wedding can't be such a tragic subject, surely?'

'It shouldn't be, but there are times— Listen, sir. You look like a man of substance and you're certainly a good customer. So I'm going to answer your question, only don't blame me if my answer doesn't seem to make much sense. I've heard nothing of any great wedding in the last three months, at least. But I have heard of a bride, a most unfortunate lady. Only no one knew who she was or where she came from.'

Gilles frowned.

'What do you mean? Can you not be more explicit?'

'No. Because, you see, sir, I've knocked about a bit in my time and I've seen a good many things, but a tale like this, it's more than I can stomach. I couldn't tell it to you. Besides, it wasn't me that saw it.'

'Someone did see it, then?'

'Yes. A cobbler from Campénéac who's a habit of poaching in the forest of Paimpont. He was hiding in a tree and he saw it all. It shook him badly and he's very willing to tell it over to anyone who'll buy him a drink.'

'What is this man called?'

'Guégan. Oh, he's not hard to find.'

At this point, one of the postilions who had been eavesdropping on the landlord's conversation with the strange gentleman, got up and came over to them.

'I'm sorry, sir, but I couldn't help overhearing. Le Coz was talking about Guégan. He's even easier to find than you think for, because I saw him arrive a short while ago with a whole sack of sabots for sale. Tomorrow is market day and he spends the night with his nephew, the baker. If you feel like paying his shot, he'll tell you all about the lovely red-haired girl and what happened to her.'

Gilles' heart missed a beat.

'Red-haired? The bride had red hair?'

'Yes. Guégan said she had hair that shone like copper. But I don't want to tell you about it first. It wouldn't be fair to Guégan, and anyway he tells it much better than I do.'

'To say nothing of the fact that you want to hear it again yourself,' Le Coz broke in, 'and get bought a few drinks yourself, as well as Guégan, eh, Joel? That's why you're ready to run and find Guégan for us!'

The postilion grinned and eyed the cask of brandy.

'I like to be helpful, that's all. Though it's true I'm not averse to a little something now and then. Especially since the Rennes coach is bound not to be here for a good hour yet.'

'Go and fetch the man,' Gilles told him. 'I'll buy anyone a drink for the sake of hearing the tale.'

'Oh, don't worry for that,' Le Coz said. 'Guégan won't come alone. He got such a fright that night that he daren't go out in the dark ever since.'

Joel had already clattered off and Gilles sat pulling furiously at his pipe and trying to fight the fear that was creeping over him. It was like a presentiment which his reason strove to throw off but could not. For God's sake, there were other red-headed girls in the world beside Judith de Saint-Mélaine! And other girls of good family in Brittany who might have become brides in the past three months. But something told him that Judith was at the centre of the tale, a dreadful one if what the little Le Coz had said was anything to go by, which he was soon to hear.

The postilion returned in ten minutes or so with two men in tow. One, dressed like a peasant in a goatskin waistcoat, boasted a fine red nose in the midst of his weatherbeaten face. The other, from the faint dusting of white that still adorned his clothes, must be his nephew the baker. The two newcomers bowed awkwardly to Gilles.

'Joel tells me,' said the one who must be Guégan, 'that you want to hear my sad tale, your honour. But I'm asking myself, is it safe to tell you?'

'Why not? If you were a mere spectator, you have nothing to fear from me.'

'What he means,' Le Coz broke in, 'is that you may be acquainted with the farmers – because he was out poaching that night.'

Gilles shrugged and drew a silver coin from his pocket.

'I didn't think I looked like a law officer. You need not fear to speak, my good man. Ask for whatever you want to drink and I'll give you this for your trouble besides.'

'I know what he likes,' Le Coz said. 'Rum.'

377

'Let it be rum all round, then.'

The arrival of the bottles was greeted with general satisfaction. The second postilion came to join the group and they formed a circle round the hearth in the time-honoured fashion of men preparing to hear a story.

Guégan swallowed a mugful of rum by way of preliminary, wiped his mouth on his sleeve and then, cradling his mug, which the landlord at a sign from Gilles had just refilled, between his hands, he embarked on his story amid an awestruck silence.

'It was coming up to Christmas and I'd been setting some traps in the forest, near the lake belonging to the Château of Trecesson, with the idea of getting a fine hare or a couple of rabbits, or even something bigger that Master Le Coz here might give me a good price for. It's a good spot, a good two leagues away from here but not far from my own village of Campénéac. The animals come down to the lake at night to drink and I know their habits.

'I went out that night after it was dark. It was cold and pitch black but I've a thick skin and I'd never been afraid of the dark. I walked fast and it was not long before I came near the château. All was quiet and there was not a light showing. I was glad of that because it meant there wasn't a lot of company up at the château. I thought that the Comte de Châteaugiron-Trecesson, who owns the place through his wife, might have decided to spend Christmas at his house in Rennes, and so I was at ease and fairly sure of not getting nabbed.

'I was just fixing my little snares when, all at once, I heard the sound of horses' hooves coming, and coming fast. I was frightened. I thought it was maybe the count arriving and I made haste to get up into the nearest tree so as not to get caught. My heart was thudding a bit. It's not that the count's a hard man, or at all close, but like all the lords of Trecesson for generations past, he likes his coverts, and all through those generations huntsmen and poachers have never got on together. Yet I'd no call to be really worried. There were no leaves left on the trees, but it was a dark night.

'But when I got up there, I wondered for a minute if I hadn't made a mistake. There was nothing more to be heard.

'I was just going to climb down again and get on with my work, when I heard cautious footsteps and the creak of wheels.

378

Then I saw two masked men come along by the moat in front of the château. They were leading their horses and behind them came a closed carriage, with the leather flaps drawn tight over its windows.

'The two men in front stopped for a moment and looked at the front of the château, which was dark and silent.

' "It's just as I hoped," one of them said. "There's no one there but the servants and they're all fast asleep at this time of night. And if they did hear anything, they'd not dare to come out. They're too frightened of ghosts and boggarts and fairies."

' "All the same, we'll not do it here, right in front of the castle," said the other man. "It'll be safer to go on a bit."

'They walked on a little farther along the edge of the lake. The carriage followed, the man on the box so muffled up that his face was completely hidden. They halted just underneath the tree where I was hiding, half dead with fright by this time, because the men with their masks, the carriage and its ghostly coachman all filled me with dread. I was all over gooseflesh and beginning to call on my guardian angel to save me.

' "Here will do very well," the taller of the two men said. He fetched one of the carriage lamps and lit it, then handed it to his companion. "You hold the light."

'The coachman got down then. He was masked, like the others, and he brought tools, picks and shovels, and the two of them set to digging a hole in the ground. They dug for a long time and I sat up in my tree and wondered what these men could be doing, digging a hole in the forest in the middle of the night. But I must admit I was beginning to be interested because to go to all that trouble, they must have something valuable to hide – gold, perhaps. Or contraband.

'The hole was long and narrow and when they decided it was deep enough they stopped and the one who seemed to be the leader, who was taller and bigger than the others, took off his hat to mop his forehead. I saw that he had red hair. Then he put his hat back again, took a flask from his pocket and took a great swig.

' "Put down the lantern," he said to the one who had done nothing but hold the light. "And go and get her."

'That was when I saw what was in the carriage. It wasn't gold or treasure – but something much more precious, so that I nearly fell out of my tree. A woman! A woman as beautiful as the day, wearing a white wedding dress, with lace and silken flowers. She was as pale as her dress, and her big, dark eyes were full of fear. Beneath her crown of orange blossom, the colour of her hair was almost red and it shone like copper, but I could not see her mouth for that was hidden by a gag. Her hands were tied and she was twisting and turning, trying to break free of the rough grip of the man who had dragged her from the carriage.

The tallest man pointed to the hole they had dug.

' "There is your marriage bed, sister. I trust you'll find it to your liking."

'They took off the gag to let her say her prayers but she was weeping so and begging them so piteously— Oh, God! I think I shall hear her pleading in my dreams for as long as I live. She pleaded so hard that they put the gag back on her again, saying that she was making too much noise.

' "If anyone in the château hears her, they won't come out because they are afraid of ghosts, but you never know. Some charcoal burner might come to see. Let's make an end!"

'They took hold of her then, by the shoulders and the feet, and they laid her in the hole. They'd not mercy enough even to throttle her, or put a dagger in her heart. From where I was, I could see her, all white in the black earth, with her hands bound on her breast and her eyes above the gag – her eyes – two dark pools filled with horror.'

Here Guégan paused and groped for a drink. Gilles filled his cup and he drained it at a draught.

'Go on,' Gilles ordered harshly.

'I didn't see much more of her. They threw her veil in over her and then they started shovelling the earth back, bigger and bigger spadefuls, going faster and faster until the hole was all filled in. I was having to cling on to my tree so as not to fall out. I wanted to throw up. I was sick with horror and dread! I couldn't see how the good God could let such monsters live.'

'And then?' Gilles asked roughly. 'What happened next?'

'They stayed there for a moment, spreading the moss and dried leaves back over their handiwork. I thought they'd never go. But in the end they got the carriage turned round and mounted their horses again and rode away into the night like the devils they were. So then I hopped out of my tree and ran to the château. I had to tell someone, the porter, a servant, anyone, and if they started asking me questions it was just too bad. I swung on the bell and rang it as loud as I could, shouting for help. Someone opened it at last, and I was in such a state that at first the porter took me for a madman. I couldn't tell you now just what I said, for I don't remember, but I suddenly found myself face to face with a gentleman in his dressing gown and nightcap with a sword tucked under his arm. It was the Comte de Châteaugiron. Contrary to what I'd thought, he and his family were at the château, only they'd gone to bed early because they were due to start for Rennes first thing in the morning.

'Seeing him there somehow helped me get my wits back and, as quickly as I could, I told him what I'd seen.

' "Come quickly, Monsieur le Comte," I begged him. "Please come! I'll show you the place. It may not be too late."

'He believed me at once, thank God! He called his servants to bring spades and torches and we all ran back to the scene of the crime. The marks of the carriage wheels were still fresh and clearly to be seen and showed that I was not making it up. So then they began to dig, six of them, with spades at first and then with their hands, as the count told them, so as not to risk hurting the young lady if, by God's will, she were still alive in the bottom of the grave. Well, they got her out of the ground at last, and, oh your honour, if you had only seen her, with her white face and her hair and her dress all stained with earth! There in the torchlight, it was a dreadful sight.

' "Hurry!" the count said. "Send a man on horseback for a physician! Her heart is still beating faintly. We'll carry her to the château."

'We all set off in a body and in the courtyard of the château I saw madame the countess and her maids and the chaplain, all crying out for pity. They carried the young lady into the house and then the count came over to me. He gave me a gold piece and said I was a stout fellow and that he did not grudge me the poaching, and that now I might go home in peace. But I asked him if I might wait a while to see how the poor young lady did. Alas, when it was getting light they came to tell me that it was all over. She had finally passed on, in spite of all the lady of the house and the chaplain could do to save her. The physician from Ploermel that they had sent the man on the horse for came just in time to learn that there was no more need for him. Well, I went home after that. But ever since then, I've kept on seeing that lovely bride lying in her grave. It's a nasty story, isn't it, sir, and a sad one?'

A silence followed. The group of rough men looked at one another and in all their eyes there was the same horror. Gilles loosened his collar uneasily, for he felt as if it were choking him.

'Does anyone know the name of the young lady?' he asked. 'Or of her murderers?'

'Why, no, sir,' Guégan said. 'No one at the château knew the young lady at all. I heard the countess say that she had never set eyes on her, nor had she even heard tell of a wedding in the neighbourhood on that day. While as to the men, they wore masks. And now, by your leave, your honour, I'll take just one more little sup and then be off home. It's getting late, and I don't care to be out much after dark these days.'

One by one, the drinkers bade farewell to the stranger and left. But he had ceased to notice them. He was standing before the fire, with his back turned to the room and his arms folded, the fingers of one hand playing nervously with the folds of his cravat, striving to fight off a growing sense of despair. He seemed to see Judith in the flames on the hearth, as Guégan had described her in that hideous scene. Judith, wearing a wedding dress, with flowers in her flaming hair, Judith cast living into that muddy hole in the ground. For he could no longer doubt the identity of the bride of Trecesson. It was Judith, basely murdered by her vile brothers. The poacher's description had been recognizable enough for him, that and the panic beating of his own heart. But why had those two villains killed her on her wedding night, when it was for that wedding that they had wanted her and had taken her from her convent? And what of the husband? Where was he while they were burying his wife? Already dead, perhaps?

The gruff voice of the landlord roused him from his dismal meditations.

'You ought to get some sleep, sir. Here, drink this. It's my turn.'

Gilles turned. Le Coz was standing there, holding out a glass. It seemed to the young man that he read sympathy and something like pity in his grey eyes. He took the glass and drained it. The liquor scorched his throat without warming his body. He felt cold to the marrow of his bones.

'And you?' he asked abruptly. 'Have you no idea either as to the identity of the participants in this horrible crime?'

The landlord's face retained its stony expression.

'It doesn't do for an innkeeper to go having ideas, not if he wants to make old bones. But something tells me, young sir, that you've some ideas of your own. You looked like death, just now, when Guégan described the beautiful young lady with the copper-coloured hair.'

'Perhaps – only I am not certain. If you know anything that may help me to find the means to punish her murderers, if you know who she was – I beg you to tell me.'

'I do not know. As God is my judge, I swear I never saw her. But a villain with red hair and one that has a brother with the same – I think that you and I can both put a name to him. Or else why did you ask me earlier if I knew the whereabouts of Le Frêne? Only I did not know there was a girl in the family. I daresay she must have been living somewhere else. But will you let me give you a piece of advice?'

'If you must. But I can't promise to act on it.'

The landlord smiled and began wiping down the tables with a cloth.

'You'll do as you please. But rather than rushing off hotfoot to Le Frêne first thing in the morning, as I can see you're burning to, you'd do better to go first to Trecesson. I know the count is there. He may be able to add something which will make you quite certain. For there is still some possibility of doubt, however small.'

The church clock was striking nine. The chimes were lost suddenly in the clatter of a heavy vehicle arriving at speed. The air was full of the noise of hooves, the jingle of bells and the shouts of postilions. A door slammed. The Rennes coach had arrived.

'Good night to you,' Gilles said, turning to the stairs. The wooden treads creaked under his feet.

'Good night, sir. God send you have no bad dreams,' Le Coz returned, already hurrying out to greet the travellers.

Back in his own room, the Chevalier de Tournemine got out his pistols and checked them coolly. Then he drew his sword and examined it carefully, testing the edge and the point. Finally, he turned to the black wooden crucifix on the wall and addressed it sternly.

'Lord, if you have allowed this abominable crime to happen, know that by this time tomorrow both Saint-Mélaines will be dead – or I shall. And either way, I shall be guiltless.'

16

Aultre n'auray

Gilles sat motionless in the saddle, while Merlin pawed the ground impatiently. He was gazing at Trecesson with mingled pain and wonderment, surprised to find the place so attractive, despite the horrid associations that clung to it.

Despite the austerity of the bare, wintry woods all around, the feudal look of its castellated gatehouse, its six-sided tower and deep, gothic archway, the lowering skies, heavy with rain, which hung above its slate roofs, the château, built of pink stone softly mantled with ivy, stood dreaming with the proud grace of a fairytale prince beside its lake. There was no sign now of the events to which it had formed the background on that dreadful night. It was as though nothing could touch it behind its rampart of quiet waters, the home of ducks and croaking frogs.

Gilles lingered for a moment before the castle, as though on the verge of a certainty, perhaps to give the nervousness tightening his stomach muscles time to subside. During the sleepless night he had just passed, he had been through a hell of regrets, combined with hatred and the thirst for vengeance. He had dreamed of a death for the Saint-Mélaine brothers that would equal the worst that the Iroquois could do. A sword thrust or pistol shot were too good for monsters capable of smothering the grace of such a child as his sunny little siren of the estuary beneath the dark earth. When he pictured the agony of her death, buried alive in that grave, the last descendant of the bloody Tournemines yearned to hear the brothers screaming under long-drawn-out tortures.

Merlin, tired of standing still, tossed his graceful head and whinnied, rousing Gilles from his gloomy meditations.

'You're quite right,' he sighed. 'We're wasting time. We must go on – and find out. We have to make sure. I may yet be wrong.' But he did not really believe it.

The pealing of the bell brought a groom running, to bow deferentially before the haughty gentleman. No, he said, the count was not at home, but the countess was in.

'Then ask her if she will be good enough to grant me a few moments of her time. My name is the Chevalier de Tournemine de la Hunaudaye and my business is a matter of some gravity.'

The man led Gilles over the drawbridge, through the arched gateway and out into a neat courtyard which opened on to a terraced garden bounded by the dense mass of the forest. From there, he gave Merlin's bridle into the groom's hands and followed the butler indoors. In another moment he was being ushered into a pretty little sitting-room on the ground floor. It had pale panelled walls and looked out on the courtyard on one side and the lake on the other. A bright fire burned in the hearth and a selection of family portraits gazed down, somewhat fixedly, from the walls.

A young woman was seated in a flowered tapestry armchair by the fire. She had a lace cap on her head and her brown velvet dress was cunningly designed so that its fullness concealed the bulge about her waist. She was winding a large skein of wool which a young peasant girl seated on a stool at her feet was holding in both hands. She greeted her visitor with an inclination of her head.

'I am told that you wish to see me on some grave business, sir, and I will not conceal from you that you come at a most inopportune moment. My husband left early this morning to go to Coëtquidan about a matter of boundaries and I cannot tell when he will return, and I am afraid that I am not at all sure that I can take his place. But, please, do come in. Come in and sit down.' She indicated an armchair placed near her own.

Gilles bowed and took the seat she offered.

'I ask you to believe me, madame, when I say that I should never have ventured to thrust myself upon you in this way if my business was not of too serious a nature to be postponed even for a moment. Forgive me – and remember that it concerns the thing that matters most in all the world to me.'

Agathe de Trecesson, wife to René Joseph Le Prestre, Comte de Châteaugiron and Marquis d'Espinay was some twenty-five or twenty-six years old. She was not strictly beautiful but her serious little face, under its magnificent crown of chestnut hair, was the picture of gentleness. There was a touch of weariness also, in the shadows round her brown eyes which just then were studying her visitor in some perplexity.

'Is it so grave?' she said at last.

'More than I can tell you, madame.'

She sighed. 'Well then, you had better leave us, Perrine. The wool can wait.'

The girl rose, looking for somewhere to put down the big skein in her hands. Gilles held out his own without thinking.

'Permit me. I have done this many times as a child.'

A spark of amusement flickered in the eyes of the mother-to-be as Gilles got up from his armchair and came instead to fold his long legs on to the little stool.

'It will be the first time I have had a soldier to hold my wool for me,' she said with a smile. 'For you are a military man, chevalier, are you not? I can tell it by your bearing.'

'Yes indeed, madame. Lieutenant in the Queen's Dragoons.'

The countess picked up her ball again and went on winding the coarse natural wool as it slipped easily from the young man's hands.

'Do you know, it surprised me a little when I heard your name just now?' she said after a moment. 'I did not know that there were any Tournemines still left. I thought the name had died out.'

'It had, madame. Or rather would have died out with my father, Count Pierre, mortally wounded in the battle for York-town, if he had not, on the battlefield, solemnly recognized me in the presence of all the chiefs of the army. The King has been good enough to endorse that recognition of a youth who, until that moment, was no more than – an accident.'

Her face lit with sudden interest.

'Yorktown? Where is that?'

'In America, madame. In Virginia, to be precise. Have you heard nothing of our army's successes in America?'

'America? You have been there, sir?'

'I returned two months since, with the Duc de Lauzun who was entrusted by Count Rochambeau and General Washington with bringing the news of their victory to Versailles.'.

'A victory! In America! Indeed, we are as ignorant as savages here. Oh, chevalier, you must certainly wait and meet my husband. He will be very cross with me if I let such an interesting person go. Positively, you shall not escape.'

'Alas, madame, I fear I cannot wait. Must I remind you that my business here is grave – and also urgent.'

The countess blushed and smiled apologetically.

'Pardon me. I was forgetting. I find you so sympathetic that already I am treating you like an old friend.'

'I hope you will continue to do so when you have heard my story. Although I must remind you of an unpleasant affair, madame. Not long ago, just before Christmas, the woods not far from here were the scene of an appalling crime. A young woman, dressed as for a wedding—'

Madame de Châteaugiron rose abruptly, so that the ball of wool rolled off her lap and across the floor. She had turned so pale that Gilles thought for a moment she was going to faint. She put both hands over her ears, as if to shut out screams that only she could hear.

'For the love of God, sir, do not speak to me of that abominable business! I do not want to discuss it – I cannot bear it. It haunts my dreams—'

'Yet now it is for me to say for the love of God, madame, take pity on me. I know how painful it must be for you to recall it, but only think that it is killing me. Ever since I first heard it, I have been afraid – oh God! I should rather say I have been half dead with the fear of learning that the victim was the girl I loved, for whose sake I went to fight in America and whom I had come to find. Only listen to me, madame. Do not refuse to hear what I have to say! You must help me.'

He had slipped easily from his stool and was half kneeling at the countess' feet. Slowly, she let fall her hands and a little colour returned to her cheeks.

'If you have already heard the story, sir, I do not see what else I can tell you,' she said in an exhausted voice. 'From whom, by the way, did you hear it?'

'From one Guégan, a cobbler from Campénéac.'

'The man who was up the tree? I see.'

'He, too, has been losing sleep over it, poor man. He drinks, and in his cups he talks. I implore you, madame, I have no wish to make you suffer any more, only I must have your answer to one question – only one!'

'What is it?'

'According to Guégan, the victim was not quite dead when they got her out. It was some time before your husband gave out the news that she was no more. Is it possible that she recovered consciousness at all – that she was able to tell you her name?'

'If that is your question, sir, I am not going to answer it.'

Gilles came slowly to his feet, until his eyes were gazing straight into hers.

'No. That is not my question. You would not answer it, of course, because you may not altogether trust me yet. I will put my question in a minute. I am going to give you a name, countess. All I ask of you in return is one little word. Yes or no. That is all.'

He was standing over her, taller by a head, striving to hold her eyes which persistently refused to meet his. But, little by little, she gave in, and the horror he read in them was not feigned. Neither was the fear.

'But, chevalier, what makes you think that I will be able to answer your question? What makes you think that poor child was able—'

'Nothing, madame. Nothing but my own heart and my faith in God. He could not have let such an infamous thing happen and leave no trace behind, however small, to avenge her.'

'Vengeance! Do you mean that if I could answer yes to your question—?'

'Before tonight I shall have seen that justice is done. That I swear, by my father's memory. Will you give me your answer?'

Madame de Châteaugiron bowed her head and turned away as if to escape from the commanding gaze that seemed to be trying to search out the depths of her consciousness. She was silent for a moment, then she moved towards the door.

'Come,' she said simply.

Once out in the hall, she took a great hooded cloak from a maidservant and wrapped herself in it.

'Where are we going?' Gilles asked.

'To the chapel. As you see, it is on the far side of the court-yard.'

A fine rain had started to fall and the building showed up, looming through the damp, misty air.

The chapel was a small one, dating from renaissance times, slim and exquisite despite the two massive buttresses that supported it, and the single window in the east wall was adorned with a fleur de lys. The arched doorway opened easily at a touch from the countess, revealing an interior of dark flagstones, a number of carved benches and a simple altar before which an aged, white-haired priest was kneeling in prayer.

Walking on tiptoe so as not to disturb him, the countess led Gilles into the miniature sacristy. There, she opened a chest and took out a soiled veil and a coronet of withered flowers at the sight of which, for all his self-control, Gilles felt himself grow pale.

'We buried her beneath the stones of the chapel but we kept these as proof,' the countess said softly. 'Now, I am ready to answer your question. But remember that I shall not answer more than one.'

'There will be no more. The only thing I want to know is this. Was the name of the unhappy child whose murdered body you received here Judith de Saint-Mélaine?'

'Yes.'

For all that he had been expecting it, the shock of that yes was almost too much for him. He clenched his teeth and was forced to shut his eyes for a moment. When he opened them again, he saw the countess staring at him in amazement.

'Is it so painful?' she asked.

'More than I could have believed – more than I can say! I loved her – I did not even know myself how much! Forgive me, madame.'

Abruptly, he seized the faded flowers which Judith had worn in her hair and the veil which had been a shroud for the lovely form which, he now knew, would haunt him all his life long. He pressed them passionately to his lips, then, with a harsh sob, rammed them blindly into the countess' hands again and rushed without leave-taking out of the chapel into the court-yard. She hurried after and her voice followed him, calling:

'Chevalier! Please, wait! Do not go like this . . . Come back!'

But Gilles was past hearing anything but the crying of his own heart, howling with grief and despair. He came to the archway where the groom had tethered Merlin, leapt on his back and rode like a whirlwind out of the château, wholly forgetting that he had left his hat and cloak behind him.

He rode up the valley through the thickening drizzle, feeling his horse lift like a bird to every obstacle. He was unaware of rain or cold, of anything but the burning hell in his breast which made him feel as if he were about to burst, like an overheated boiler. He even snatched off his white wig, letting his own hair fly in the wind of his mad career. He had only one idea in mind, one fixed object, which was to get to Le Frêne and slaughter Judith's murderers like the vile beasts they were.

He rode through the dormant woods, over rocks, streams and gulleys. Before leaving Ploermel that morning, he had obtained precise directions how to reach Le Frêne from the landlord, Le Coz.

'It's a lot nearer to Trecesson than to here,' he had said. 'Look out for a village called Néant.'

The word had made him grimace at the time. Now, he found it almost soothing. Néant, oblivion, was where he meant to send the murderers but if he himself were to fall in the approaching fray, if death came to him in that house which had been the scene of Judith's childhood, he would gladly go with the Saint-Mélaines to oblivion, if only to stand before God and demand their damnation. Life had ceased to mean anything to him since he had heard Guégan's tale. What good was an ancient name to him, titles, rank, fame and fortune, if they could do no more than adorn his loneliness?

At the edge of a mere, he met two men cutting reeds and reining Merlin in with both hands so that he reared up and whinnied in protest, he called out: 'Is this the road to Néant?'

'Straight ahead as far as the next fork. After that, it's on your right!'

He plunged his hand into his pocket, tossed them a coin at random and rode on like the wind, leaving the man pulling off his blue woollen cap and crossing himself, convinced that what he had just seen was the demon rider on his way back down to hell. Which did not stop him hunting in the grass until he found the coin.

Once through the village, where he sent a group of black-cloaked women emerging from the church scuttling in panic, he was easily able to recognize the landmarks which Le Coz had mentioned. He left the Dinan road for a sunken lane full of ruts which soon forced him to slow down his pace considerably lest Merlin should stumble and break a leg. In any case, he had not far to go now and it was necessary to keep his eyes open so as not to fall into any of the traps with which, no doubt, the two villains had safeguarded the approaches to their lair. It was not long before he had his first glimpse of the house through a gap in the hedge.

It was built of heavy, dark-red stone against a background of sombre trees. A row of handsome dormer windows and a flight of broad stone steps in front, leading up to the first floor which rose above the surrounding farm buildings, gave it an air of nobility. No lights shone in the tall windows and there was no reflection from their dusty panes, but a thread of smoke was rising from one of the chimneys. Over to the right of the house was the dull, mercurial glint of water from the surface of a wide pool and near it the big ash tree from which the house evidently got its name. Seen from a distance it looked more like a large farm than a manor house.

The rain had stopped. Gilles looked up at the sky. It was a uniform depressing light grey with no sign of cloud. It was not going to be dark for some time yet. His eyes returned to the woods behind the house. He was wondering if it might not be better to go round and approach from that side, so as to have the advantage of surprise.

Before he could make up his mind, he heard the quick click-clack of a pair of sabots and a woman appeared round a bend in the sunken lane. She was covered from head to foot in a long, hooded cloak and was leaping over the puddles as lightly as a wagtail. She paused for a moment as she caught sight of the horse and its rider and then came on again without haste, swaying slightly from the hips.

She looked up, her face framed in the black oval of her hood. She had a broad face with a strongly defined bone structure and the hair that fell over her wide forehead was so fair as to be almost white. Her full lips were red as an open wound and she would have been beautiful but that one eye was half closed by a swelling bruise. She stared boldly up at Gilles.

'I've not seen you before? Are you a friend of theirs?'

'Do I look like it?'

'No – o. No, you don't really. And if that's so, you'd best be off. They don't like strangers round here.'

'I don't need your advice. Just answer my question. Are the brothers at home?'

The girl shrugged derisively and made a move to go on. But Gilles had swung himself to the ground and caught her by the cloak, so roughly that she gave a scream of fright and would have fallen but for his firm grip on her arm.

'I asked you a question. Try and answer it. I am not a patient man.'

'You're hurting me,' she whined. 'And – don't look at me like that! As though you were trying to see right through me. You've eyes in your head like cold steel. Let me go. I've had enough of that house and the people in it.'

'So they are there! Answer me! I'll not let you go until you do.'

'What have you got against them?'

'I might tell you that's none of your business but, since you seem none too fond of them yourself, I'll tell you. I've come to kill them both! And if you'll tell me what you know, I'll give you a silver piece.'

The girl's undamaged eye, which was green and very pretty, shone with a fierce joy.

'You're telling me the truth? You really mean to kill them?'

'On my honour!'

'Come on then! I'll not only answer you, I'm going to help you! I know a way of getting into the house without going through the courtyard. There are three men always on watch there, and a kennel with dogs that could tear you to pieces. Lead your horse. I'll show you where to hide him, or they could kill you just to steal him.'

He tried to slip the coin into her hand but she would not take it.

'Keep your money, handsome sir! I've dreamed for too long

of seeing those two rotten carcasses stone dead. Look!' she added, pointing to her eye. 'Who do you think did that?'

'One of them?'

'Yes. That swine Tudal, the elder. I've been his mistress for two years now. His mistress!' she repeated bitterly. 'His dog, I should say! His slave! Whenever he wants another girl, he beats me and throws me out. Here, look at this!'

She pulled up her sleeve and showed him her arm, oddly misshapen by a badly mended break.

'Then why do you go back to him? Two years is a long time.'

'I don't go back. He sends for me. He likes my body, when he's nothing else to get his teeth in! And it's the worse for me if I don't obey, or if I merely keep him waiting. I've a sick mother in the village and he threatens to kill her if I don't go. Sometimes he will let me alone for a month or two, depending on the girl he fancies at the moment. This time, it's a kid not yet fifteen. They took her to him yesterday, like a cow to bull. I don't know where he found her. But keep quiet. We're nearly there.'

She led him across country, keeping in the shelter of the trees, to skirt the house, keeping on the far side of the pond with the ash tree, and then across an alley between two holly trees into the shelter of the wood. The red walls of the house loomed very close.

'Leave your horse here. No one will see him and I will take you in by way of the cellar door,' the girl whispered. 'And that reminds me, I forgot to tell you. Tudal is alone in the house. It won't be hard for you to kill him. He's got an attack of gout which makes him yell as soon as he puts his foot to the ground, but that won't stop him drinking like a sponge and having his way with the girl.'

Gilles frowned. 'And Morvan? Where is he? My quarrel is with the pair of them.'

'He went off this morning, with two other men. I don't know where he went, but it was on some evil errand. All I can tell you is that he'll be back tonight. You have only to wait for him.'

Gilles tethered Merlin to a tree, took his pistols from their holsters and thrust them into his belt, put a powder horn and balls into his pocket and made sure that his sword was loose in its sheath.

'By the way – what's your name?'

'My mother named me Corentine,' she murmured. 'But they call me—'

'I don't want to know. Tomorrow, you shall be Corentine again to all the world. Come, now.'

He had nearly asked her about Judith but a kind of embarrassment prevented him. He could not call up the frightened figure of the little bride of Trecesson to stand between himself and this poor girl whose own days of innocence were long past. Later, perhaps, when the lair of the Saint-Mélaines had been washed clean by their blood.

Guided by Corentine, he passed back through the holly trees and then the two of them made their way down into a kind of dry ditch to where a low door stood at the far end. The girl opened the door, taking care to keep it from creaking. A foul smell of stale wine and rotting fruit assailed their nostrils and they found themselves in a cellar which, except for two fair-sized casks, seemed to contain more broken bottles than full ones. Two rats fled squeaking before them.

Without a word, Corentine pointed to some stone steps leading up to another door. She picked her way over to it, carefully avoiding the broken glass which would have crunched under her feet. When she reached the top, she paused.

'This comes out at the end of the passage. There is a door opposite that leads into the room where they mostly sit. Tudal is in there—'

'Alone?'

'Sure to be. When he's got a girl, he doesn't like to share his fun, and he's only had her since last night.'

As though to give the lie to her words, the thin sound of a Breton bagpipe broke out suddenly, so close at hand that Corentine started. Her hand clutched at Gilles' arm and she pulled him back hurriedly into the cellar.

'No! I was wrong. Yann Wooden Head is there too. It is he who is playing.'

'Who is he?'

'Their boon companion. They call him that because he is bald. He recruits their men for them, and gets them girls and robs right and left. There's no task too low for him. He'll do anything.'

'Does he drive their coach for them as well?'

The girl's eyes widened.

'Yes – he has done that. Not long ago either. How did you know?'

'The same way as I know many other things. One doesn't come to kill a man for no reason, you know. When was it you saw Yann drive the coach?'

'Last Christmas. The brothers came back in the middle of the night with a carriage which they must have stolen somewhere. Yann was driving it.'

'What did they do with the carriage? Did they put it in a coach house?'

'No. That was the funny thing. They burned it. There was nothing left but the iron rims off the wheels.'

Then Gilles could no longer hold back the question that was on the tip of his tongue.

'Tell me, did you, at any time before that night, see their sister come here?'

The surprise on Corentine's face was complete and genuine.

'Their sister? Lord, no! I know they have one, because she used to be seen about here a lot before the old baron's wife died and he went away. She was a pretty little thing, too – and a proper wild cat, but she hasn't been here for a long time. They say she is a nun somewhere.'

Gilles wasted no time wondering what the Saint-Mélaines had done with their sister in between the convent at Hennebont and the grave of Trecesson. That was something he was going to get the answer to from Tudal, if he had to force it out of him! Up above, the bagpipe was still playing, accompanied now by the rhythmic click of sabots. Corentine uttered a short, contemptuous laugh.

'Tudal must be making the girl dance for him. He likes that.'

'Well, we'll go and interrupt his party.'

Grasping both pistols, Gilles sprang up the steps, opened the door, which creaked, and crossed the passage to another door he saw on the far side. This he kicked inwards, revealing a huge, low-ceilinged room. Shutters had been drawn across the windows and the only light came from candles and the fire in the hearth.

Seated in an armchair before it, a table laden with the remains of a meal and a number of empty bottles at his side, and his gouty foot, swathed in bandages, propped on a stool with a pillow on it, Tudal de Saint-Mélaine was clapping his hands in time to the music. A young girl, dressed in nothing but a headscarf and a pair of clogs, was dancing in front of the leaping flames. The firelight glinted on the bald head of the musician in the corner.

At Gilles' entry, all three figures froze momentarily. The bagpipe emitted a piercing squeak, the girl stood with one foot in the air, as though fearing the levelled pistols would go off if she set it down. Saint-Mélaine himself sat with his jaw dropping and his hands still parted like a mechanical toy whose spring had gone. But he recovered himself quickly and frowned, while his face went from something near the colour of his hair to a dull purple.

'Who are you?' he barked. 'And what do you want?'

'To talk to you. After that, we shall see.'

'You've a funny way of talking, pointing your guns at a man.'

'Just so. I should have made myself clearer. To ask you a few questions, I meant. A few questions, Tudal de Saint-Mélaine, concerning the death of your sister, basely murdered by you.'

Behind him, Gilles heard Corentine gasp. Then her gasp changed to a yell.

'Look out!'

A knife, thrown by a sure hand, hissed like a snake out of the corner where Yann Wooden Head was sitting. Gilles jerked his head aside instinctively, avoiding it, although it scratched his cheek as it flew past. He reacted instantly. One of the pistols spat and the man with the bagpipe folded over, blood spurting from his mouth.

'One,' Gilles said coolly.

Tudal, dull-eyed, had watched his henchman die with a kind of indifference which was probably the result of the drink he had imbibed. Then, with a sudden access of mad rage, he reached across the table for the pistol, the butt of which was just beyond his grasp. But Corentine was quicker. She slid, snakelike, between table and chair, snatched up the gun and vanished beneath the thick, oak board.

Tudal swore furiously. Disarmed, he crouched in his armchair like a wild boar brought to bay.

'Harlot! Slut! You'll pay for that, my girl! I'll see your mother dies!'

'You'll not have time,' Gilles said icily. 'Corentine, shut the doors and barricade them well, so that this fat swine's loyal servants can't get in to help him. As for you, little clog dancer, get your clothes on. You're too young for that kind of exhibition. And what are you crying for?'

'I – I'm cold! And I'm hungry! He w-wouldn't let me have anything to eat since yesterday.'

'I see. Well, get your clothes on and help yourself to some food. There must be something left on the table.'

While Corentine, with unexpected strength, was dragging a large chest across one door and drawing the heavy bolts across the other, which led out into the yard, Tudal sat watching her evilly. But the shock had sobered him and he said with a sneer : 'That's right, barricade yourselves in! You'll have to get out sometime! I've three more men outside as well as the dogs and my brother will be coming back with more.'

'We'll take care of him later. It's between us two now. I told you I had some questions to ask you.'

'By what right? I don't know you. Who are you?'

'My name is Gilles de Tournemine of La Hunaudaye. As for what brings me here – I loved Judith and she loved me!'

He broke off as a violent banging on the door drowned his words. Saint-Mélaine's servants had come to their master's aid, alerted, presumably, by the sound of the shot.

'Not so much noise, there!' Gilles called in the Breton tongue. 'I am holding your master at gunpoint. I'll kill him this moment if you don't keep quiet.'

The noise ceased instantly. The only sounds to be heard were the crackle of the fire and the champing of the girl's jaws as she guzzled the remains of a game stew out of the dish.

'Never heard of you,' Tudal snarled. 'Where have you come from?'

'From America, where I've had the opportunity of seeing

398

something of your brother's ways. Not that it's any concern of yours. I'm asking the questions.'

'Go on, then. Ask away, if it gives you any pleasure. But something tells me I shan't please to answer.'

'We'll see about that. You forced Madame de la Bourdonnaye to let you take Judith away, pretending you were going to marry her to a rich old man. So will you tell me how it comes about that on the night of her wedding you thought fit to murder her? Murder? It's a poor word to describe the horror of your deed. You buried her alive, didn't you, alive in the dark earth, with her wedding dress for a shroud. I want to know why.'

The red-headed man laughed, revealing teeth that would have been good but for the ravages of decay. The slate-grey eyes beneath his red brows gleamed with malice.

'So you think you can carry on like this in folks' houses, loosing off pistols all round and then set yourself up as a righter of wrongs, a judge—'

'And executioner, too! Are you going to talk?'

'Go—'

'Very well.'

Coolly returning the unused pistol to his belt, Gilles held the other out to Corentine, along with the powder and balls.

'You know how to load?'

'Of course. Give it to me.'

His hands thus freed, he walked over to the hearth and took down the long coachman's whip he had seen on the wall above it as he came in. He weighed it in his hand, tightened his grip and struck like lightning. The lash hissed through the air and was followed a fraction of a second later by a scream of agony. With diabolical accuracy, the thong had wound itself round Tudal's gouty leg and with a sharp jerk Gilles had dragged him from his seat on to the floor. The big man sprawled there, sweating profusely and bellowing like an injured bull. He tried to struggle up but he was in too much pain. Moreover, Gilles was on him in a flash, turning him over like a pancake, which made him scream again, and then holding him down with a knee in the small of his back.

'Get me a rope,' he ordered Corentine, who had been watching the scene delightedly out of her good eye.

She ran to a chest and brought out a whole assortment of them. In a trice, Tudal's hands were tied behind his back. He slavered and cursed with his face to the floor, half insane with rage and pain.

'You villain! You'll not get out of here alive,' he roared. 'My brother will deal with you!'

'I'm not afraid of your brother. I've had occasion to chastize him once before this and his turn will come. Now talk, or I'll put your foot in the fire.'

And, while Tudal continued to deliver himself of a stream of abuse, Gilles set about dragging his big body close enough to the fire for him to feel the heat. Meanwhile, a muffled hammering had been resumed without.

'Take care,' Corentine breathed. 'The men are taking advantage of his screams to attack the shutters.'

'If you've finished loading that pistol, fire it at the first man who shows himself. And you, Tudal, talk quickly or I'll heave the whole of you into the fire without more ado.'

'All right. I'll tell you what happened. After all, I've no call to conceal it. I was within my rights. The bitch cheated us. She got what she deserved. We'd found a fine match for her, a man of great wealth who had seen her in the convent parlour one day when he went to visit a cousin.'

'Vauferrier. I know. What then?'

'He fell madly in love with her. He was determined to have her and he offered a fortune to marry her. So we went to fetch her to him. He has a big place over towards Malestroit. That was where the wedding was to take place and so that was where we took the bride, naturally. Vauferrier received her like a queen. He had ordered clothes and jewels for her – he threw a fortune at her feet and got nothing but contemptuous glances for his pains. She said she didn't want to marry him and that nothing and no one could make her, the little fool—'

'Insult her once more and I'll start on that foot of yours,' Gilles warned.

'Go to the devil! I wanted to drag her to the altar there and then, only that fool Vauferrier still thinks he's an Adonis. He wanted to win her by gentleness. He said she'd come round to him in the end, that he'd tamed harder cases than her and all he needed was time. She was put in the best room in the house,

400

with a governess and an army of servants. But she was as cunning as a fox. She pretended to be coming round so that the watch on her was relaxed and then, one morning, as she was going to mass in a little chapel on the far side of the grounds, she knocked the poor woman down with a branch of wood and ran away.

'Oh, we searched for a long time. But to no avail. It was as if she had vanished into the landscape with the morning mist. In the end, Vauferrier lost his temper and threw us out, Morvan and me. It was only after we came back here that we found out by accident what had become of her. A physician from Vannes, a man named Job Kernoa, had taken her in, after finding her half dead with hunger, almost under his carriage wheels. She told him her story and he hid her in a house of his, on the heath at Lanvaux. He was young, prosperous – and not ill-looking. He persuaded her that the only way for her to keep out of our clutches was to marry him. It seems he told her he had relatives in the Parliament and in high positions. At all events, she agreed. Yes, she agreed. That hurts, does it? You come here, shouting and carrying on about how you loved one another, and your rights? It's not worth playing Sir Galahad, Tournemine. She never cared for you—'

'Go on,' Gilles ordered coldly.

Tudal's jeering eyes could read nothing in his face, which was as hard as stone, or in his icy glance, but the pain had reawakened in his heart, joined to a bitter jealousy, for which he reproached himself as sacrilege. Disappointed, Tudal shrugged his shoulders.

'We caught up with her just in time. On the day of the wedding we were there, on the heath, Morvan, Yann and I, with the rest. We let them get the ceremony over. There were not many there, only the priest and two witnesses. It was a very quiet wedding. And then, when we were quite sure that everyone had gone – and the turtle doves were pretty well alone, we went into action. It wasn't difficult, and it didn't take long. The bride was still in her wedding clothes. She was drinking a glass of champagne with her husband. The poor fellow hadn't even time enough to drain his. My sword went through his body like a needle through silk. He fell without a sound. There was a carriage in the stables. We got Madame Kernoa into it, weeping like a fountain – and then the next night, you know what happened to her.'

'Why the next night, then? And why the woods at Trecesson?'

Tudal's laughter rasped the young man's raw nerves.

'To kill two birds with one stone! First because it would never occur to anyone to look for her there, and secondly because we liked the idea of making a present of her to the Comte de Châteaugiron. We'd had some trouble with him the year before. Now, I hope you're satisfied, for something tells me that your troubles are just beginning.'

At that moment one of the shutters was torn away and a shot rang out, missing Corentine by a hair's breadth. She let out a cry which was echoed by Tudal's maniacal laugh. But Gilles was already at the outer door, pulling back the bolts and dragging it wide open, while keeping himself out of the line of fire. He found himself face to face with a man and fired. The man dropped like a stone. Meanwhile, Corentine had crept bravely over to the broken window then stood up suddenly and, holding Tudal's heavy pistol in both hands, fired blindly. She was rewarded by a shriek which ended in a gurgle.

'Got him!' Gilles cried. 'Well done, lass!'

He saw her smile for the first time, a funny shy little smile that sat crookedly on her bruised face.

'It's easy to feel like a heroine with someone like you around, chevalier,' she called back. 'If you ever need to raise hell in Brittany, remember Corentine! My father was a marine. It was he taught me to shoot. But we'd better not go to sleep yet. There's still one more outside and Morvan can't be far off.'

'The dogs!' Tudal was bellowing. 'Why don't the fools go for the dogs?'

Gilles was already outside. He saw a man running towards a barn from which came a chorus of frantic barking.

'Stop!' he cried. 'Throw down your gun and stand still or you're a dead man!'

The man, a rough-looking fellow in a goatskin waistcoat and wide, baggy trousers, with hair that stuck out stiffly from beneath his round hat, stopped dead but did not drop the gun. In one swift movement, he swung round and fired. The ball lodged in the lintel of the door but even as it did so Gilles' second pistol let loose its deadly bark. The last of Tudal's bodyguards rocked, bent at the knees and fell face downwards in the mud.

Gilles walked calmly back to the house. He fastened the door carefully and leaned against it. He let his eyes roam coolly round the room, pausing briefly on the girl who had been dancing and who was now cowering under the table with a vacant expression and a hambone clutched in one hand, and then brought them back to his strange ally, who was gazing at him as though he were the archangel Gabriel in person.

'Go home, Corentine, and take that child with you. What I am going to do now is no sight for a woman.'

The girl only laughed.

'Because the things you have done so far were? My late father taught me one thing, you know, chevalier, and that is that a good soldier doesn't go to bed before the battle is over.'

'He was right, and you are a good little soldier. But the battle is over. This is the time for justice and I would not make you an executioner's assistant.'

She came and stood before him, her hands on her hips, and her wide, red mouth parted in a smile.

'I think I'd do worse things for you, chevalier. You'll not be rid of me so easily. I'm staying. I want to see it to the end. As for her—'

She bent and hauled the girl out from under the table and forced her to stand upright. But she let go of her at once and her captive subsided on to the floor again with a hiccup.

'Pooh!' Corentine exclaimed. 'She's as drunk as an owl! She must have finished off all the bottles while we weren't looking! We need only lay her on a settle. She's half asleep already.'

Gilles shrugged and walked over to where Tudal was still lying by the fire. He was silent now, but his grey face and the sweat trickling down his cheeks spoke clearly enough of the fear that possessed him. The death of his men had taken all the braggart out of him and he looked up at the tall, dark figure standing over him with mingled hate and dread.

'If you know any prayers, Tudal de Saint-Mélaine, now is the time to say them,' Gilles said grimly.

'You're not going to kill me? Not just like that? Not without

403

giving me a chance to defend myself?' Tudal cried desperately.

'Did you give Judith a chance to defend herself?'

'I was within my rights to do what I did,' he wailed. 'She had cast off the obedience she owed me – prostituted our name with a low, common fellow. What I did was justice. A Saint-Mélaine cannot become a Madame Kernoa!'

Gilles was conscious of a slight nausea. The wretch before him still had enough pride of caste to pose even now as the guardian of justice.

'What I am going to do is justice also,' he said simply.

Watched by Tudal's starting eyes, he went over to the ropes which Corentine had got out earlier, selected the longest and, measuring the height of the ceiling with his eye, jumped on to the table, kicking aside the remains of the food, and passed the rope over the king beam.

'What are you going to do?' Saint-Mélaine croaked. 'You can't—'

'Hang you? Yes. I told you I was your executioner. And you do not deserve to die like a gentleman. Your blood would sully a good sword.'

'Coward! You are nothing but a coward! Fight, at least! Oh, you're taking advantage of my helplessness!'

'I'll do your brother the honour of crossing swords with him when he comes. That's more than your whole family deserves! Start praying.'

He sprang down and began calmly making a running noose on the end of the rope. Corentine almost snatched it out of his hands.

'Give it to me,' she said harshly, meeting his eyes. 'It is for me to put it round his neck. I like to pay my debts. You have set me free. I won't let you soil your hands by touching him. It is enough for you to tighten the rope.'

In a few minutes, Tudal de Saint-Mélaine was dangling like some great swollen fruit from the main beam of his house. Gilles and Corentine stood looking at each other. They were pale and a little breathless. The red-haired man had died as he lived, vilely and without dignity. To the last, he had done nothing but spew out curses, sob and beg for mercy, but never for an instant had the last of the Tournemines felt a shadow of pity cross his frozen heart. He could not forget the picture of

Judith, cast alive into that hole in the ground. With seeming calm, he walked over to the table, picked up a half-empty goblet of rum and drained it at a draught.

'Two,' he said, with a sigh as he put down the cup. 'Now we have only to wait for Morvan.'

He began reloading his pistols with hands that did not tremble. That done, he unlocked the door, set it ajar and sat down facing it in the armchair recently occupied by his victim, a pistol in either hand. Meanwhile Corentine had wrapped herself in her cloak and sat crouched on the hearth, like some weird spirit of the house. There was nothing for Gilles to do now but wait for the last of the Saint-Mélaines. After that – he did not know very clearly what he would do after that, only that he felt very tired. He had aged ten years in the past twenty-four hours. And still more in the last hour.

His boyhood love, so sweet and pure, born in the sunniest light of a September's evening, had ended in darkness, blood and horror. His vengeance had the bitter taste of fruit not left to ripen but he knew that in a little while, when Morvan appeared, he would not hesitate to gorge himself again. He had offered up five lives as sacrifices to the shade of her whom, even when he did not know it, he had never ceased to love. He needed one more, but if he sacrificed a hundred men it would not appease his grief, since he would never see Judith again on this earth. Even her farewell letter had no meaning for him now, since she had fled to other arms for refuge. He drew it from his pocket and tossed it idly into the flames. As he did so, his eye was caught by his left hand and he held it before his face. The ring of gold and blue enamel which had been his father's glowed softly on it. He caressed the design with his finger, lingering on the gothic letters of the motto *Aultre n'auray*. I will have no other. Abruptly, he thrust the ring into his mouth and bit on it, fighting back the sobs that rose to his lips. But he could not prevent one tear from creeping out from between his dry lids and rolling down his cheek.

'But you, my love,' he murmured softly. 'No other but you – if that was truly what you wished.'

He would not go back to Versailles, nor even to Hennebont or Pontivy. Tomorrow, when it was all over, he would turn Merlin's head towards Brest and take ship with him back to

America and a life of a man among men, a life of war and danger. He would be the Gyrfalcon once more, more reckless than ever, until death came to crown a legend for children to listen to in years to come.

Corentine's voice, though it was no louder than a whisper, penetrated his thoughts and brought him back to the present.

'Listen! There are horses coming. Morvan is here!'

'Hide under the table. I want you to keep out of sight as much as possible.'

She obeyed without demur, although he noticed that she still hugged Tudal's pistol underneath her arm. Gilles rose and stretched himself, then he took up his stand with legs apart, facing the door, and waited. The afternoon was drawing in. It would soon be dark. The low room was filled with dancing shadows from the firelight. The horsemen were nearer now. There must be three or four of them. Soon they were close to the house. The horses whinnied and there was a clatter of booted feet as men sprang to the ground. Footsteps approached the door, which still stood ajar, the steps of one man only.

'Come in, Morvan,' Gilles called. 'I have been waiting for you—'

The door was pushed open, creaking slowly, from outside. A man stood there.

'Morvan is not coming,' he said pleasantly. 'I saw him as I arrived. He was flying the place as if the devil were on his heels! I think he must have taken fright at what he saw in the courtyard, especially since he was alone.'

Gilles examined the stranger with a frown, but did not lower his pistols. The man was evidently a gentleman. That much was clear from his well-modulated voice and the elegance of his grey velvet hunting dress, as well as his distinguished bearing. He seemed to be about thirty, with a pleasant, open face. But what the devil was he doing here?

'May I inquire who you are, sir?'

'Certainly. My name is René La Prestre de Châteaugiron. You visited my house this morning and I think you were affected by what you heard there – if I am to judge by what I see before me. The justice you mete out is formidable, sir, and exceedingly expeditious.'

With the air of a connoisseur inspecting an exhibit in a

museum, the lord of Trecesson strolled over to where Tudal's body still hung from its beam, then glanced across at the bagpipe player stiffening in his own congealed blood. Gilles drew himself up defensively.

'After the tragedy which took place on your land, Count, do you think my hand was too heavy?'

'By no means, my friend – if I may call you so? These scoundrels have deserved death for a long time. I am even beginning to think it would have been a shame if my wife had managed to call you back. Besides, I came here purely in order to assist you and not to put the least rub in the way of your intentions.'

'And yet, if I understood you, you say that you let Morvan escape?'

'Good God yes! Time could have been precious. I wasn't going to waste it chasing after him. Remember that I did not know what might have happened inside the house. Moreover, I do really believe that the – er – temporary demise of that delightful and unfortunate young lady has been adequately avenged. Let Morvan go to the devil in his own way. At all events, it won't be long.'

'The – the temporary demise! Do you know what you are saying, sir? You seem to speak very lightly of these matters!'

'I do know, chevalier. None better. The – er – the thing we buried in our chapel – at Mademoiselle de Saint-Mélaine's own express request – was a sack of sand. She made us swear to keep her secret in order to preserve a life which God had saved by a miracle. My wife took you to the chapel this morning to test you and at the sight of your emotion she almost told you the whole. She hurried after you and called to you, but you were already out of earshot.'

Gilles was compelled to lean against the side of the hearth for support. His head was spinning and he was almost fainting, half-choked by this sudden joy coming on top of his previous grief. Judith! Could it be that Judith was still alive?

The Count laughed. 'Well,' he said. 'Surely you aren't going to swoon like a girl? May I suggest we quit this gloomy spot? My men are outside. They will attend to the – er – tidying up. We will go to my house where my wife awaits you, with a good dinner and a warm bed. We can talk as we go. Why, what are you after under the table? If it's a good-looking girl with a black eye who was crouching there with an enormous pistol, let me tell you that she left a good five minutes ago and went running off like a mad thing. I fear I may have frightened her.'

By this time the colour was beginning to creep back into Gilles' face. He managed a faint smile.

'No. But she is like all good soldiers. Once the battle is over, they go back to their billets and no questions asked. I'll go and see her before I leave these parts.'

Once again, the tide was going out. The winter was nearly over and the spring tide, strong and full, was carrying the blue-grey waters of the Blavet out into the Atlantic. Standing not far from the grassy nest where once a little barefoot peasant boy had cast his line, the Chevalier de Tournemine watched the fishing boats with their red sails going out in line to the night's fishing. Everything was as it had been, and yet nothing was the same.

On the other side of that vast expanse of water, he had won all that it was humanly possible for him to win – except love, and that fate had given to him in this very spot. Everything was as it had been, only no flaming hair floated like seaweed on the muddy waters, no imperious little voice was hurling insults at his head.

'Judith,' he murmured tenderly. 'Judith, haughty and pathetic, wise and foolish, tender and cruel – where are you now, Judith my love, while I stand here calling you?'

Who could say for sure? Very far, perhaps, or very near? She had told no one of her intentions. When she left Trecesson, which she did in the greatest secrecy, she had said nothing of where she hoped to find a refuge sufficiently remote to hide her from her brother's rage. But she had let fall one thing, a few brief words that could be significant.

'The safest place should be in the middle of the biggest city.'

And Madame de Châteaugiron had concluded: 'I believe she chose Paris.'

Perhaps it was there that he should seek.

Gilles turned back resolutely to where Merlin was tethered to a tree. On a sudden impulse, he bent his head and kissed the animal's silky cheek. Merlin rubbed his head against him affectionately and showed his great teeth.

'What do you think, old fellow? With the two of us, nothing is impossible and if we have to go to the end of the world to find her, then we'll go! But for the moment, Pontivy awaits us. Let's go and make the acquaintance of the Queen's Dragoons, to which we have been appointed with the splendid rank of supernumerary lieutenant. After that – well, we'll see how soon we can get to Paris and see what's happening there. After all, we've not yet made our bow to our colonel-in-chief, the Queen. That's not something any gentleman can overlook.'

The Chevalier de Tournemine sprang lightly on to his horse's back, to be greeted with a whinney of pleasure, rammed his hat down on his head and set off at a gallop across the heath where the bare feet of a little illegitimate boy named Gilles Goëlo had so often run before.

On the gorse bushes, the first tiny green shoots were showing, the green of hope itself. In the distance, the sweet, melancholy notes of the angelus floated on the sea air which already carried a hint of spring.

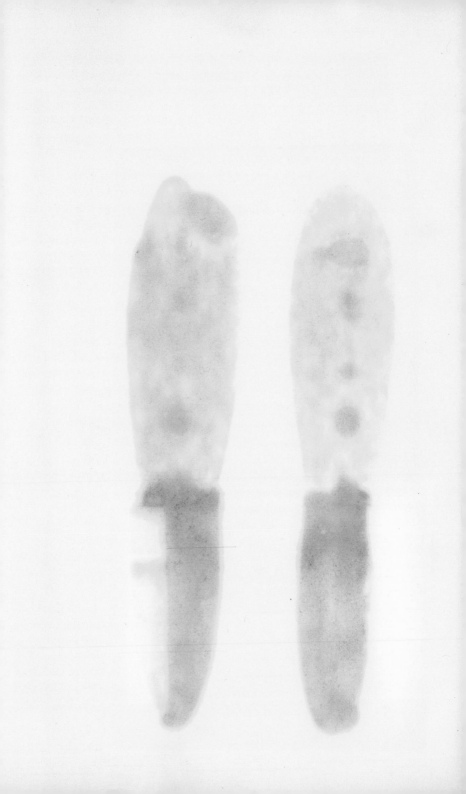

Benzoni, Juliette.
The lure of the falcon /